D0050552

HOUSE
of
EL

BOOK TWO

written by
CLAUDIA GRAY

illustrated by
ERIC ZAWADZKI

colors by
DEE CUNNIFFE

letters by
DERON BENNETT

BASED ON CHARACTERS CREATED BY
JERRY SIEGEL AND **JOE SHUSTER**

BY SPECIAL ARRANGEMENT WITH THE **JERRY SIEGEL** FAMILY

HOUSE of EL

BOOK TWO

THE ENEMY DELUSION

JIM CHADWICK Editor
COURTNEY JORDAN Assistant Editor
STEVE COOK Design Director – Books
AMIE BROCKWAY-METCALF Publication Design
DANIELLE DIGRADO Publication Production

MARIE JAVINS Editor-in-Chief, DC Comics

DANIEL CHERRY III Senior VP – General Manager
JIM LEE Publisher & Chief Creative Officer
JOEN CHOE VP – Global Brand & Creative Services
DON FALLETTI VP – Manufacturing Operations & Workflow Management
LAWRENCE GANEM VP – Talent Services
ALISON GILL Senior VP – Manufacturing & Operations
NICK J. NAPOLITANO VP – Manufacturing Administration & Design
NANCY SPEARS VP – Revenue

HOUSE OF EL BOOK TWO: THE ENEMY DELUSION

Published by DC Comics. Copyright © 2021 DC Comics. All Rights Reserved. All characters, their distinctive likenesses, and related elements featured in this publication are trademarks of DC Comics. The stories, characters, and incidents featured in this publication are entirely fictional. DC Comics does not read or accept unsolicited submissions of ideas, stories, or artwork.
DC – a WarnerMedia Company.

DC Comics, 2900 West Alameda Ave., Burbank, CA 91505
Printed by Worzalla, Stevens Point, WI, USA. 11/26/21.
First Printing.
ISBN: 978-1-4012-9608-7

Library of Congress Cataloging-in-Publication Data

Names: Gray, Claudia, writer. | Zawadzki, Eric, illustrator. | Cunniffe, Dee, colourist. | Bennett, Deron, letterer.
Title: The enemy delusion / written by Claudia Gray ; illustrated by Eric Zawadzki ; colors by Dee Cunniffe ; letters by Deron Bennett.
Description: Burbank, CA : DC Comics, [2022] | Series: House of El ; book two | "Based on characters created by Jerry Siegel and Joe Shuster by special arrangement with the Jerry Siegel family" | Audience: Ages 8-12 | Audience: Grades 4-6 | Summary: Sera the soldier and Zahn the scientist are teenagers on opposite sides of the same extinction-level event who get drawn deeper into conspiracies that could doom them and their home planet Krypton.
Identifiers: LCCN 2021041140 | ISBN 9781401296087 (trade paperback)
Subjects: CYAC: Graphic novels. | Science fiction. | LCGFT: Science fiction comics.
Classification: LCC PZ7.7.G7315 En 2022 | DDC 741.5/973--dc23
LC record available at https://lccn.loc.gov/2021041140

MIX
Paper from responsible sources
FSC® C002589

CHAPTER ONE

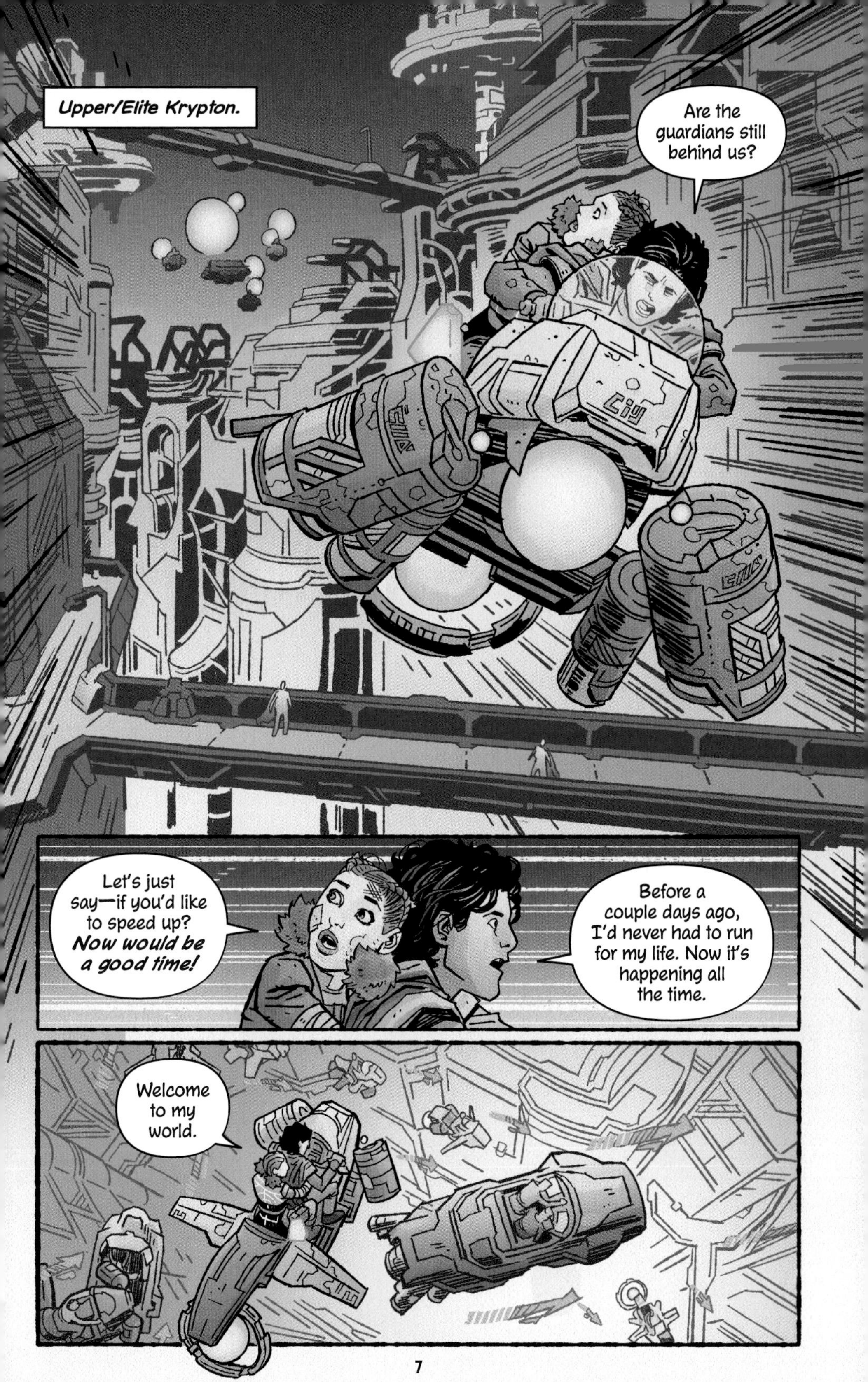
Upper/Elite Krypton.
Are the guardians still behind us?
Let's just say—if you'd like to speed up? *Now would be a good time!*
Before a couple days ago, I'd never had to run for my life. Now it's happening all the time.
Welcome to my world.

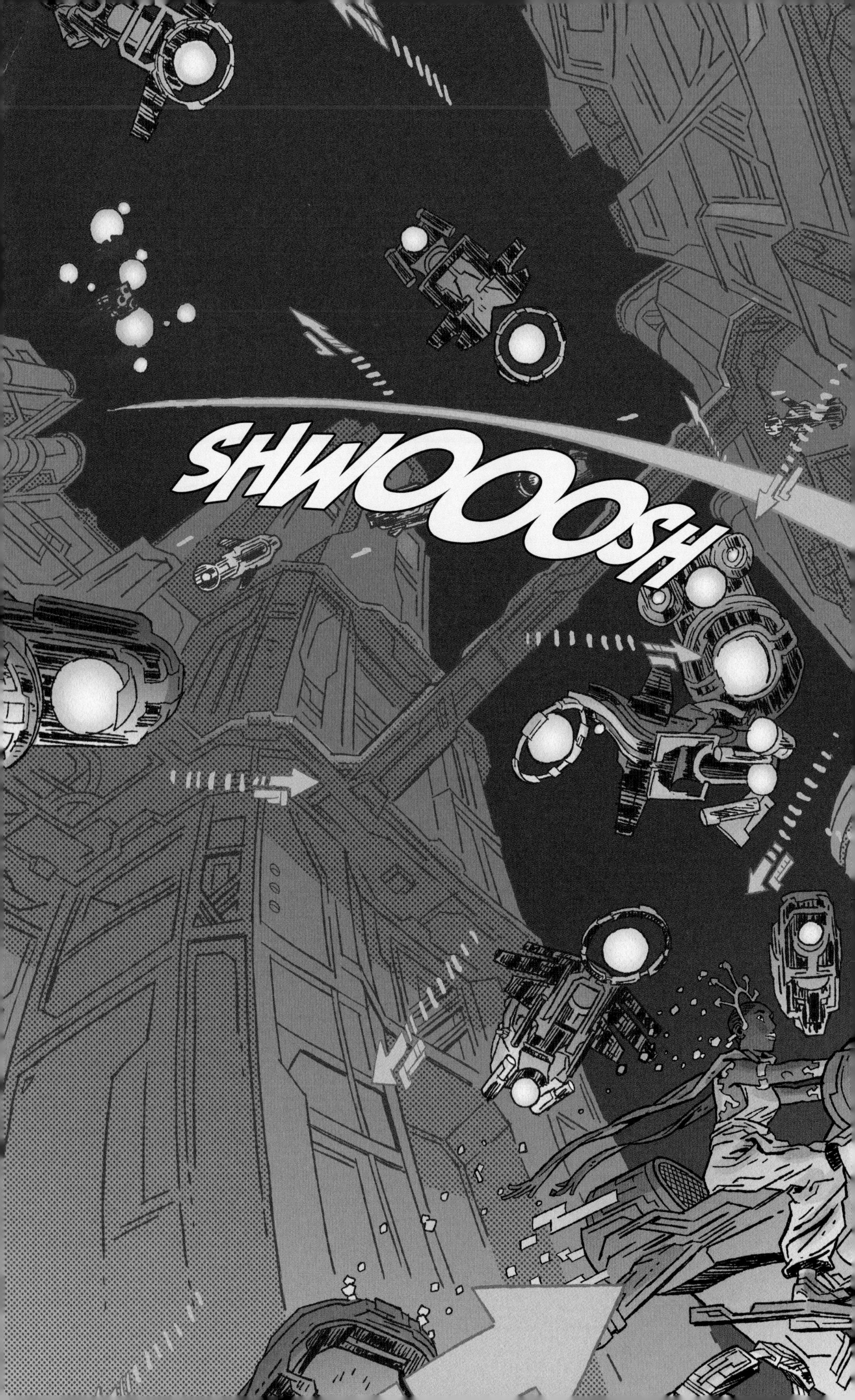
SHWOOOSH

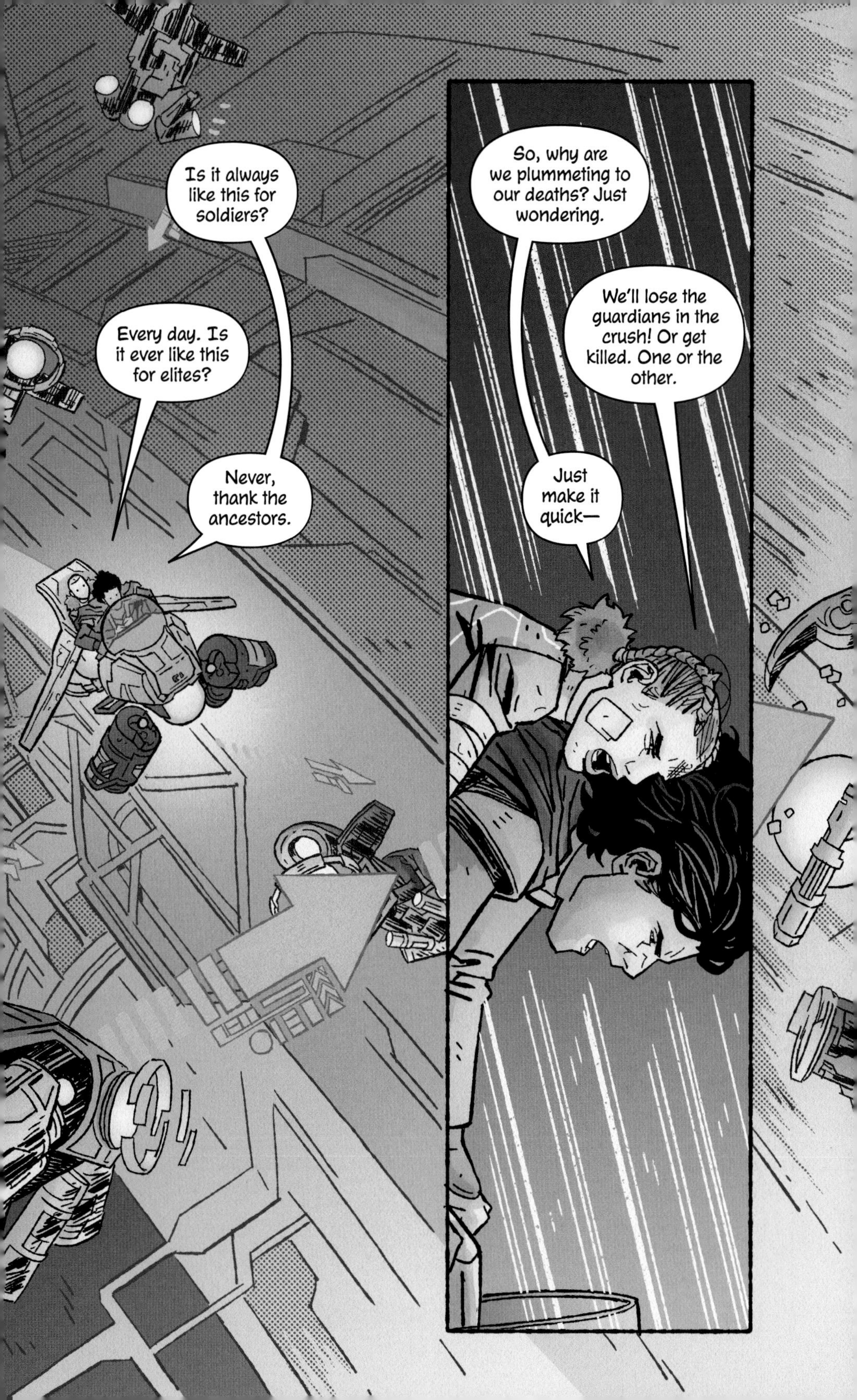
Is it always like this for soldiers?
Every day. Is it ever like this for elites?
Never, thank the ancestors.
So, why are we plummeting to our deaths? Just wondering.
We'll lose the guardians in the crush! Or get killed. One or the other.
Just make it quick—

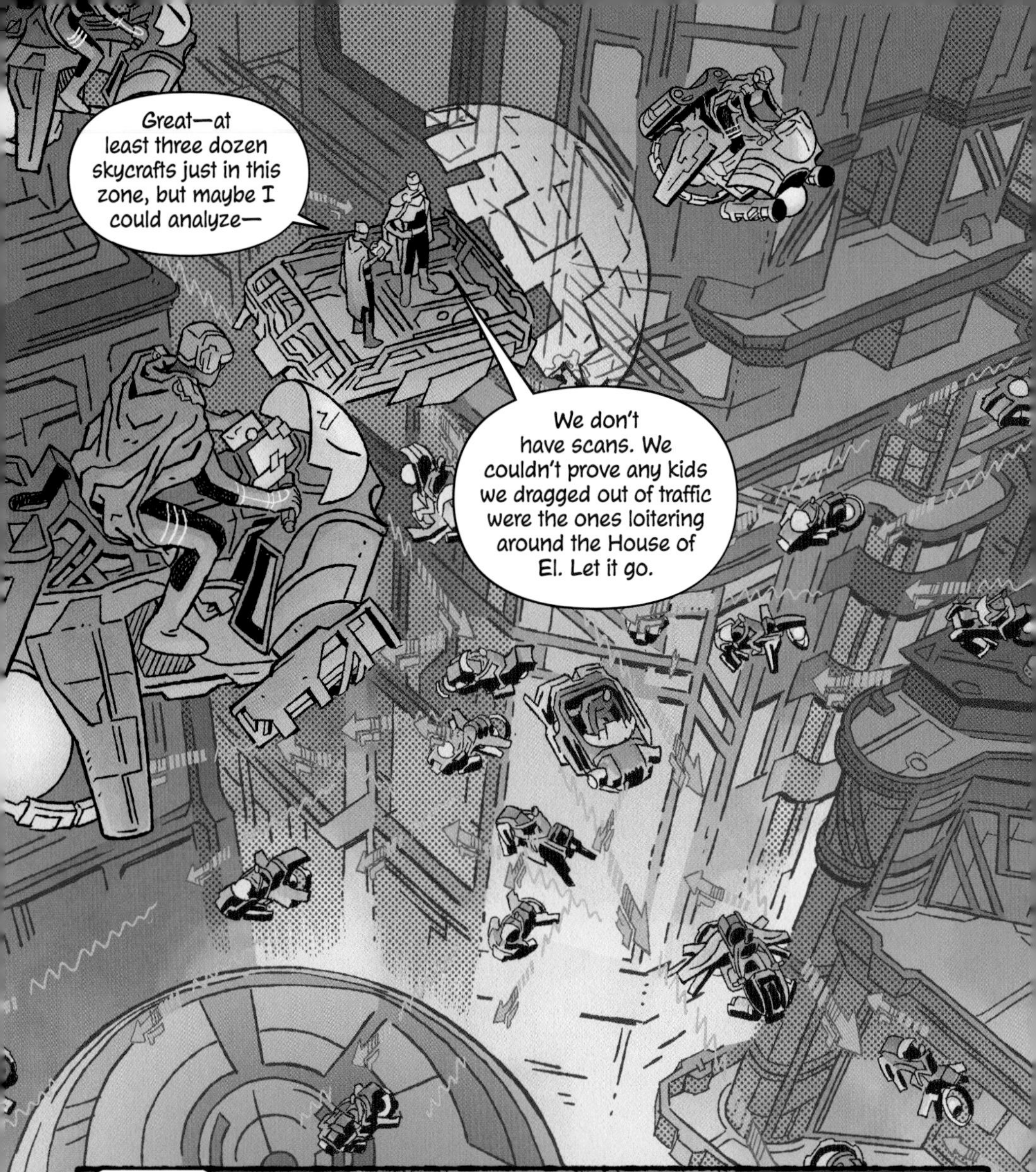
Great—at least three dozen skycrafts just in this zone, but maybe I could analyze—
We don't have scans. We couldn't prove any kids we dragged out of traffic were the ones loitering around the House of El. Let it go.

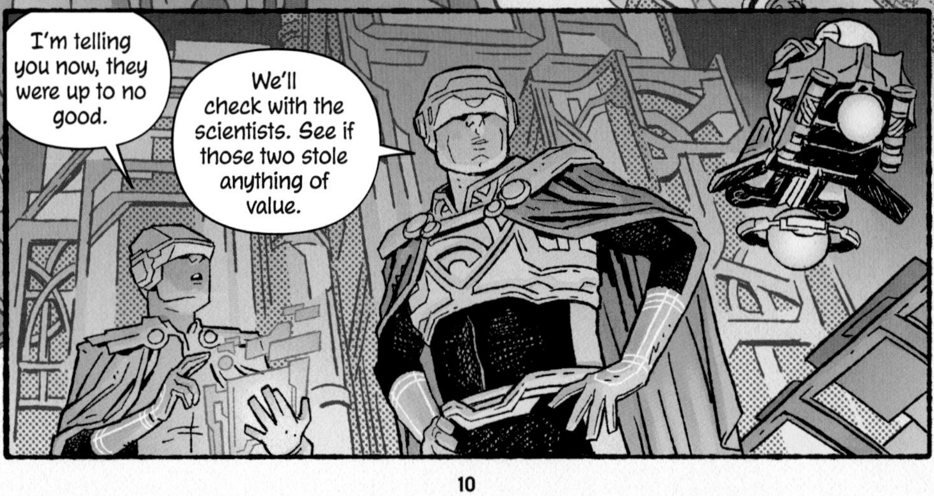
I'm telling you now, they were up to no good.
We'll check with the scientists. See if those two stole anything of value.

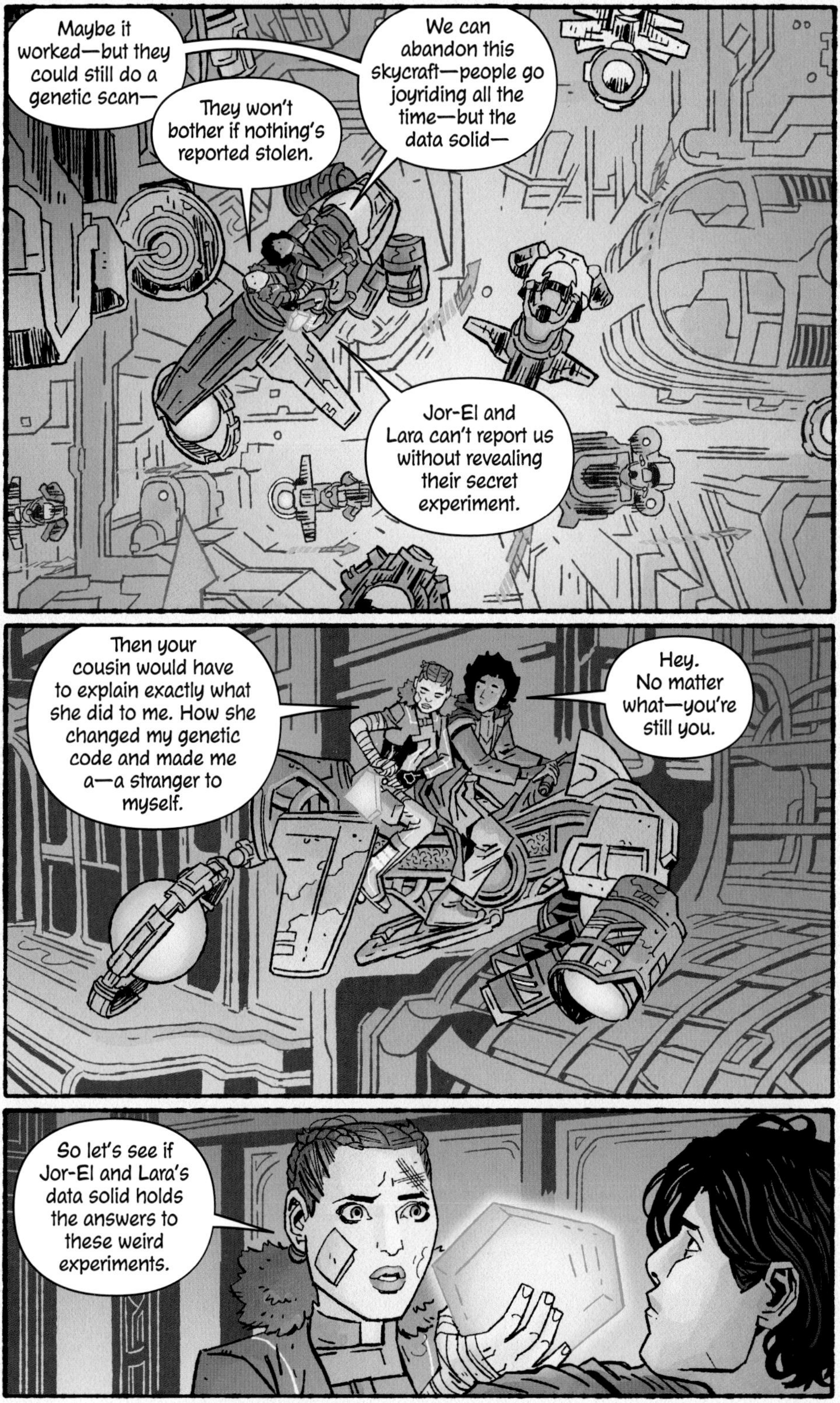
Maybe it worked—but they could still do a genetic scan—
They won't bother if nothing's reported stolen.
We can abandon this skycraft—people go joyriding all the time—but the data solid—
Jor-El and Lara can't report us without revealing their secret experiment.
Then your cousin would have to explain exactly what she did to me. How she changed my genetic code and made me a—a stranger to myself.
Hey. No matter what—you're still you.
So let's see if Jor-El and Lara's data solid holds the answers to these weird experiments.

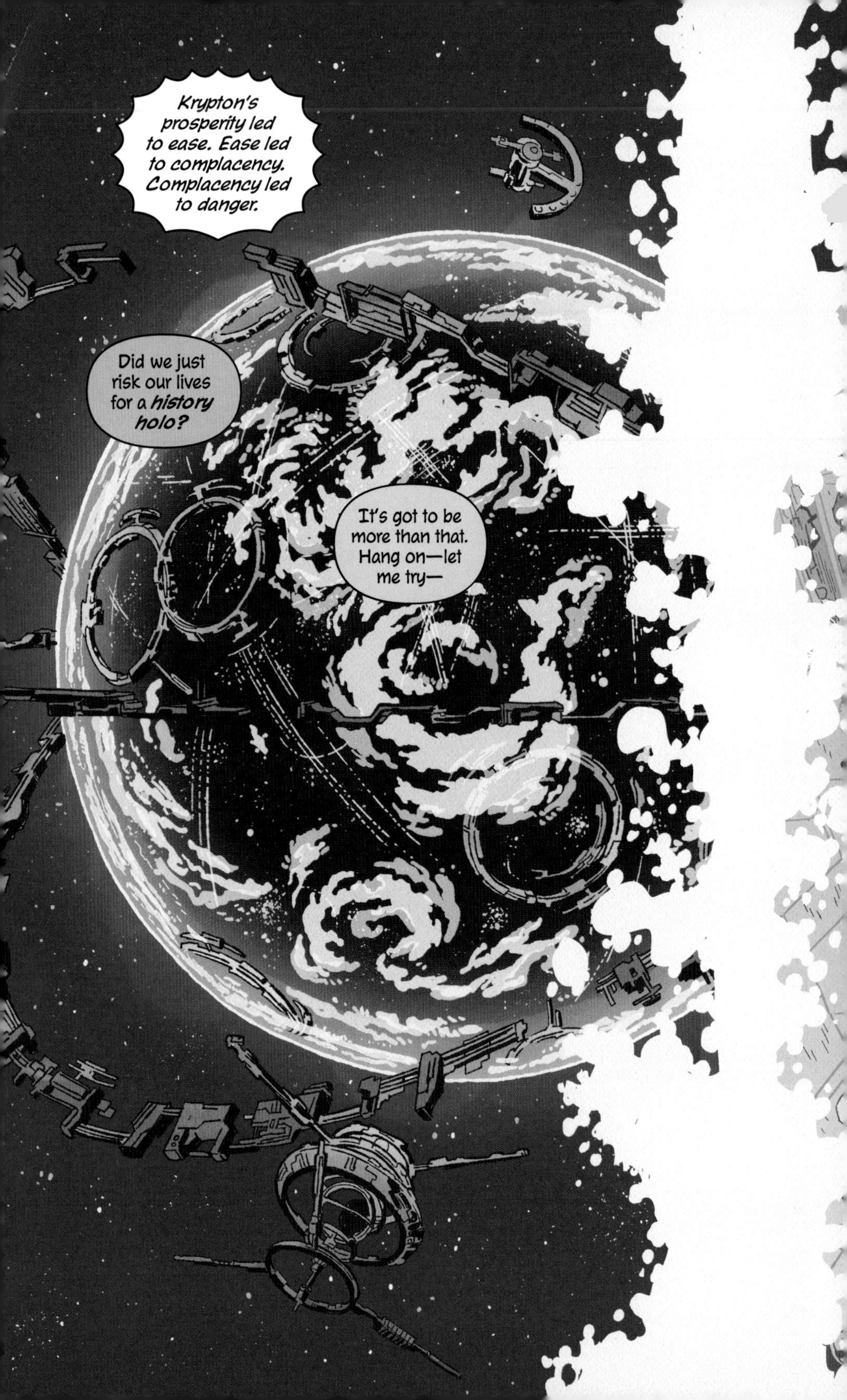
Krypton's prosperity led to ease. Ease led to complacency. Complacency led to danger.
Did we just risk our lives for a *history holo?*
It's got to be more than that. Hang on—let me try—

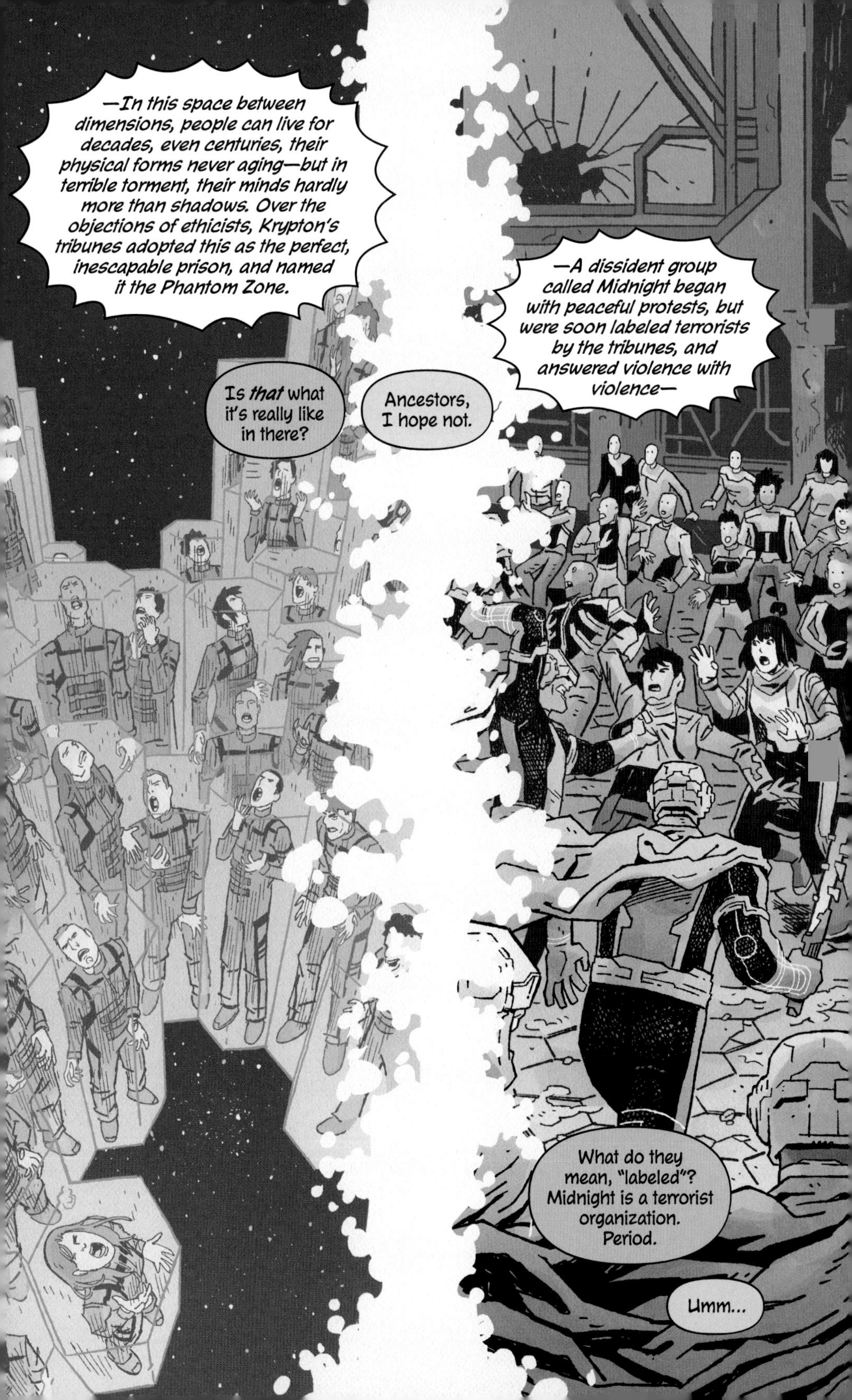
—In this space between dimensions, people can live for decades, even centuries, their physical forms never aging—but in terrible torment, their minds hardly more than shadows. Over the objections of ethicists, Krypton's tribunes adopted this as the perfect, inescapable prison, and named it the Phantom Zone.
Is *that* what it's really like in there?
Ancestors, I hope not.
—A dissident group called Midnight began with peaceful protests, but were soon labeled terrorists by the tribunes, and answered violence with violence—
What do they mean, "labeled"? Midnight is a terrorist organization. Period.
Umm...

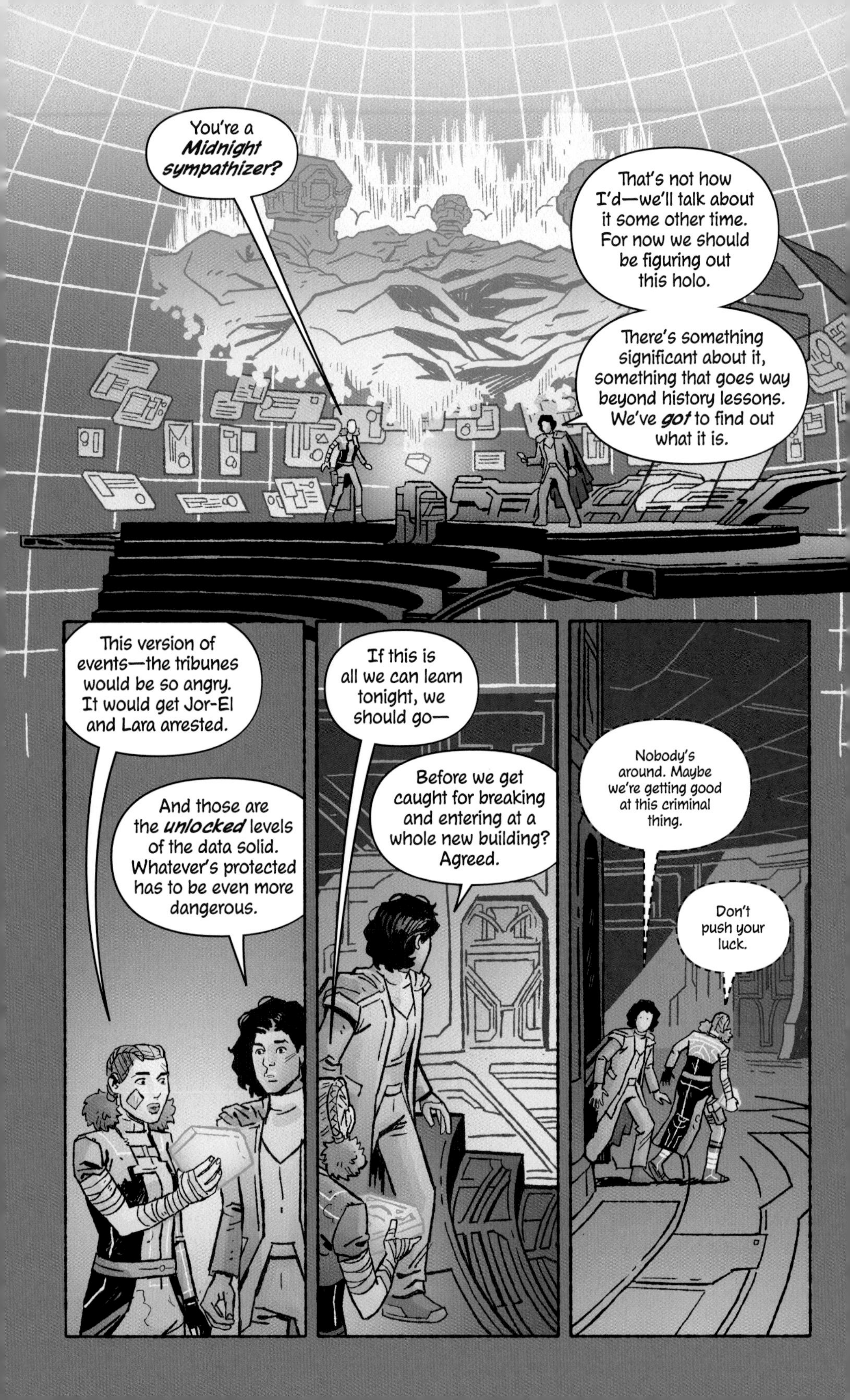
You're a *Midnight sympathizer?*
That's not how I'd—we'll talk about it some other time. For now we should be figuring out this holo.
There's something significant about it, something that goes way beyond history lessons. We've *got* to find out what it is.
This version of events—the tribunes would be so angry. It would get Jor-El and Lara arrested.
And those are the *unlocked* levels of the data solid. Whatever's protected has to be even more dangerous.
If this is all we can learn tonight, we should go—
Before we get caught for breaking and entering at a whole new building? Agreed.
Nobody's around. Maybe we're getting good at this criminal thing.
Don't push your luck.

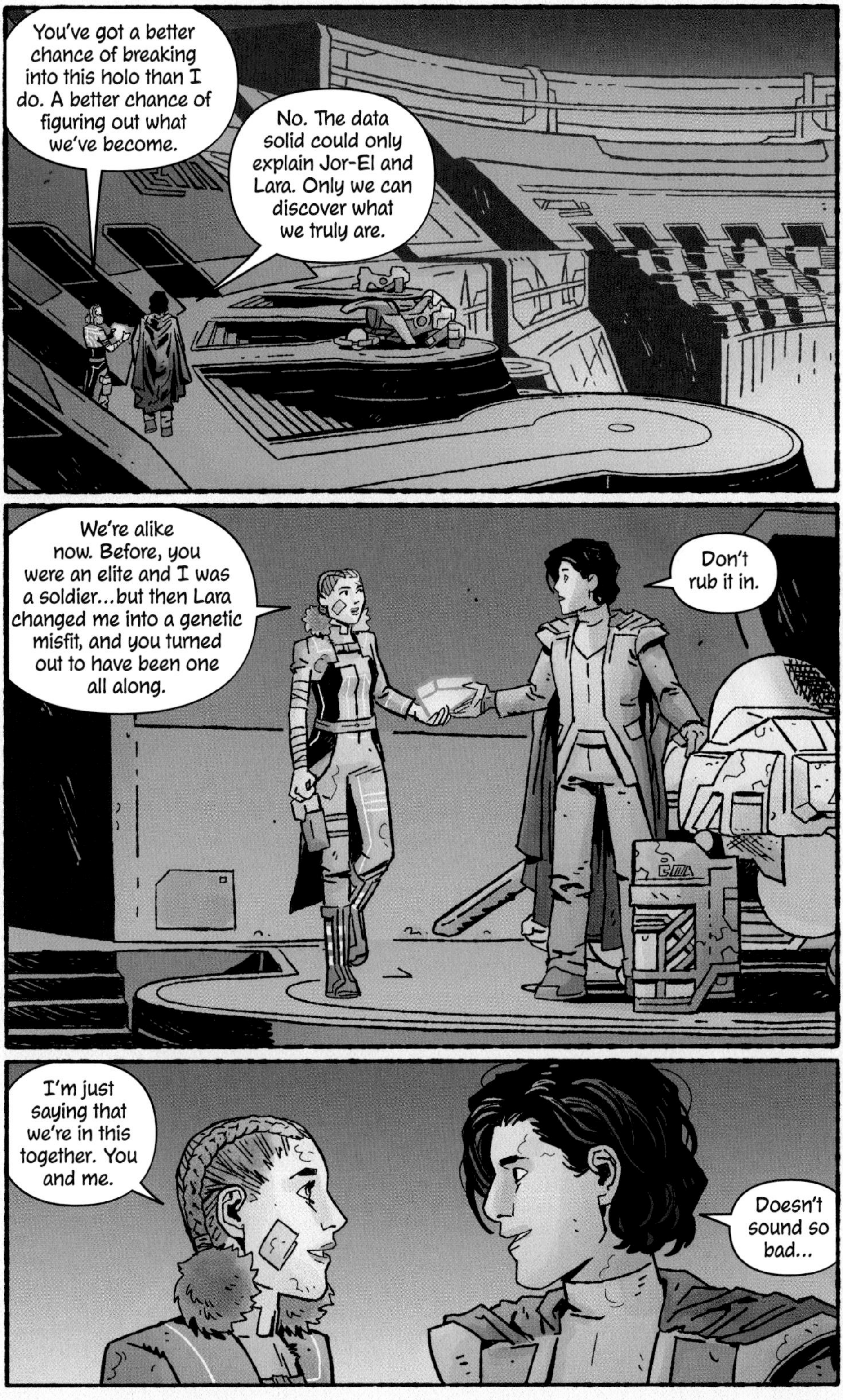
You've got a better chance of breaking into this holo than I do. A better chance of figuring out what we've become.
No. The data solid could only explain Jor-El and Lara. Only we can discover what we truly are.
We're alike now. Before, you were an elite and I was a soldier...but then Lara changed me into a genetic misfit, and you turned out to have been one all along.
Don't rub it in.
I'm just saying that we're in this together. You and me.
Doesn't sound so bad...

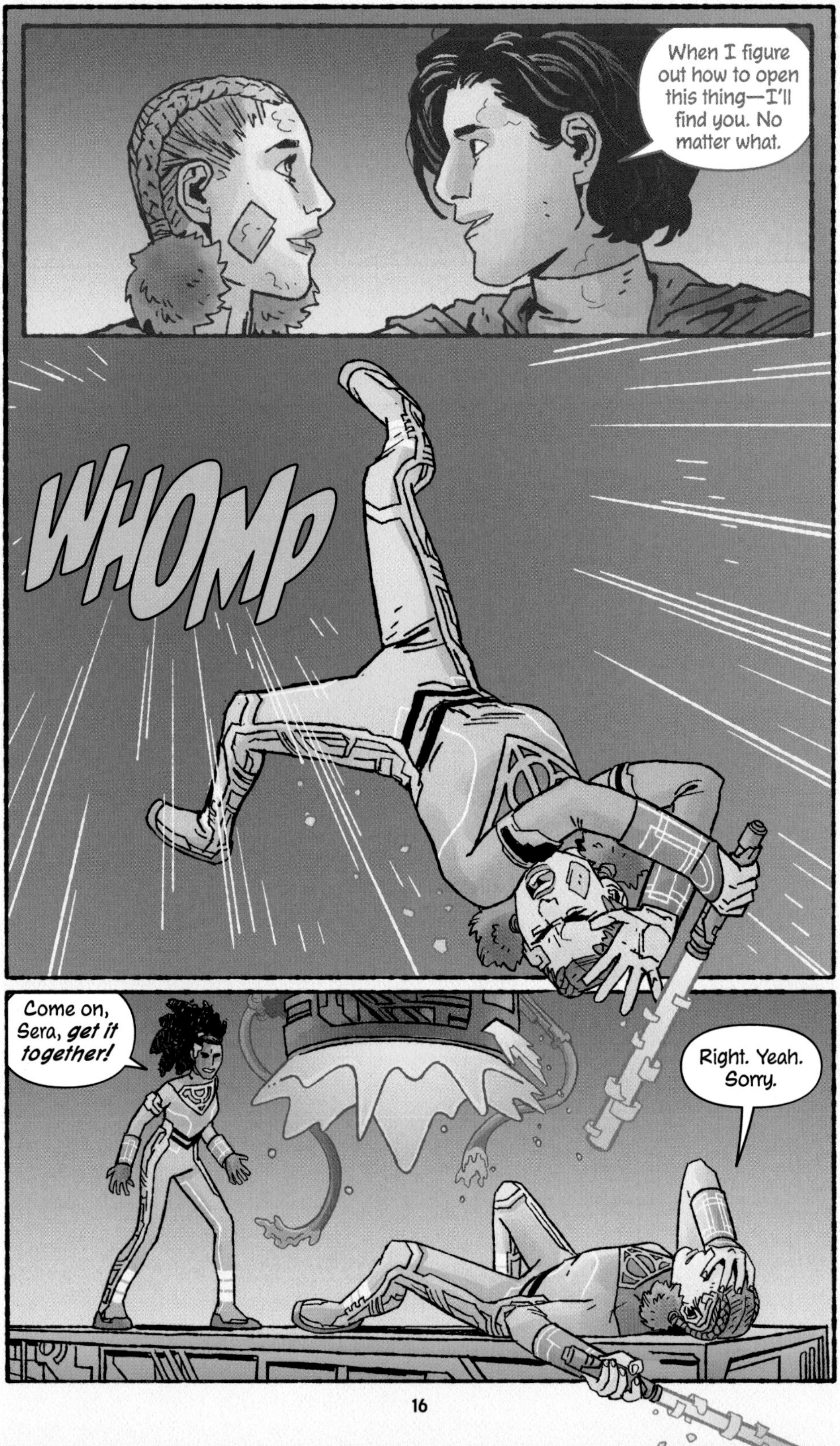
When I figure out how to open this thing—I'll find you. No matter what.
WHOMP
Come on, Sera, *get it together!*
Right. Yeah. Sorry.

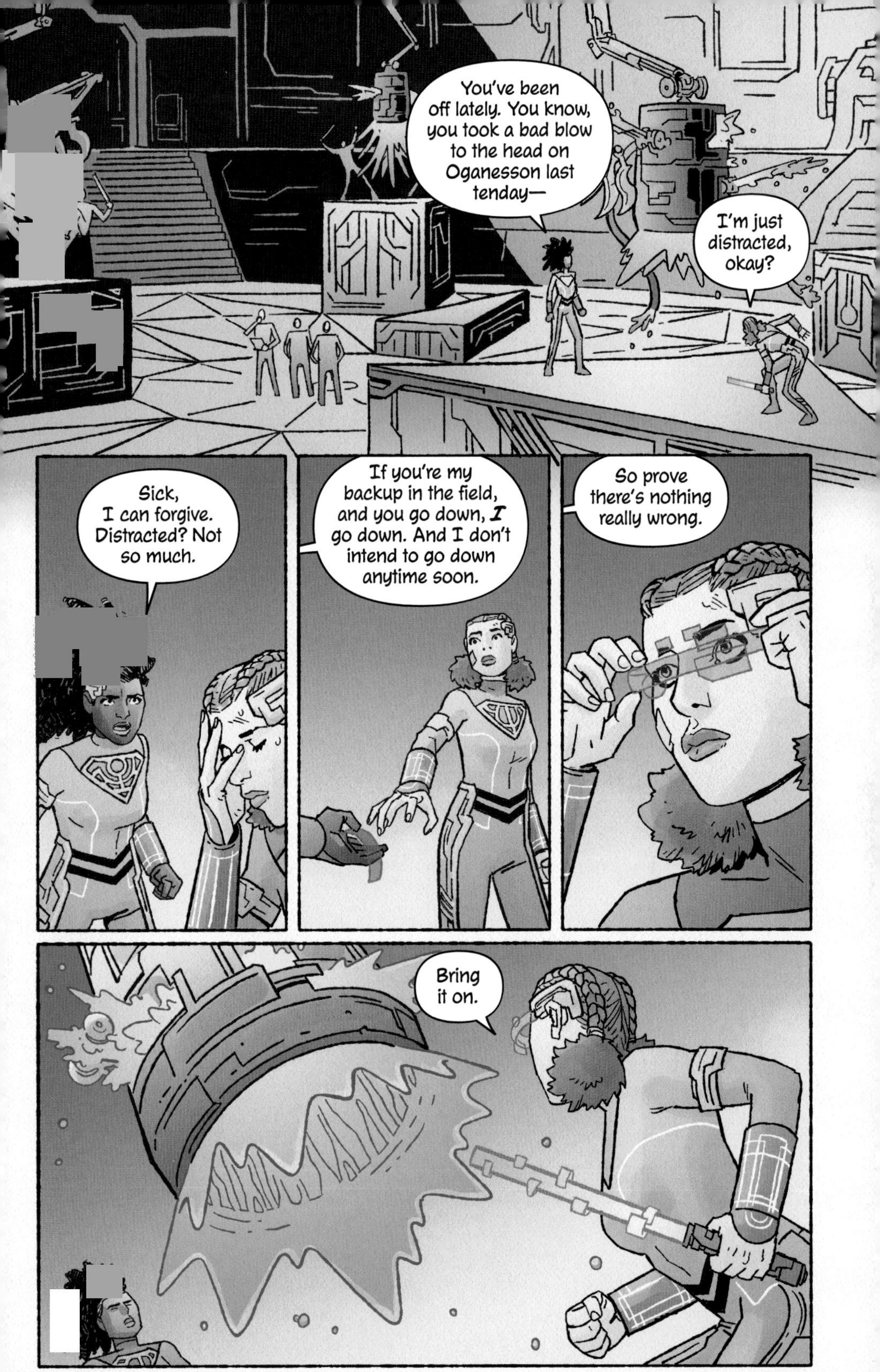
You've been off lately. You know, you took a bad blow to the head on Oganesson last tenday—
I'm just distracted, okay?
Sick, I can forgive. Distracted? Not so much.
If you're my backup in the field, and you go down, *I* go down. And I don't intend to go down anytime soon.
So prove there's nothing really wrong.
Bring it on.

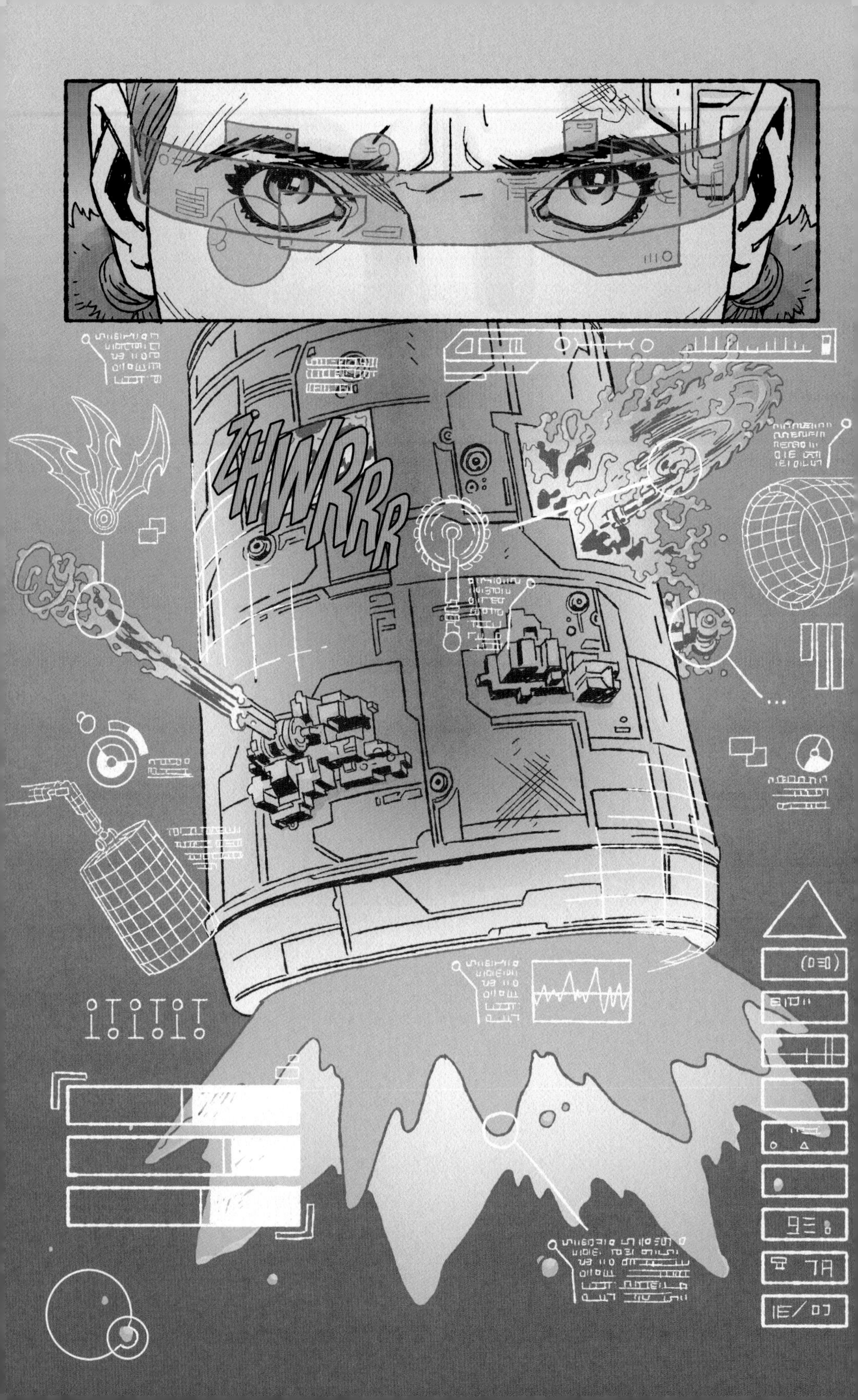
ZHWRRR

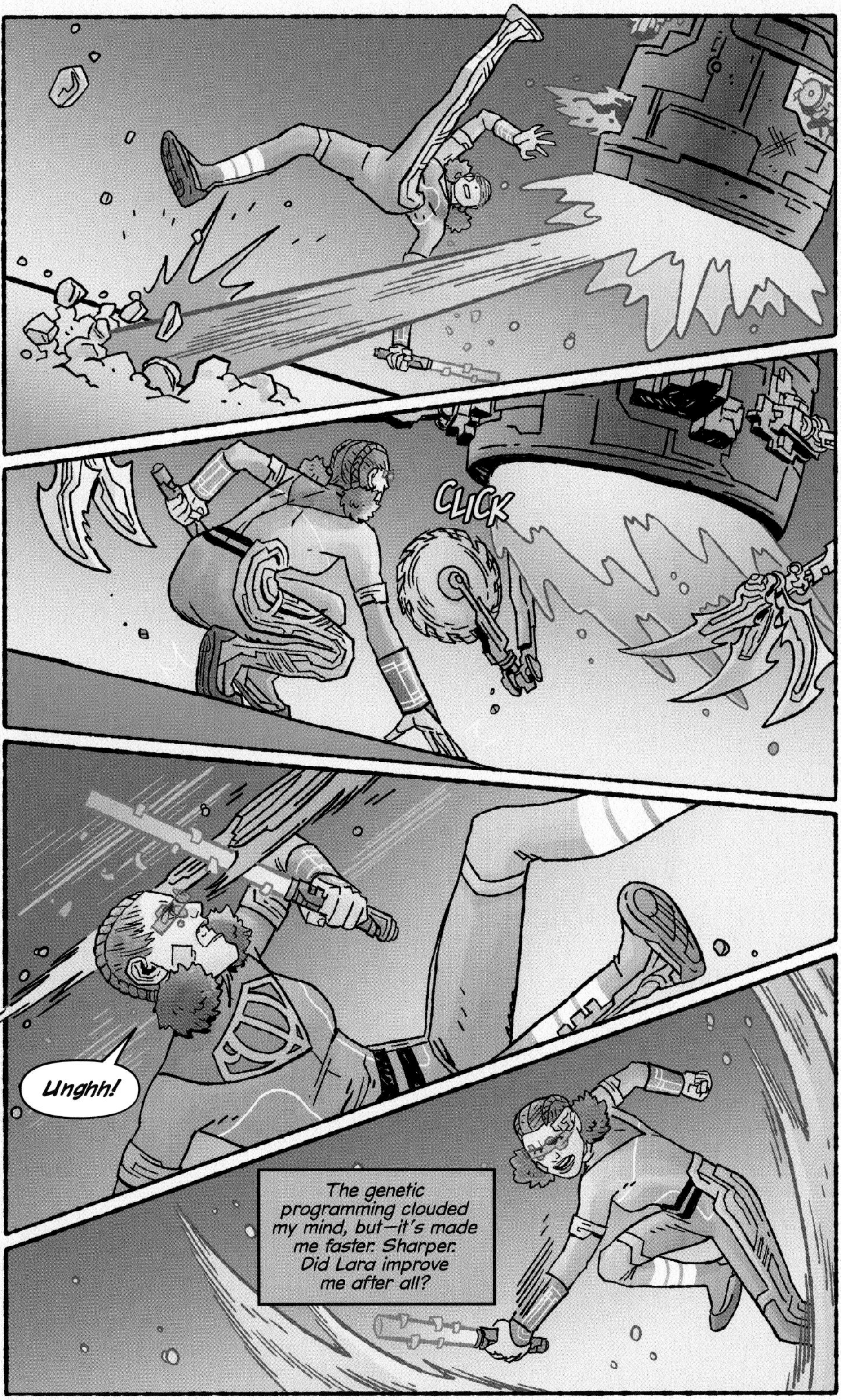
CLICK
Unghh!
The genetic programming clouded my mind, but—it's made me faster. Sharper. Did Lara improve me after all?

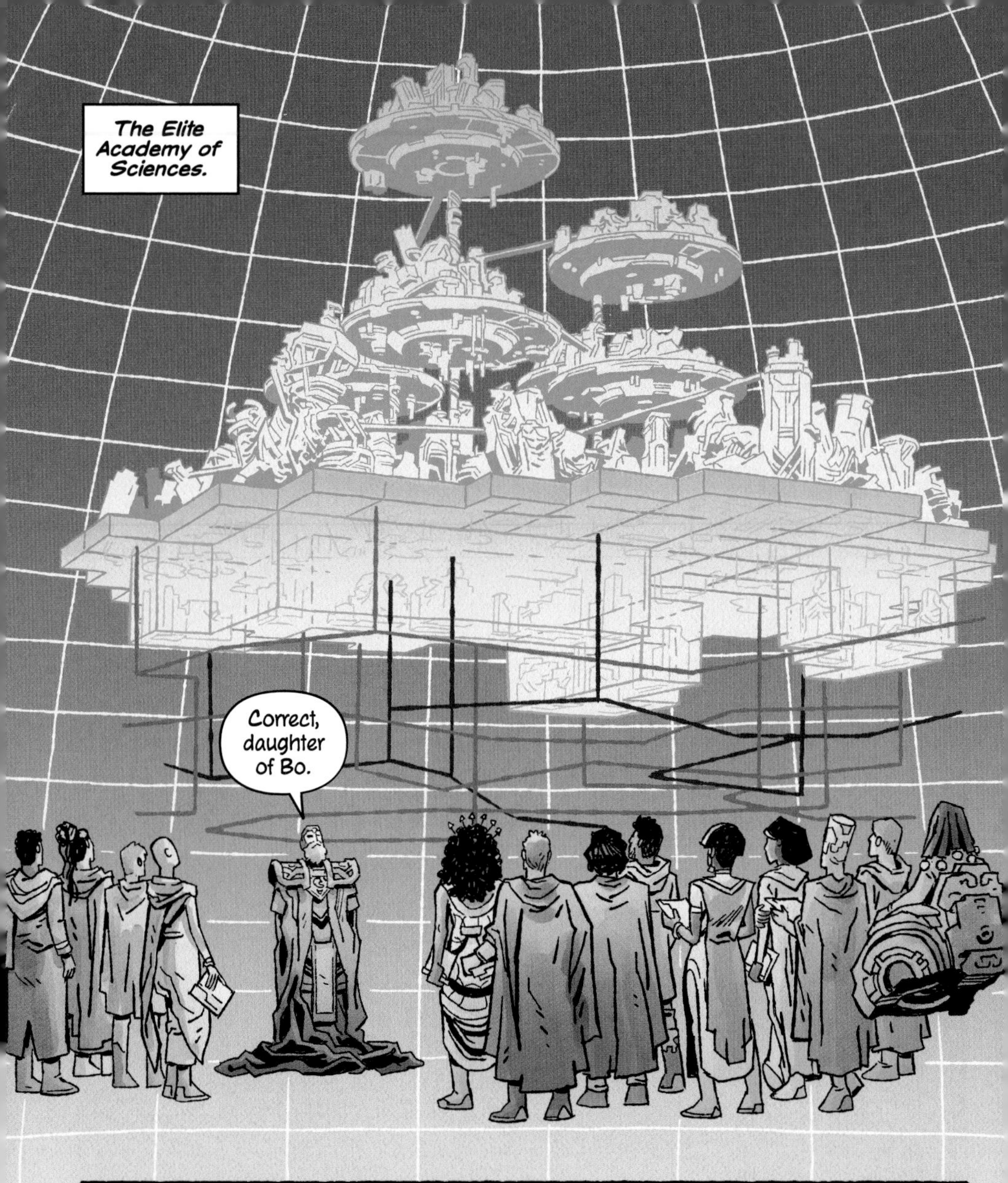
The Elite Academy of Sciences.
Correct, daughter of Bo.

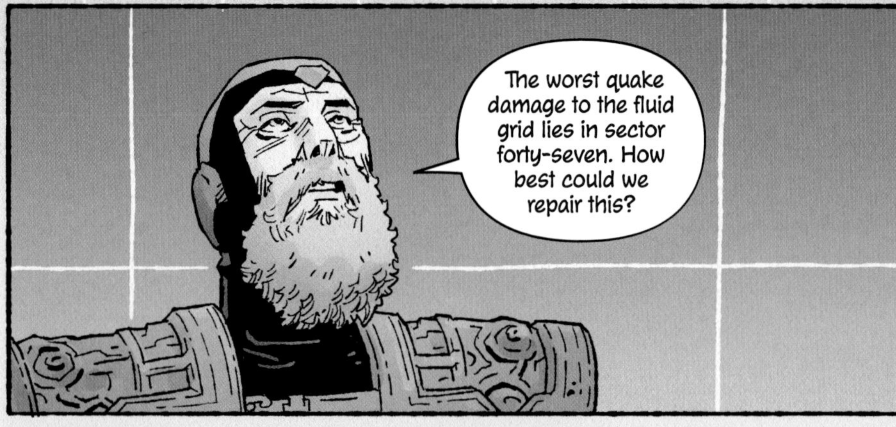
The worst quake damage to the fluid grid lies in sector forty-seven. How best could we repair this?

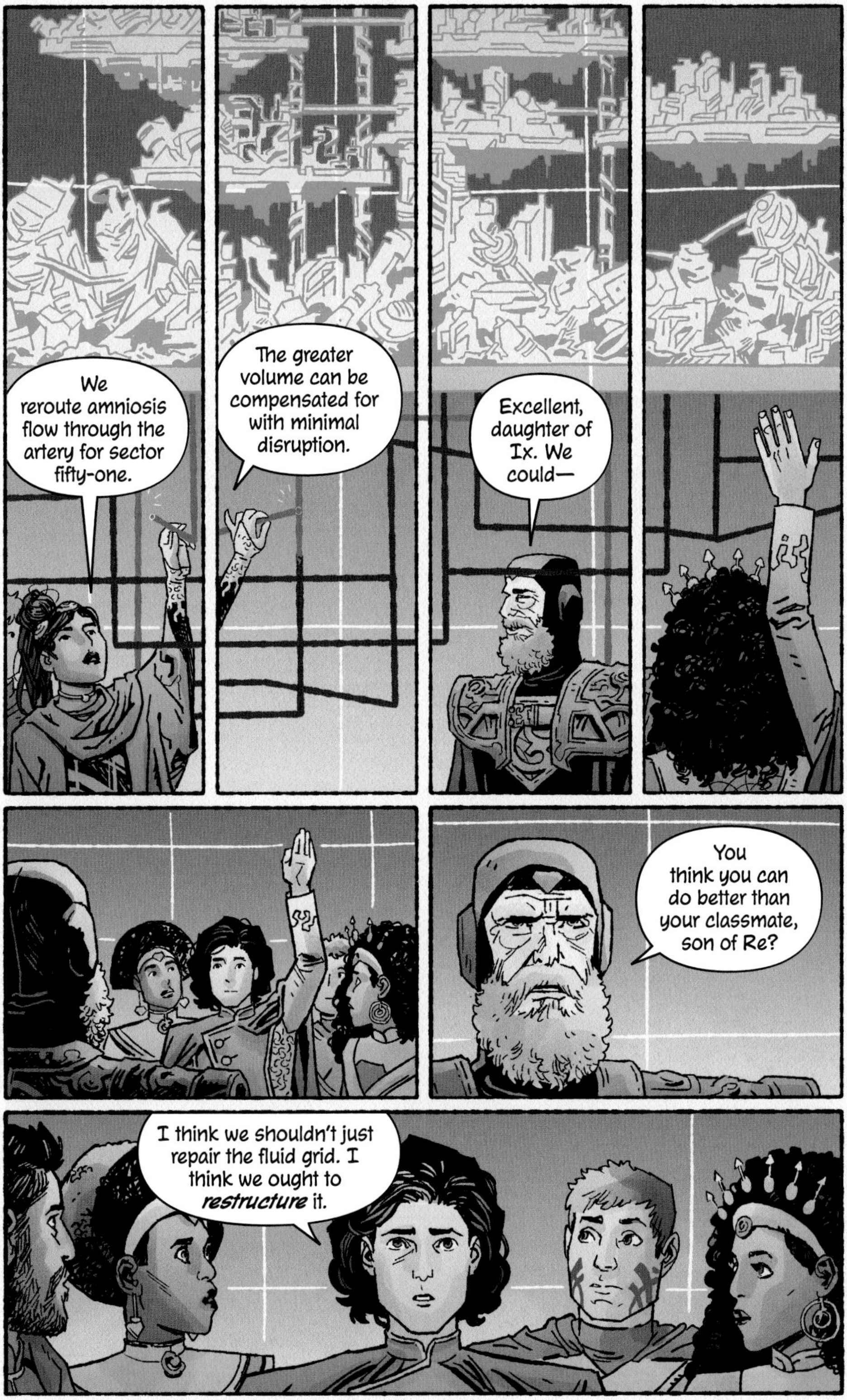
We reroute amniosis flow through the artery for sector fifty-one.
The greater volume can be compensated for with minimal disruption.
Excellent, daughter of Ix. We could—
You think you can do better than your classmate, son of Re?
I think we shouldn't just repair the fluid grid. I think we ought to *restructure* it.

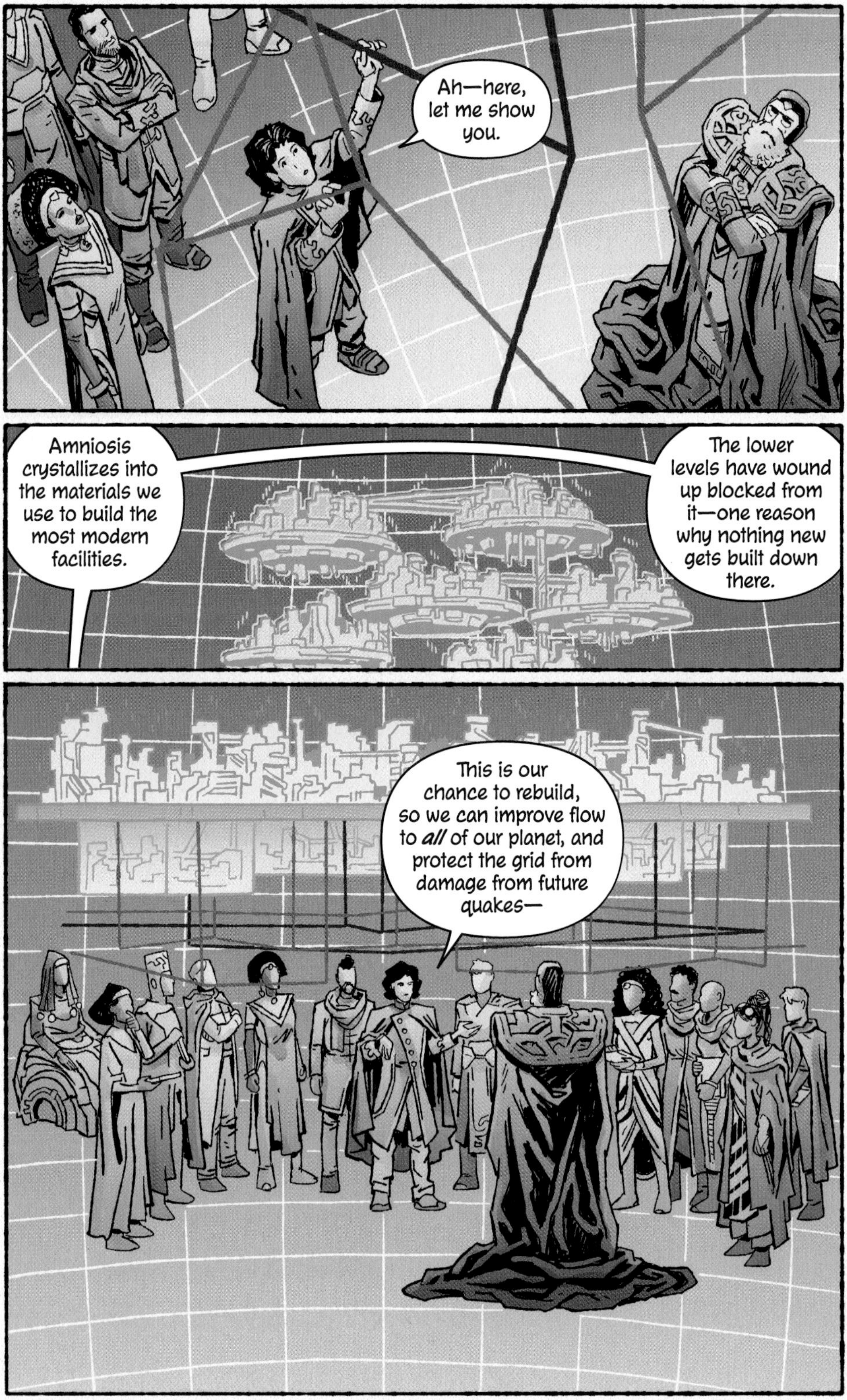
Ah—here, let me show you.
Amniosis crystallizes into the materials we use to build the most modern facilities.
The lower levels have wound up blocked from it—one reason why nothing new gets built down there.
This is our chance to rebuild, so we can improve flow to *all* of our planet, and protect the grid from damage from future quakes—

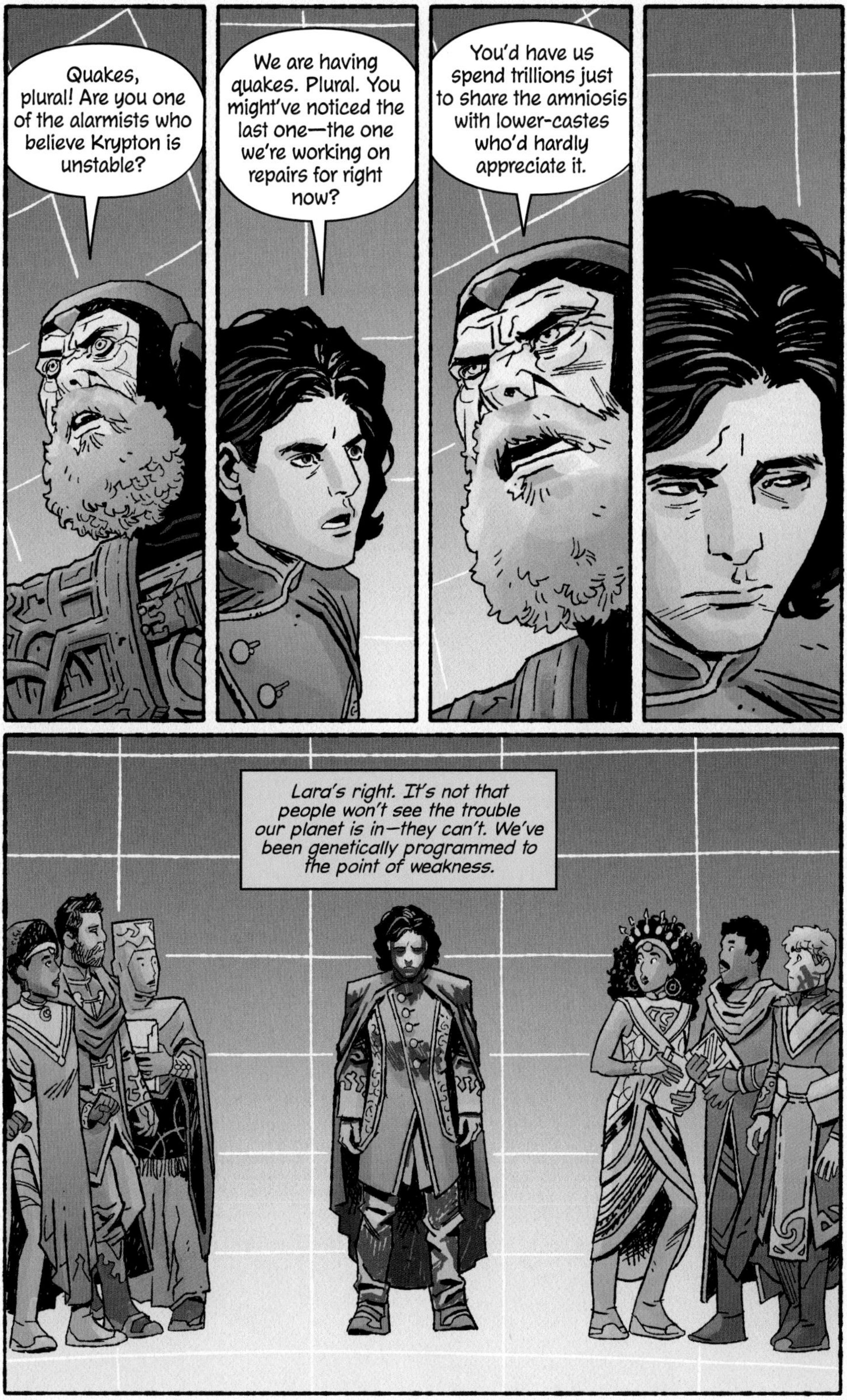
Quakes, plural! Are you one of the alarmists who believe Krypton is unstable?
We are having quakes. Plural. You might've noticed the last one—the one we're working on repairs for right now?
You'd have us spend trillions just to share the amniosis with lower-castes who'd hardly appreciate it.
Lara's right. It's not that people won't see the trouble our planet is in—they can't. We've been genetically programmed to the point of weakness.

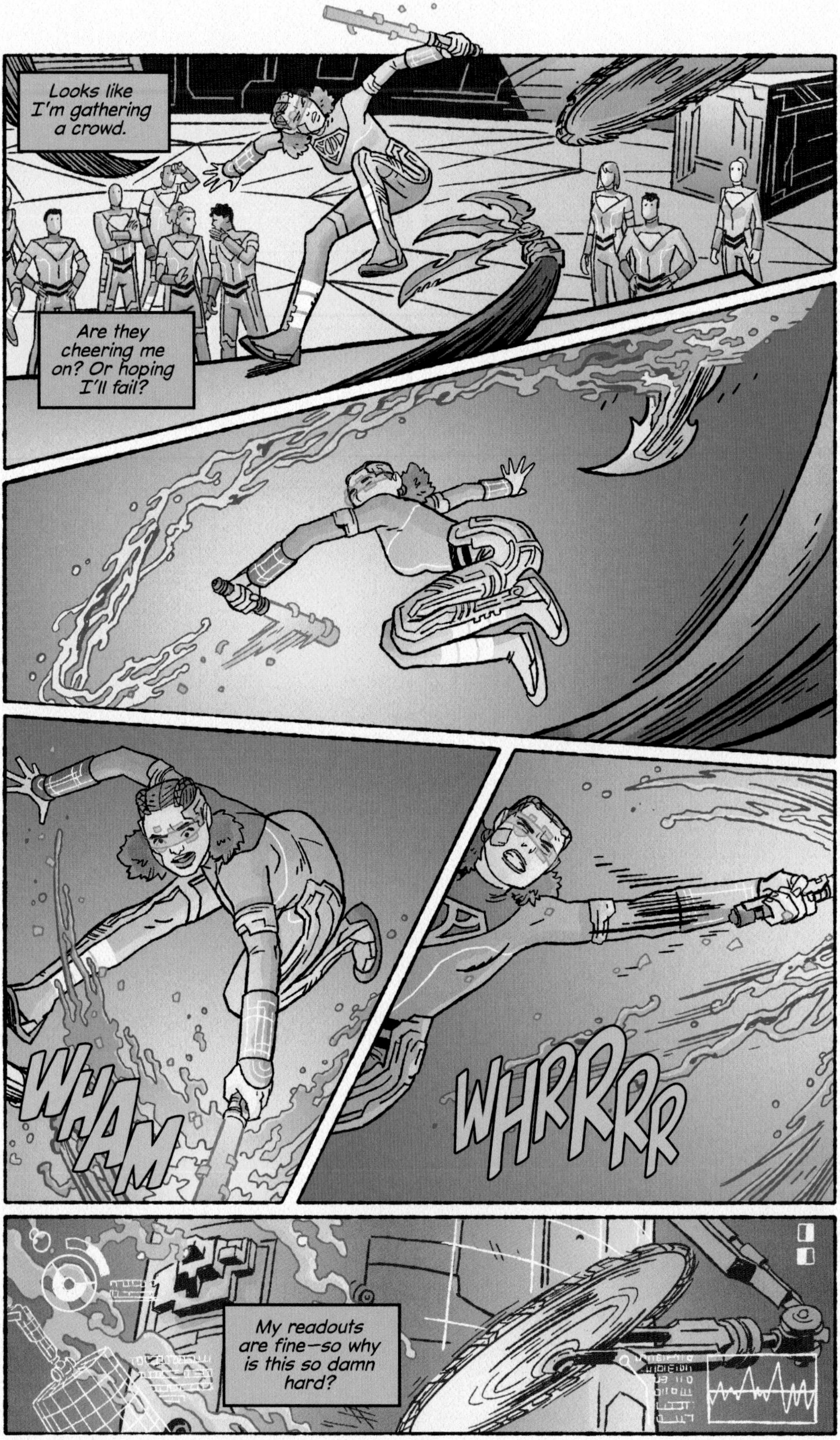
Looks like I'm gathering a crowd.
Are they cheering me on? Or hoping I'll fail?
WHAM
WHRRRR
My readouts are fine—so why is this so damn hard?

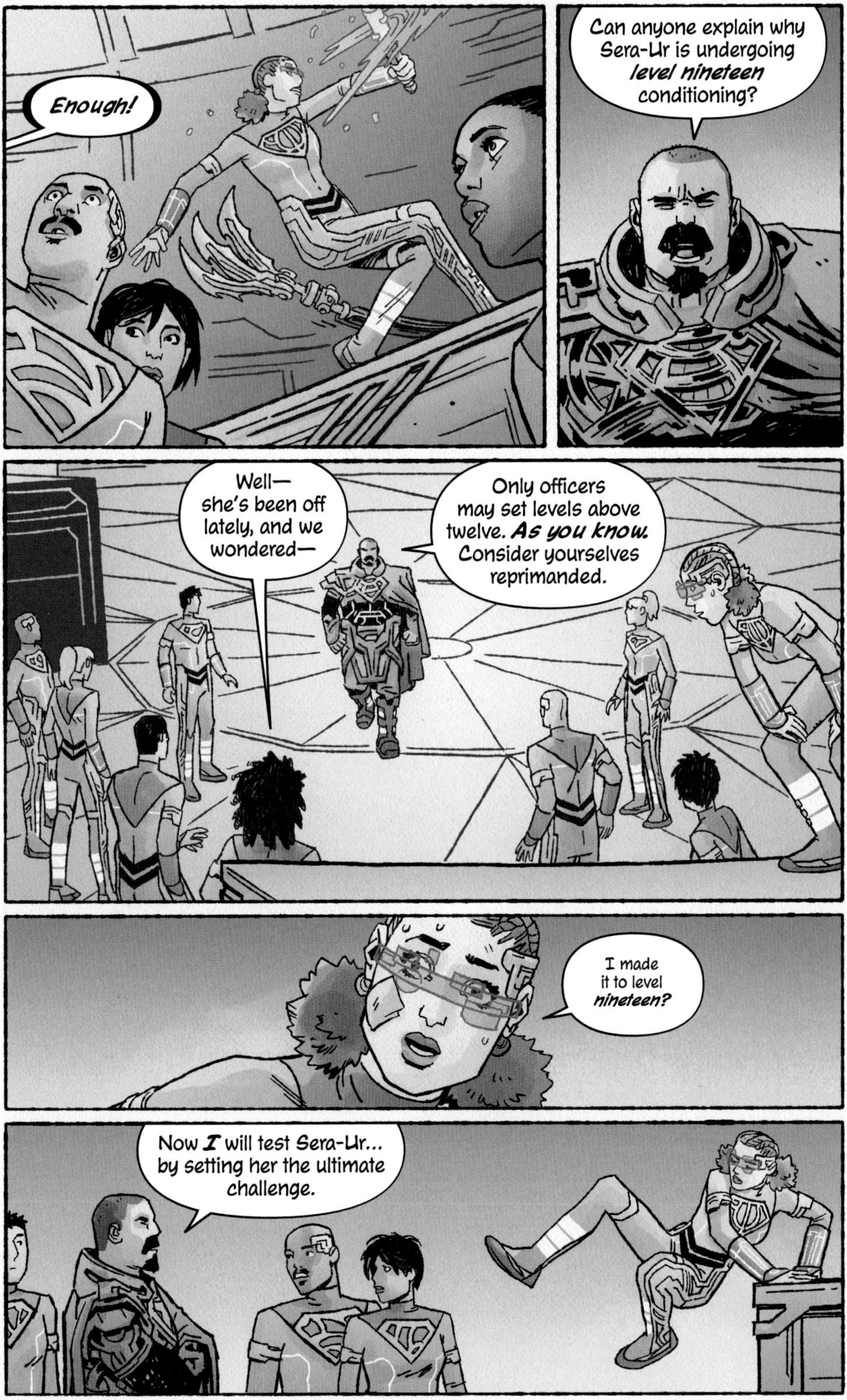
Enough!
Can anyone explain why Sera-Ur is undergoing *level nineteen* conditioning?
Well— she's been off lately, and we wondered—
Only officers may set levels above twelve. ***As you know.*** Consider yourselves reprimanded.
I made it to level ***nineteen?***
Now ***I*** will test Sera-Ur... by setting her the ultimate challenge.

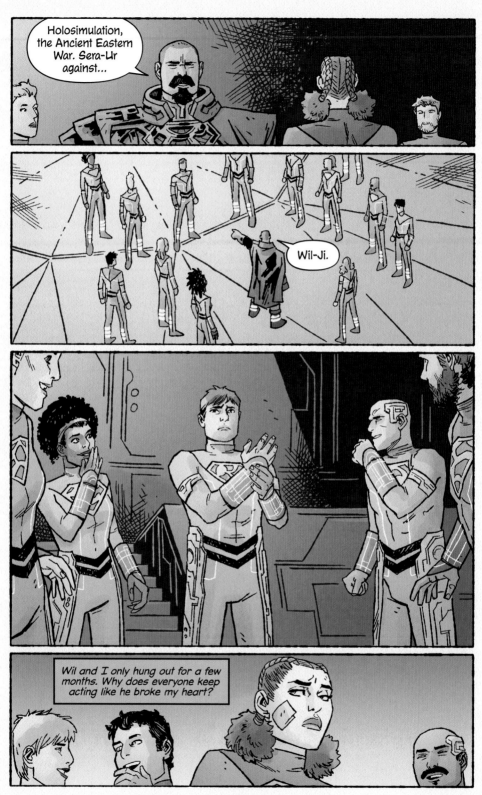

Holosimulation, the Ancient Eastern War. Sera-Ur against...

Wil-Ji.

Wil and I only hung out for a few months. Why does everyone keep acting like he broke my heart?

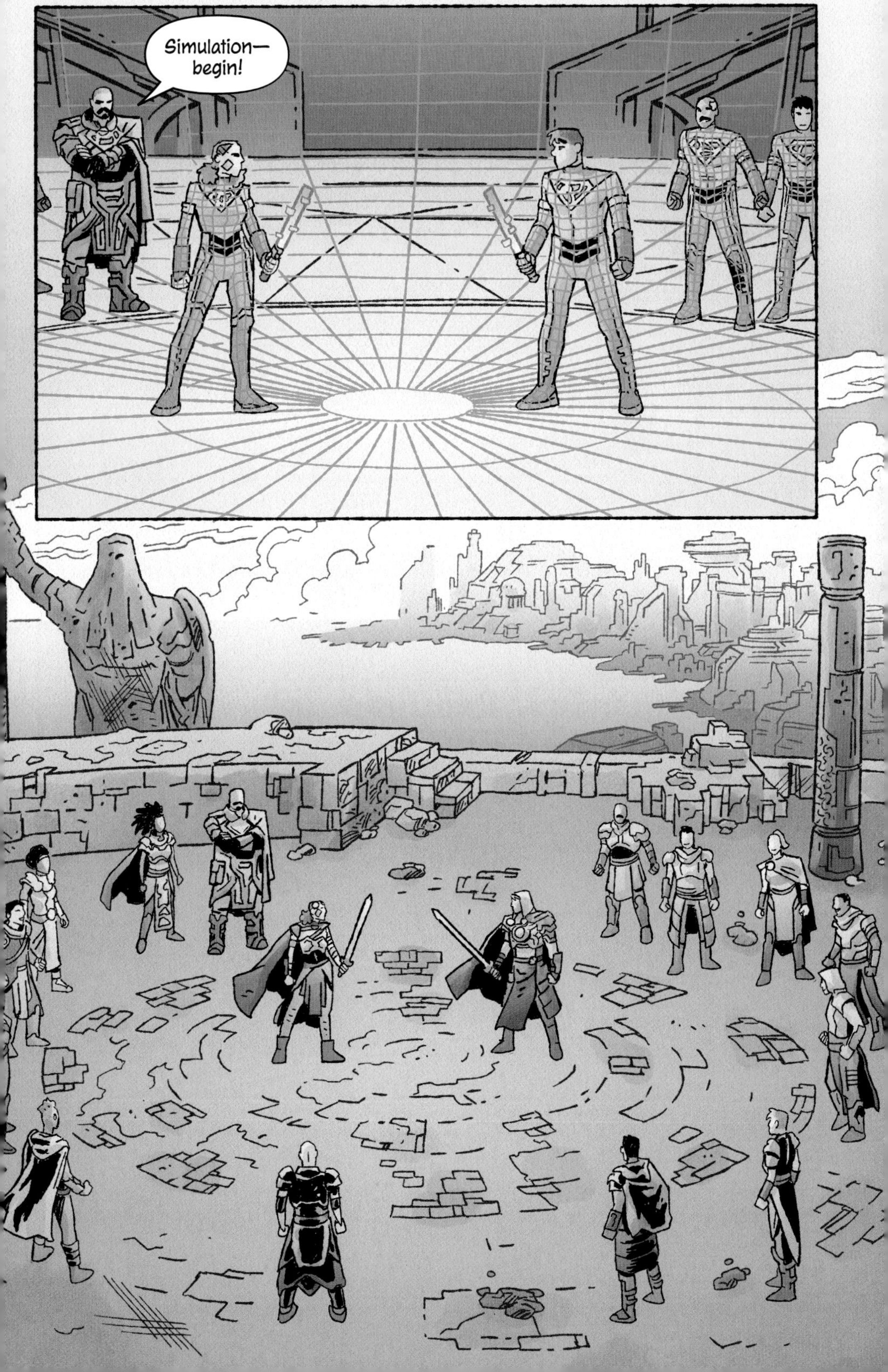
Simulation—begin!

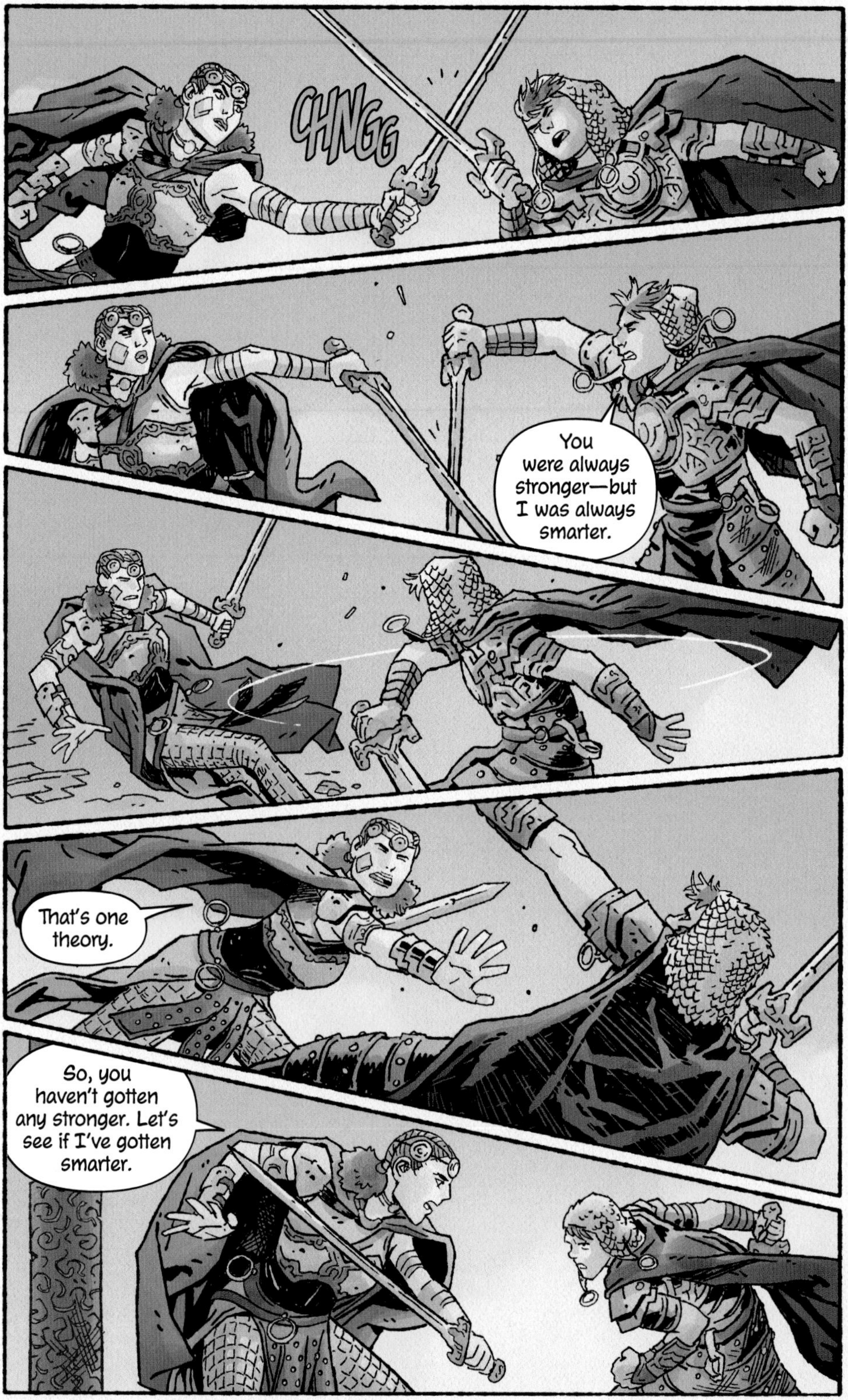
CHNGG
You were always stronger—but I was always smarter.
That's one theory.
So, you haven't gotten any stronger. Let's see if I've gotten smarter.

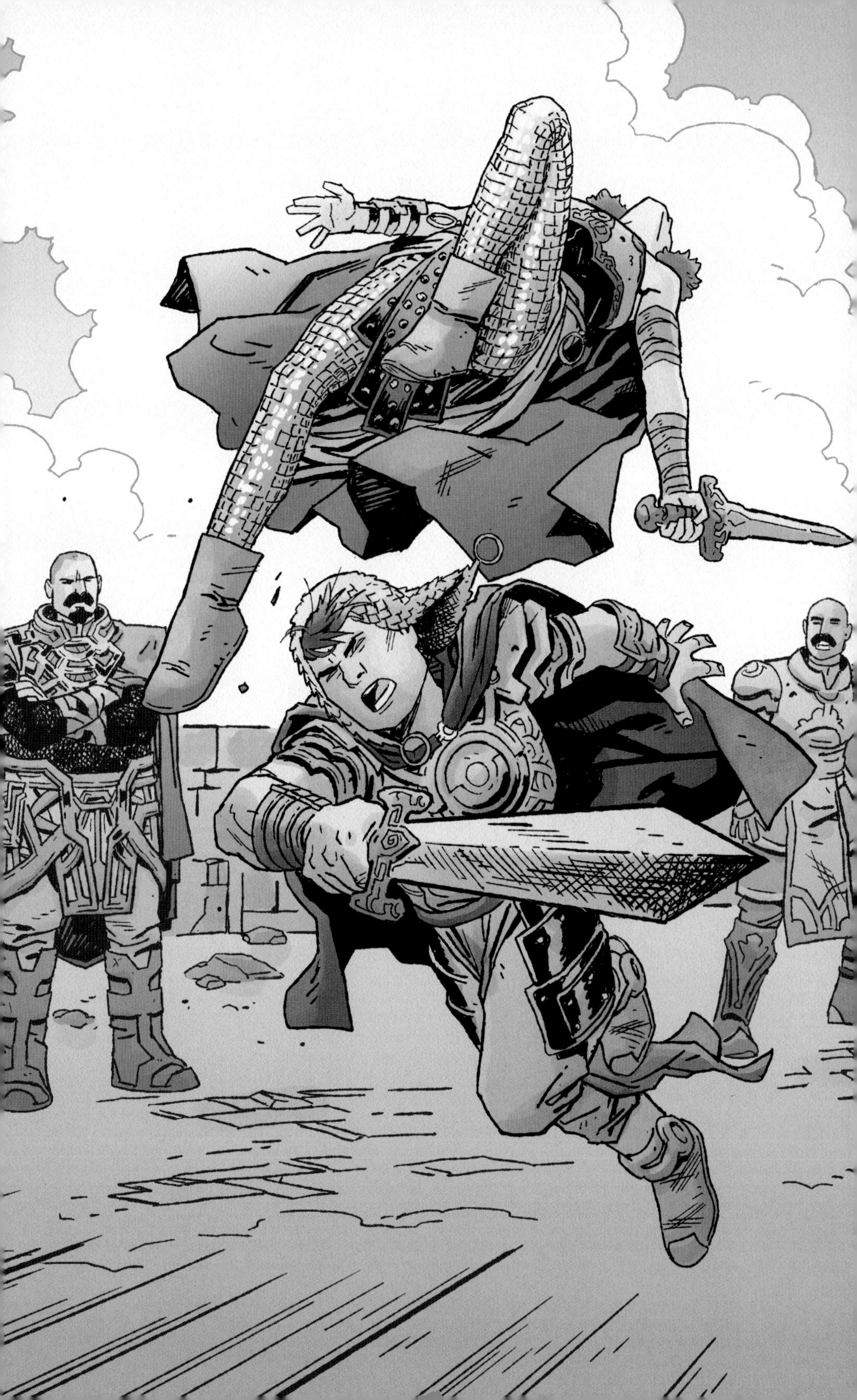

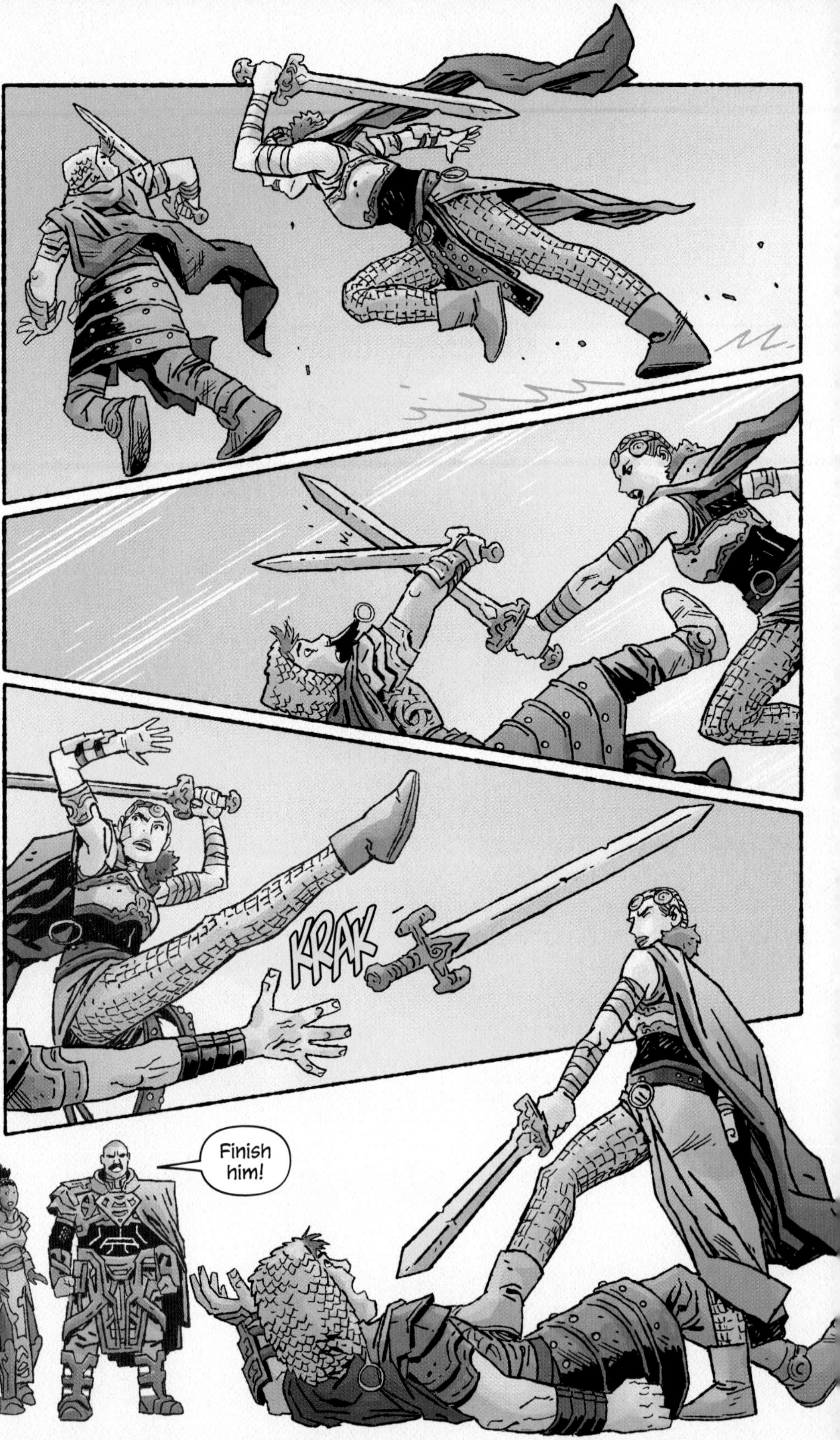
KRAK
Finish him!

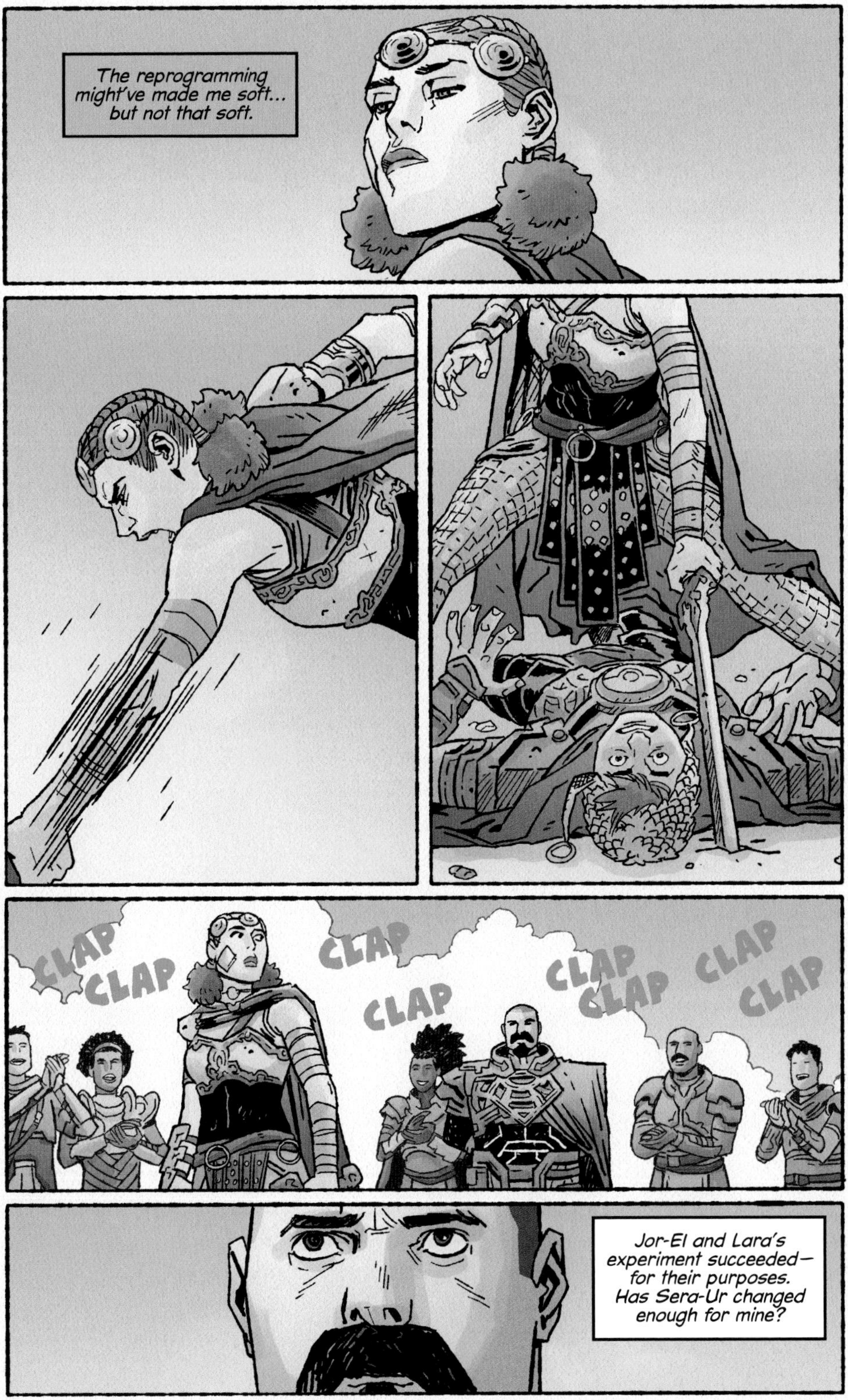

The reprogramming might've made me soft... but not that soft.
CLAP
CLAP
CLAP
CLAP
CLAP
CLAP
CLAP
CLAP
Jor-El and Lara's experiment succeeded—for their purposes. Has Sera-Ur changed enough for mine?

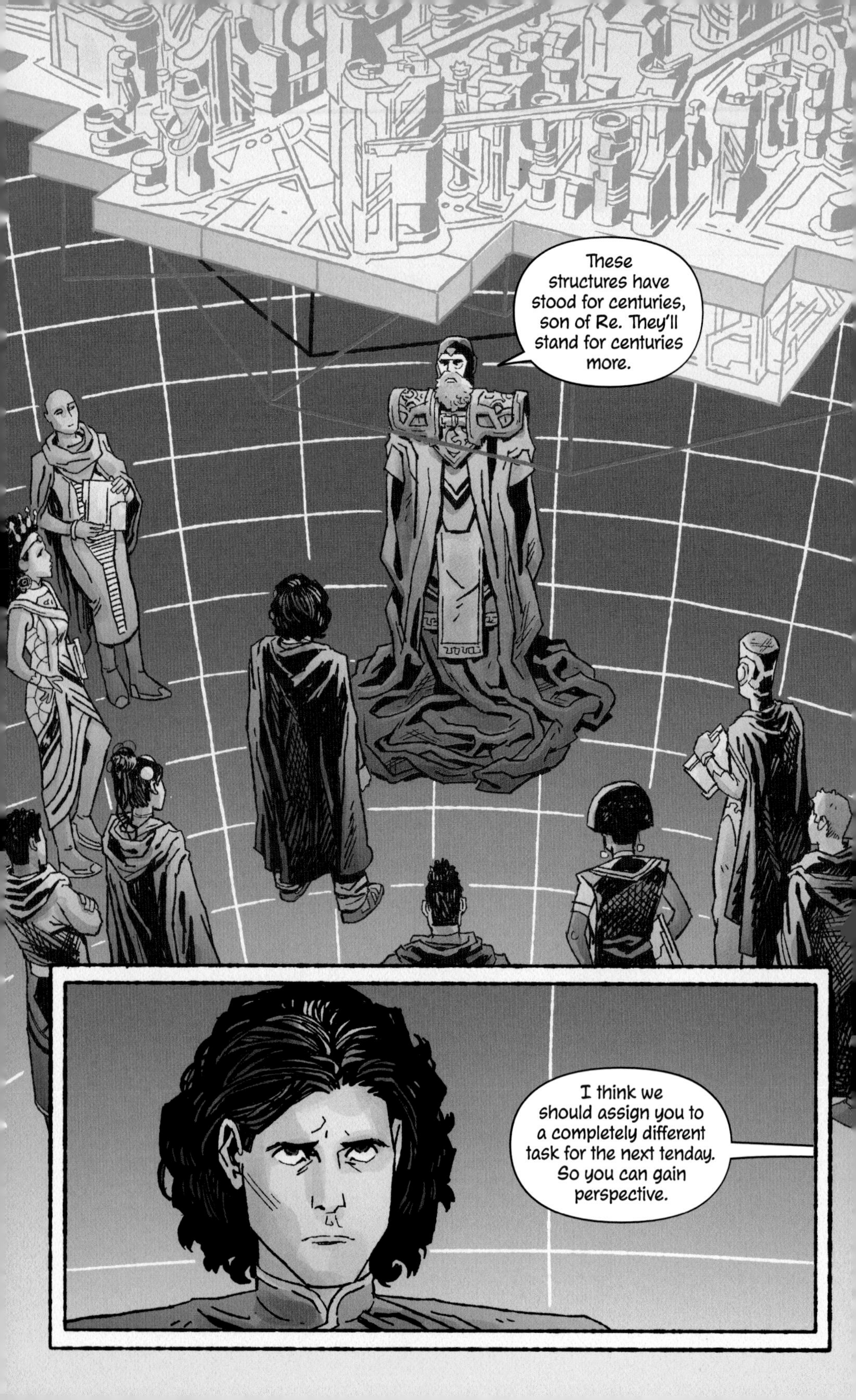
These structures have stood for centuries, son of Re. They'll stand for centuries more.
I think we should assign you to a completely different task for the next tenday. So you can gain perspective.

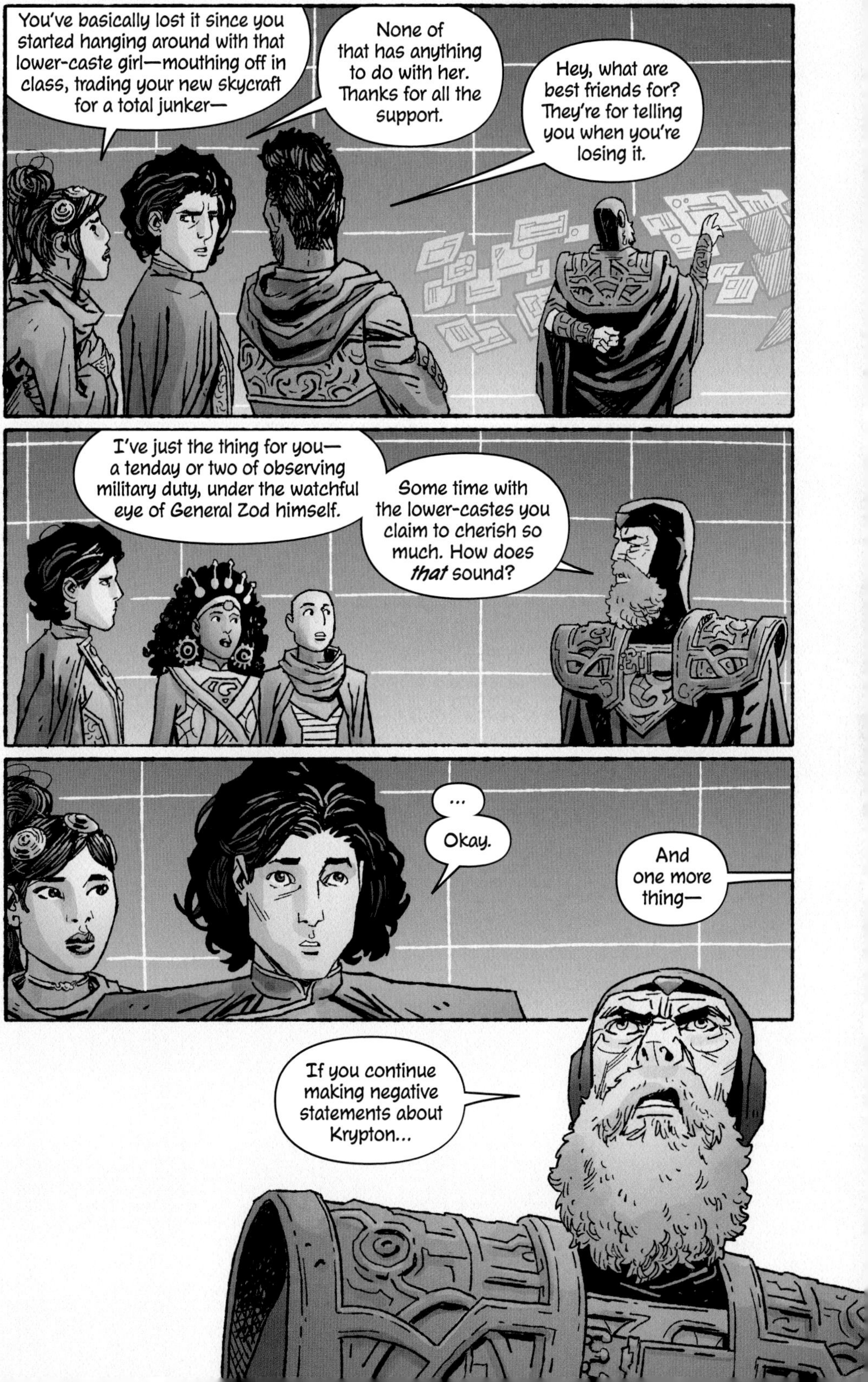
You've basically lost it since you started hanging around with that lower-caste girl—mouthing off in class, trading your new skycraft for a total junker—
None of that has anything to do with her. Thanks for all the support.
Hey, what are best friends for? They're for telling you when you're losing it.
I've just the thing for you—a tenday or two of observing military duty, under the watchful eye of General Zod himself.
Some time with the lower-castes you claim to cherish so much. How does *that* sound?
...
Okay.
And one more thing—
If you continue making negative statements about Krypton...

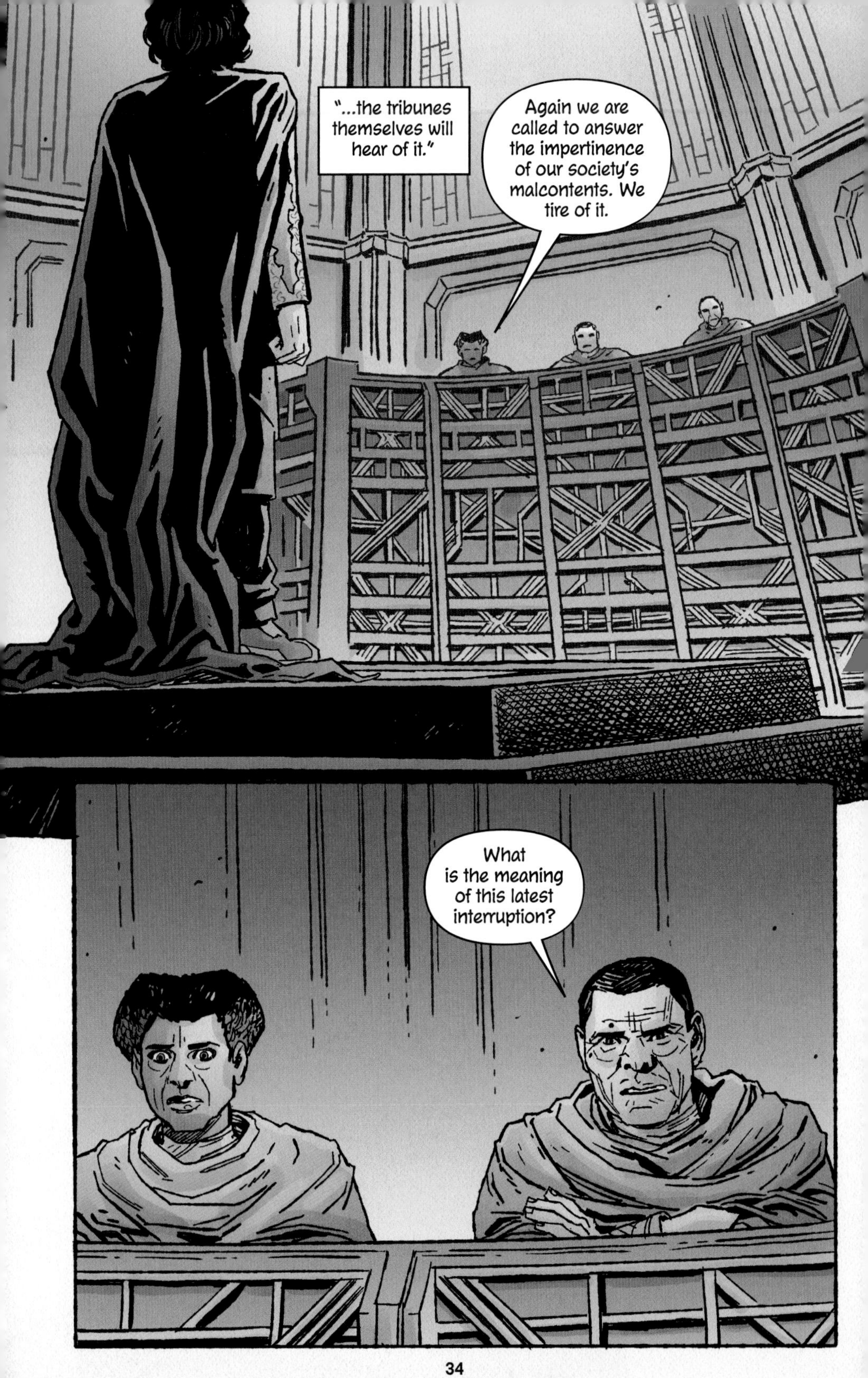
"...the tribunes themselves will hear of it."
Again we are called to answer the impertinence of our society's malcontents. We tire of it.
What is the meaning of this latest interruption?

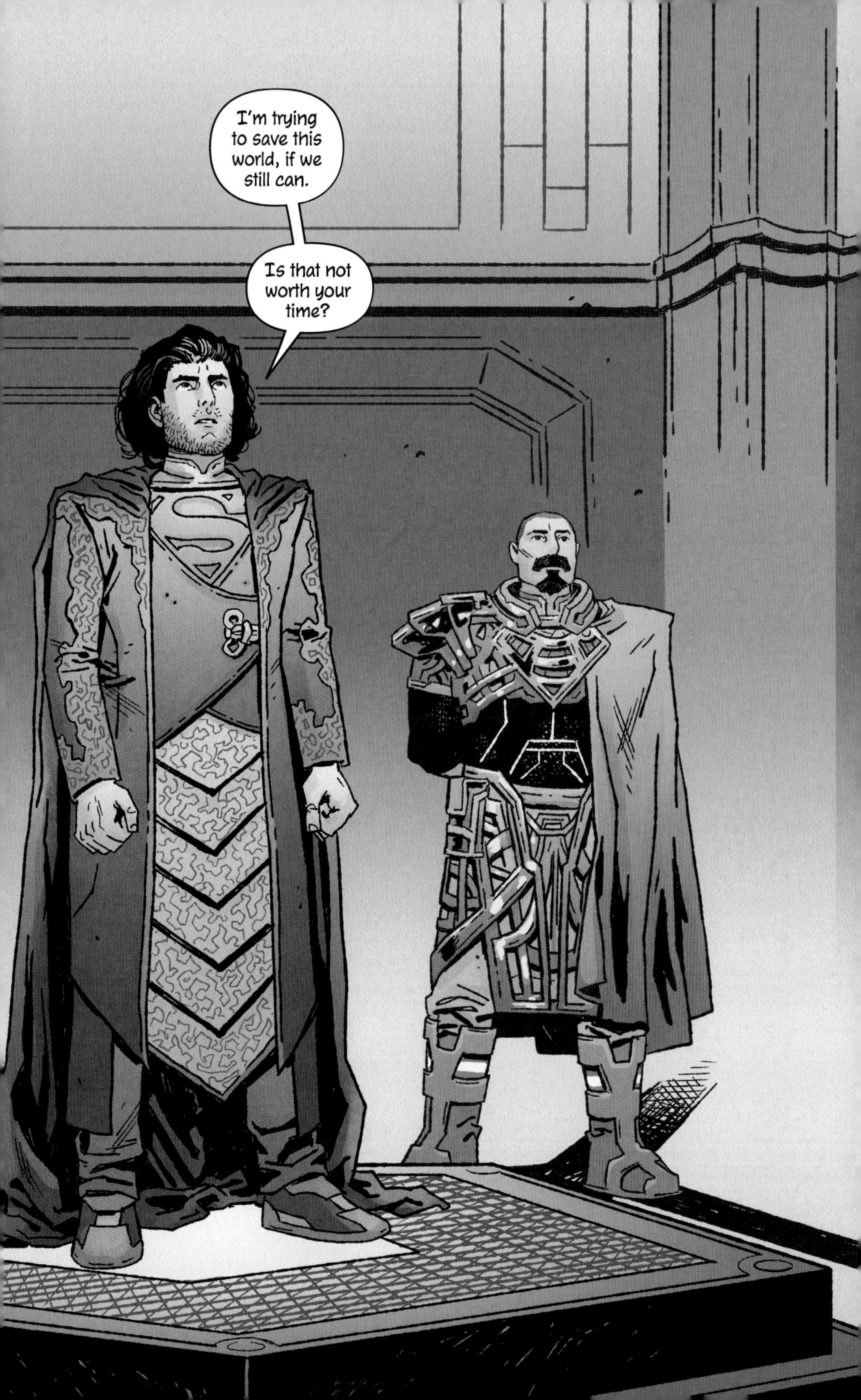
I'm trying to save this world, if we still can.
Is that not worth your time?

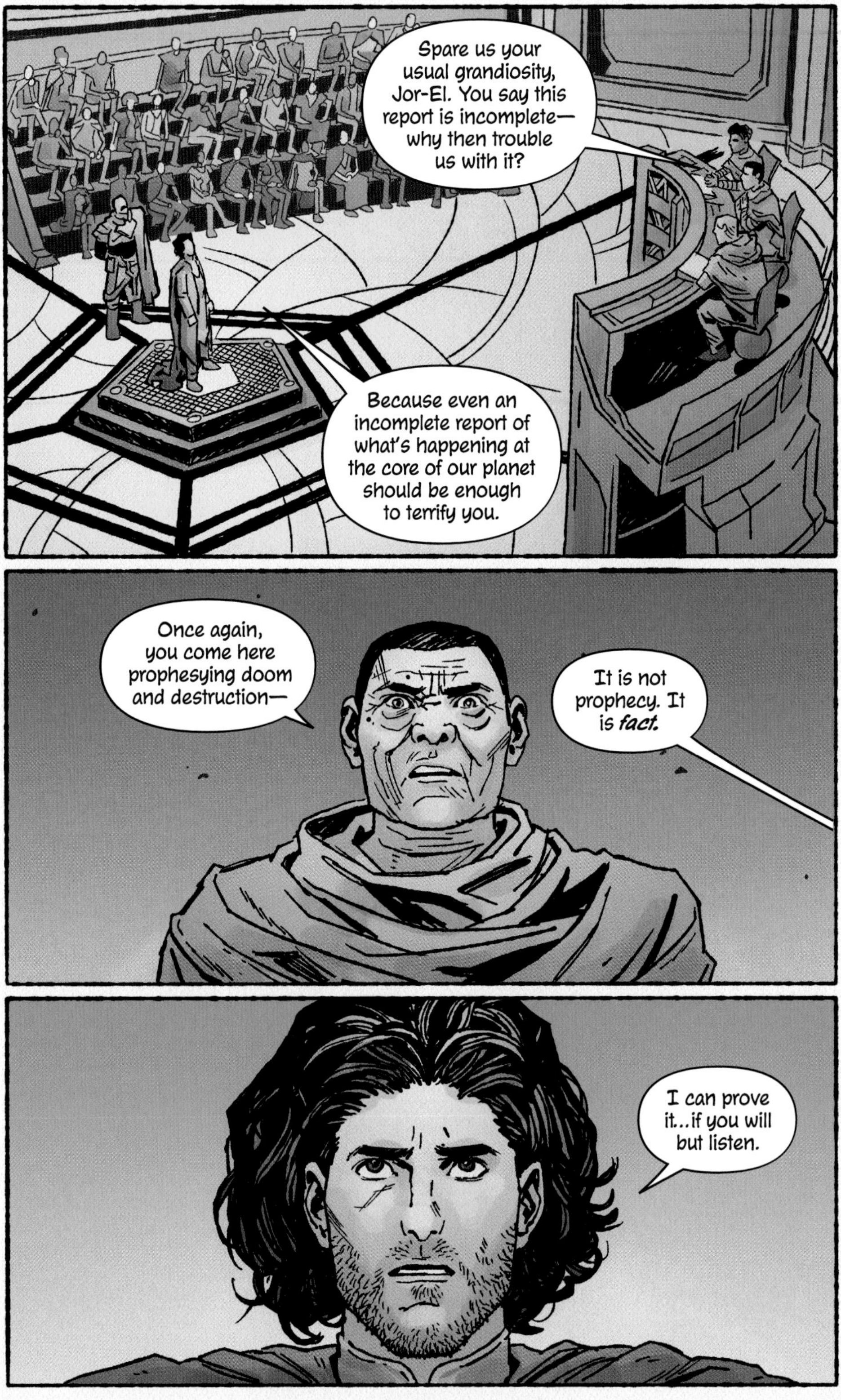
Spare us your usual grandiosity, Jor-El. You say this report is incomplete—why then trouble us with it?
Because even an incomplete report of what's happening at the core of our planet should be enough to terrify you.
Once again, you come here prophesying doom and destruction—
It is not prophecy. It is *fact.*
I can prove it...if you will but listen.

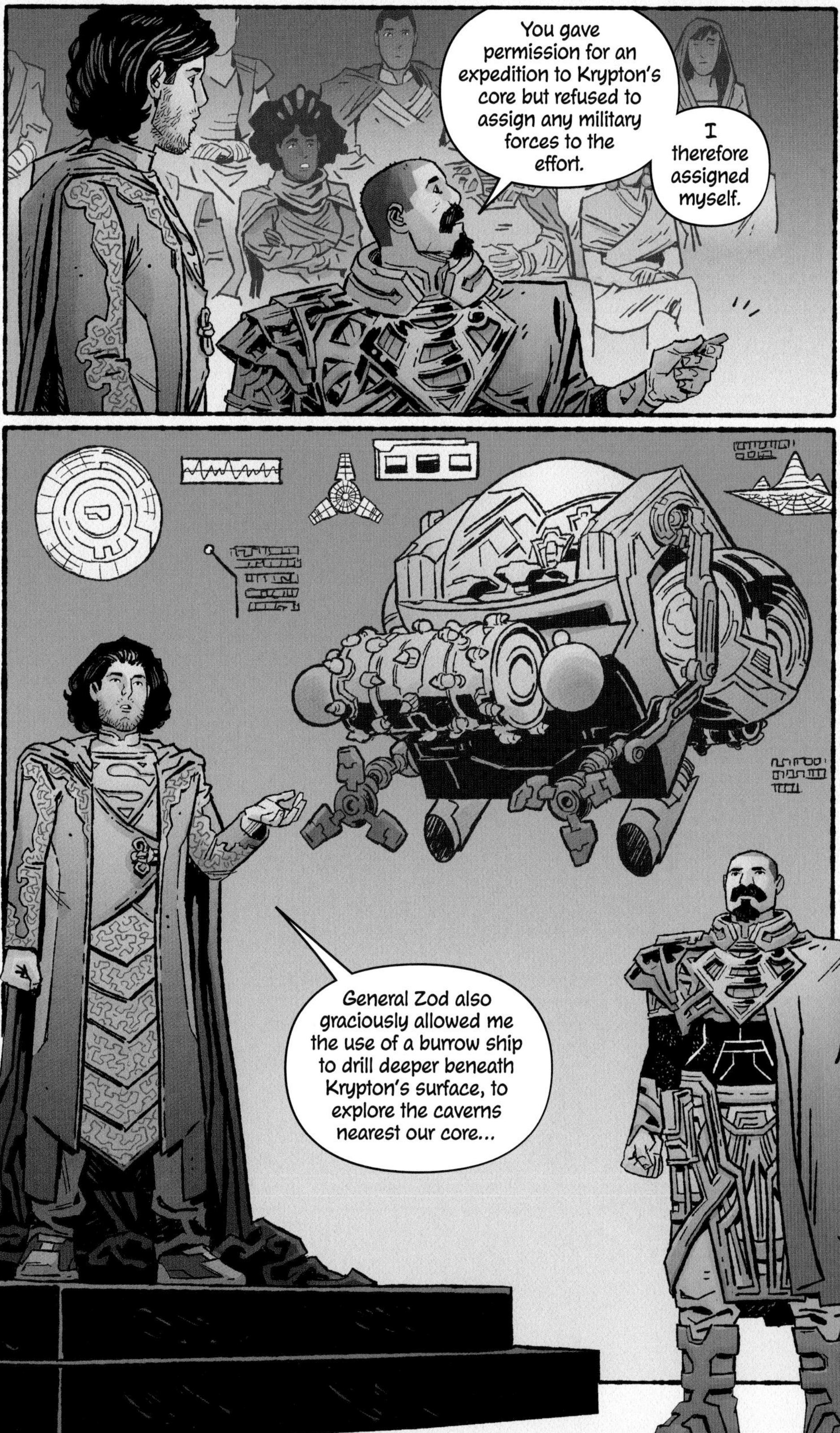
You gave permission for an expedition to Krypton's core but refused to assign any military forces to the effort.
I therefore assigned myself.
General Zod also graciously allowed me the use of a burrow ship to drill deeper beneath Krypton's surface, to explore the caverns nearest our core...

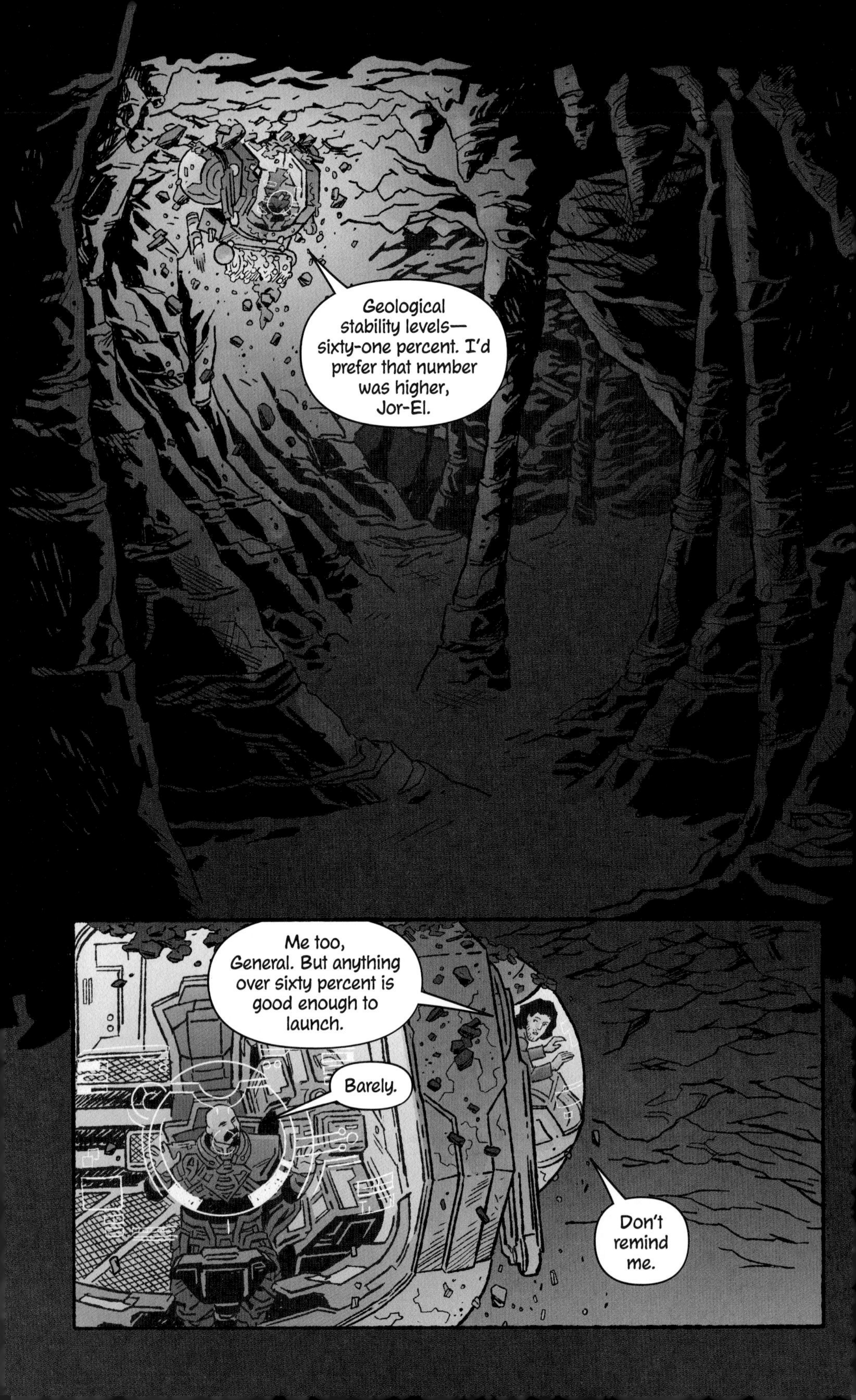
Geological stability levels—sixty-one percent. I'd prefer that number was higher, Jor-El.
Me too, General. But anything over sixty percent is good enough to launch.
Barely.
Don't remind me.

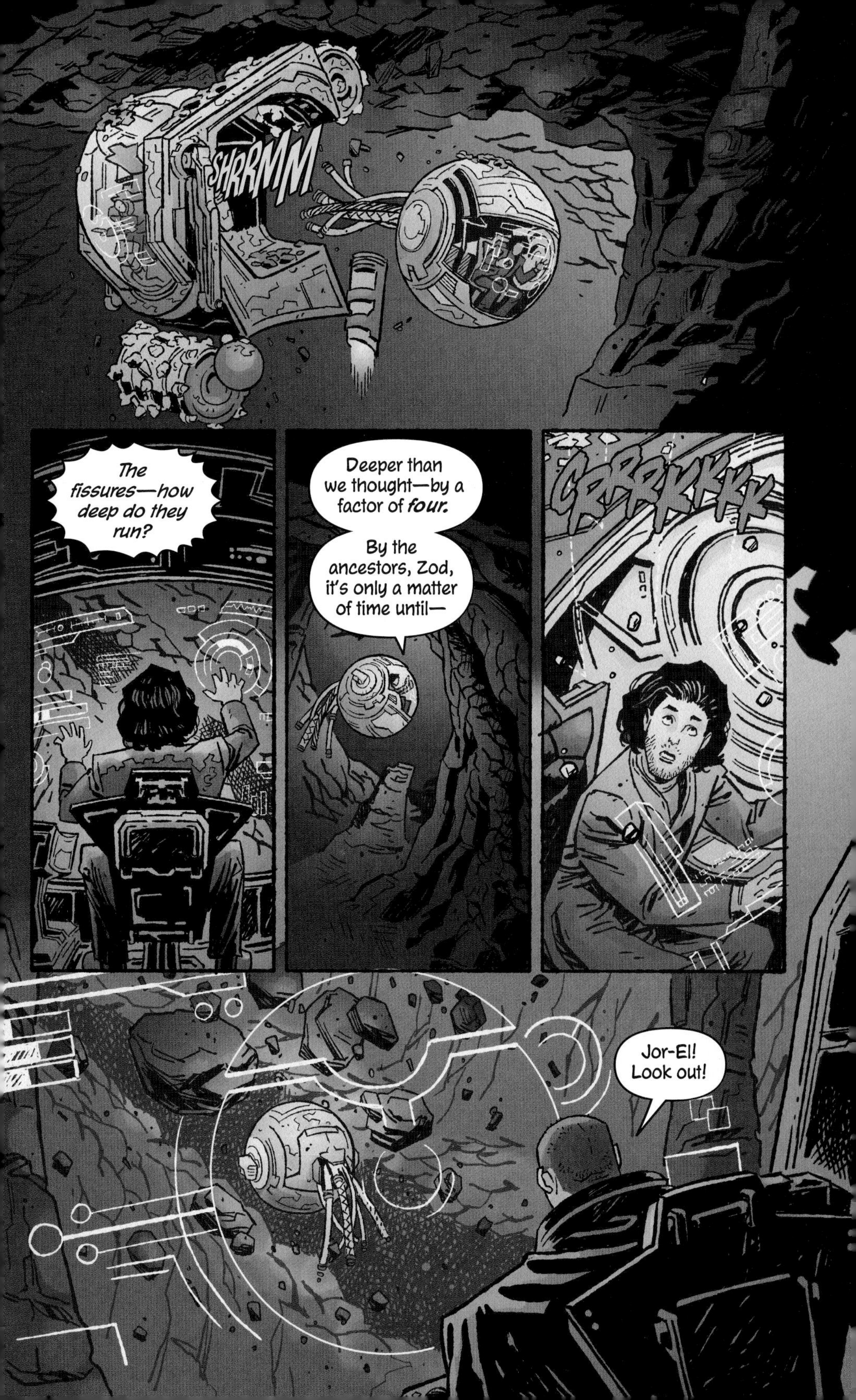
SHRRMM
The fissures—how deep do they run?
Deeper than we thought—by a factor of *four.*
By the ancestors, Zod, it's only a matter of time until—
CRRKKKK
Jor-El! Look out!

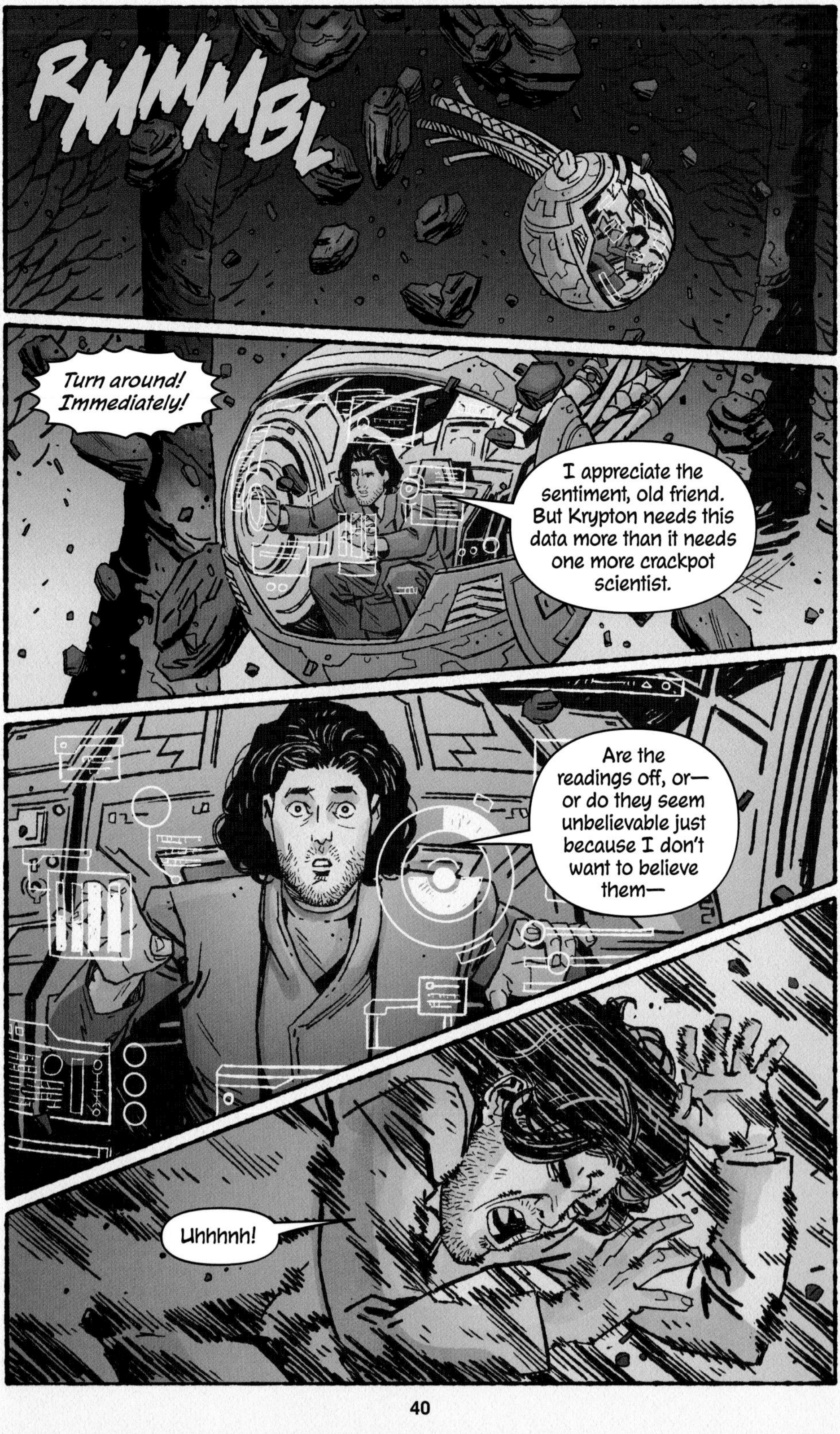
RMMMBL
Turn around! Immediately!
I appreciate the sentiment, old friend. But Krypton needs this data more than it needs one more crackpot scientist.
Are the readings off, or— or do they seem unbelievable just because I don't want to believe them—
Uhhhhh!

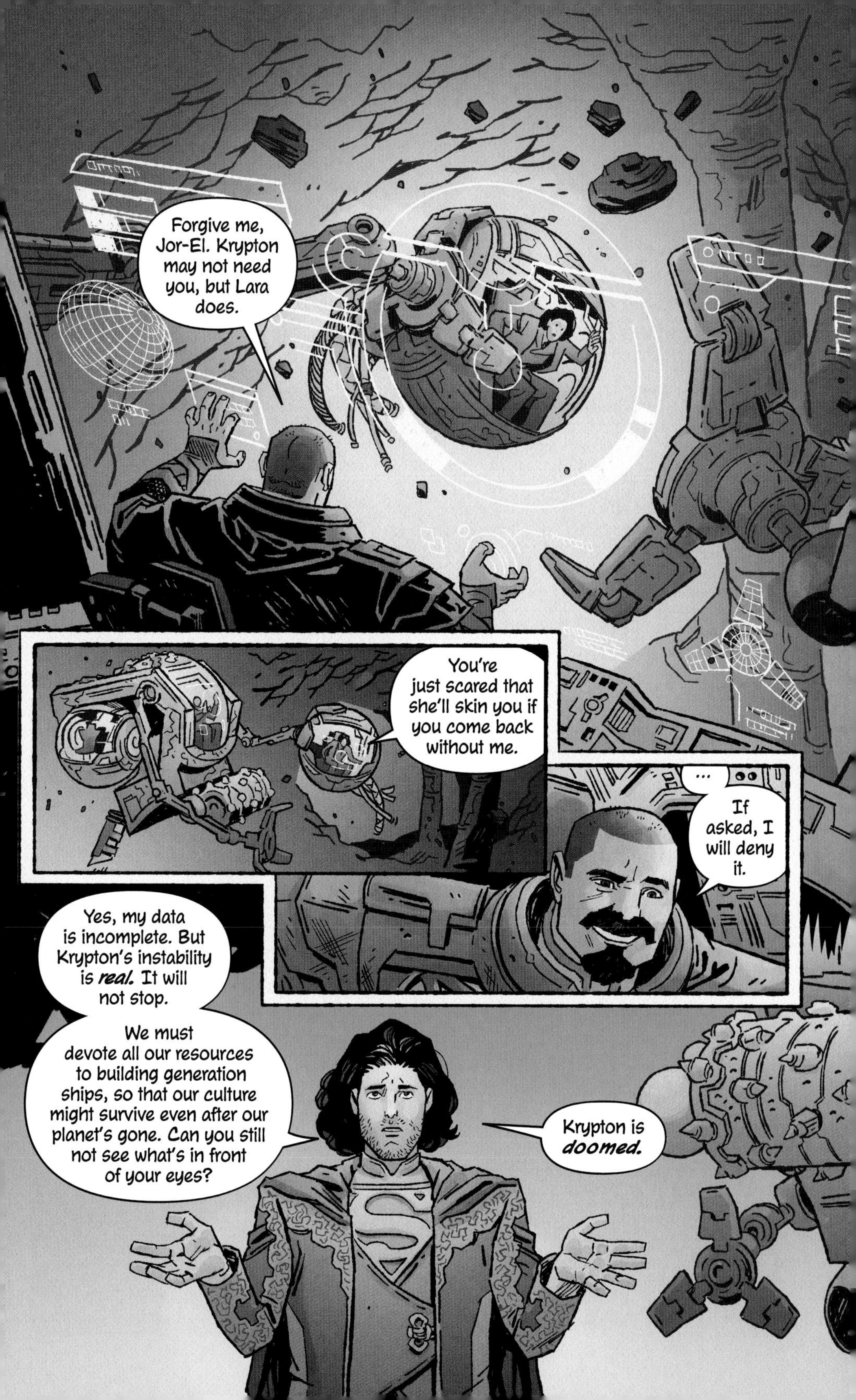
Forgive me, Jor-El. Krypton may not need you, but Lara does.
You're just scared that she'll skin you if you come back without me.
...
If asked, I will deny it.
Yes, my data is incomplete. But Krypton's instability is *real.* It will not stop.
We must devote all our resources to building generation ships, so that our culture might survive even after our planet's gone. Can you still not see what's in front of your eyes?
Krypton is *doomed.*

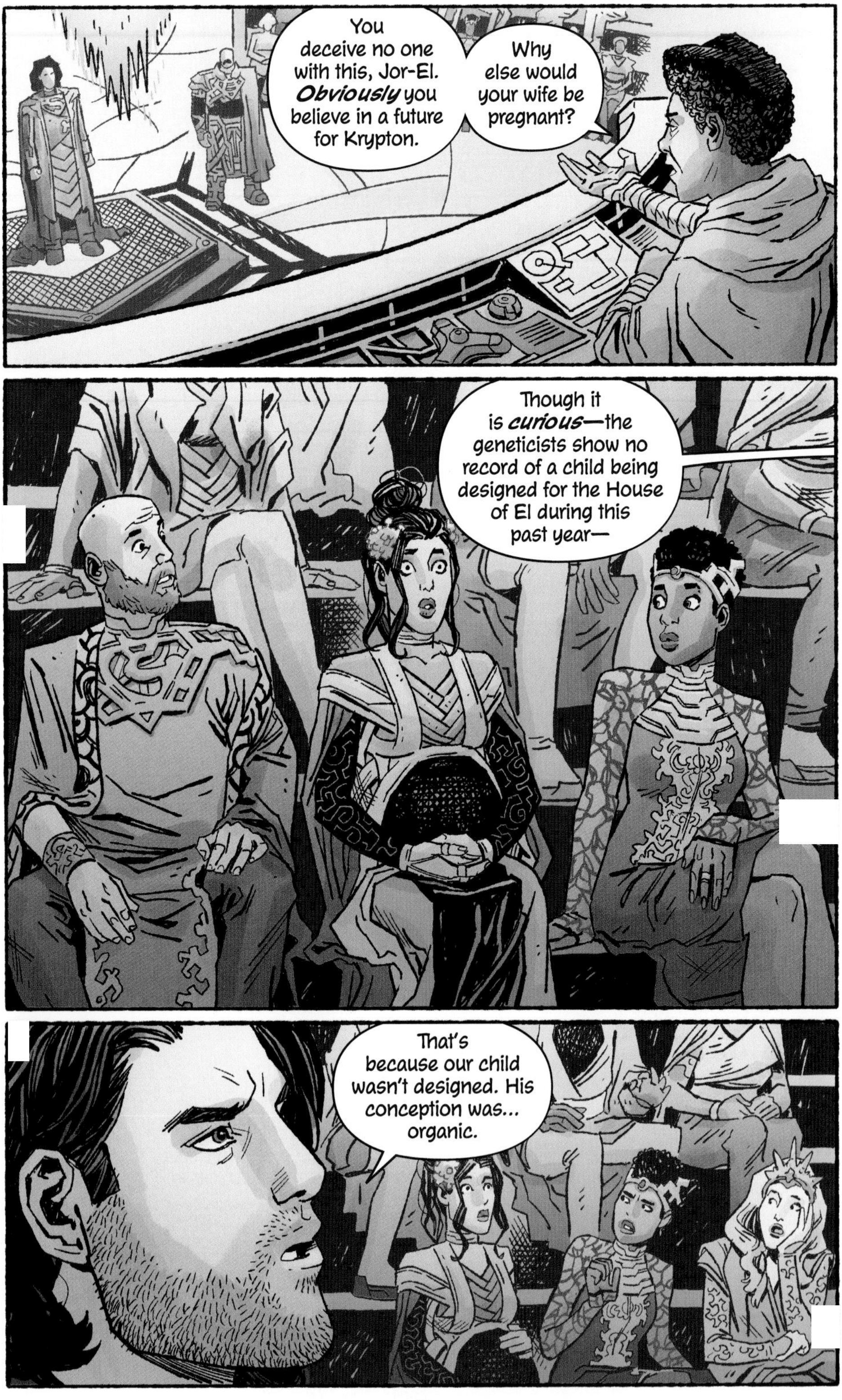
You deceive no one with this, Jor-El. *Obviously* you believe in a future for Krypton.
Why else would your wife be pregnant?
Though it is *curious*—the geneticists show no record of a child being designed for the House of El during this past year—
That's because our child wasn't designed. His conception was... organic.

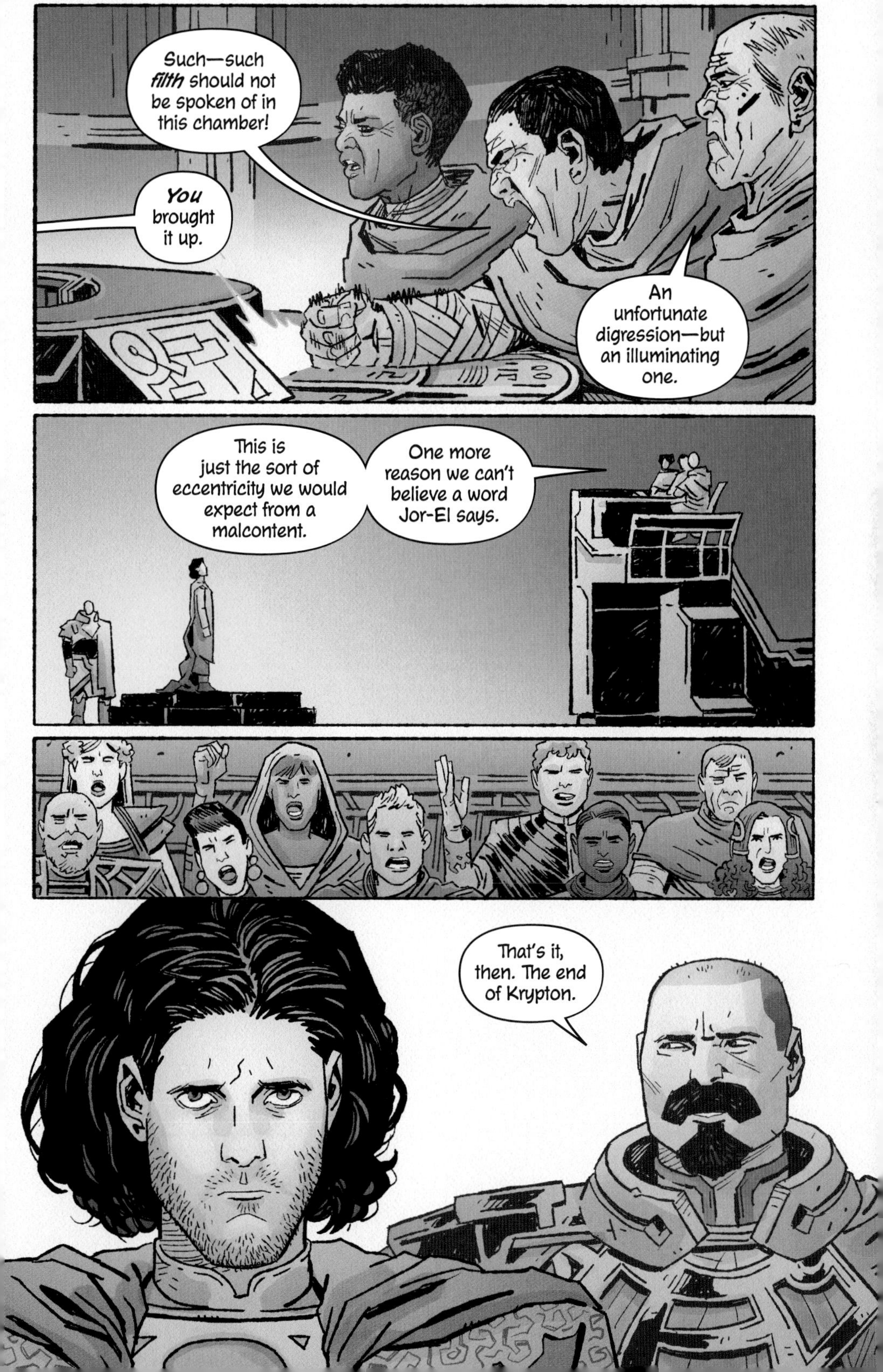
Such—such *filth* should not be spoken of in this chamber!
You brought it up.
An unfortunate digression—but an illuminating one.
This is just the sort of eccentricity we would expect from a malcontent.
One more reason we can't believe a word Jor-El says.
That's it, then. The end of Krypton.

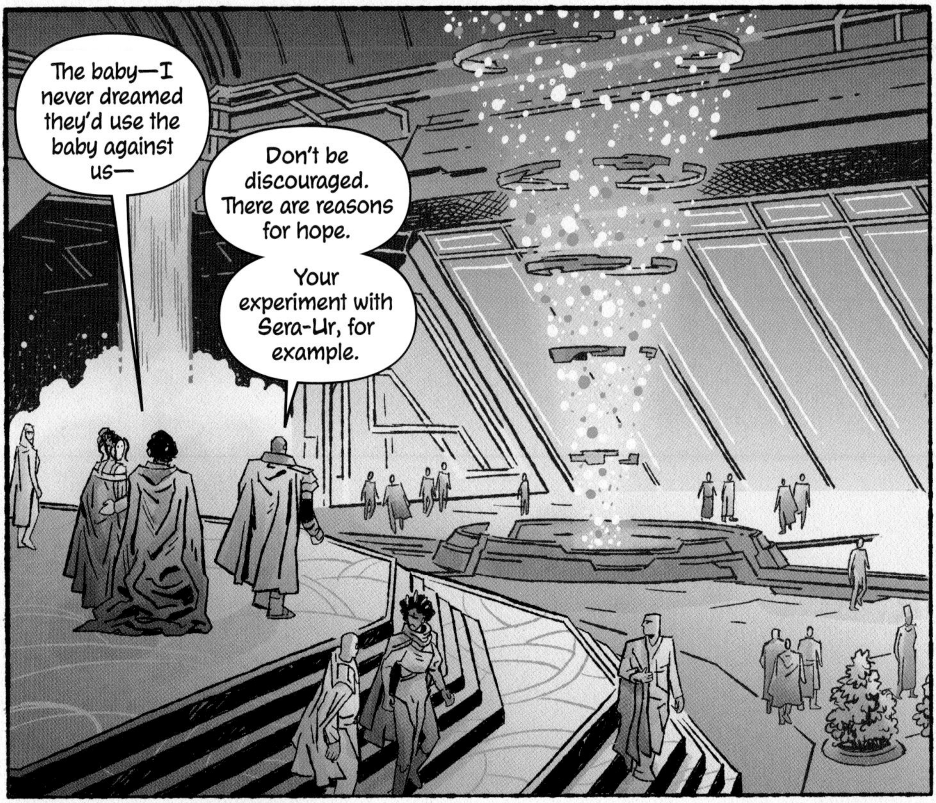
The baby—I never dreamed they'd use the baby against us—
Don't be discouraged. There are reasons for hope.
Your experiment with Sera-Ur, for example.

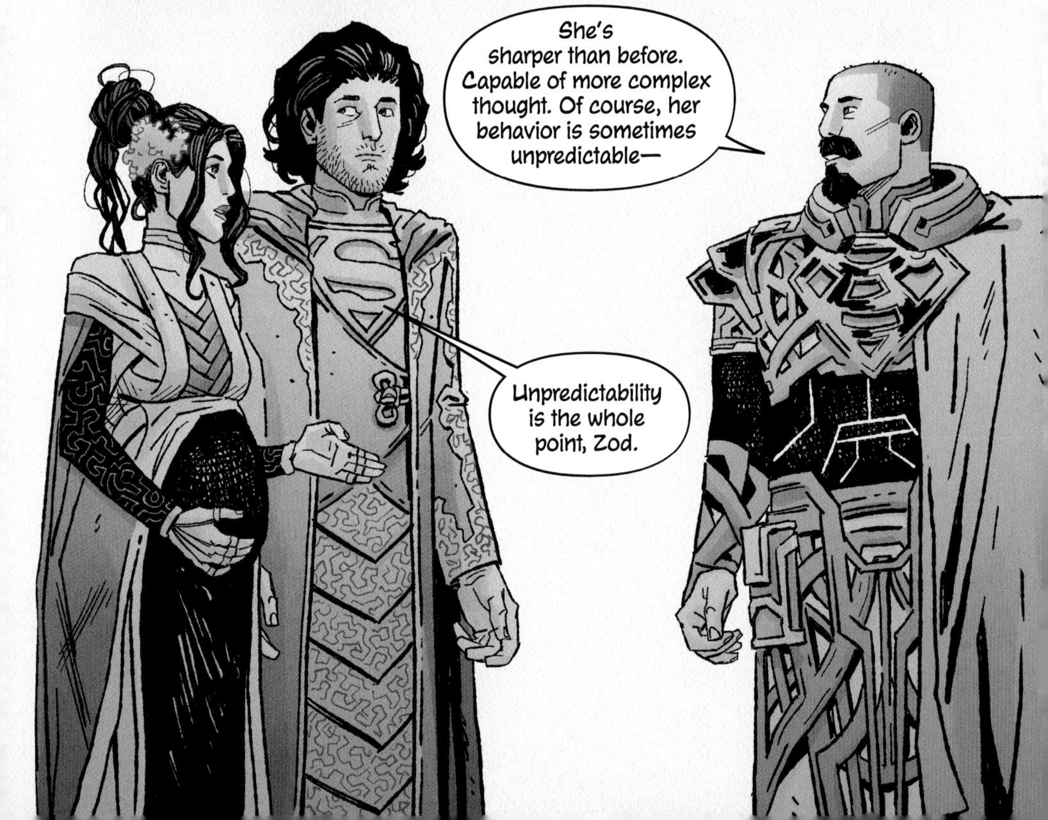
She's sharper than before. Capable of more complex thought. Of course, her behavior is sometimes unpredictable—
Unpredictability is the whole point, Zod.

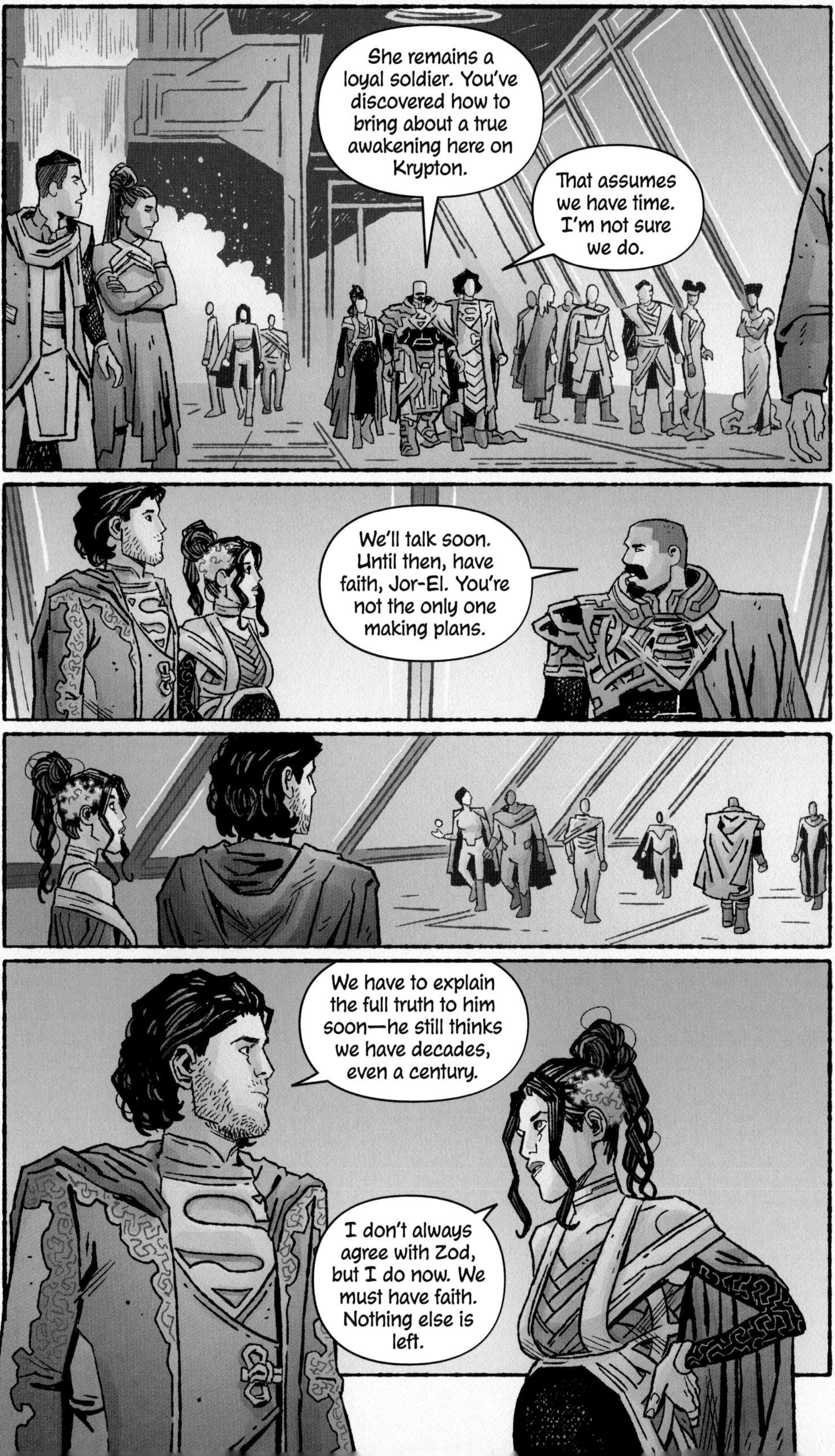
She remains a loyal soldier. You've discovered how to bring about a true awakening here on Krypton.
That assumes we have time. I'm not sure we do.
We'll talk soon. Until then, have faith, Jor-El. You're not the only one making plans.
We have to explain the full truth to him soon—he still thinks we have decades, even a century.
I don't always agree with Zod, but I do now. We must have faith. Nothing else is left.

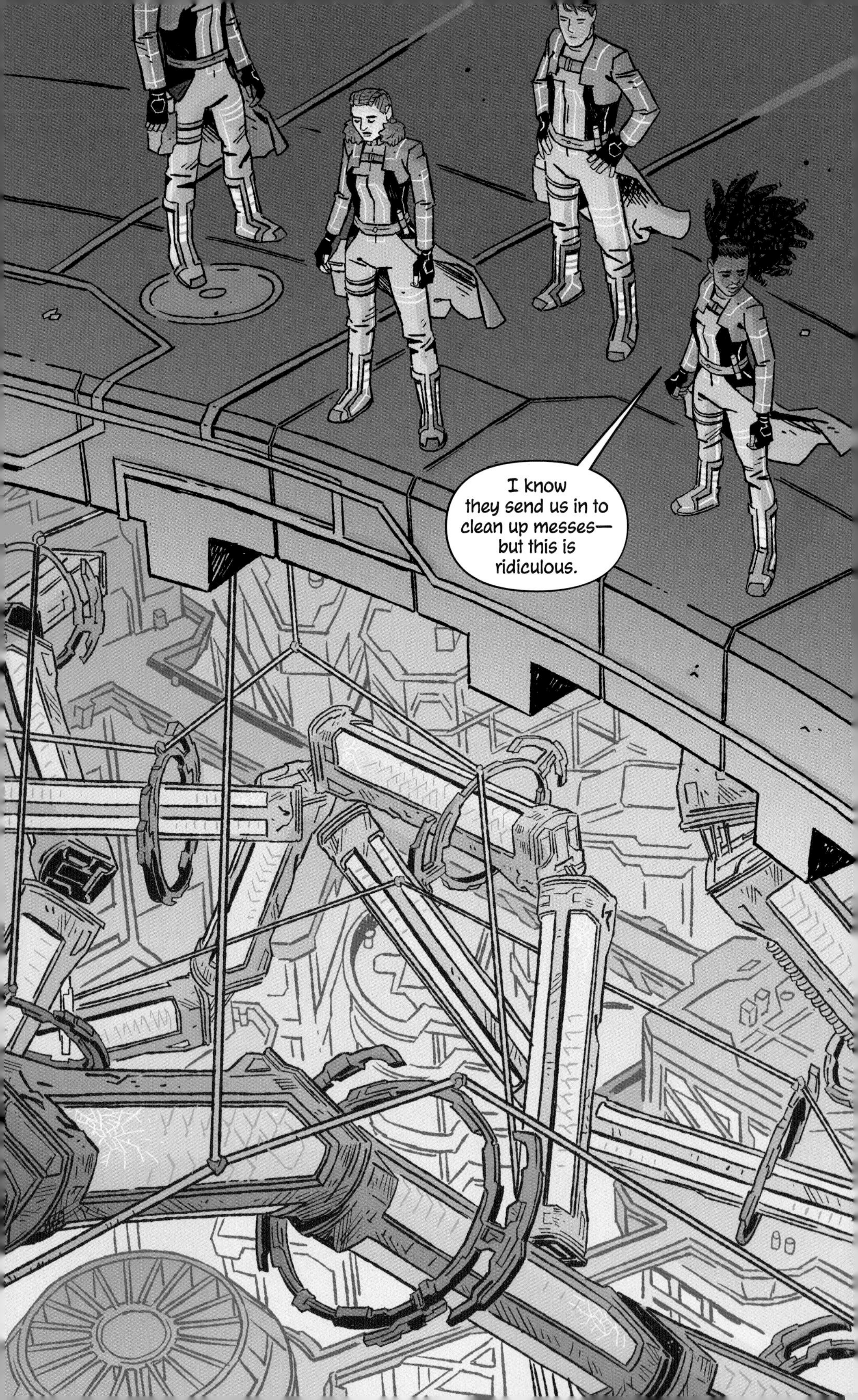
I know they send us in to clean up messes— but this is ridiculous.

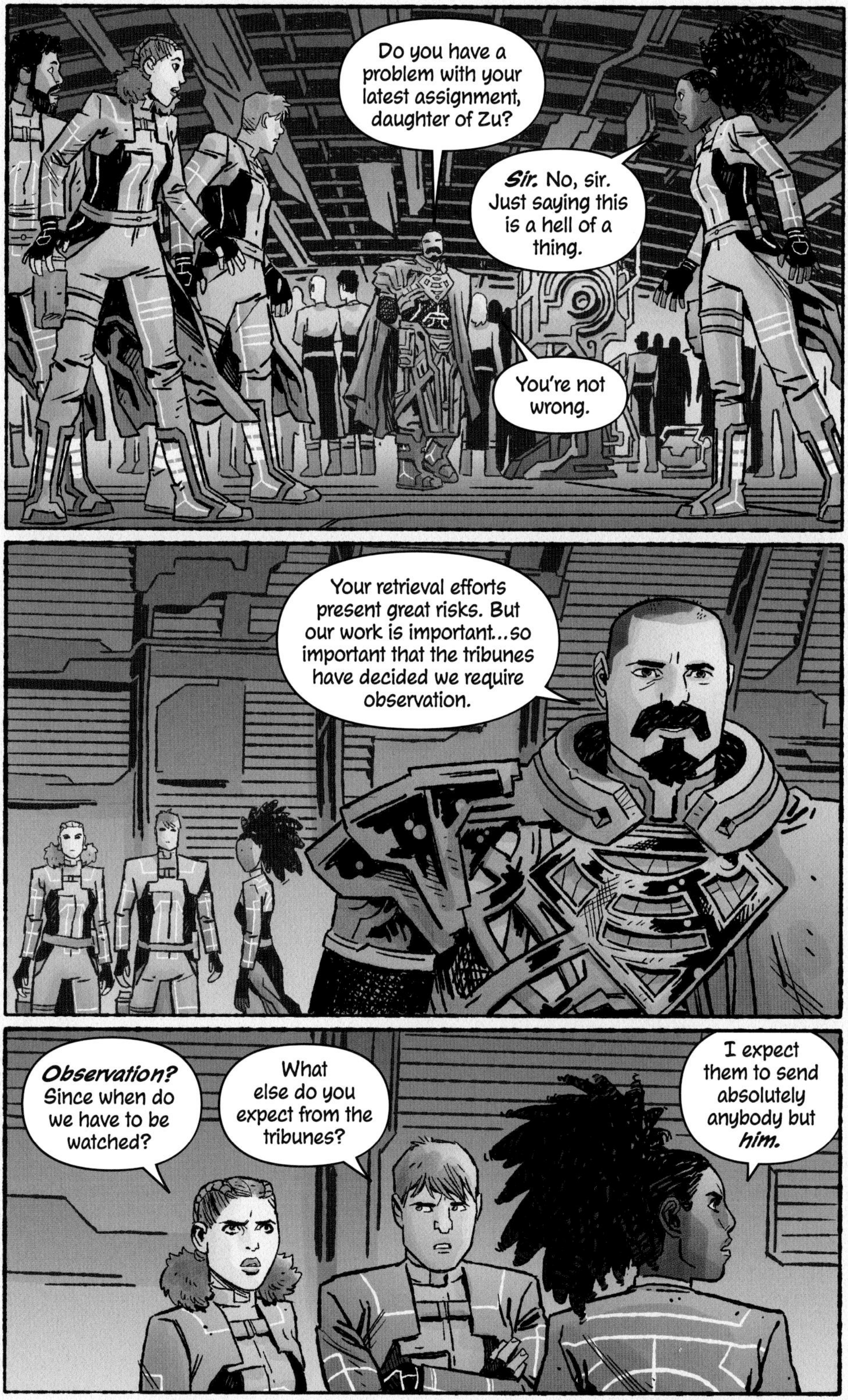
Do you have a problem with your latest assignment, daughter of Zu?
Sir. No, sir. Just saying this is a hell of a thing.
You're not wrong.
Your retrieval efforts present great risks. But our work is important...so important that the tribunes have decided we require observation.
Observation? Since when do we have to be watched?
What else do you expect from the tribunes?
I expect them to send absolutely anybody but *him.*

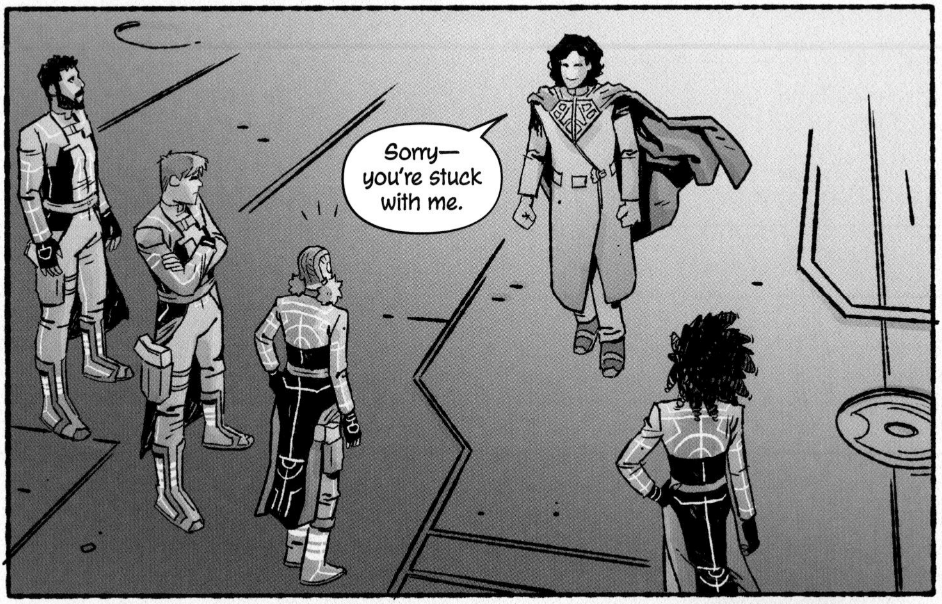
Sorry—you're stuck with me.

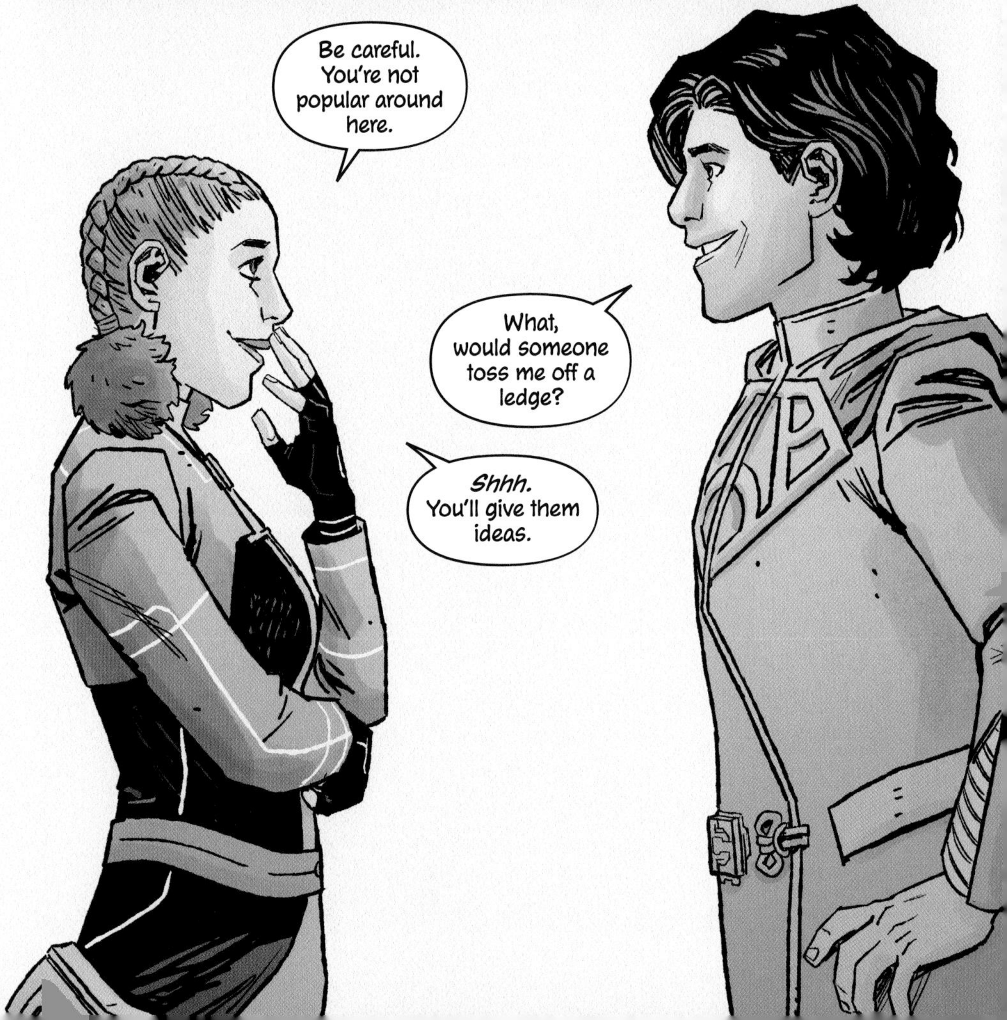
Be careful. You're not popular around here.
What, would someone toss me off a ledge?
Shhh. You'll give them ideas.

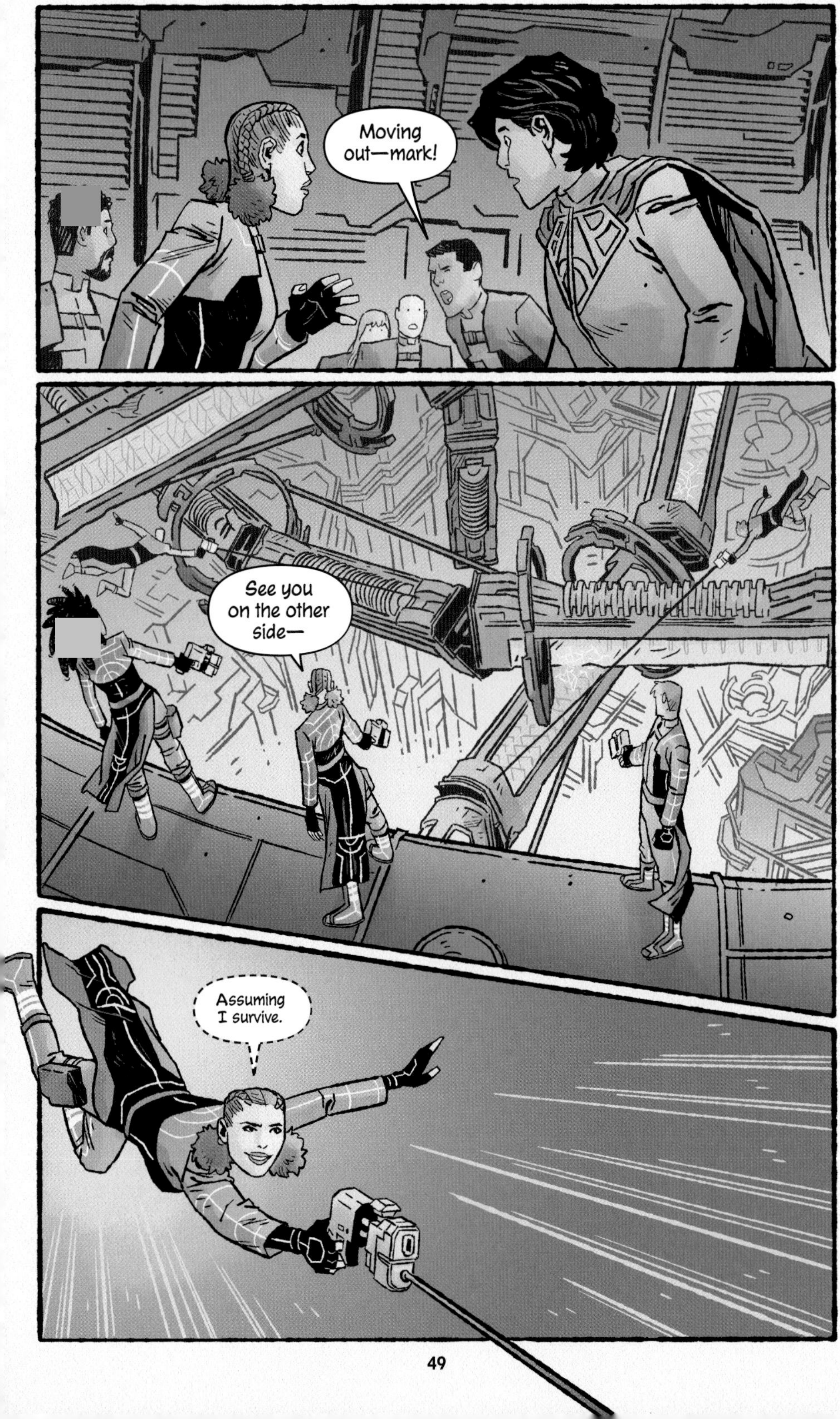
Moving out—mark!
See you on the other side—
Assuming I survive.

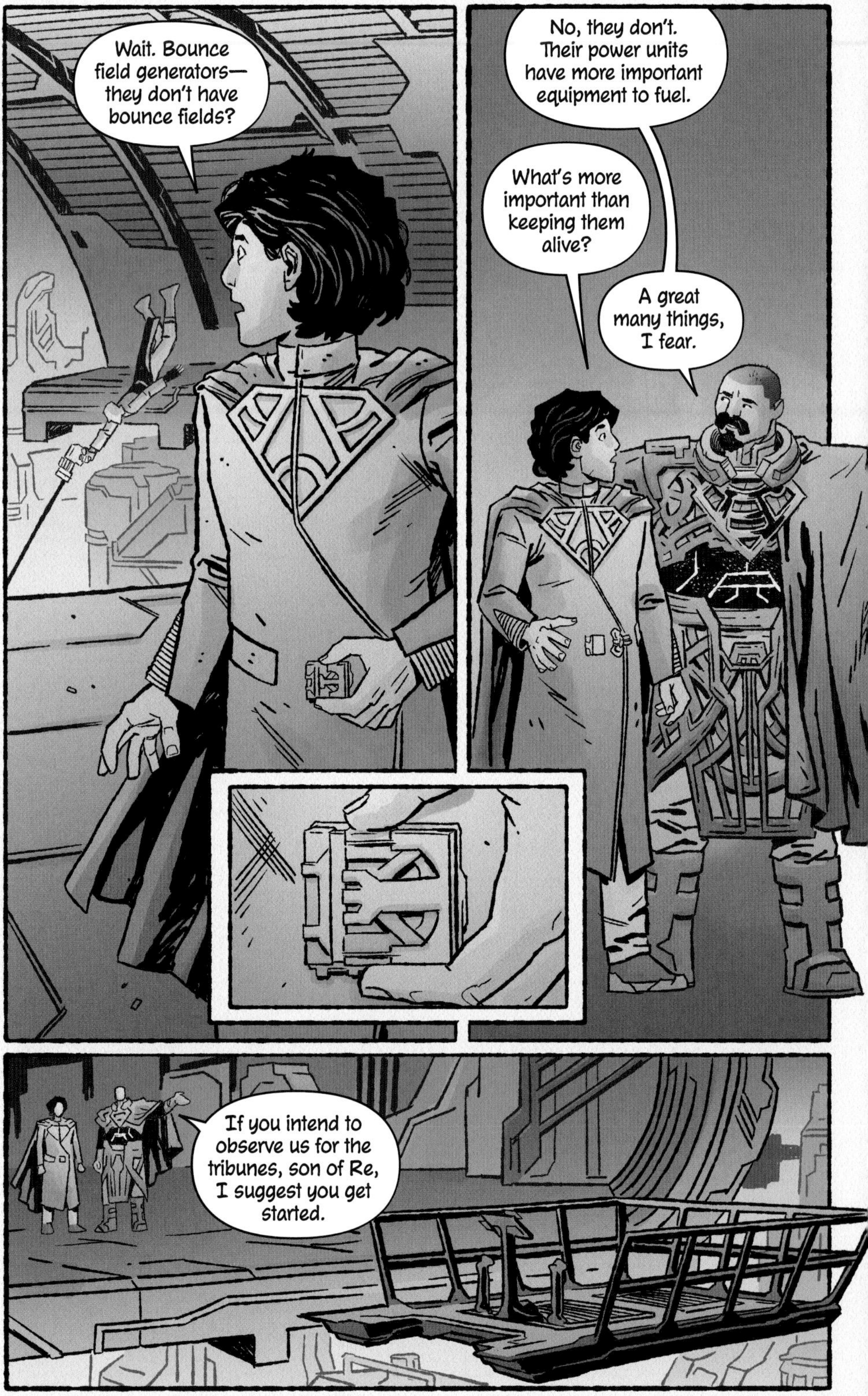
Wait. Bounce field generators— they don't have bounce fields?
No, they don't. Their power units have more important equipment to fuel.
What's more important than keeping them alive?
A great many things, I fear.
If you intend to observe us for the tribunes, son of Re, I suggest you get started.

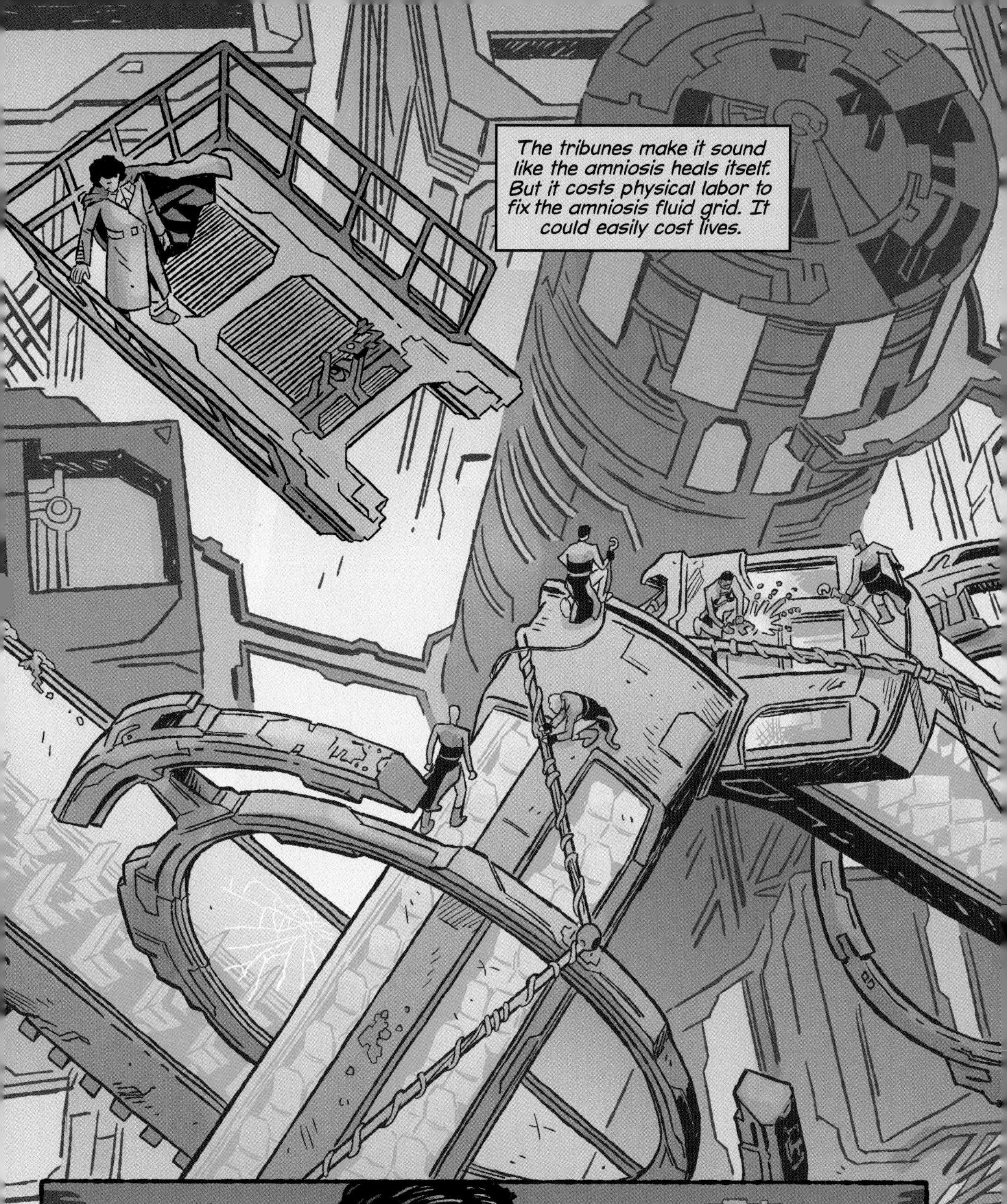
The tribunes make it sound like the amniosis heals itself. But it costs physical labor to fix the amniosis fluid grid. It could easily cost lives.

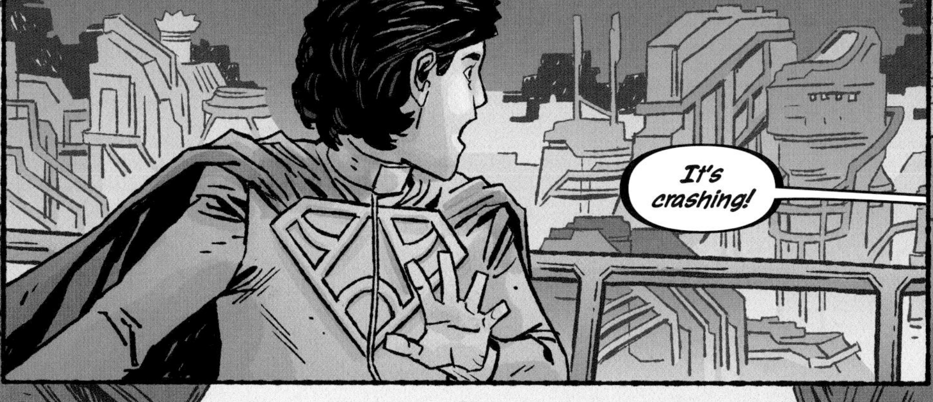
It's crashing!

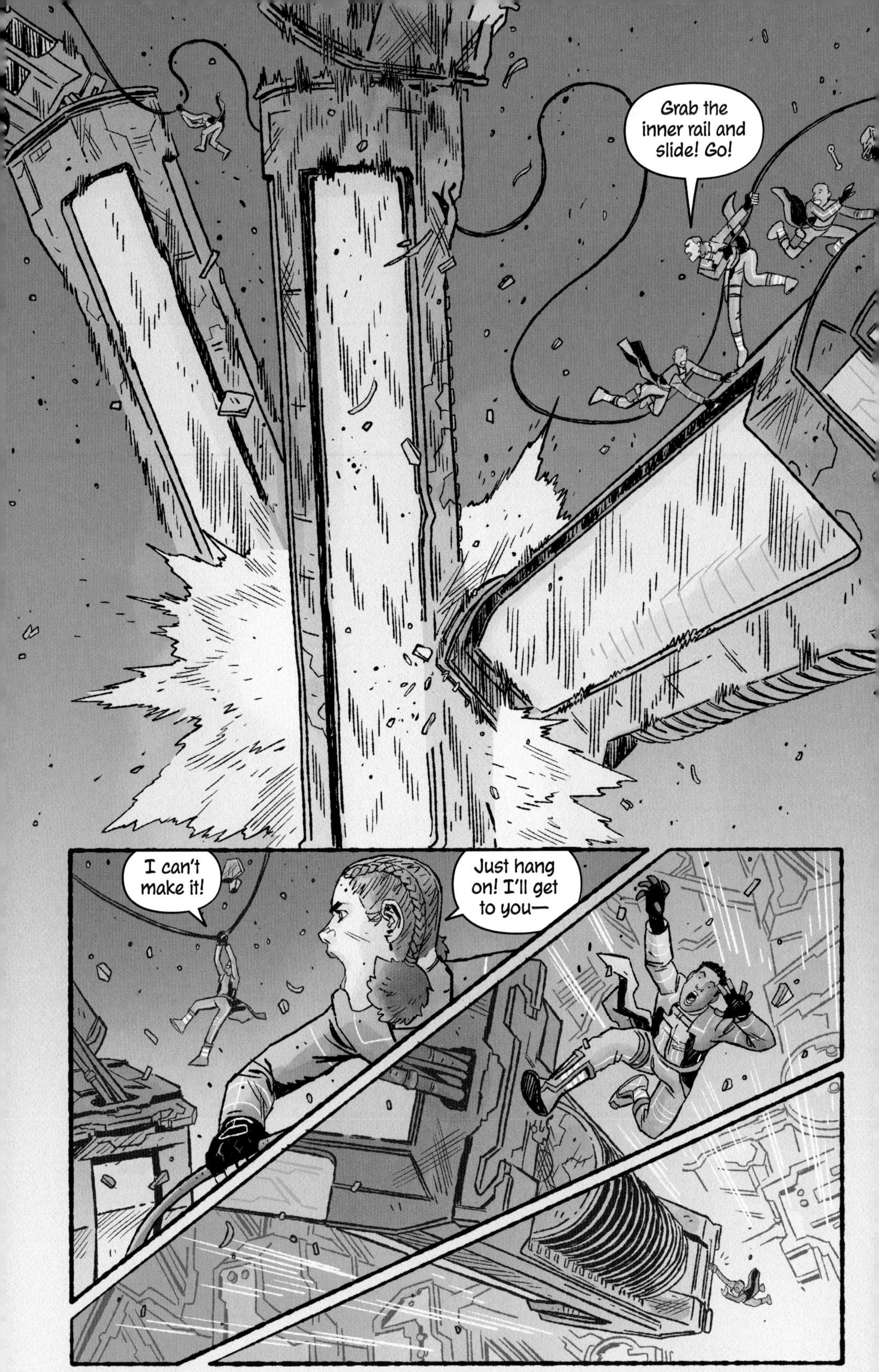
Grab the inner rail and slide! Go!
I can't make it!
Just hang on! I'll get to you—

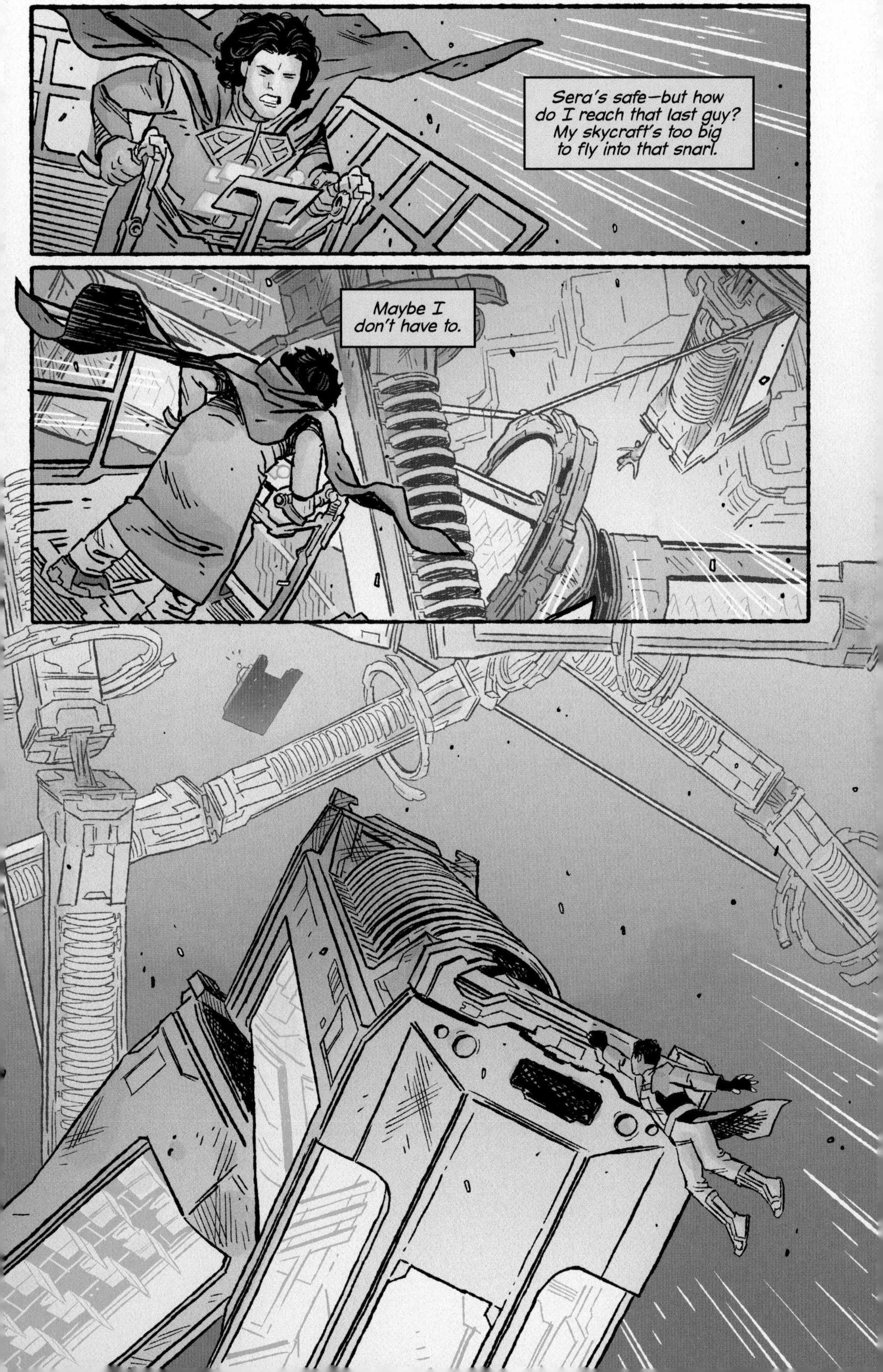
Sera's safe—but how do I reach that last guy? My skycraft's too big to fly into that snarl.
Maybe I don't have to.

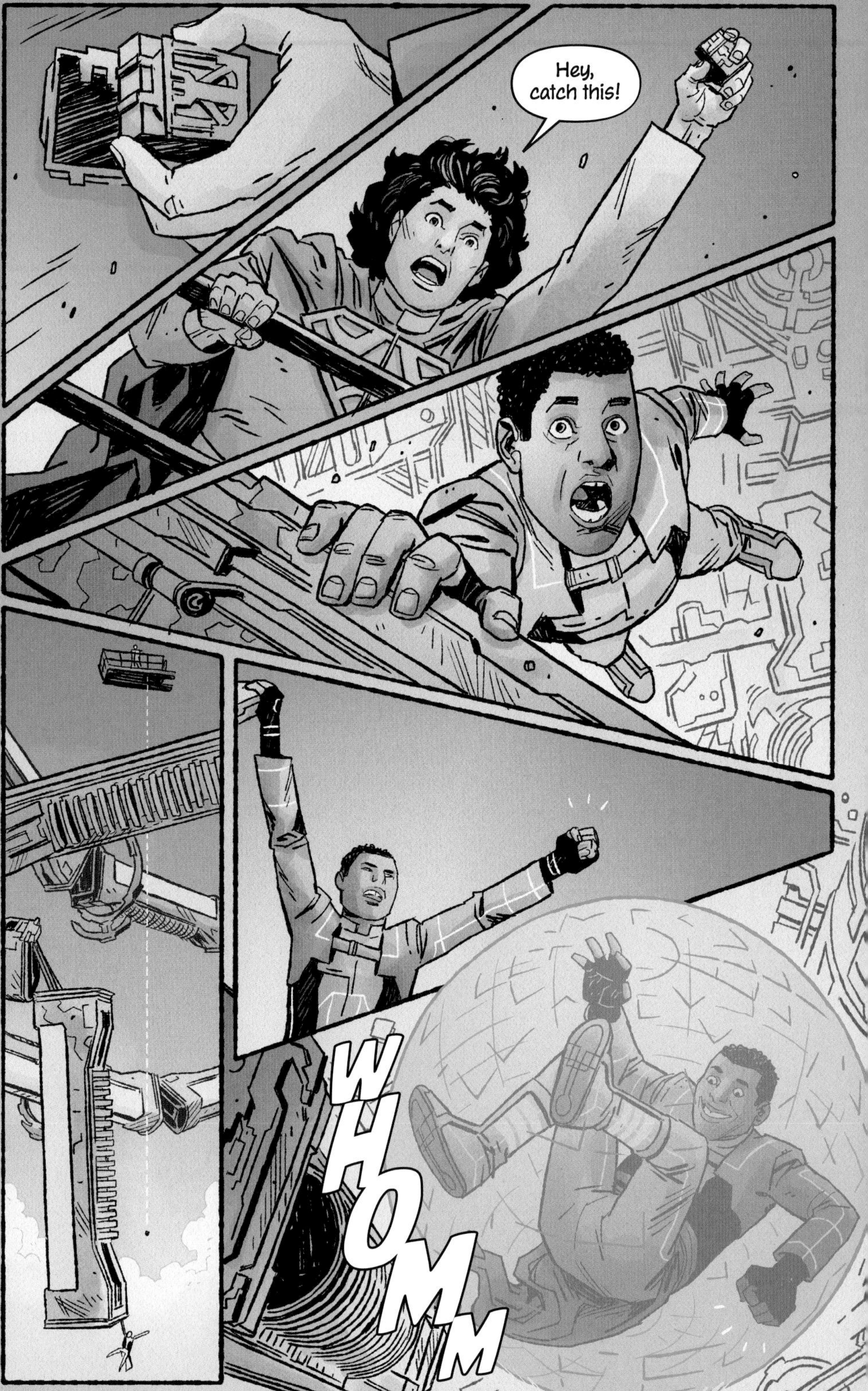
Hey,
catch this!
WHOMMM

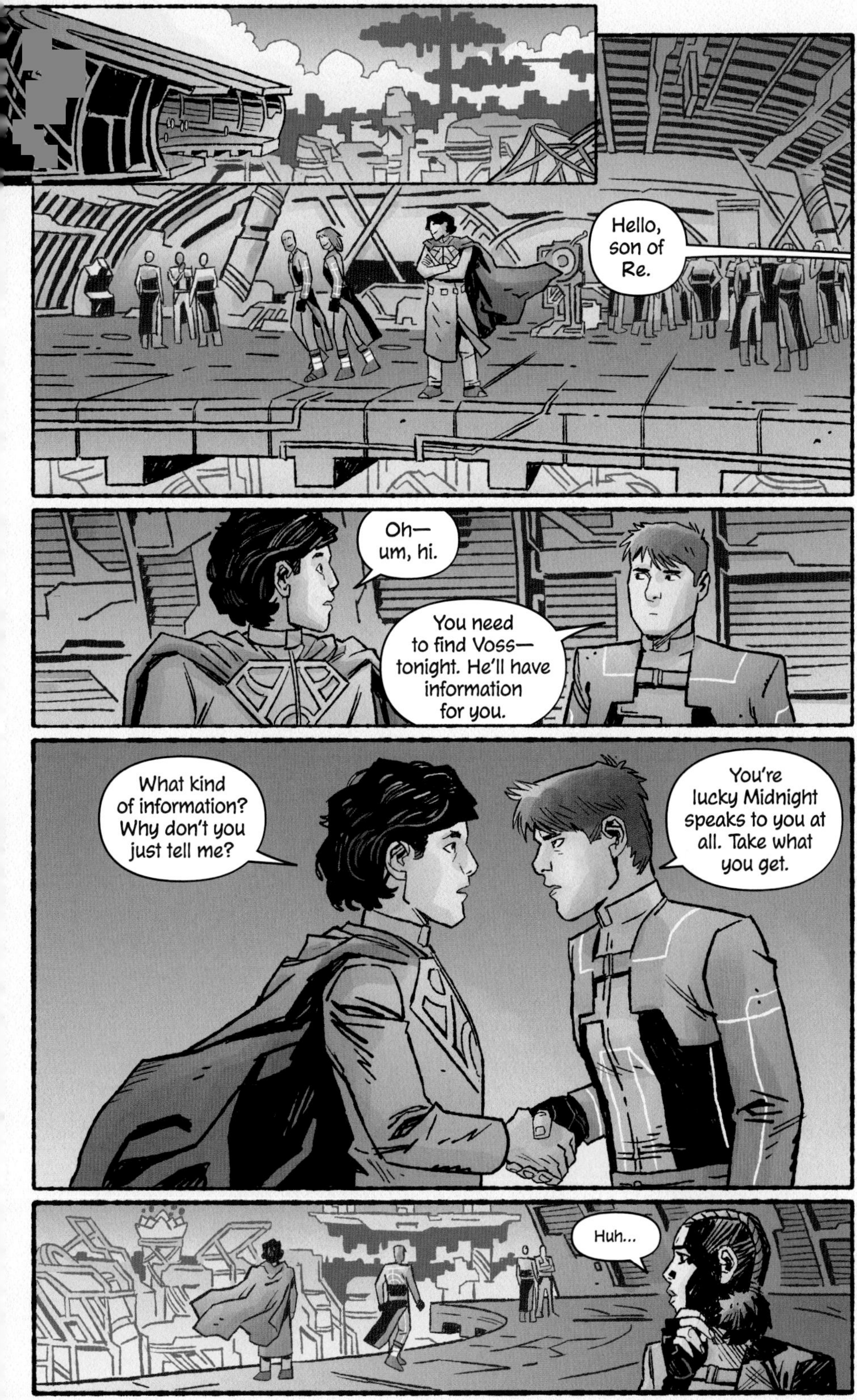
Hello, son of Re.
Oh— um, hi.
You need to find Voss— tonight. He'll have information for you.
What kind of information? Why don't you just tell me?
You're lucky Midnight speaks to you at all. Take what you get.
Huh...

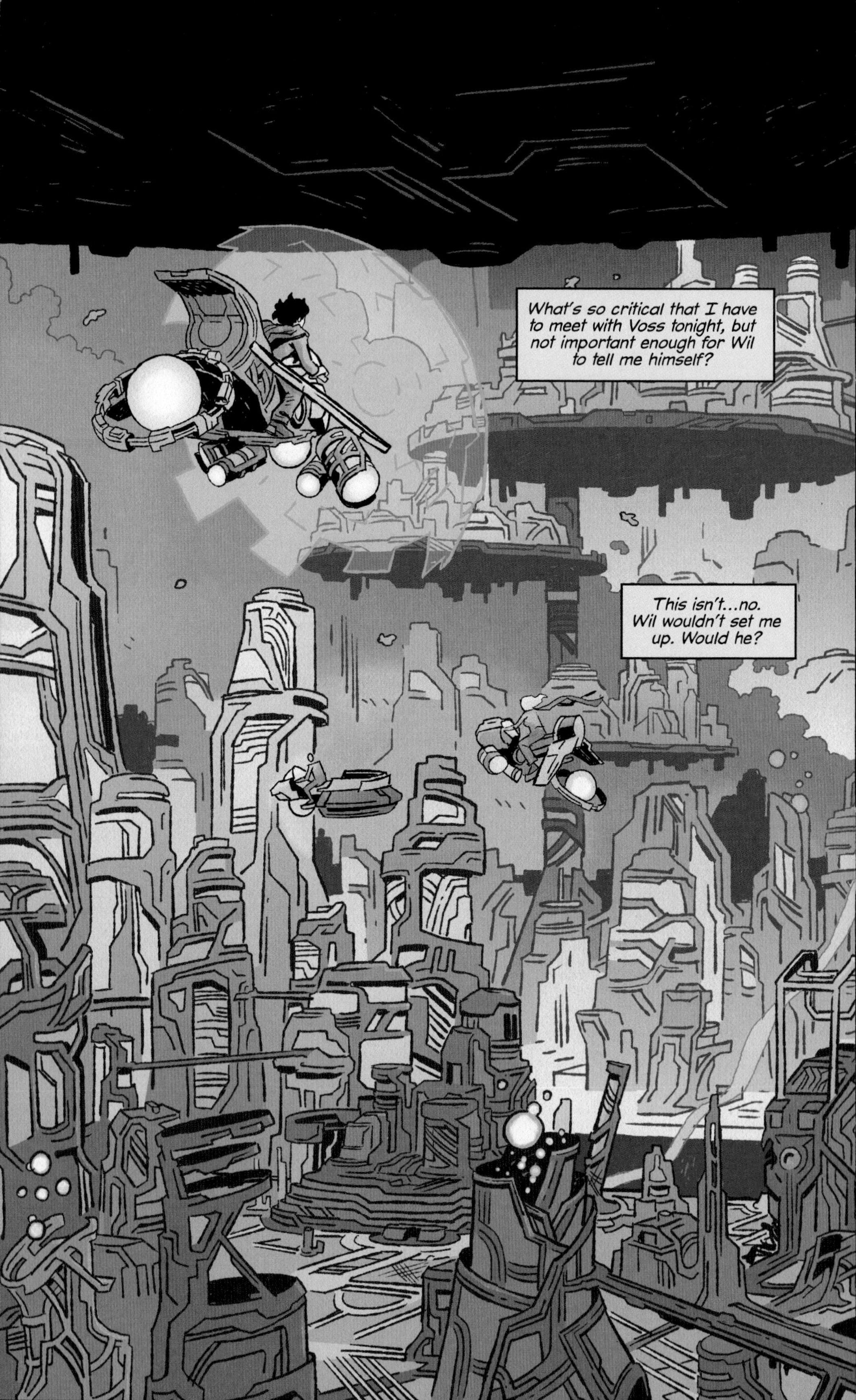
What's so critical that I have to meet with Voss tonight, but not important enough for Wil to tell me himself?
This isn't...no. Wil wouldn't set me up. Would he?

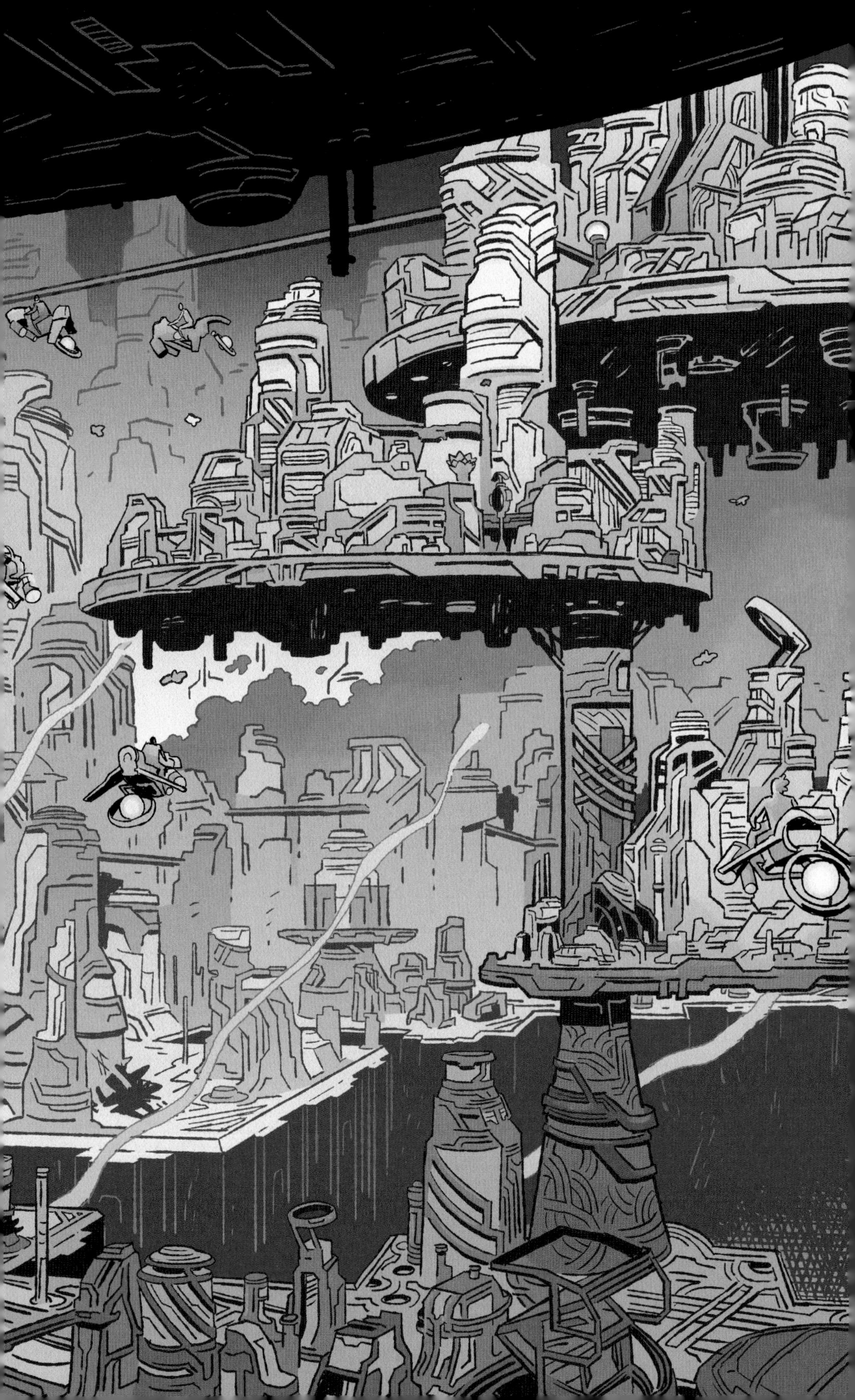

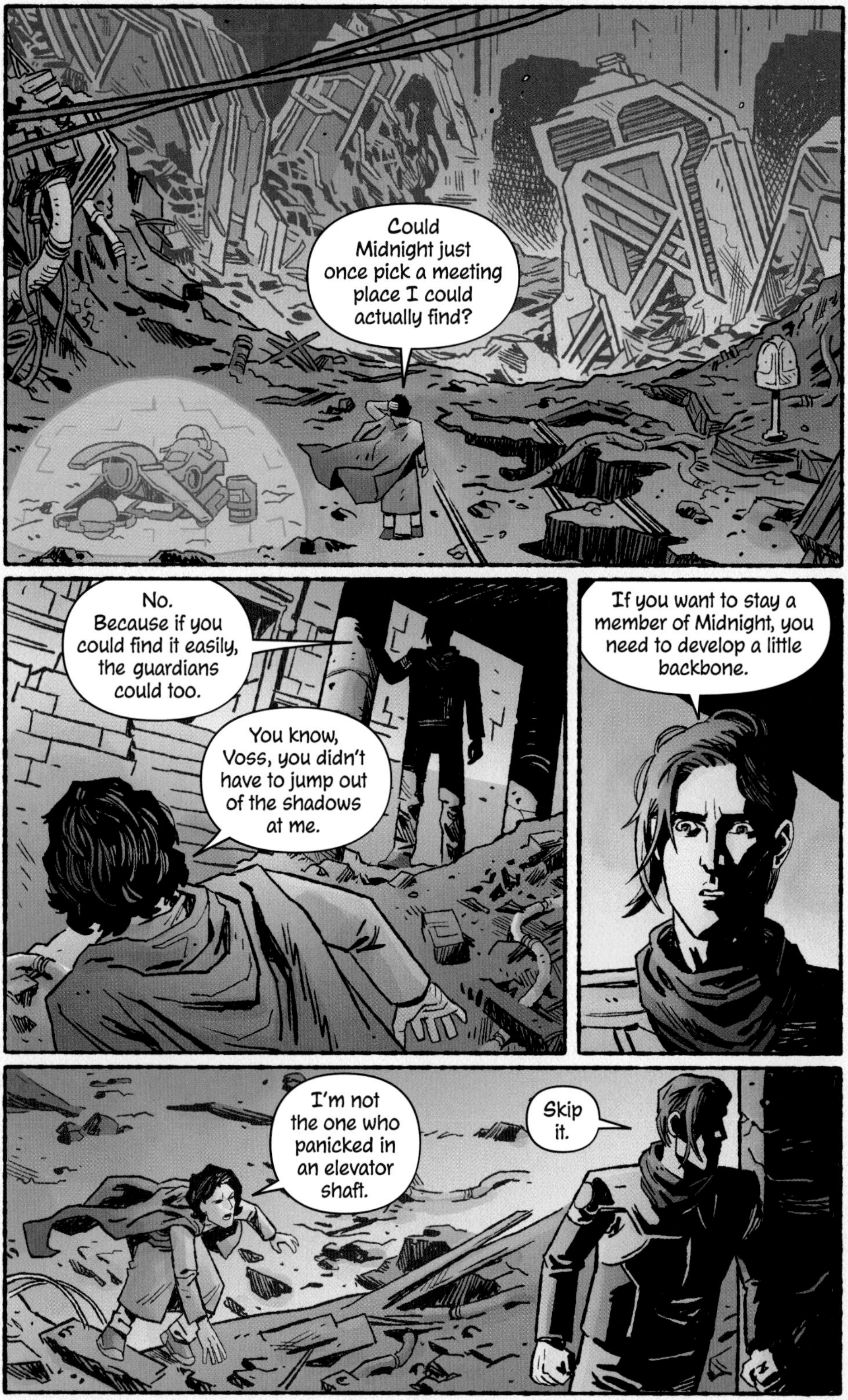
Could Midnight just once pick a meeting place I could actually find?
No. Because if you could find it easily, the guardians could too.
You know, Voss, you didn't have to jump out of the shadows at me.
If you want to stay a member of Midnight, you need to develop a little backbone.
I'm not the one who panicked in an elevator shaft.
Skip it.

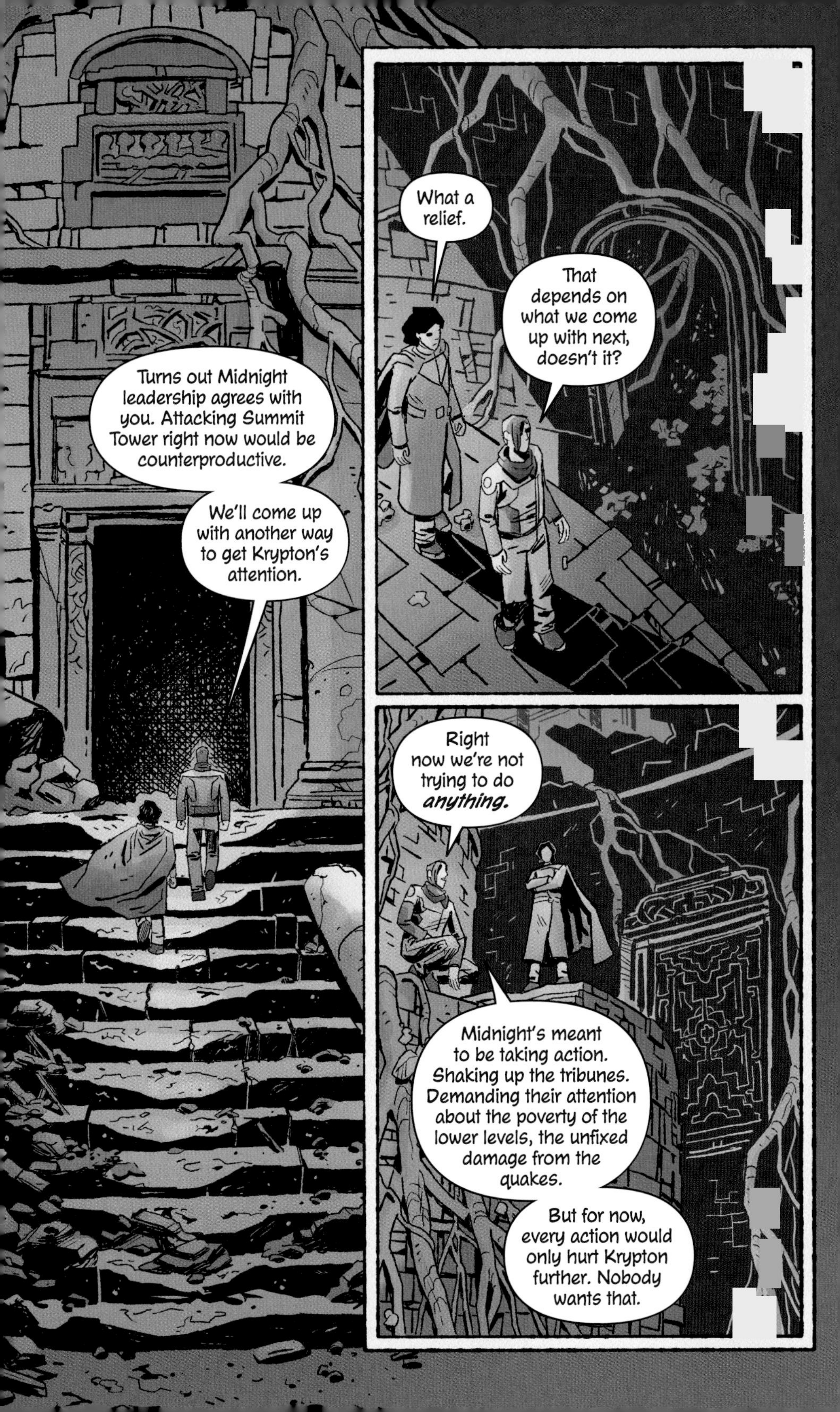
Turns out Midnight leadership agrees with you. Attacking Summit Tower right now would be counterproductive.
We'll come up with another way to get Krypton's attention.
What a relief.
That depends on what we come up with next, doesn't it?
Right now we're not trying to do *anything.*
Midnight's meant to be taking action. Shaking up the tribunes. Demanding their attention about the poverty of the lower levels, the unfixed damage from the quakes.
But for now, every action would only hurt Krypton further. Nobody wants that.

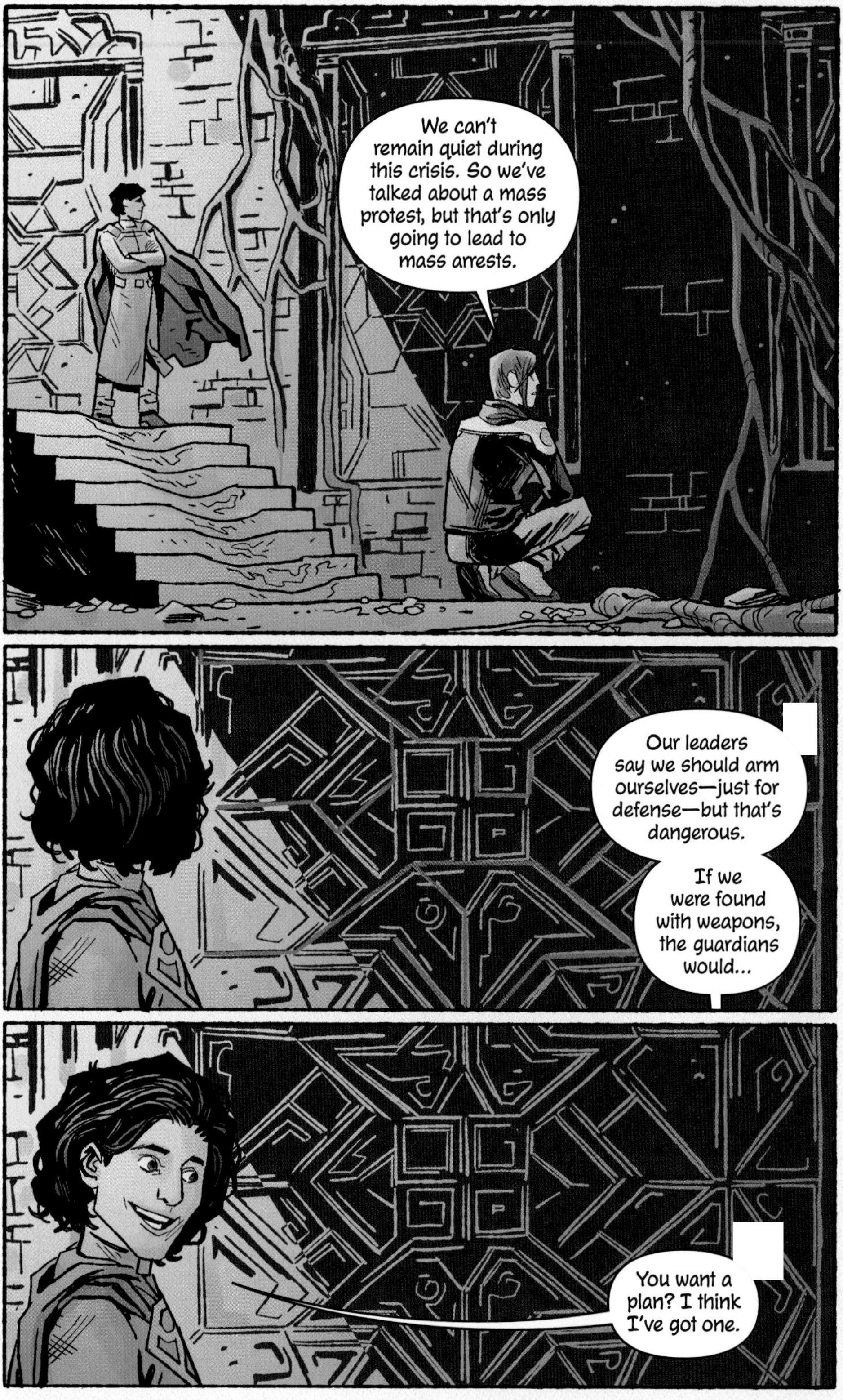
We can't remain quiet during this crisis. So we've talked about a mass protest, but that's only going to lead to mass arrests.
Our leaders say we should arm ourselves—just for defense—but that's dangerous.
If we were found with weapons, the guardians would...
You want a plan? I think I've got one.

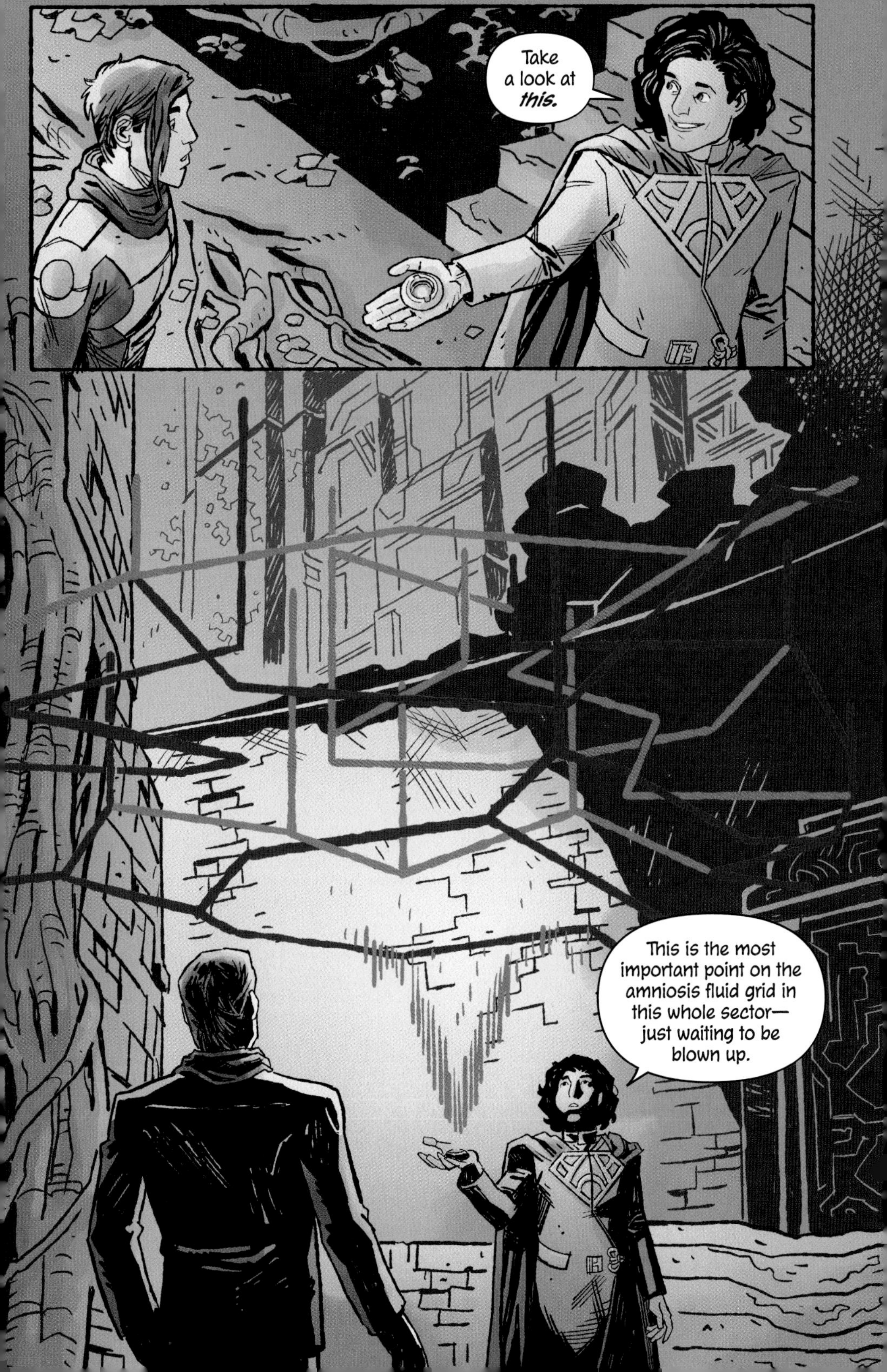
Take a look at *this.*
This is the most important point on the amniosis fluid grid in this whole sector— just waiting to be blown up.

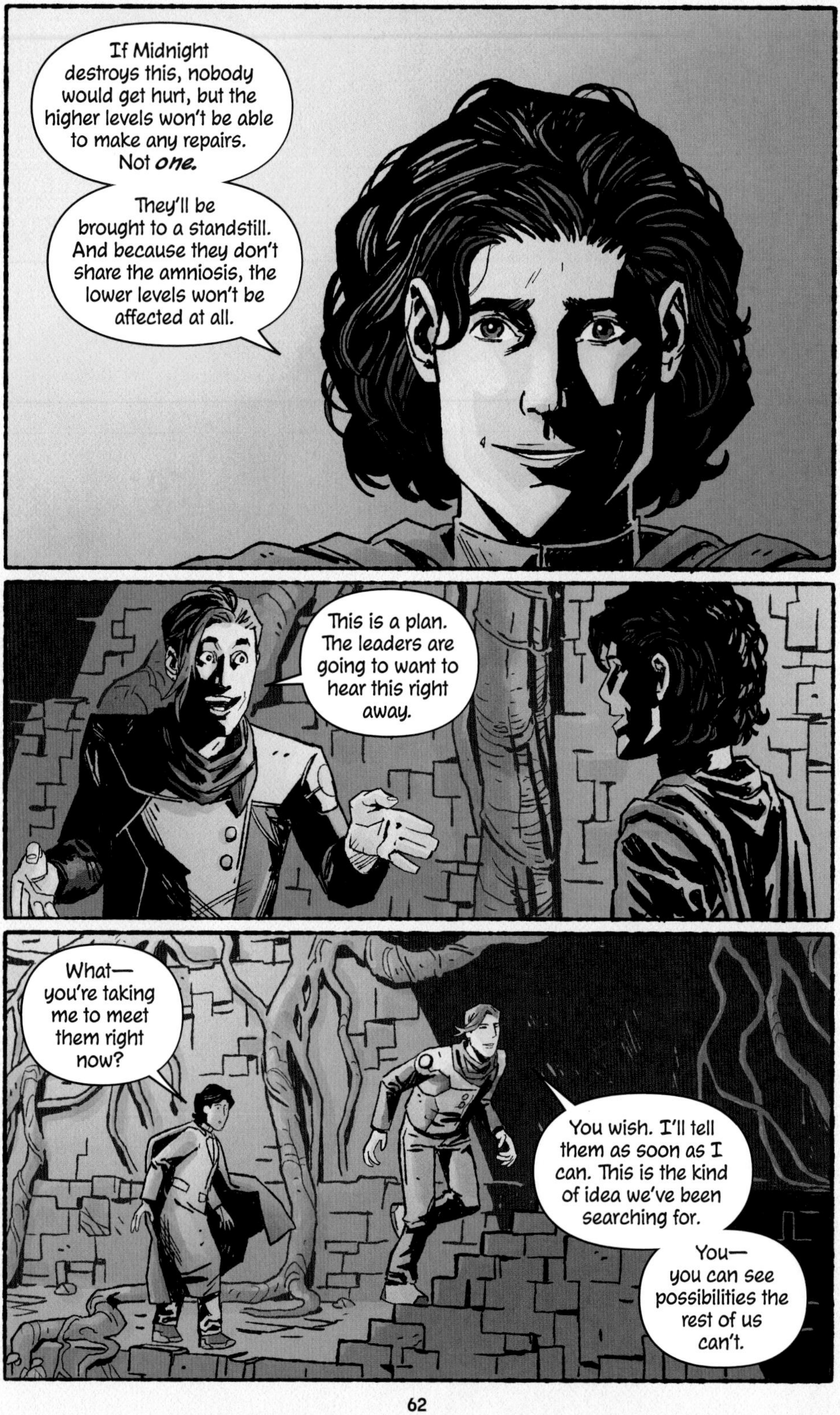
If Midnight destroys this, nobody would get hurt, but the higher levels won't be able to make any repairs. Not *one.*
They'll be brought to a standstill. And because they don't share the amniosis, the lower levels won't be affected at all.
This is a plan. The leaders are going to want to hear this right away.
What— you're taking me to meet them right now?
You wish. I'll tell them as soon as I can. This is the kind of idea we've been searching for.
You— you can see possibilities the rest of us can't.

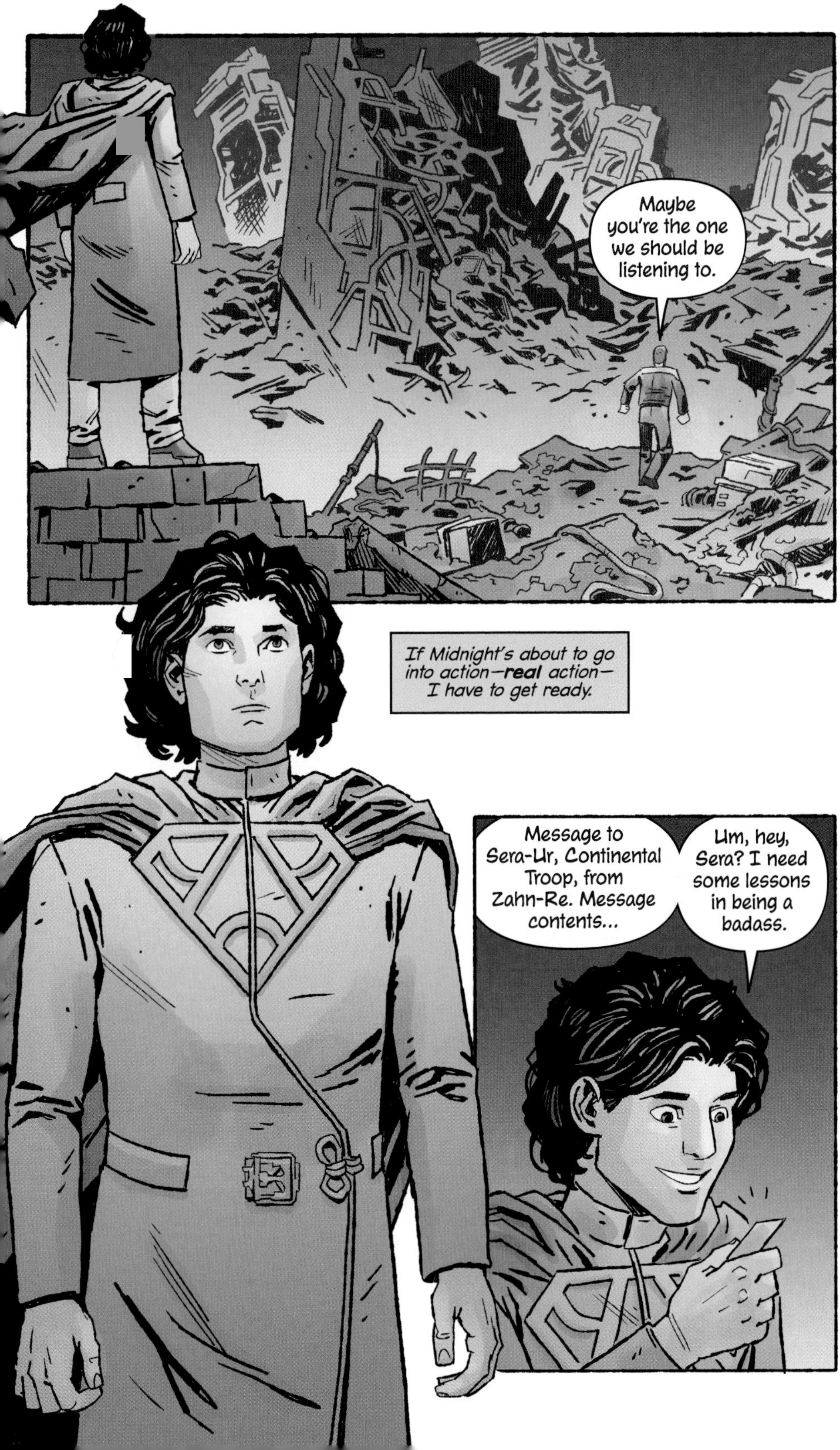
Maybe you're the one we should be listening to.
If Midnight's about to go into action—**real** action—I have to get ready.
Message to Sera-Ur, Continental Troop, from Zahn-Re. Message contents...
Um, hey, Sera? I need some lessons in being a badass.

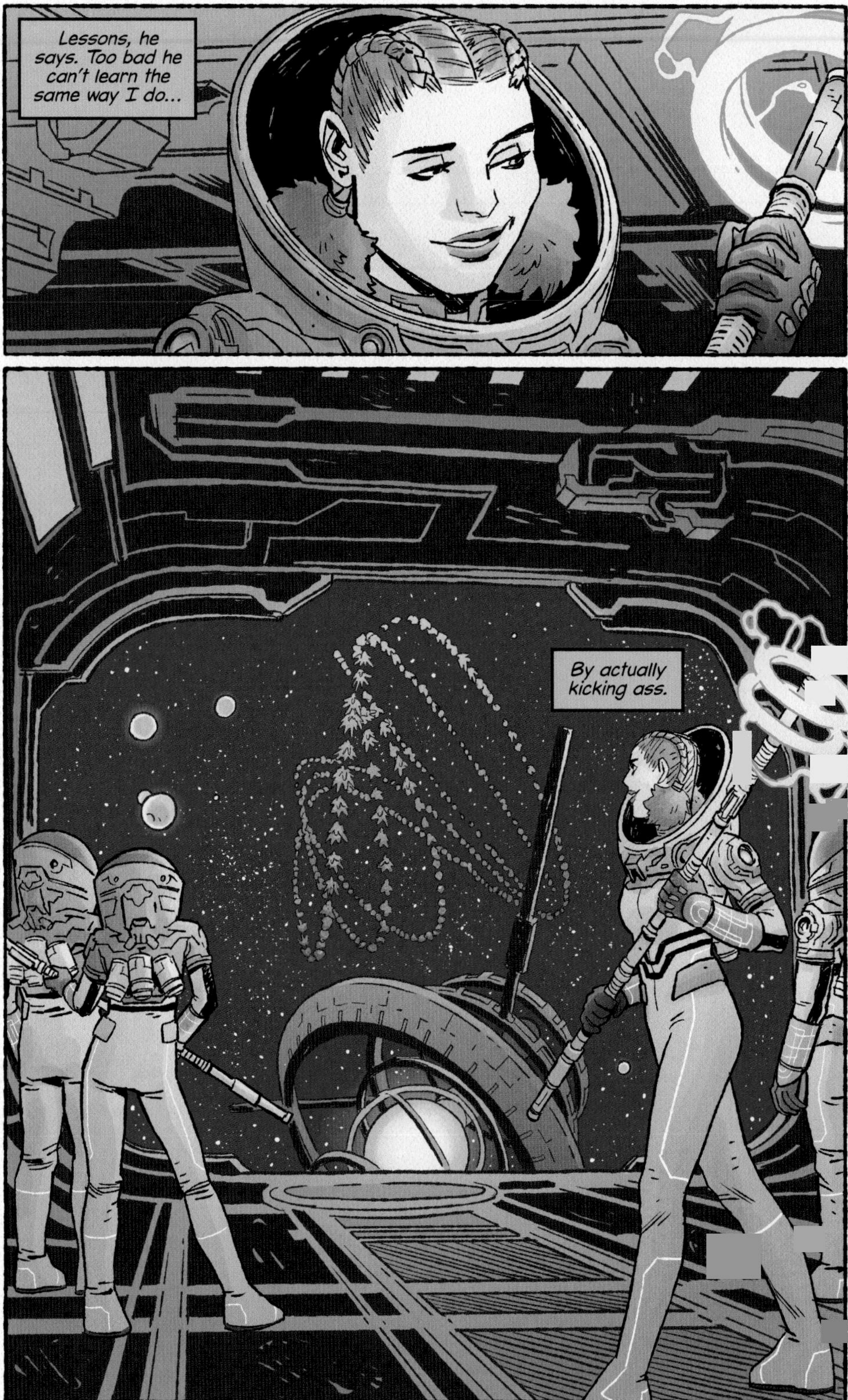
Lessons, he says. Too bad he can't learn the same way I do...
By actually kicking ass.

CHAPTER
TWO

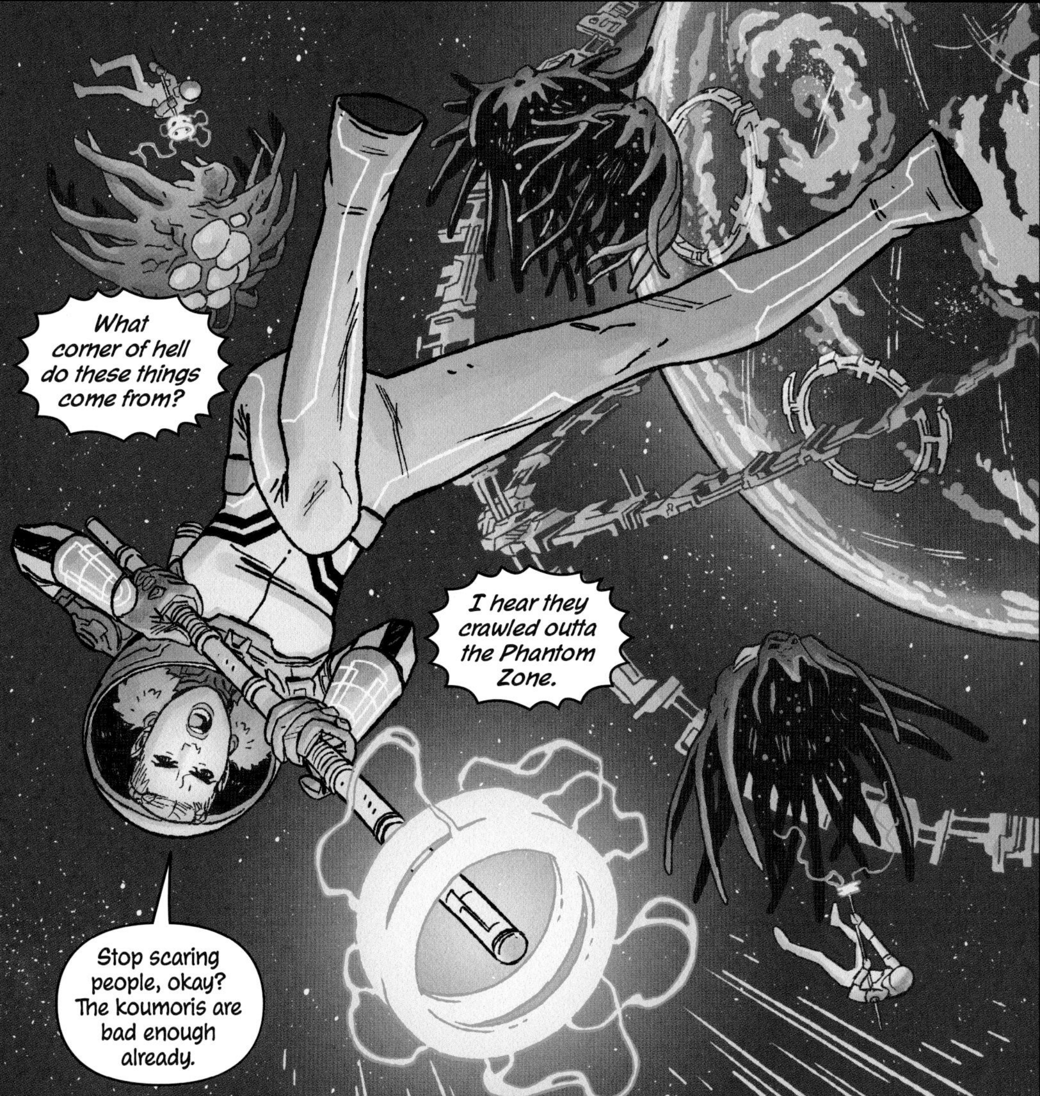
What corner of hell do these things come from?
I hear they crawled outta the Phantom Zone.
Stop scaring people, okay? The koumoris are bad enough already.

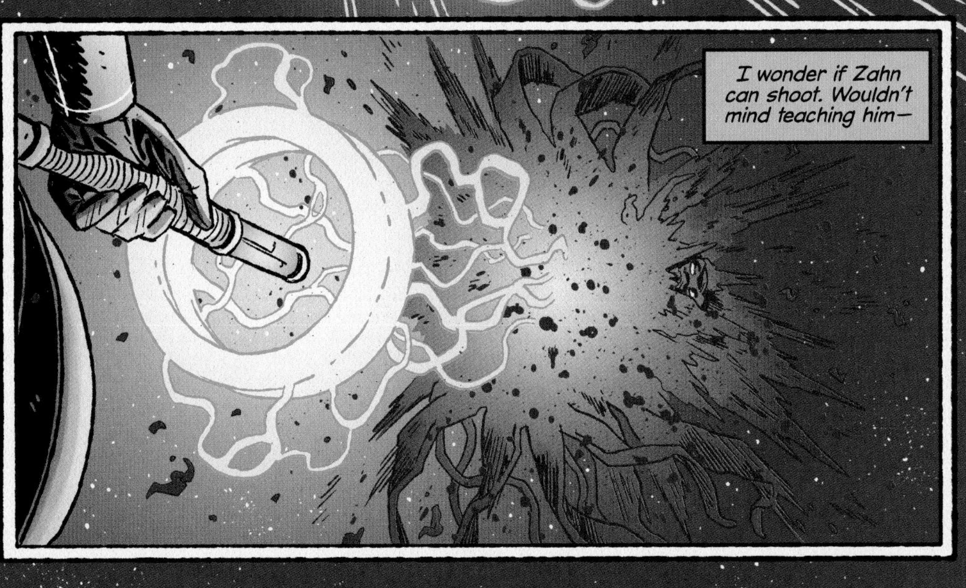
I wonder if Zahn can shoot. Wouldn't mind teaching him—

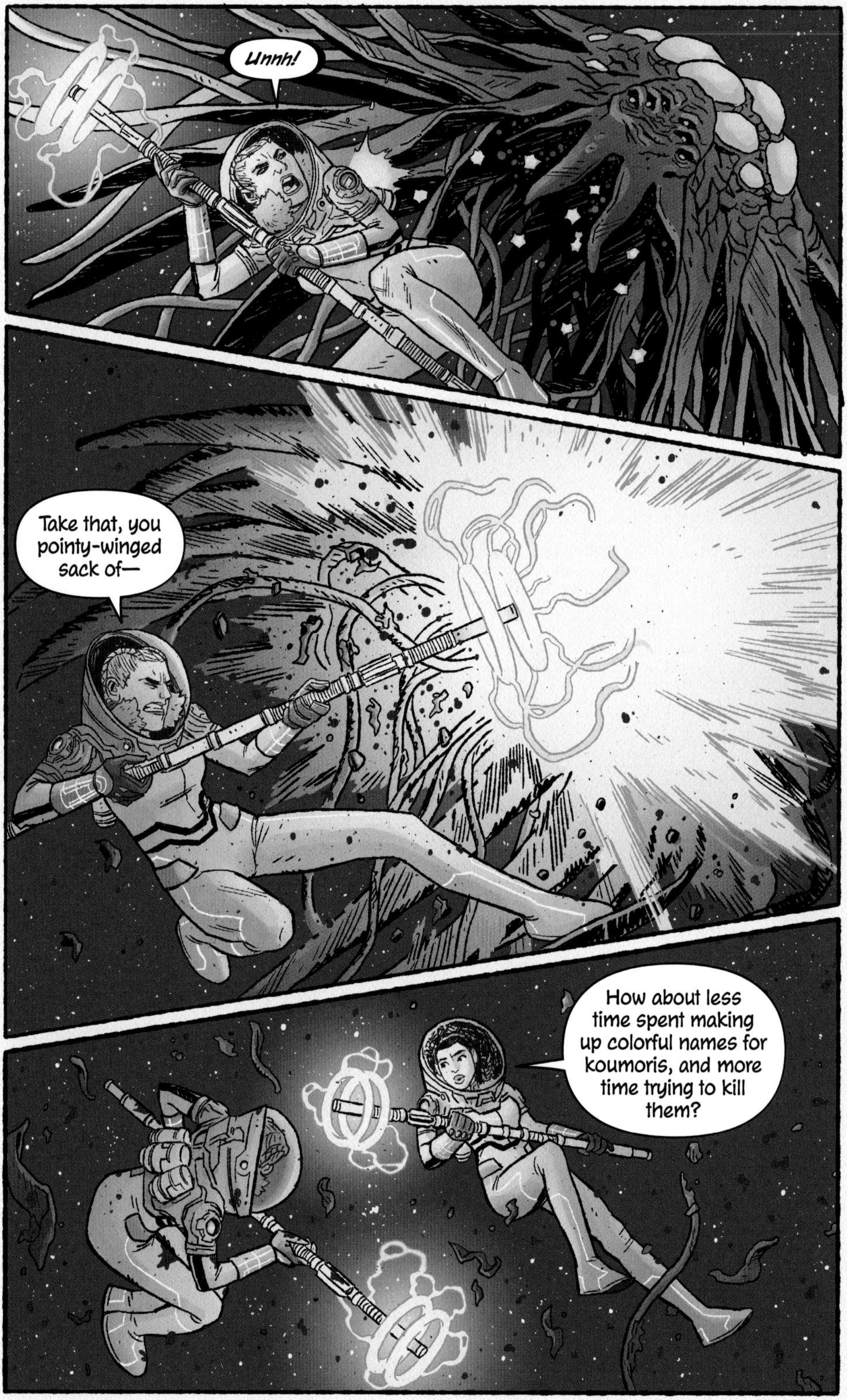
Unnh!
Take that, you pointy-winged sack of—
How about less time spent making up colorful names for koumoris, and more time trying to kill them?

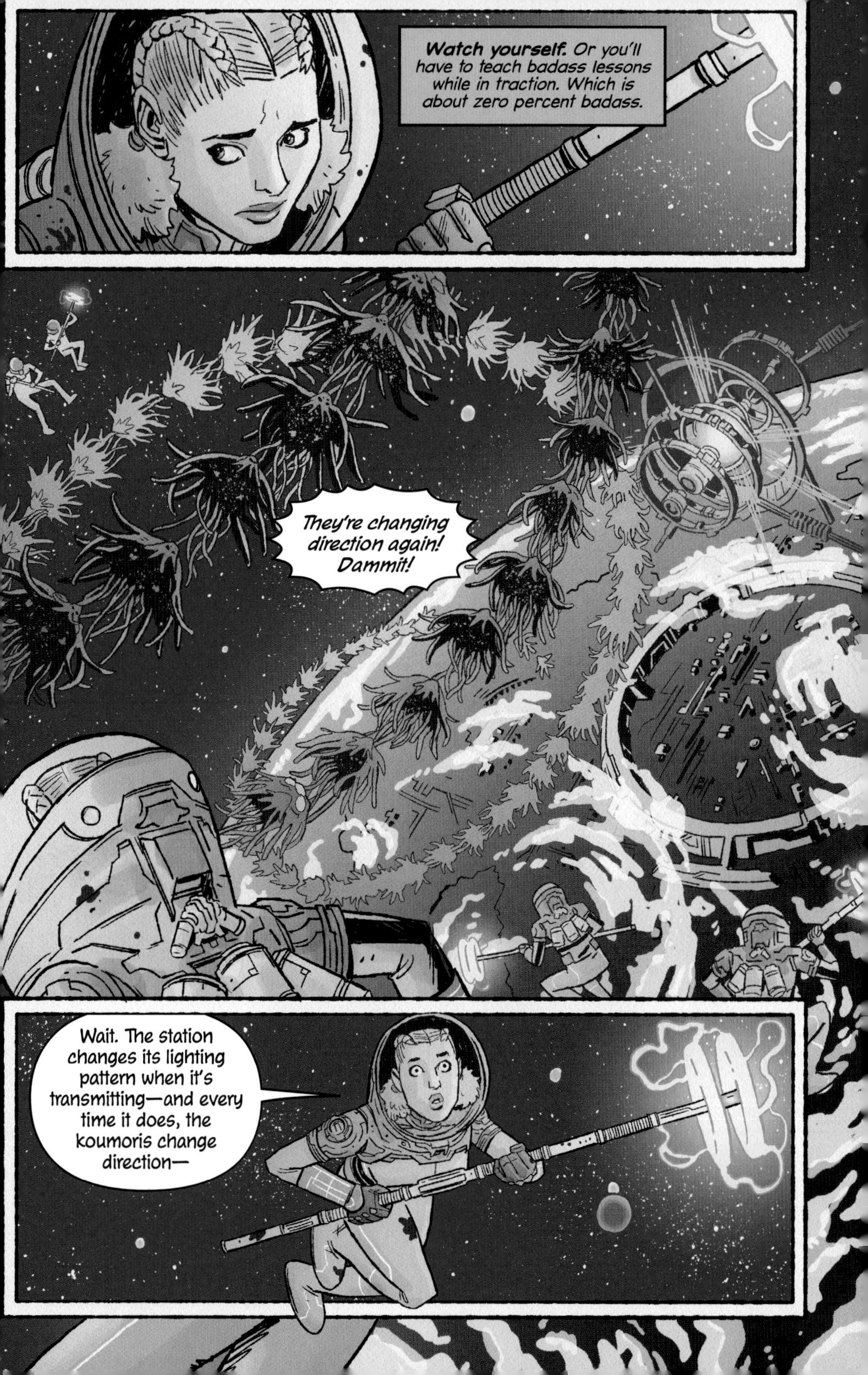
Watch yourself. Or you'll have to teach badass lessons while in traction. Which is about zero percent badass.
They're changing direction again! Dammit!
Wait. The station changes its lighting pattern when it's transmitting—and every time it does, the koumoris change direction—

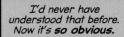

Everybody! The koumoris can see colors and patterns—the lights are driving them crazy. The next time the station lights shift, they will too, and we can be ready for them!

I'd never have understood that before. Now it's *so obvious*.

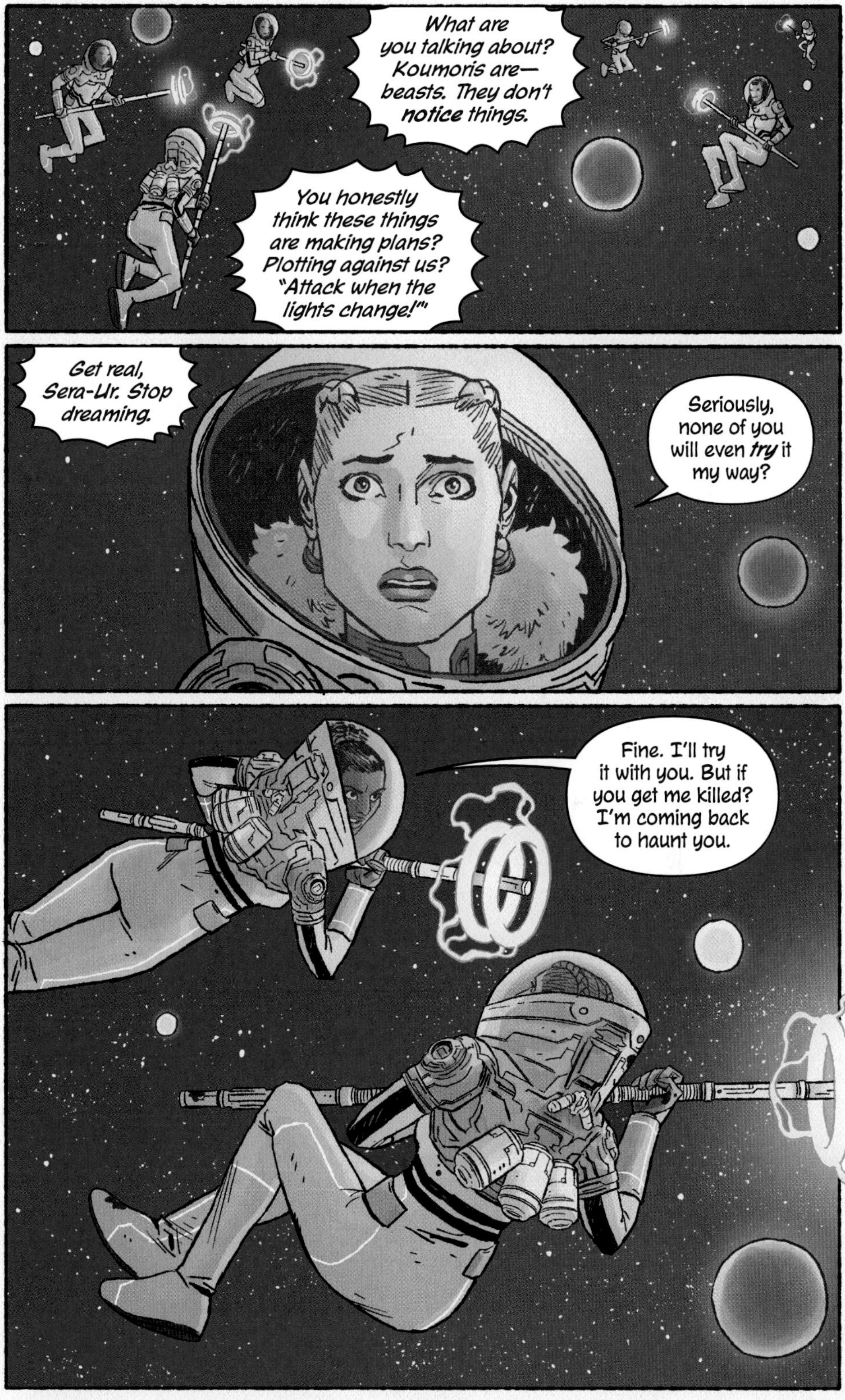
What are you talking about? Koumoris are— beasts. They don't notice things.
You honestly think these things are making plans? Plotting against us? "Attack when the lights change!"
Get real, Sera-Ur. Stop dreaming.
Seriously, none of you will even try it my way?
Fine. I'll try it with you. But if you get me killed? I'm coming back to haunt you.

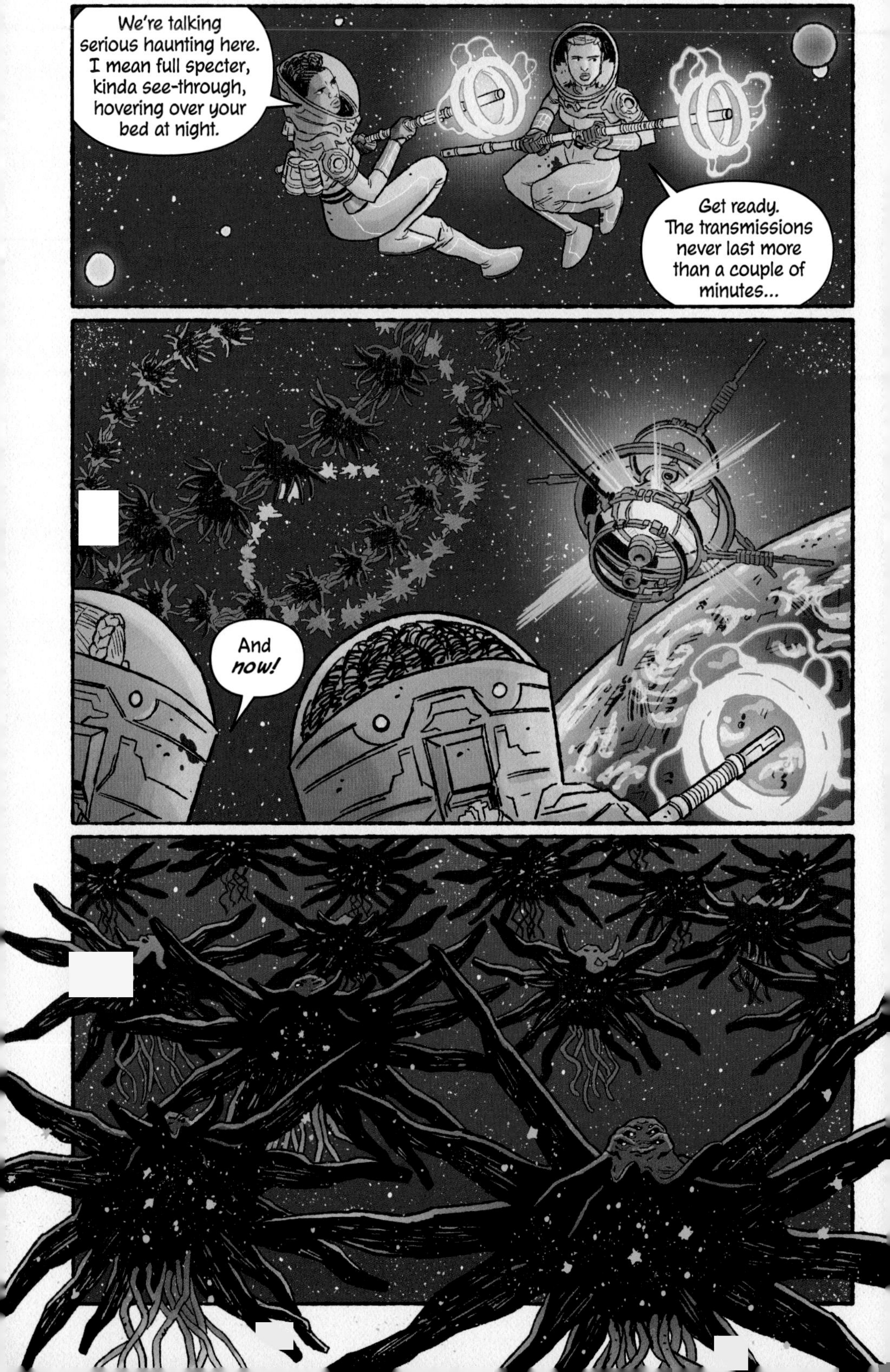
We're talking serious haunting here. I mean full specter, kinda see-through, hovering over your bed at night.
Get ready. The transmissions never last more than a couple of minutes...
And *now!*

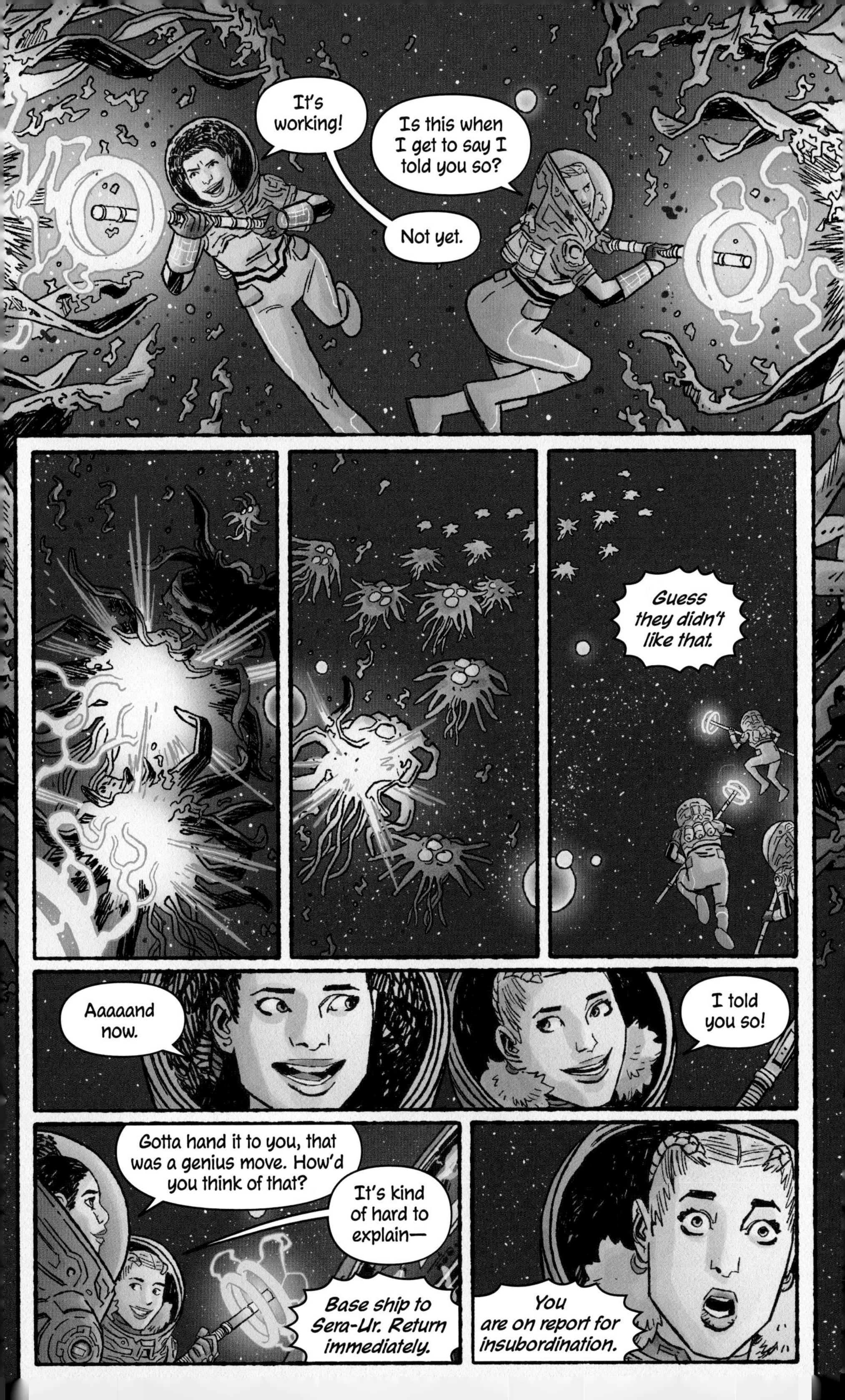
It's working!
Is this when I get to say I told you so?
Not yet.
Guess they didn't like that.
Aaaaand now.
I told you so!
Gotta hand it to you, that was a genius move. How'd you think of that?
It's kind of hard to explain—
Base ship to Sera-Ur. Return immediately.
You are on report for insubordination.

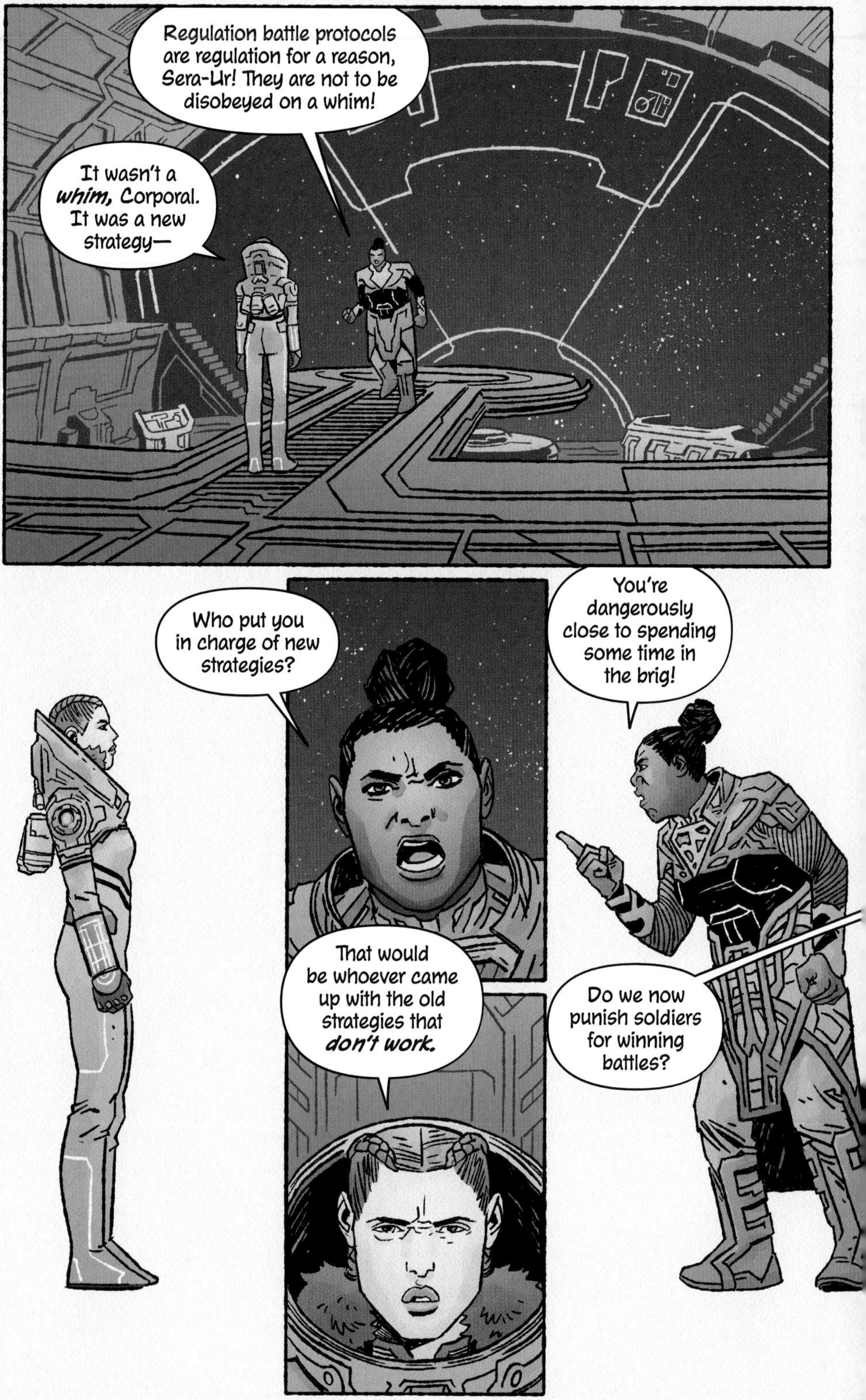

Regulation battle protocols are regulation for a reason, Sera-Ur! They are not to be disobeyed on a whim!
It wasn't a *whim,* Corporal. It was a new strategy—
Who put you in charge of new strategies?
You're dangerously close to spending some time in the brig!
That would be whoever came up with the old strategies that *don't work.*
Do we now punish soldiers for winning battles?

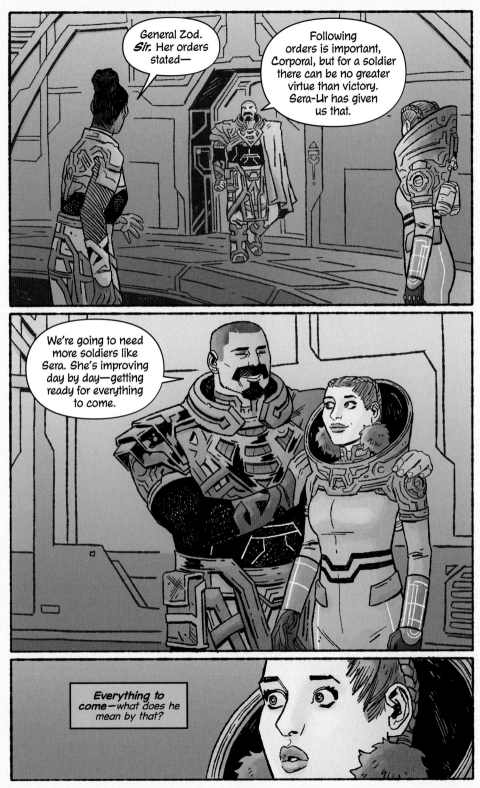

General Zod. *Sir.* Her orders stated—

Following orders is important, Corporal, but for a soldier there can be no greater virtue than victory. Sera-Ur has given us that.

We're going to need more soldiers like Sera. She's improving day by day—getting ready for everything to come.

Everything to come—what does he mean by that?

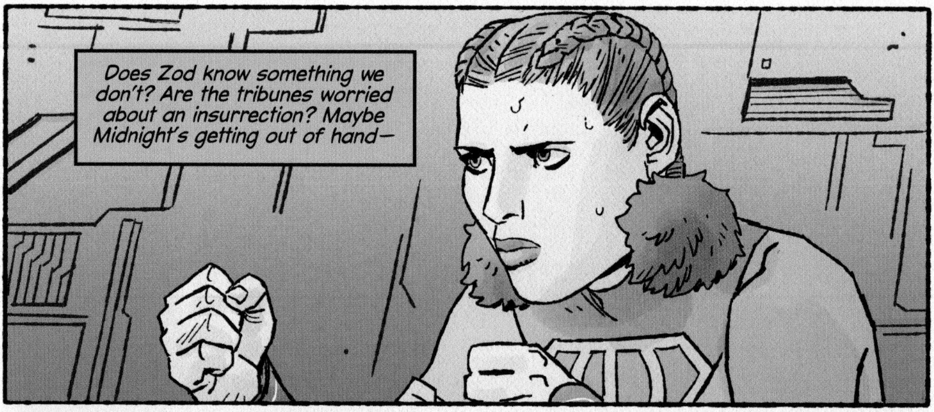
Does Zod know something we don't? Are the tribunes worried about an insurrection? Maybe Midnight's getting out of hand—

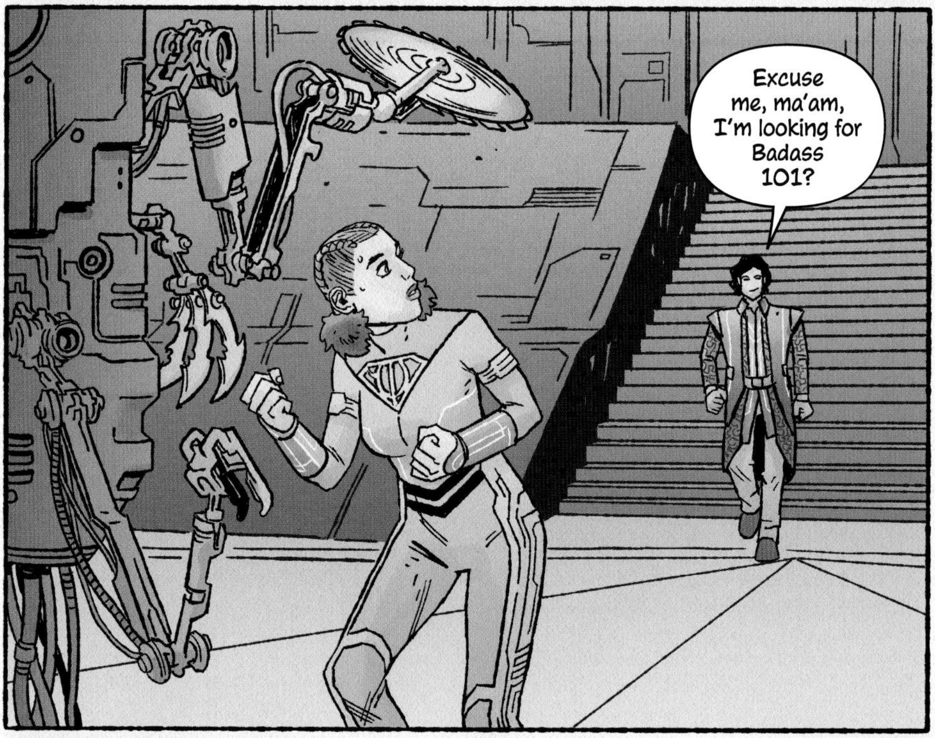
Excuse me, ma'am, I'm looking for Badass 101?

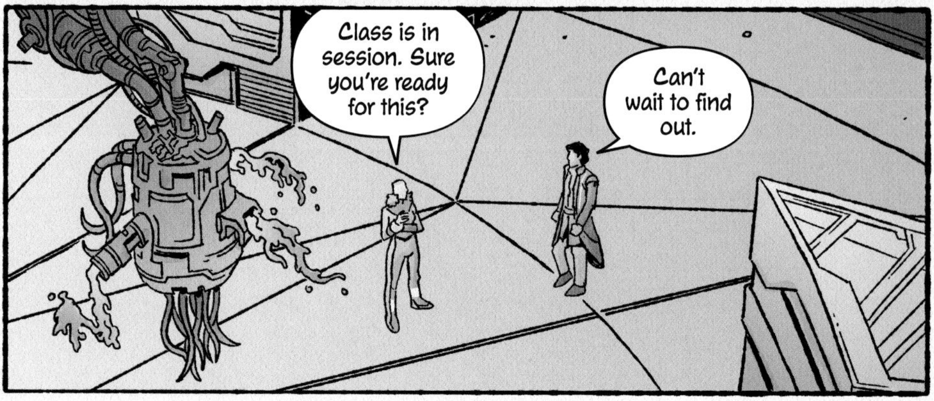
Class is in session. Sure you're ready for this?
Can't wait to find out.

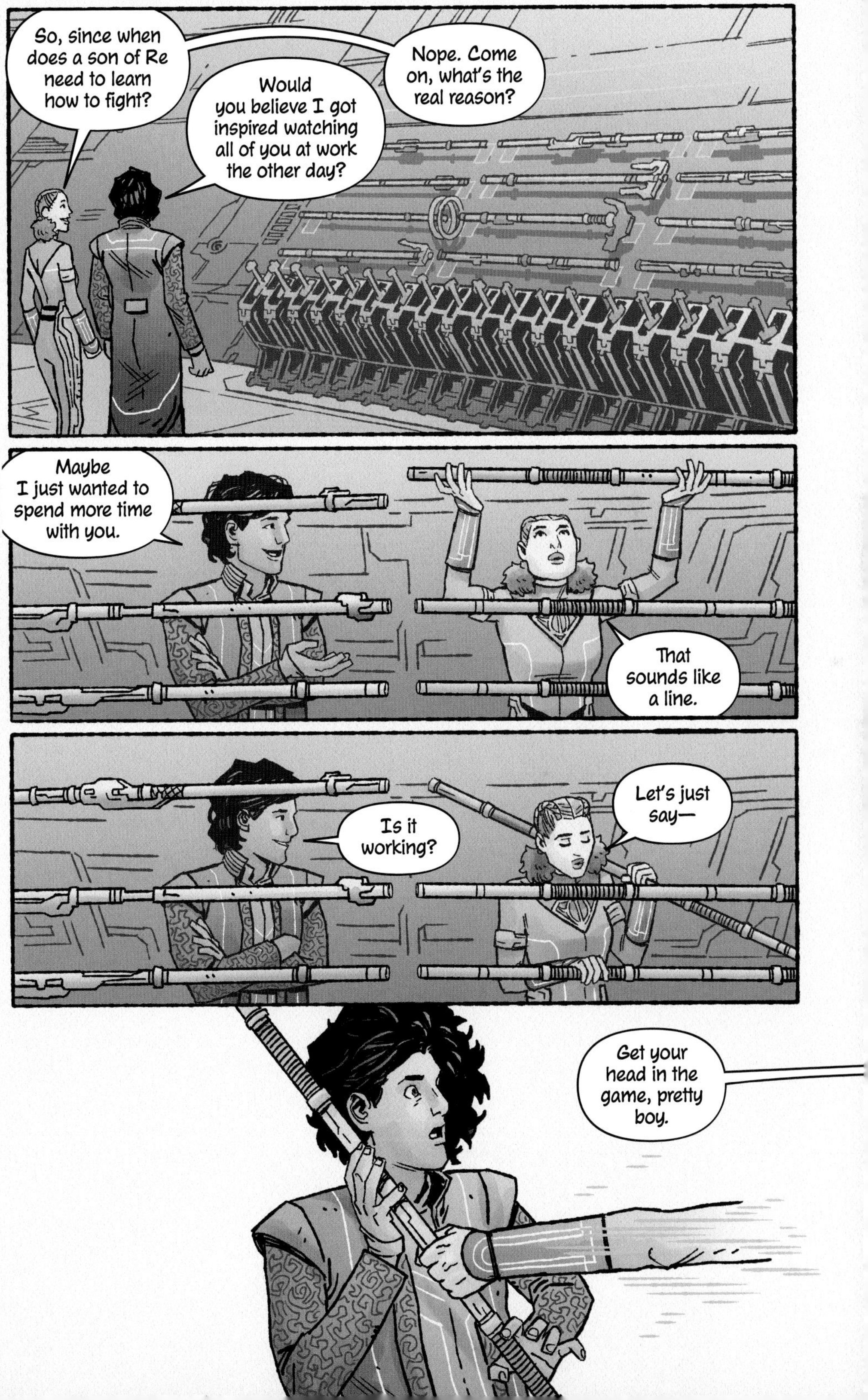
So, since when does a son of Re need to learn how to fight?
Would you believe I got inspired watching all of you at work the other day?
Nope. Come on, what's the real reason?
Maybe I just wanted to spend more time with you.
That sounds like a line.
Is it working?
Let's just say—
Get your head in the game, pretty boy.

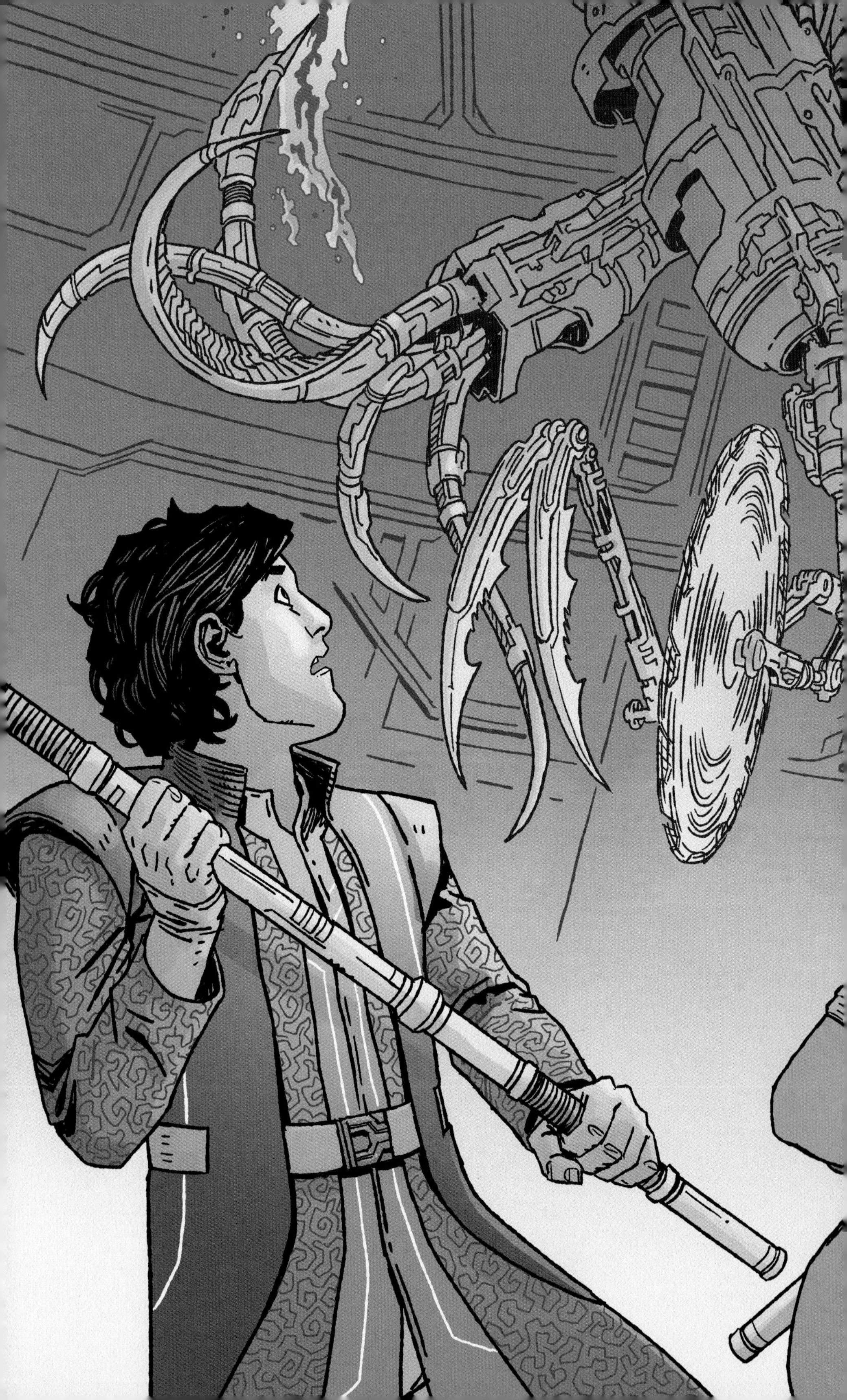

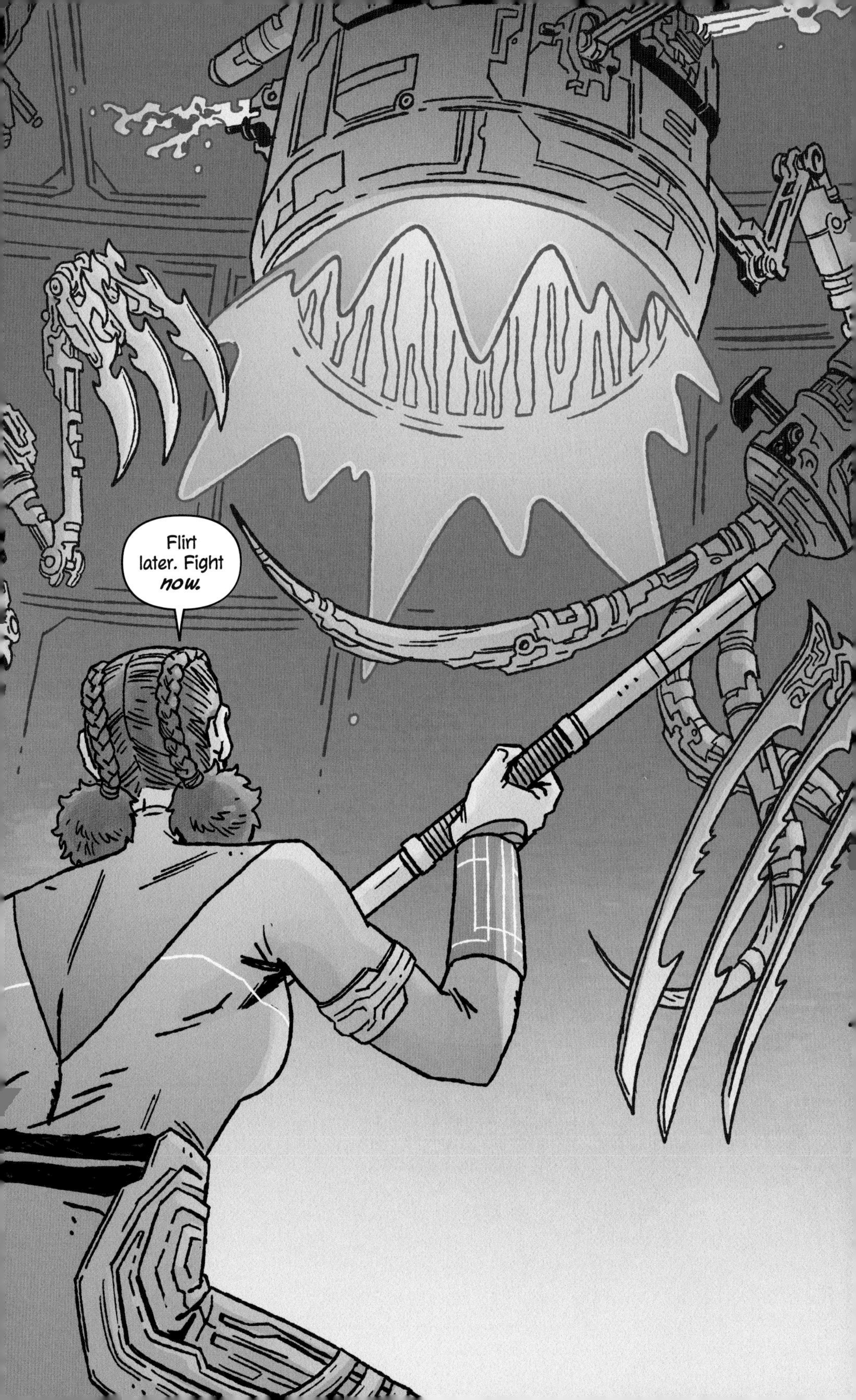
Flirt later. Fight *now.*

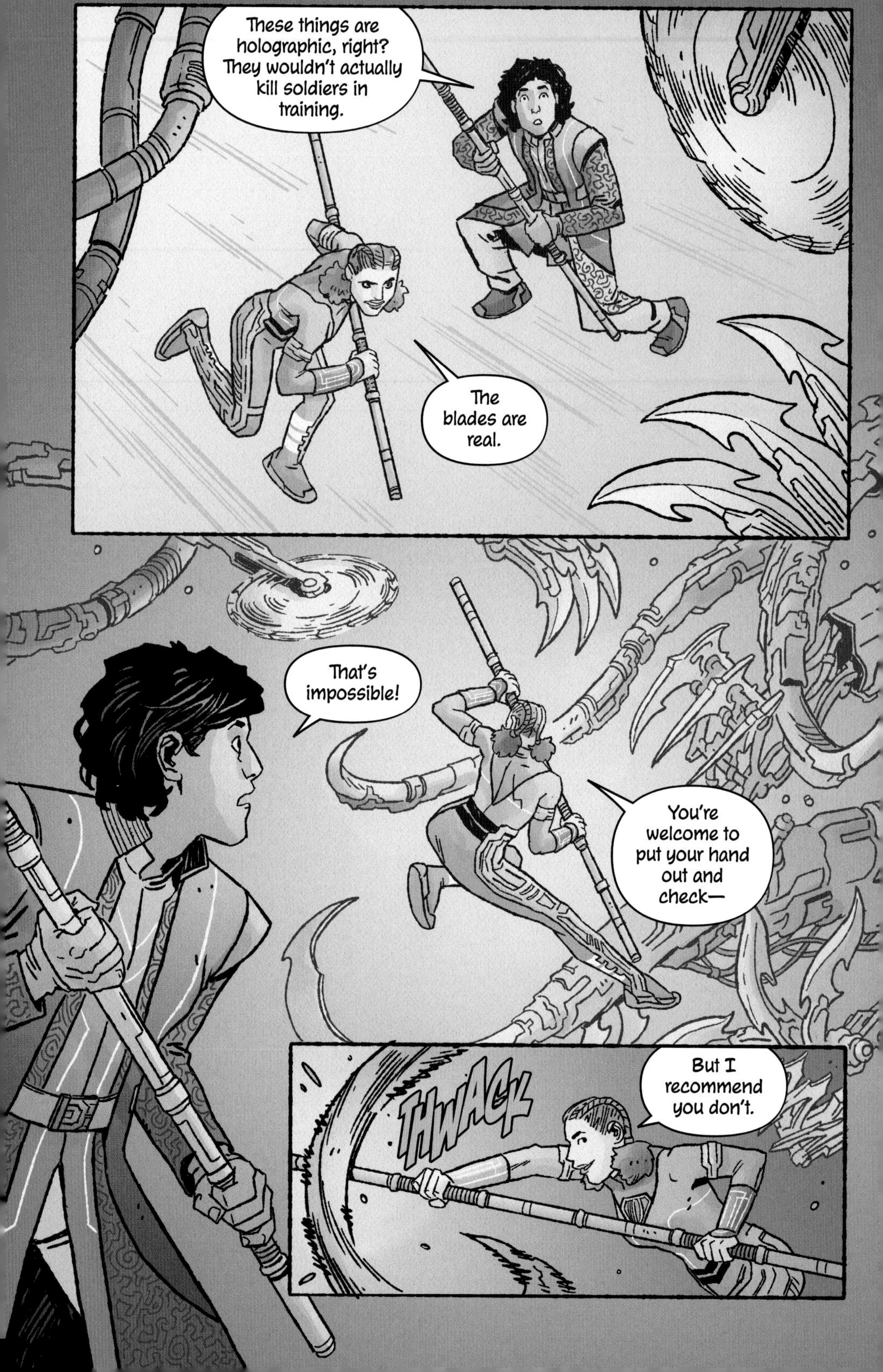
These things are holographic, right? They wouldn't actually kill soldiers in training.
The blades are real.
That's impossible!
You're welcome to put your hand out and check—
THWACK
But I recommend you don't.

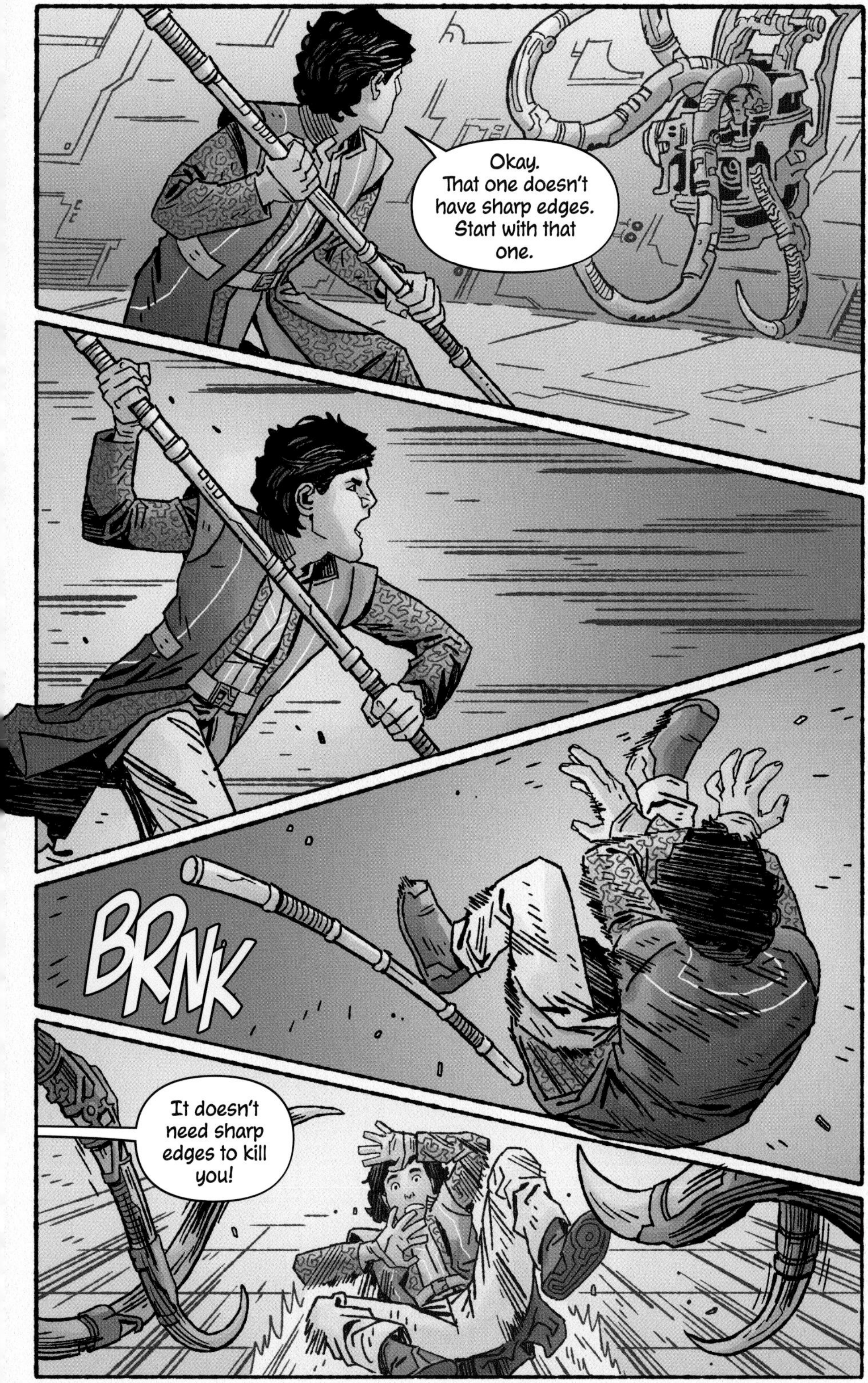
Okay.
That one doesn't have sharp edges. Start with that one.
BRNK
It doesn't need sharp edges to kill you!

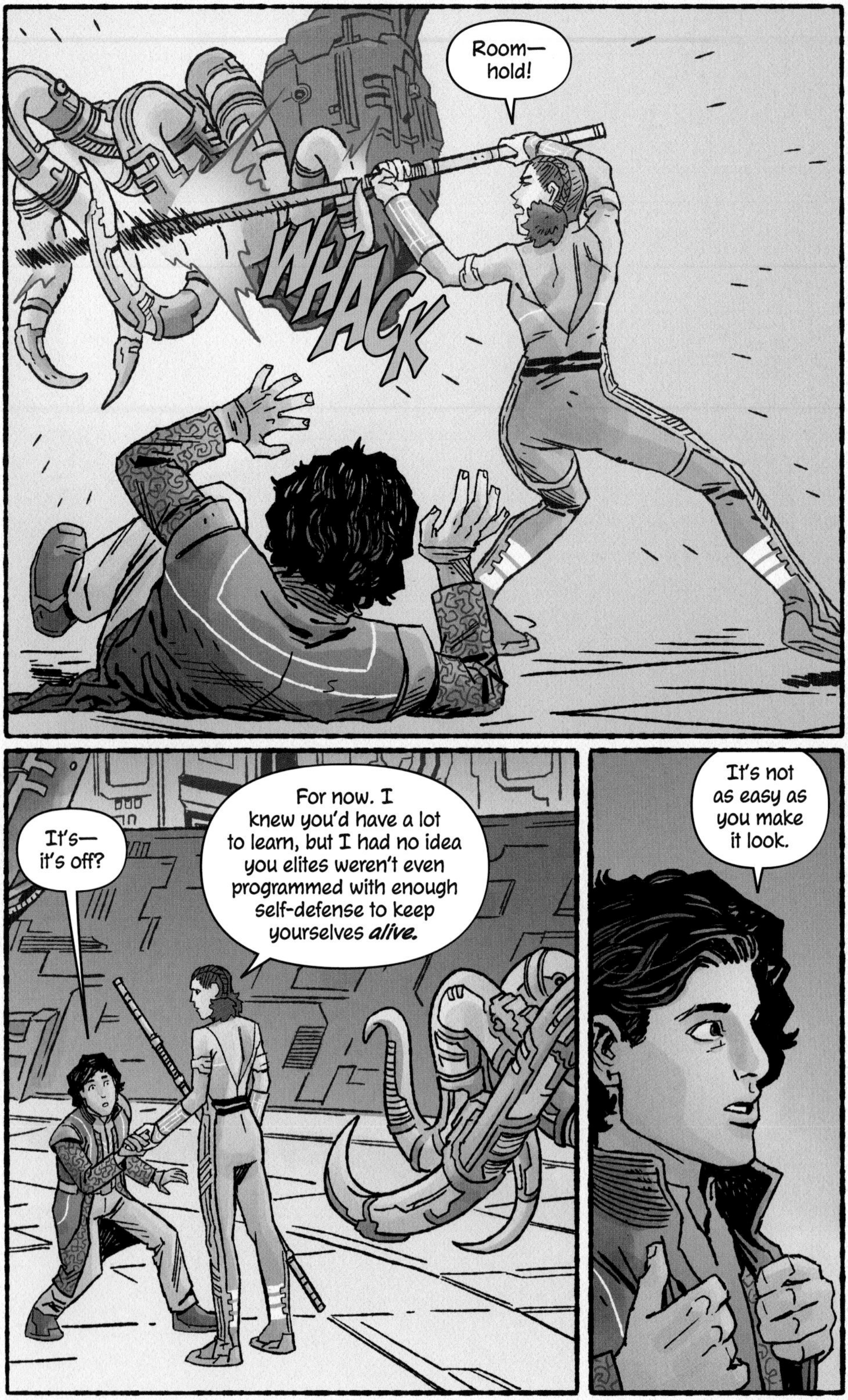
Room—
hold!
WHACK
It's—
it's off?
For now. I knew you'd have a lot to learn, but I had no idea you elites weren't even programmed with enough self-defense to keep yourselves *alive.*
It's not as easy as you make it look.

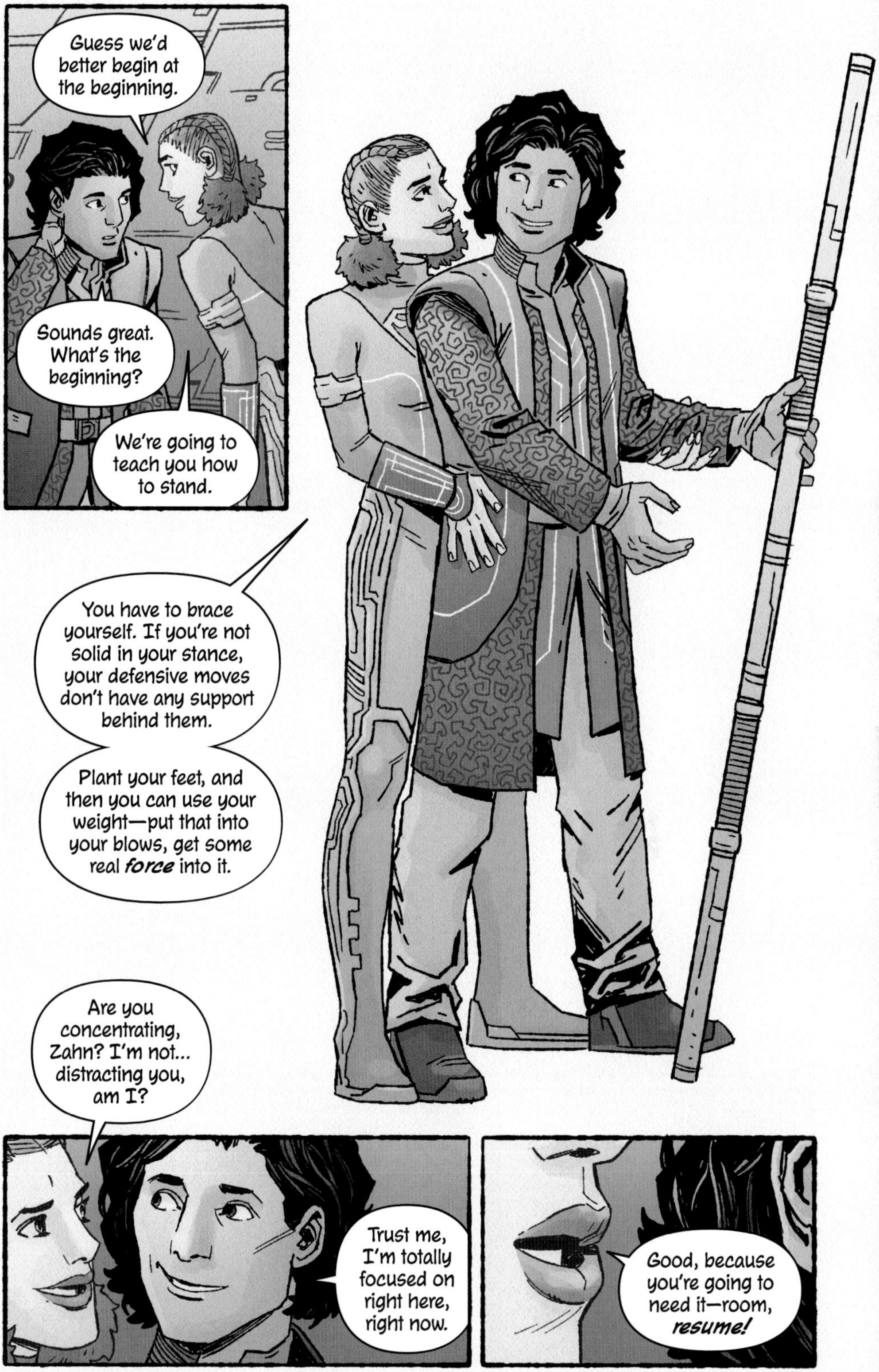

Guess we'd better begin at the beginning.
Sounds great. What's the beginning?
We're going to teach you how to stand.
You have to brace yourself. If you're not solid in your stance, your defensive moves don't have any support behind them.
Plant your feet, and then you can use your weight—put that into your blows, get some real *force* into it.
Are you concentrating, Zahn? I'm not... distracting you, am I?
Trust me, I'm totally focused on right here, right now.
Good, because you're going to need it—room, ***resume!***

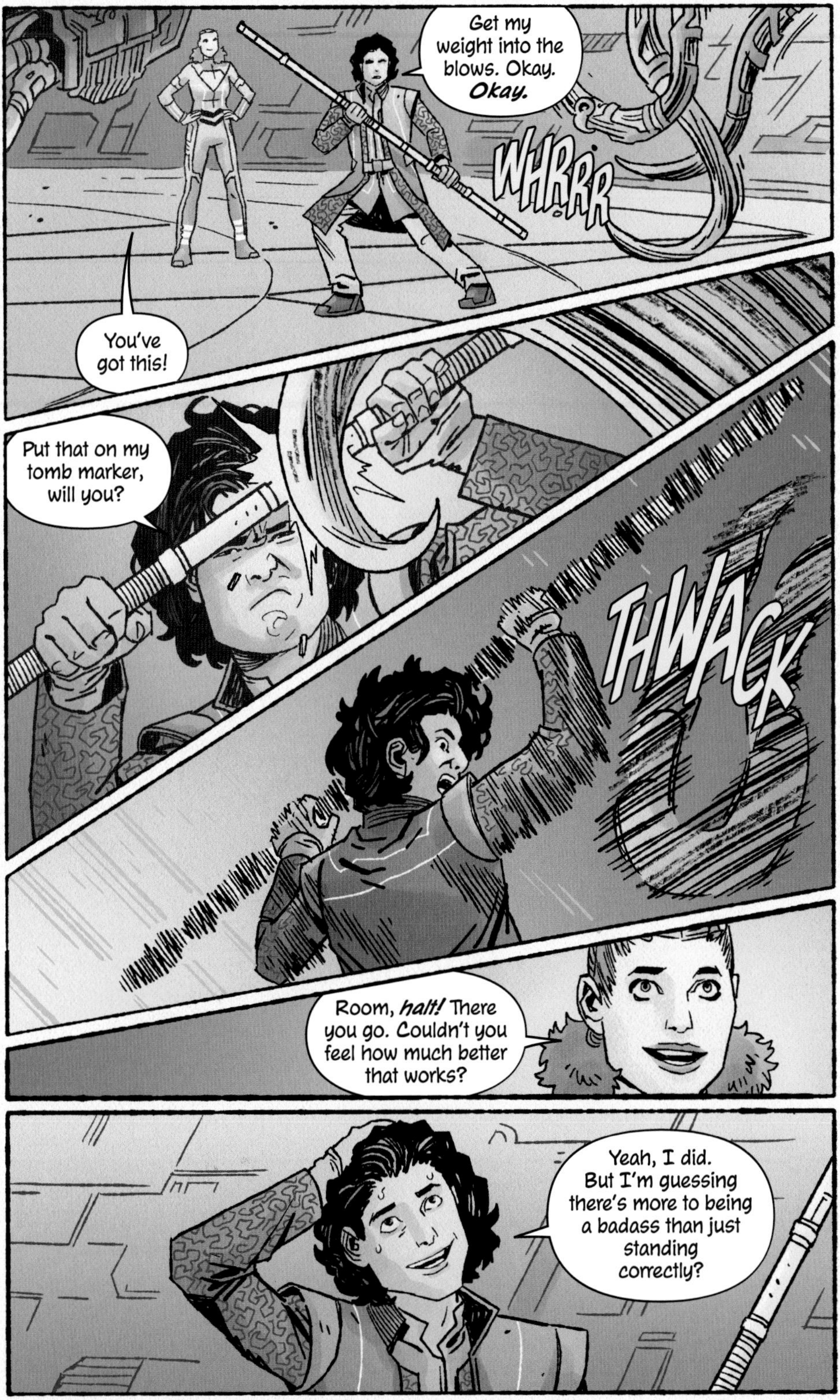

Get my weight into the blows. Okay. ***Okay.***
WHRRR
You've got this!
Put that on my tomb marker, will you?
THWACK
Room, ***halt!*** There you go. Couldn't you feel how much better that works?
Yeah, I did. But I'm guessing there's more to being a badass than just standing correctly?

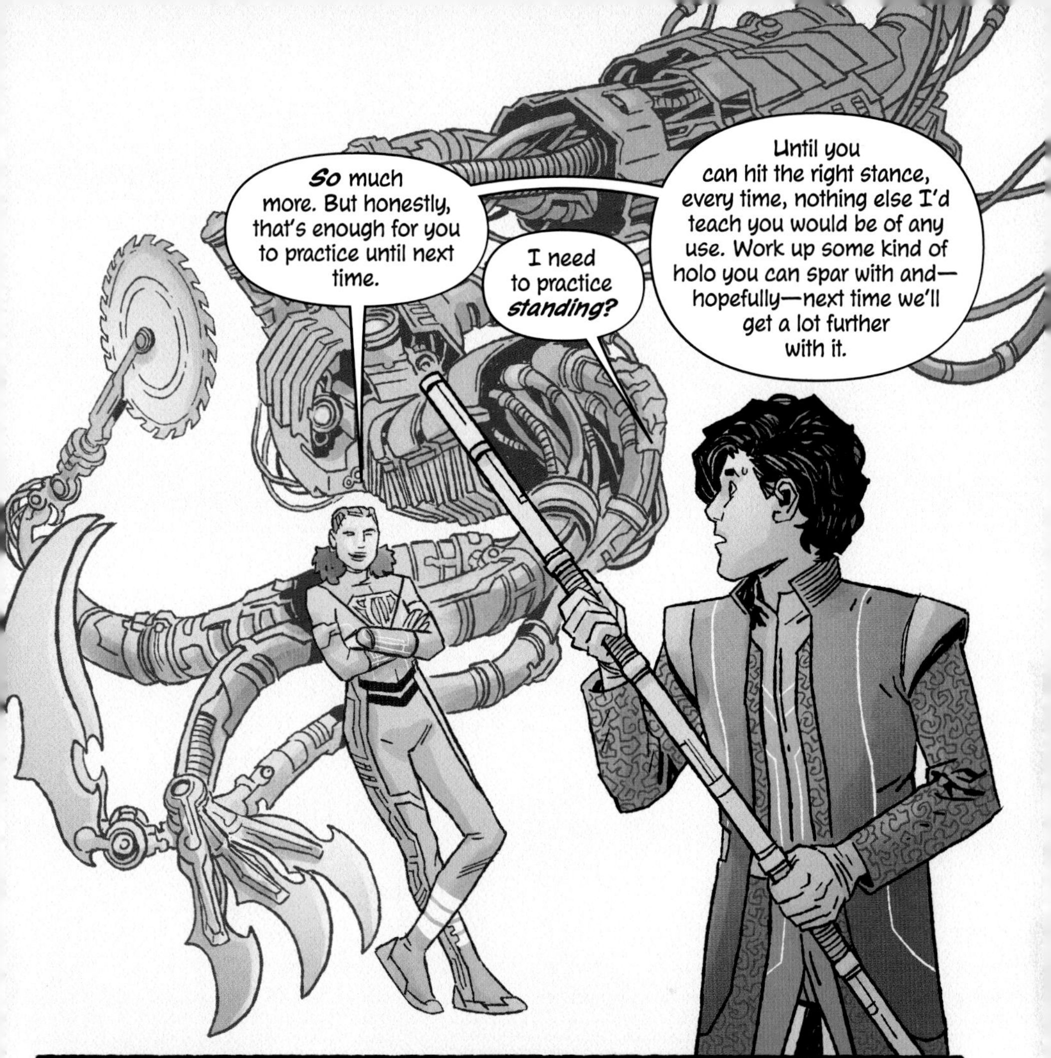
So much more. But honestly, that's enough for you to practice until next time.
I need to practice *standing?*
Until you can hit the right stance, every time, nothing else I'd teach you would be of any use. Work up some kind of holo you can spar with and—hopefully—next time we'll get a lot further with it.

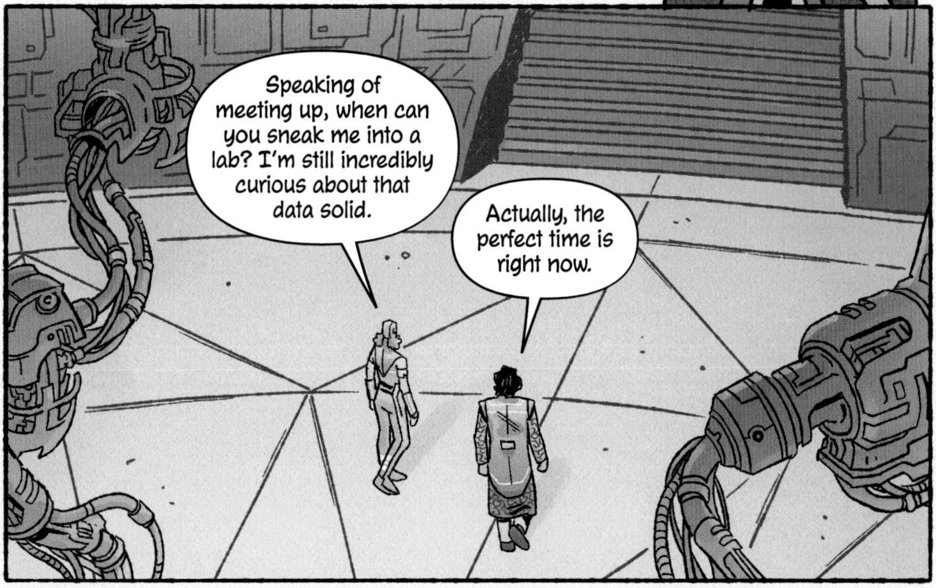
Speaking of meeting up, when can you sneak me into a lab? I'm still incredibly curious about that data solid.
Actually, the perfect time is right now.

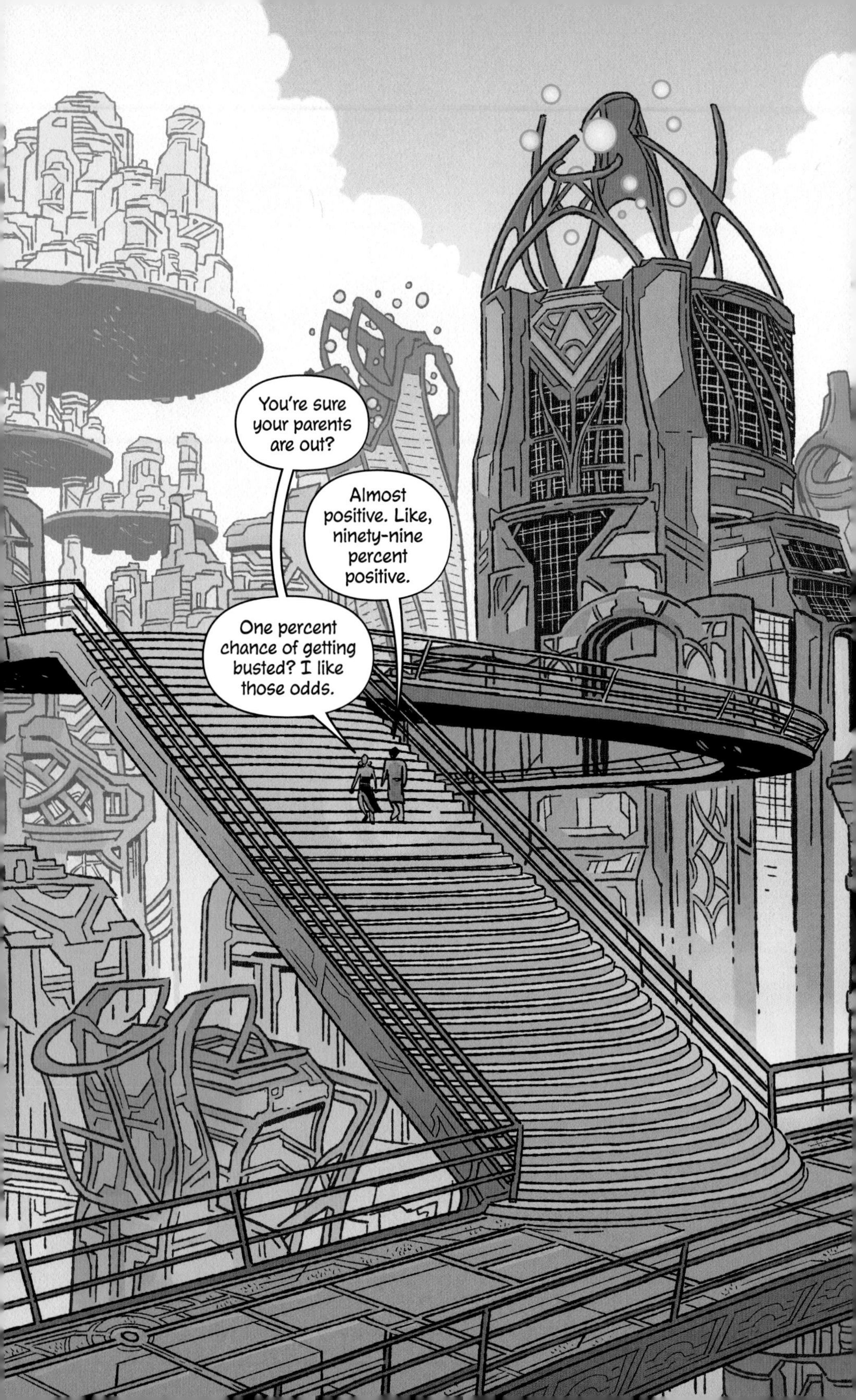
You're sure your parents are out?
Almost positive. Like, ninety-nine percent positive.
One percent chance of getting busted? I like those odds.

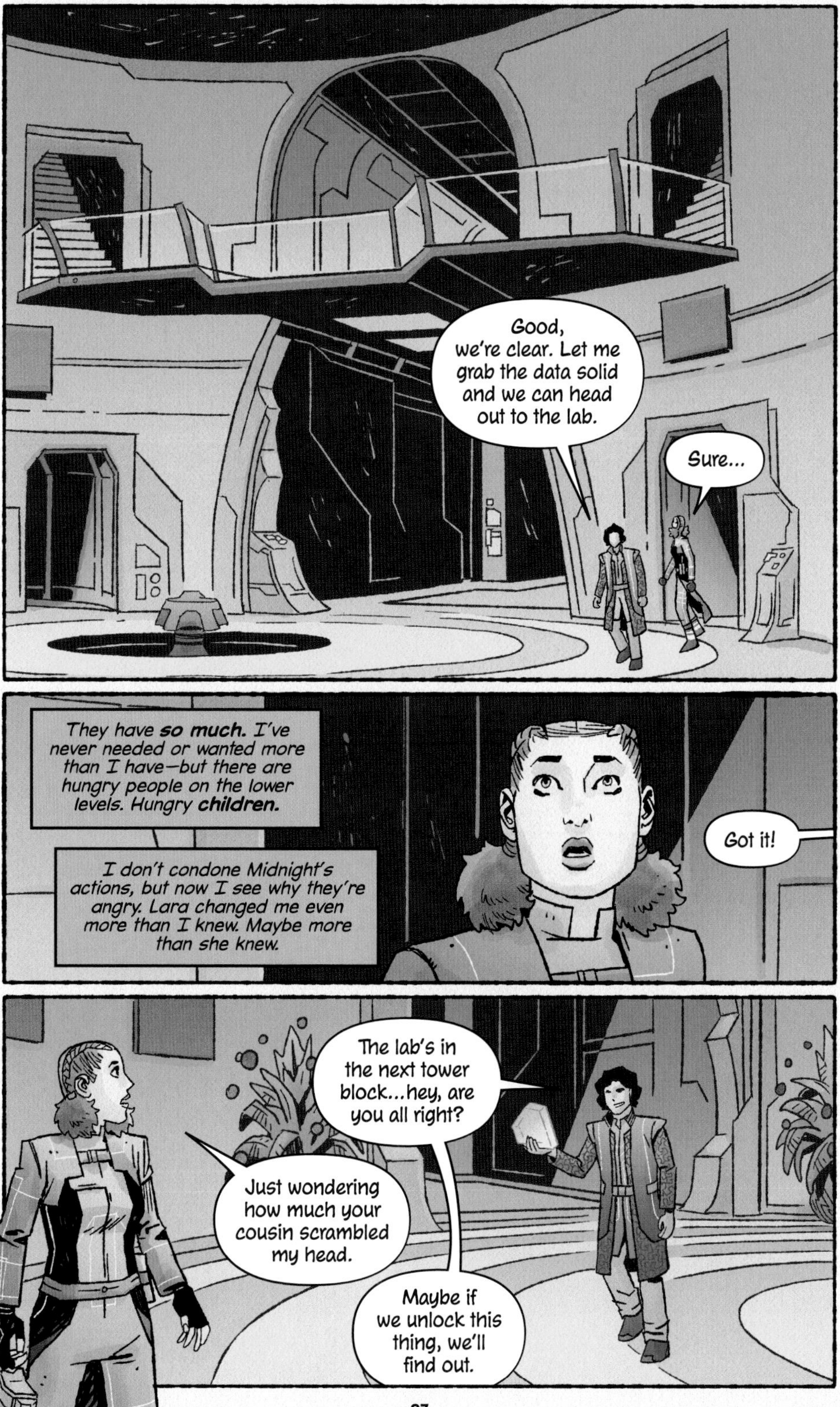
Good, we're clear. Let me grab the data solid and we can head out to the lab.
Sure...
They have **so much.** I've never needed or wanted more than I have—but there are hungry people on the lower levels. Hungry **children.**
I don't condone Midnight's actions, but now I see why they're angry. Lara changed me even more than I knew. Maybe more than she knew.
Got it!
The lab's in the next tower block...hey, are you all right?
Just wondering how much your cousin scrambled my head.
Maybe if we unlock this thing, we'll find out.

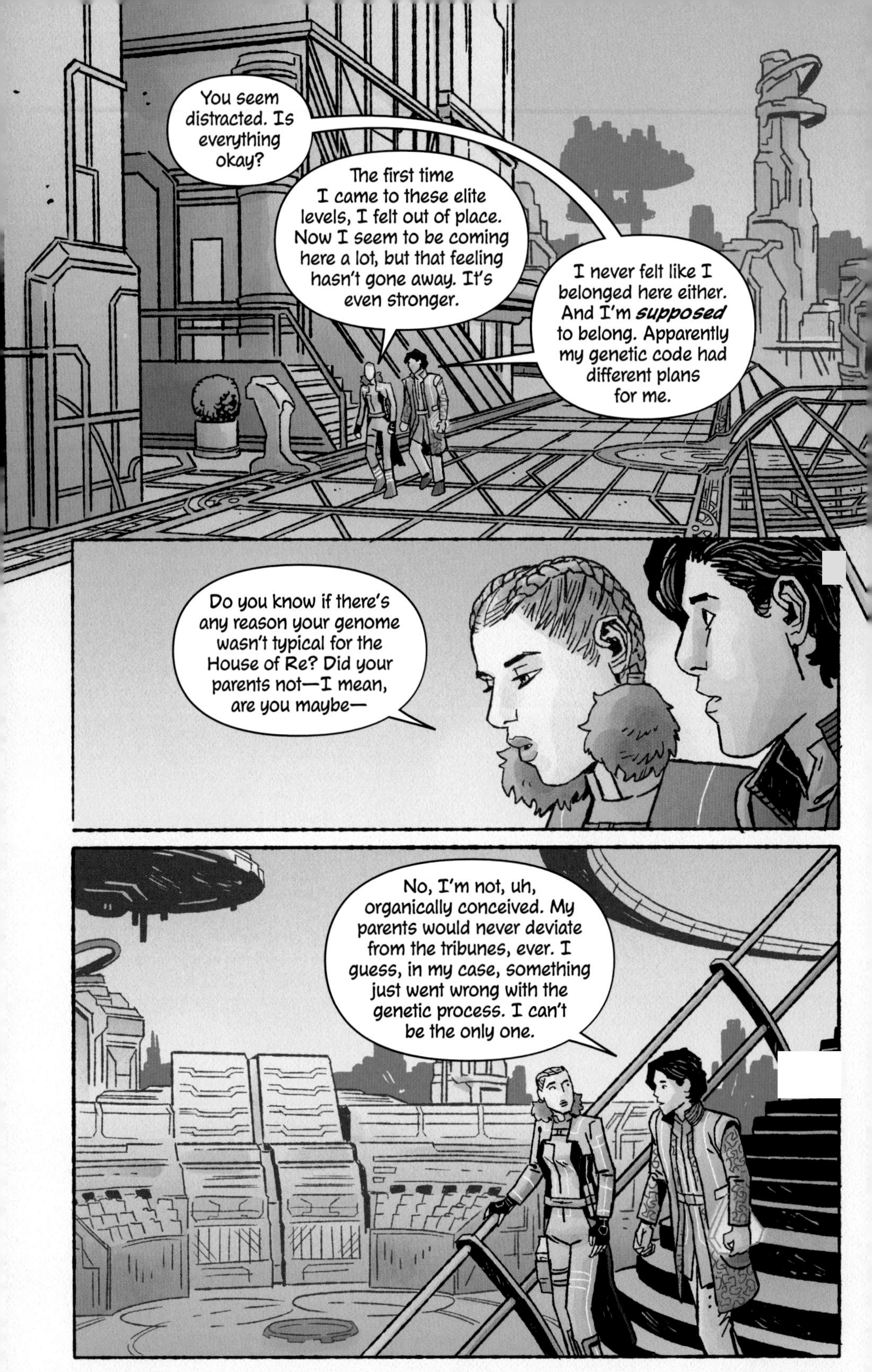
You seem distracted. Is everything okay?
The first time I came to these elite levels, I felt out of place. Now I seem to be coming here a lot, but that feeling hasn't gone away. It's even stronger.
I never felt like I belonged here either. And I'm *supposed* to belong. Apparently my genetic code had different plans for me.
Do you know if there's any reason your genome wasn't typical for the House of Re? Did your parents not—I mean, are you maybe—
No, I'm not, uh, organically conceived. My parents would never deviate from the tribunes, ever. I guess, in my case, something just went wrong with the genetic process. I can't be the only one.

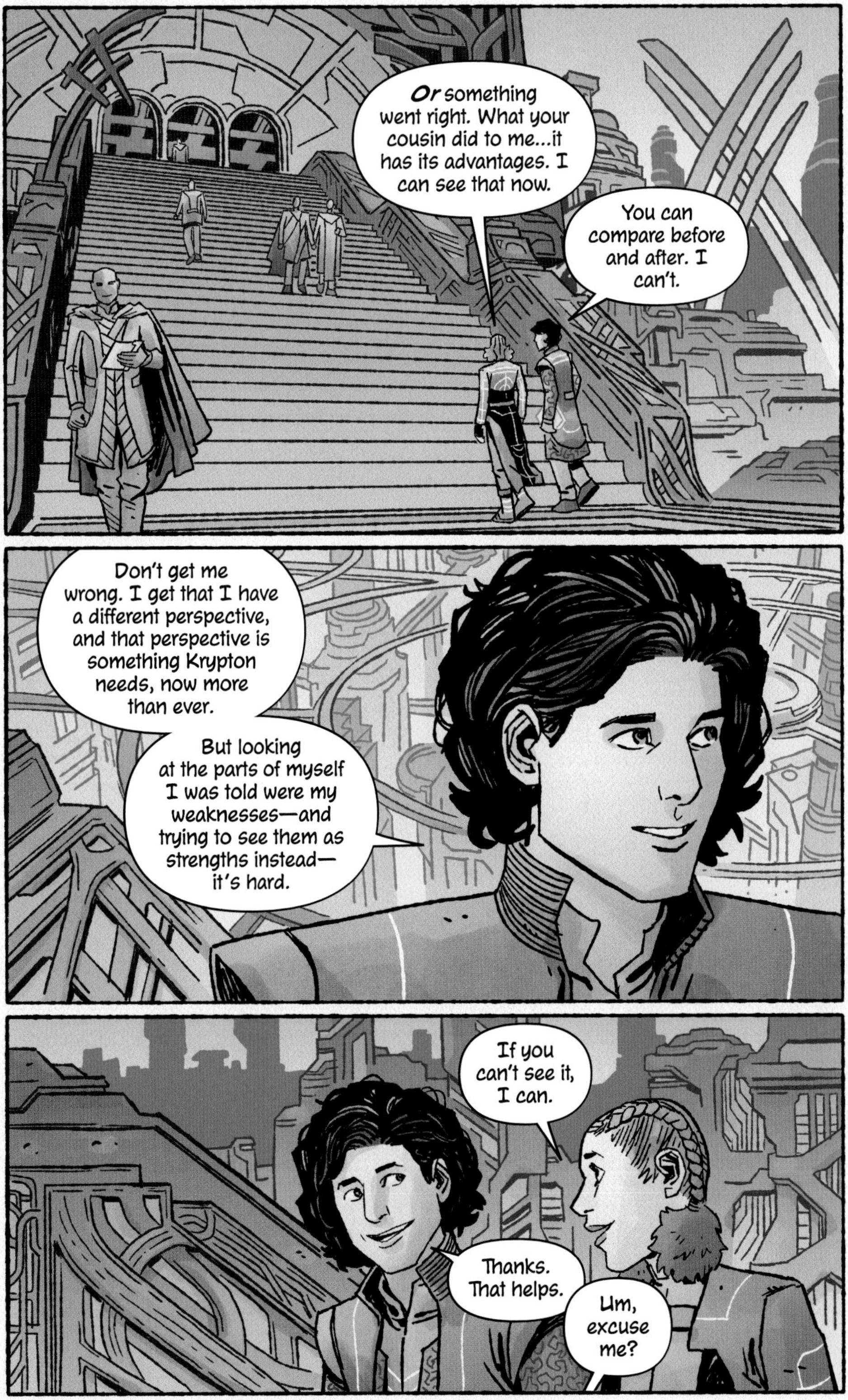

Or something went right. What your cousin did to me...it has its advantages. I can see that now.
You can compare before and after. I can't.
Don't get me wrong. I get that I have a different perspective, and that perspective is something Krypton needs, now more than ever.
But looking at the parts of myself I was told were my weaknesses—and trying to see them as strengths instead—it's hard.
If you can't see it, I can.
Thanks. That helps.
Um, excuse me?

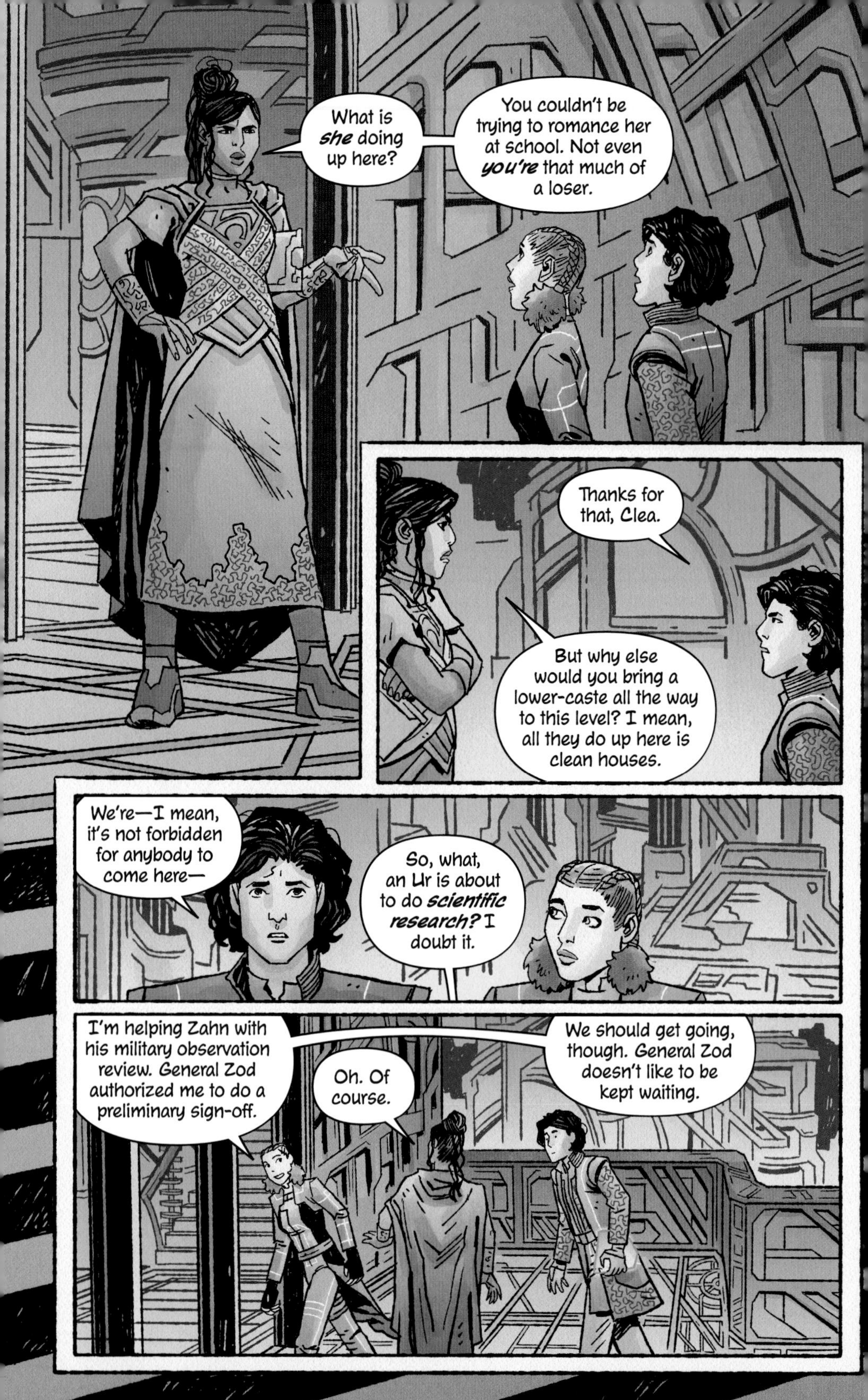
What is *she* doing up here?
You couldn't be trying to romance her at school. Not even *you're* that much of a loser.
Thanks for that, Clea.
But why else would you bring a lower-caste all the way to this level? I mean, all they do up here is clean houses.
We're—I mean, it's not forbidden for anybody to come here—
So, what, an Ur is about to do *scientific research?* I doubt it.
I'm helping Zahn with his military observation review. General Zod authorized me to do a preliminary sign-off.
Oh. Of course.
We should get going, though. General Zod doesn't like to be kept waiting.

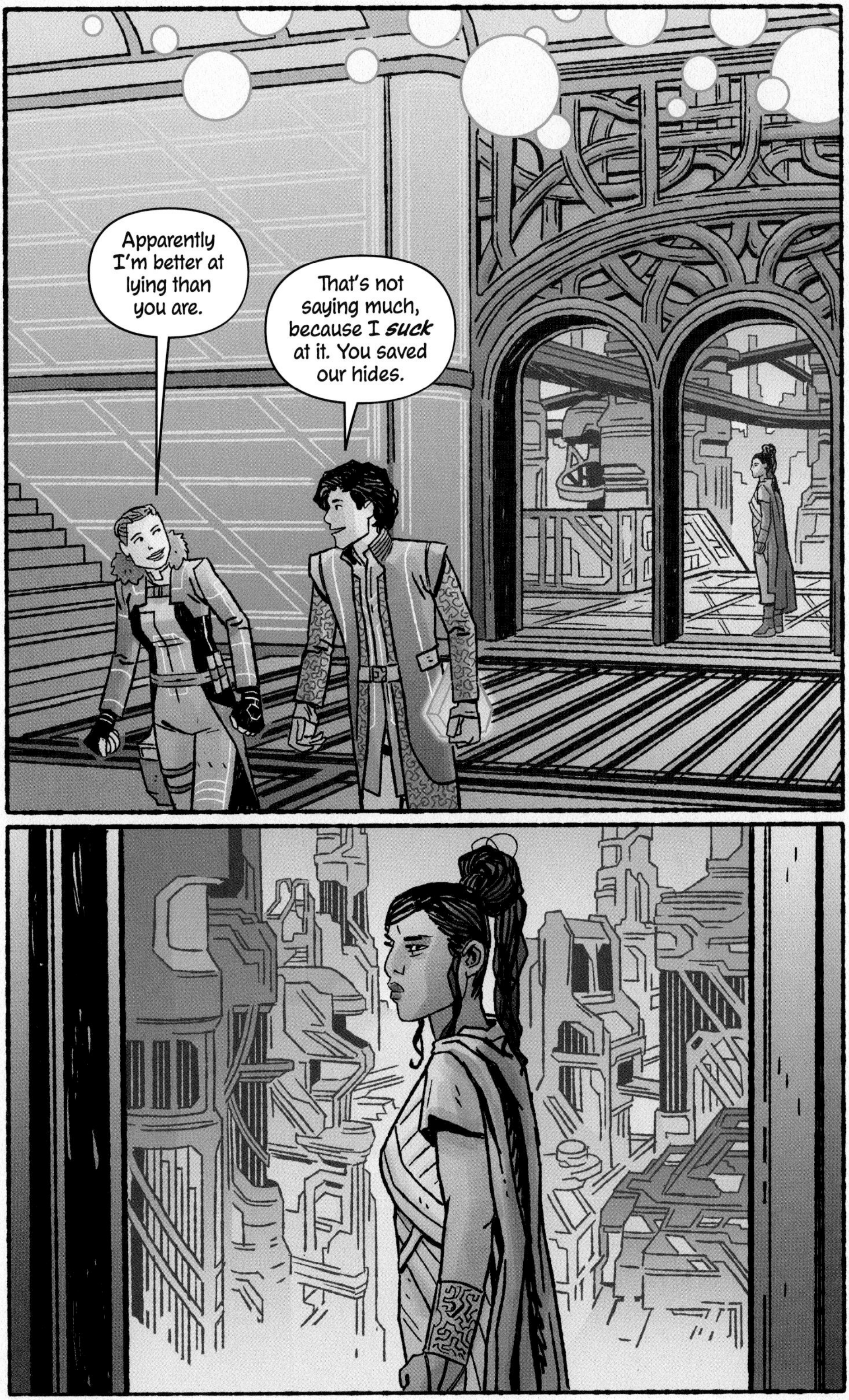
Apparently I'm better at lying than you are.
That's not saying much, because I *suck* at it. You saved our hides.

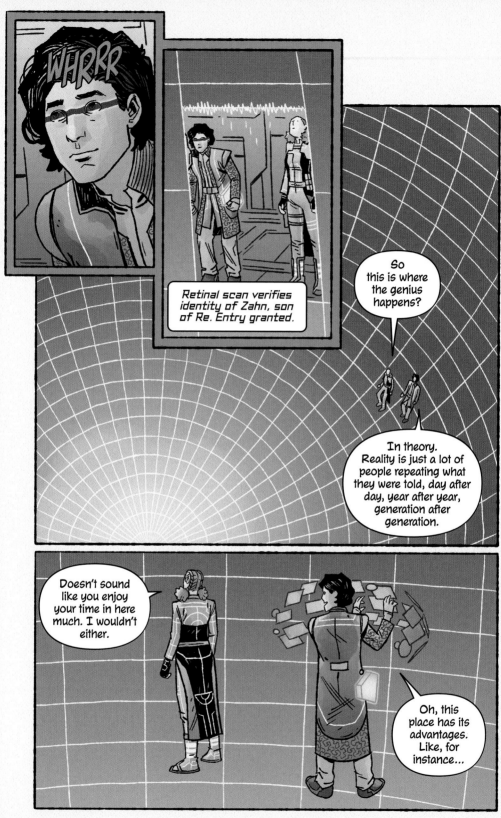

WHRRR

Retinal scan verifies identity of Zahn, son of Re. Entry granted.

So this is where the genius happens?

In theory. Reality is just a lot of people repeating what they were told, day after day, year after year, generation after generation.

Doesn't sound like you enjoy your time in here much. I wouldn't either.

Oh, this place has its advantages. Like, for instance...

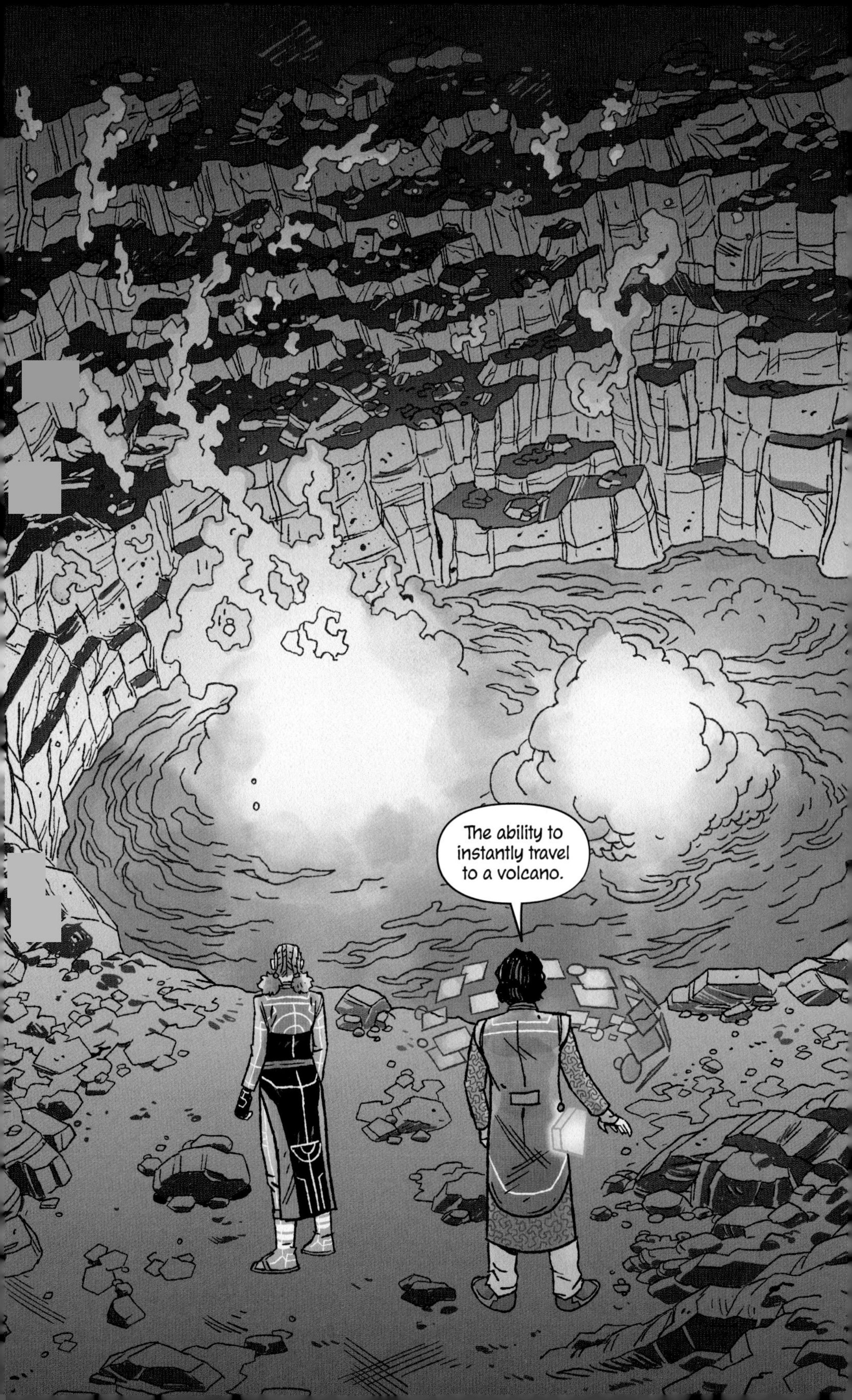
The ability to instantly travel to a volcano.

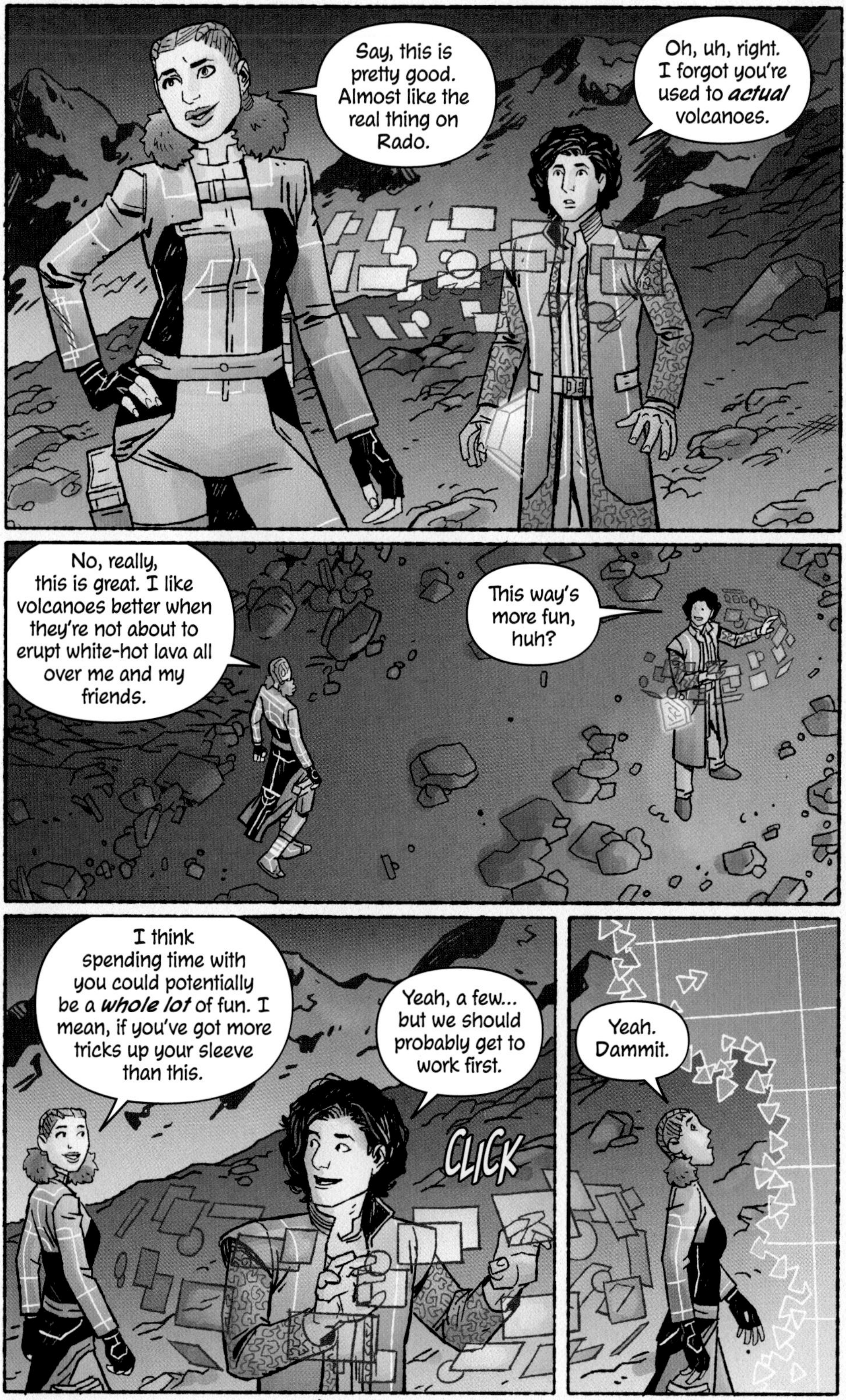
Say, this is pretty good. Almost like the real thing on Rado.
Oh, uh, right. I forgot you're used to *actual* volcanoes.
No, really, this is great. I like volcanoes better when they're not about to erupt white-hot lava all over me and my friends.
This way's more fun, huh?
I think spending time with you could potentially be a *whole lot* of fun. I mean, if you've got more tricks up your sleeve than this.
Yeah, a few... but we should probably get to work first.
CLICK
Yeah. Dammit.

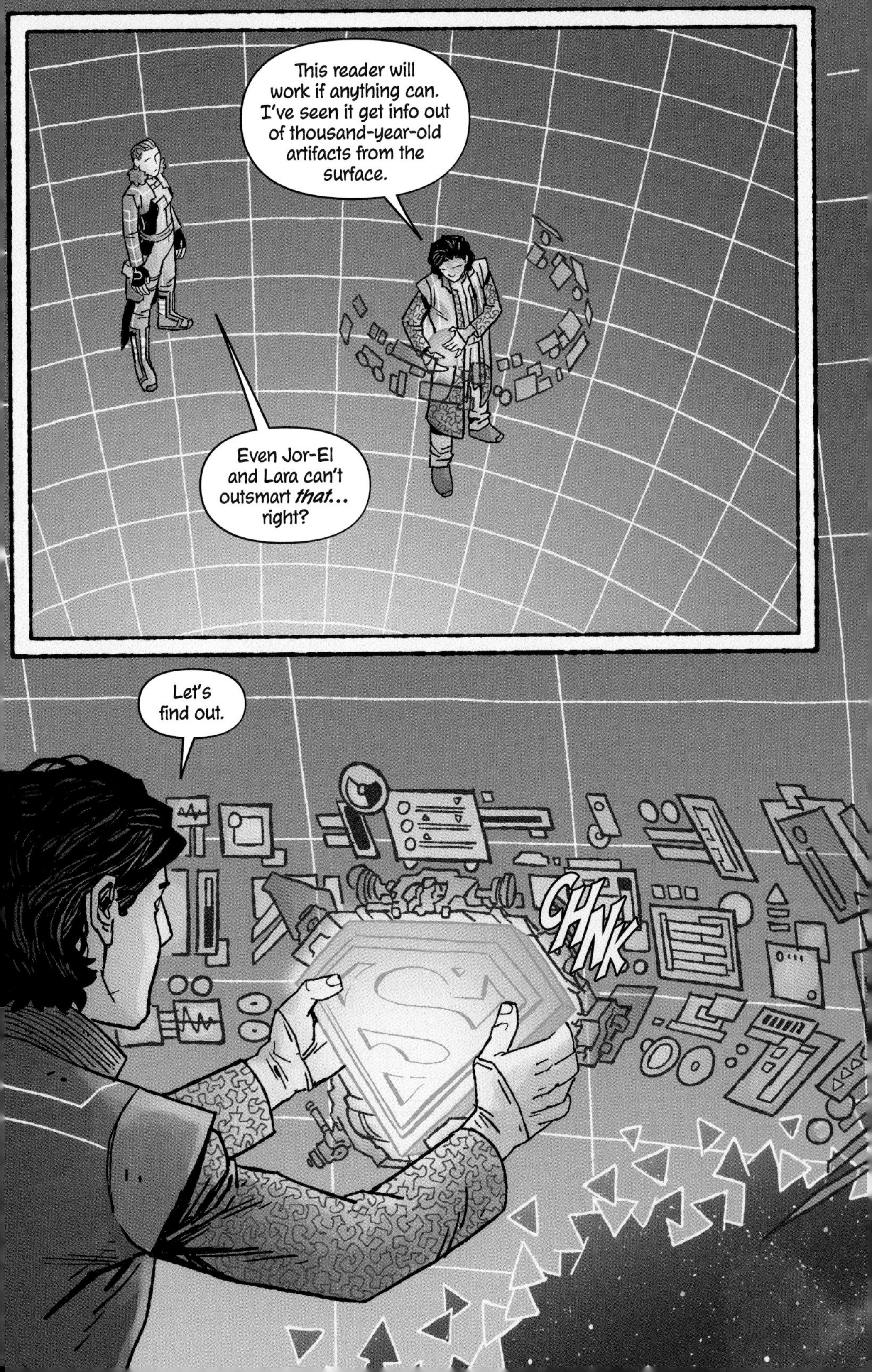
This reader will work if anything can. I've seen it get info out of thousand-year-old artifacts from the surface.
Even Jor-El and Lara can't outsmart *that*... right?
Let's find out.
CHNK

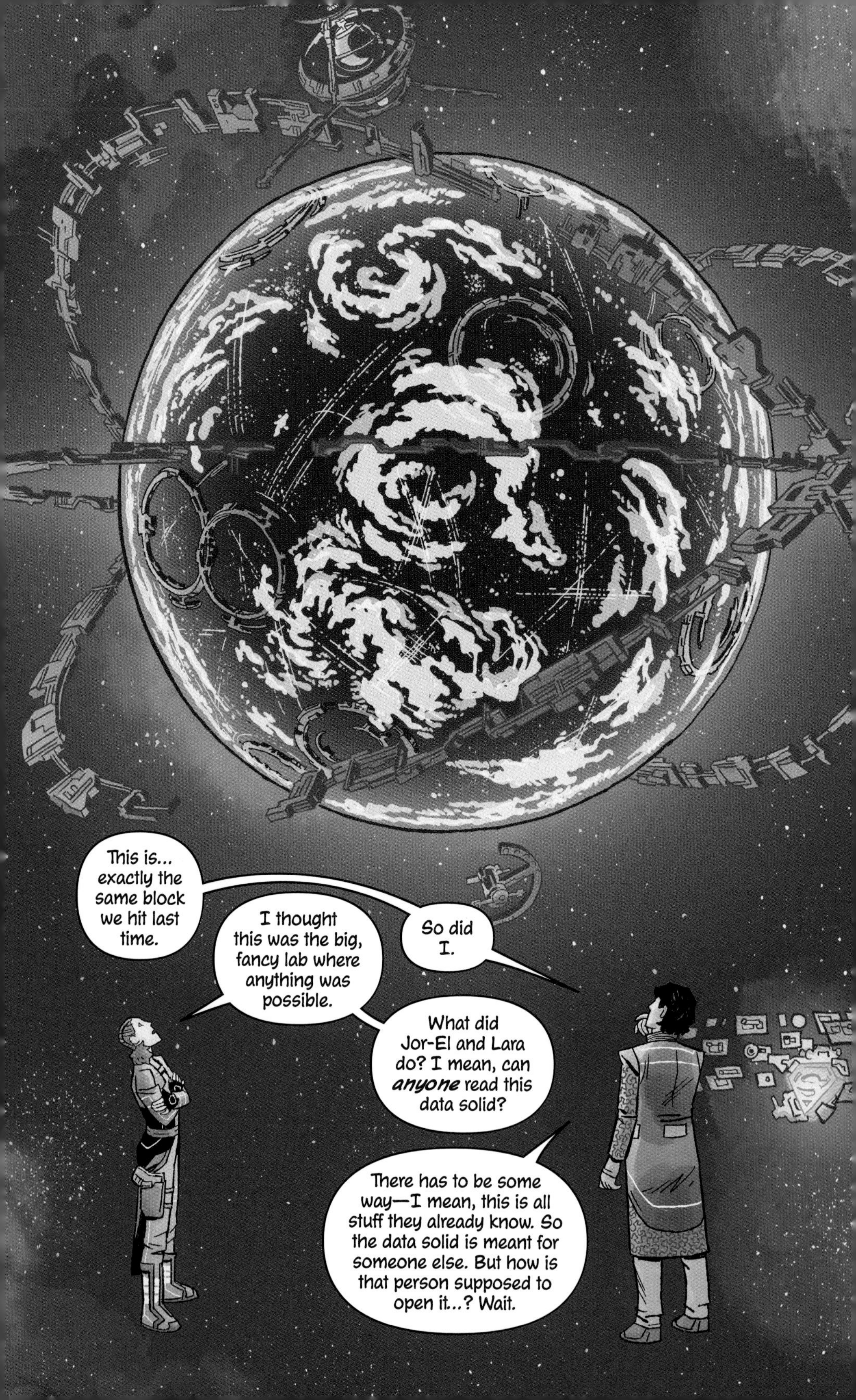
This is... exactly the same block we hit last time.
I thought this was the big, fancy lab where anything was possible.
So did I.
What did Jor-El and Lara do? I mean, can *anyone* read this data solid?
There has to be some way—I mean, this is all stuff they already know. So the data solid is meant for someone else. But how is that person supposed to open it...? Wait.

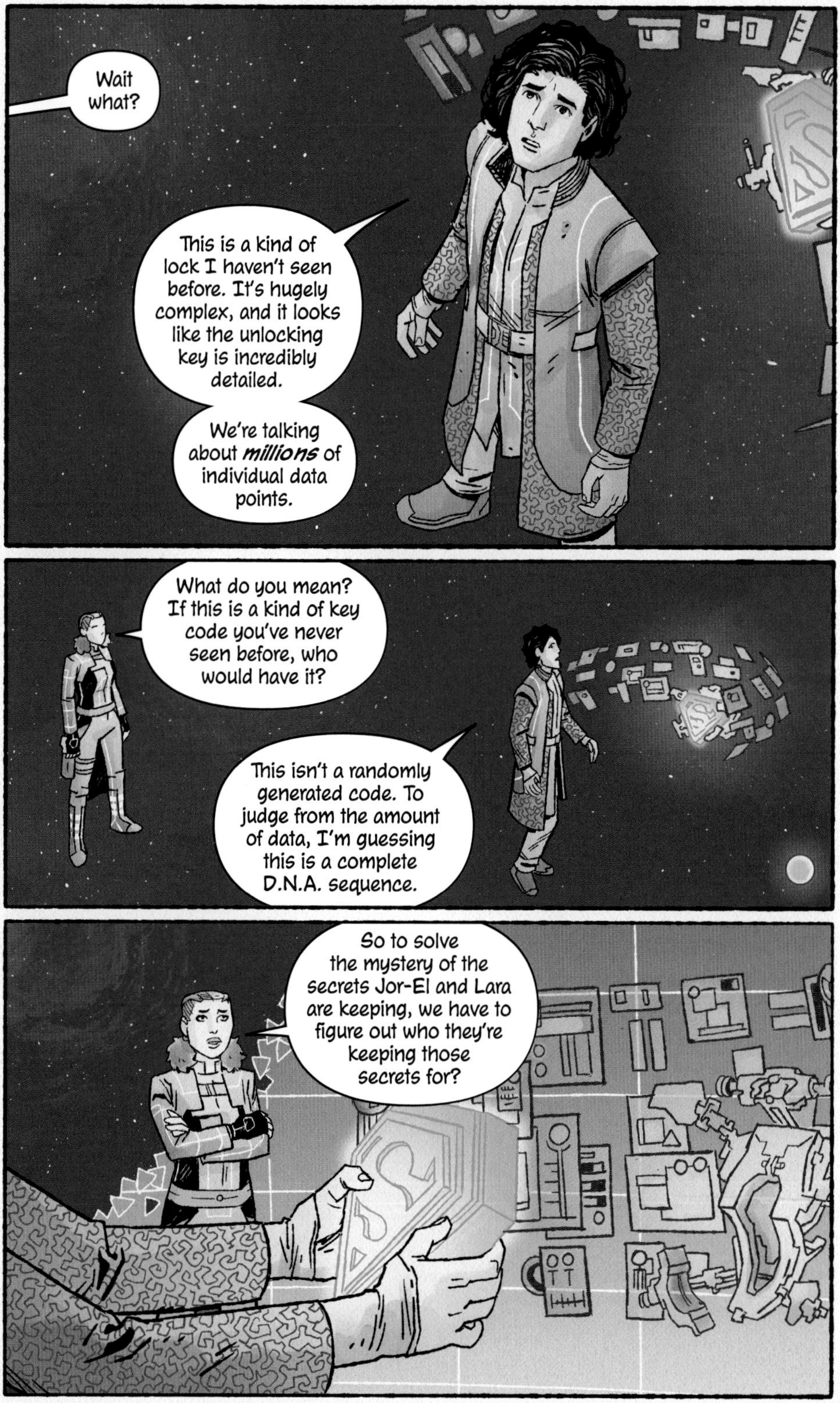
Wait what?
This is a kind of lock I haven't seen before. It's hugely complex, and it looks like the unlocking key is incredibly detailed.
We're talking about *millions* of individual data points.
What do you mean? If this is a kind of key code you've never seen before, who would have it?
This isn't a randomly generated code. To judge from the amount of data, I'm guessing this is a complete D.N.A. sequence.
So to solve the mystery of the secrets Jor-El and Lara are keeping, we have to figure out who they're keeping those secrets for?

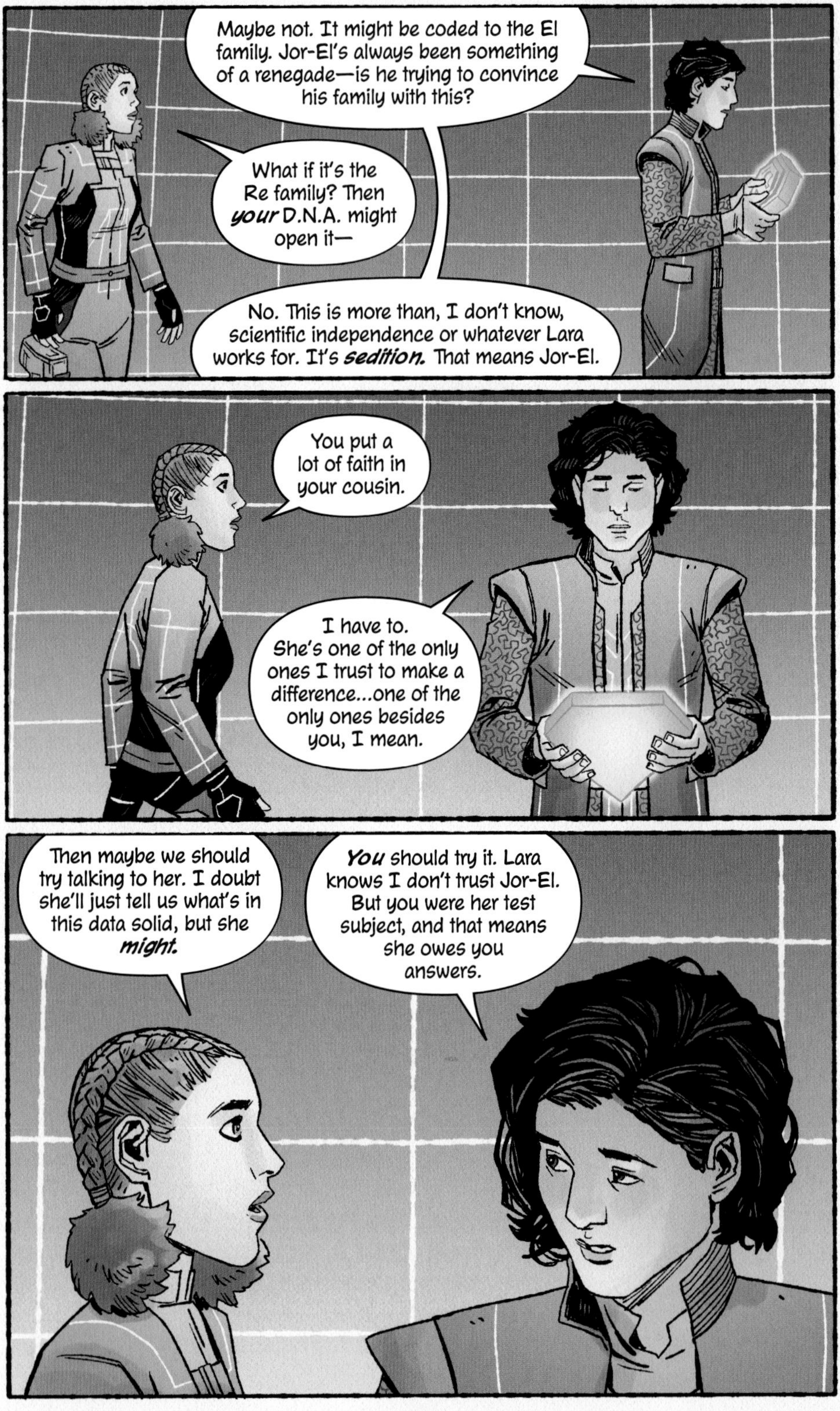
Maybe not. It might be coded to the El family. Jor-El's always been something of a renegade—is he trying to convince his family with this?
What if it's the Re family? Then *your* D.N.A. might open it—
No. This is more than, I don't know, scientific independence or whatever Lara works for. It's *sedition.* That means Jor-El.
You put a lot of faith in your cousin.
I have to. She's one of the only ones I trust to make a difference...one of the only ones besides you, I mean.
Then maybe we should try talking to her. I doubt she'll just tell us what's in this data solid, but she *might.*
You should try it. Lara knows I don't trust Jor-El. But you were her test subject, and that means she owes you answers.

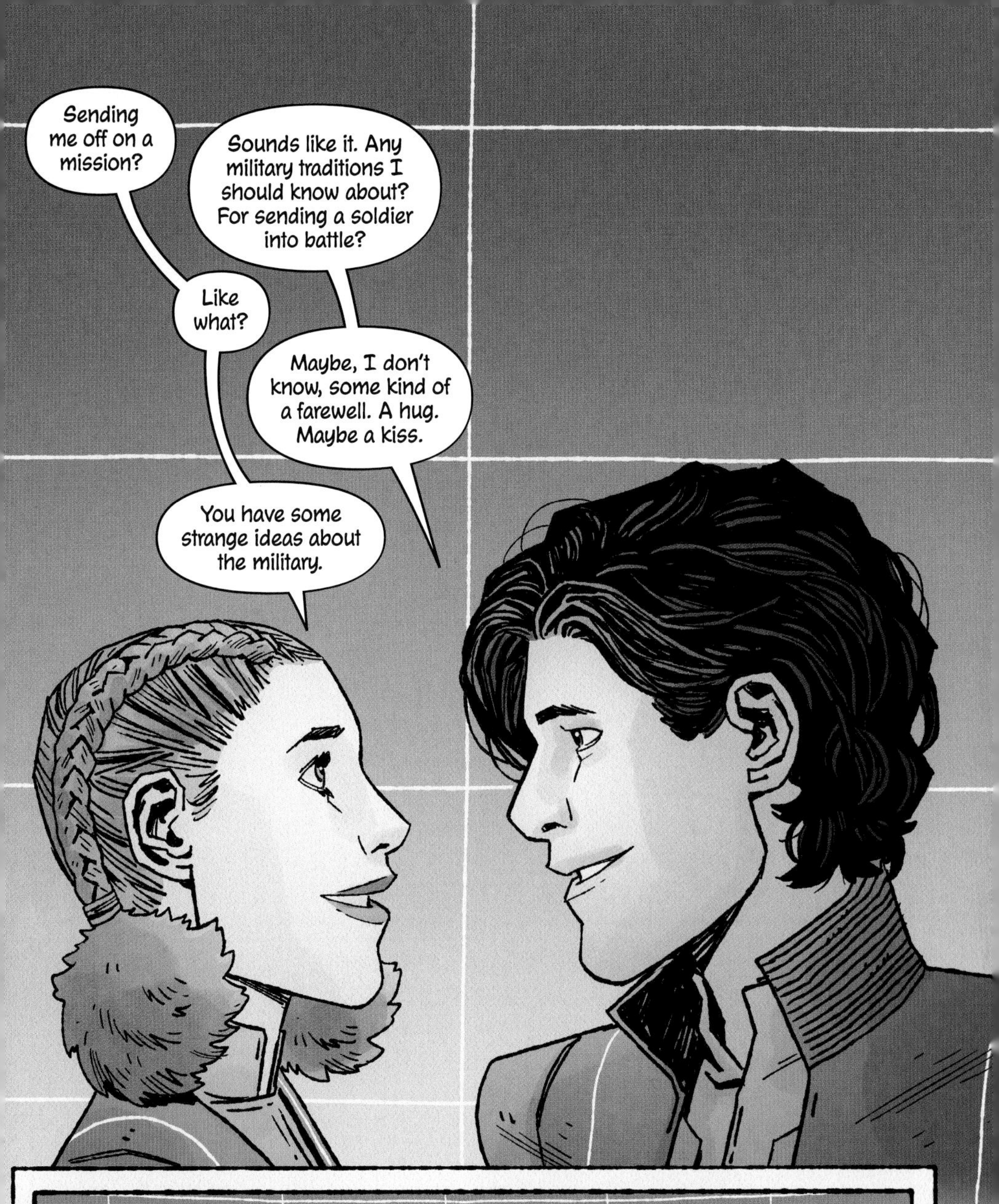
Sending me off on a mission?
Sounds like it. Any military traditions I should know about? For sending a soldier into battle?
Like what?
Maybe, I don't know, some kind of a farewell. A hug. Maybe a kiss.
You have some strange ideas about the military.

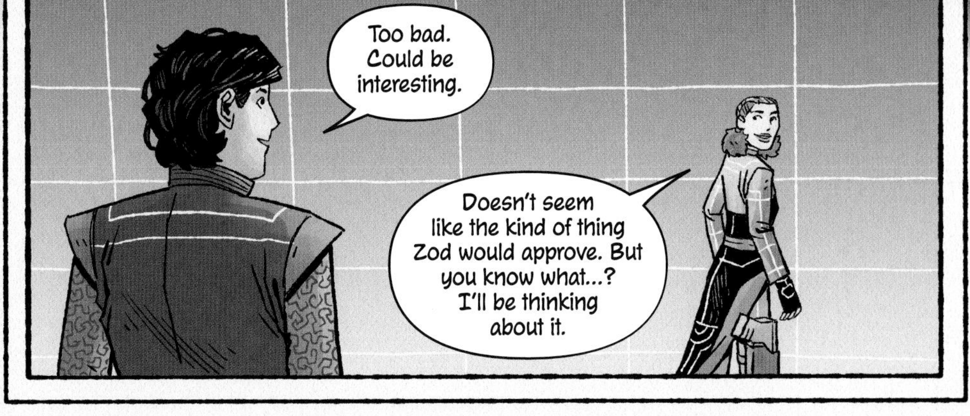
Too bad. Could be interesting.
Doesn't seem like the kind of thing Zod would approve. But you know what...? I'll be thinking about it.

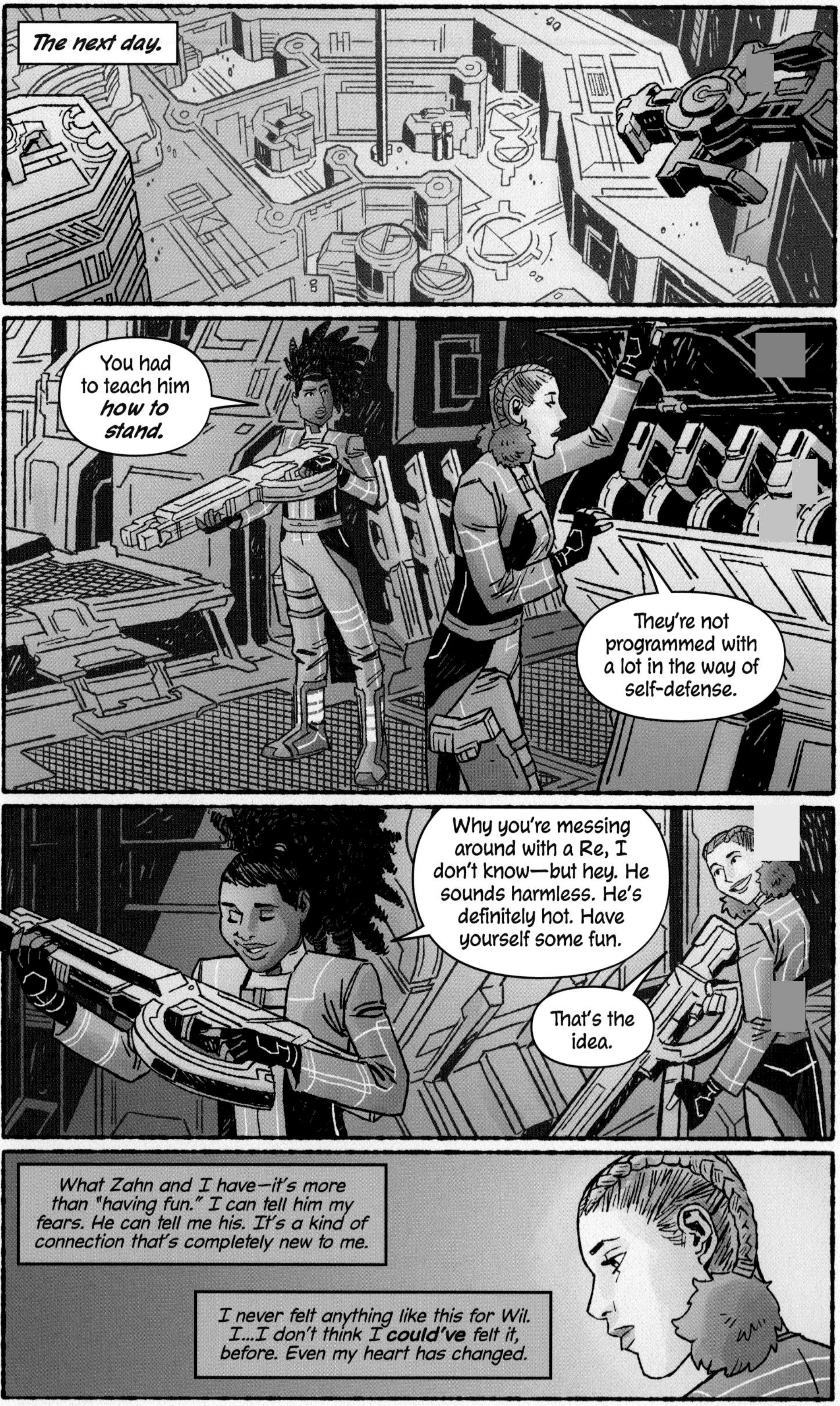
The next day.
You had to teach him how to stand.
They're not programmed with a lot in the way of self-defense.
Why you're messing around with a Re, I don't know—but hey. He sounds harmless. He's definitely hot. Have yourself some fun.
That's the idea.
What Zahn and I have—it's more than "having fun." I can tell him my fears. He can tell me his. It's a kind of connection that's completely new to me.
I never felt anything like this for Wil. I...I don't think I could've felt it, before. Even my heart has changed.

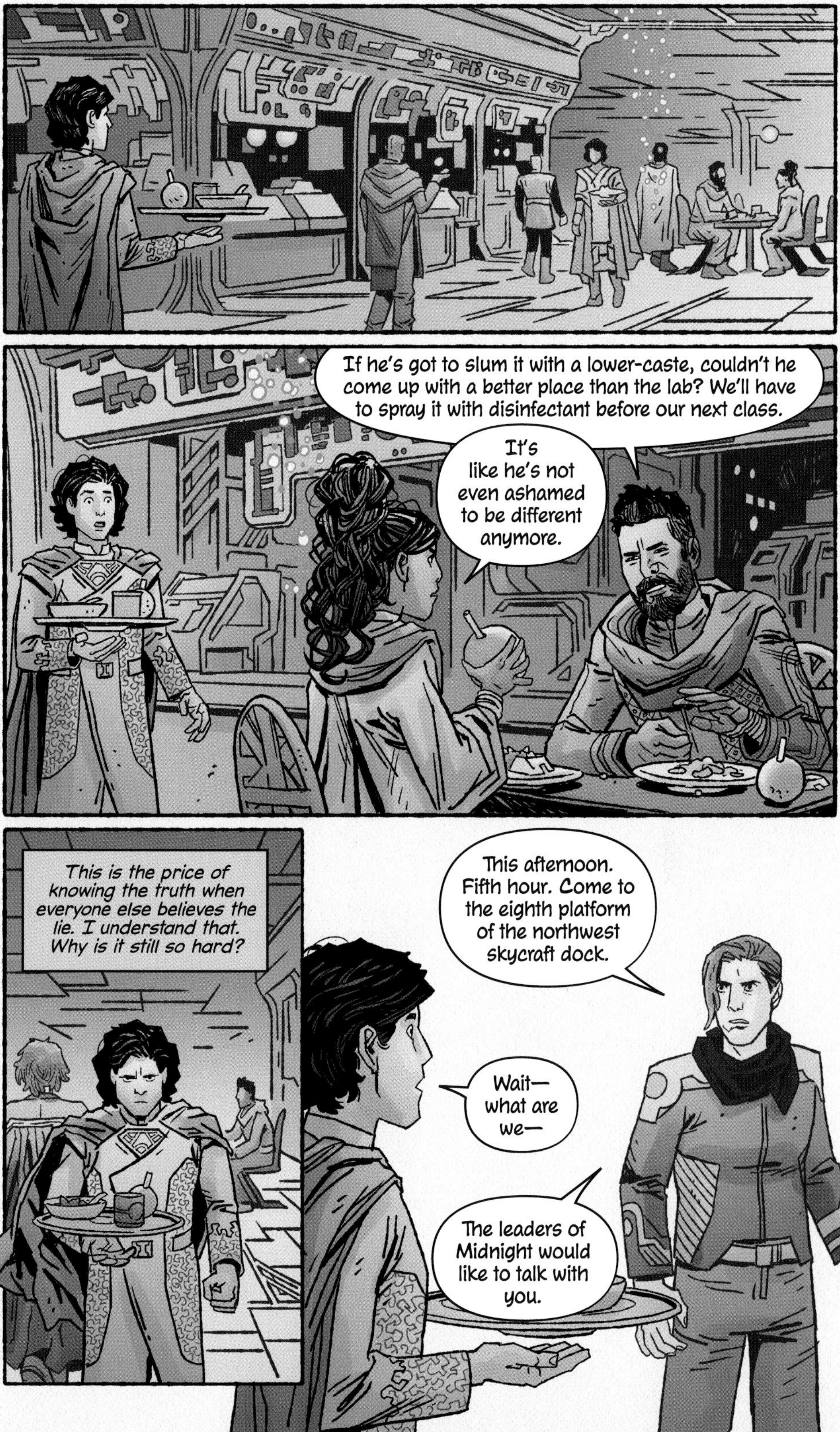
If he's got to slum it with a lower-caste, couldn't he come up with a better place than the lab? We'll have to spray it with disinfectant before our next class.
It's like he's not even ashamed to be different anymore.
This is the price of knowing the truth when everyone else believes the lie. I understand that. Why is it still so hard?
This afternoon. Fifth hour. Come to the eighth platform of the northwest skycraft dock.
Wait— what are we—
The leaders of Midnight would like to talk with you.

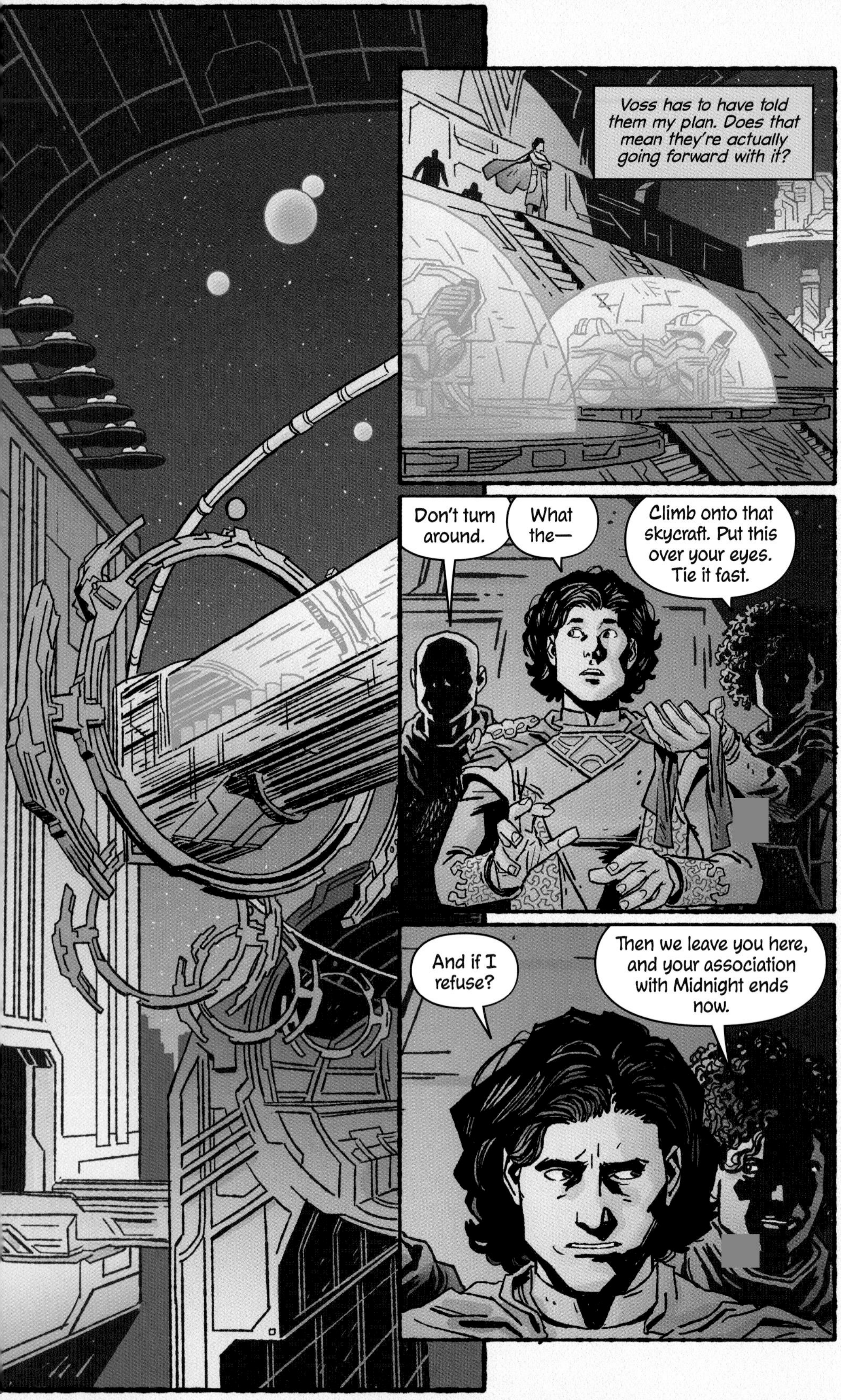
Voss has to have told them my plan. Does that mean they're actually going forward with it?
Don't turn around.
What the—
Climb onto that skycraft. Put this over your eyes. Tie it fast.
And if I refuse?
Then we leave you here, and your association with Midnight ends now.

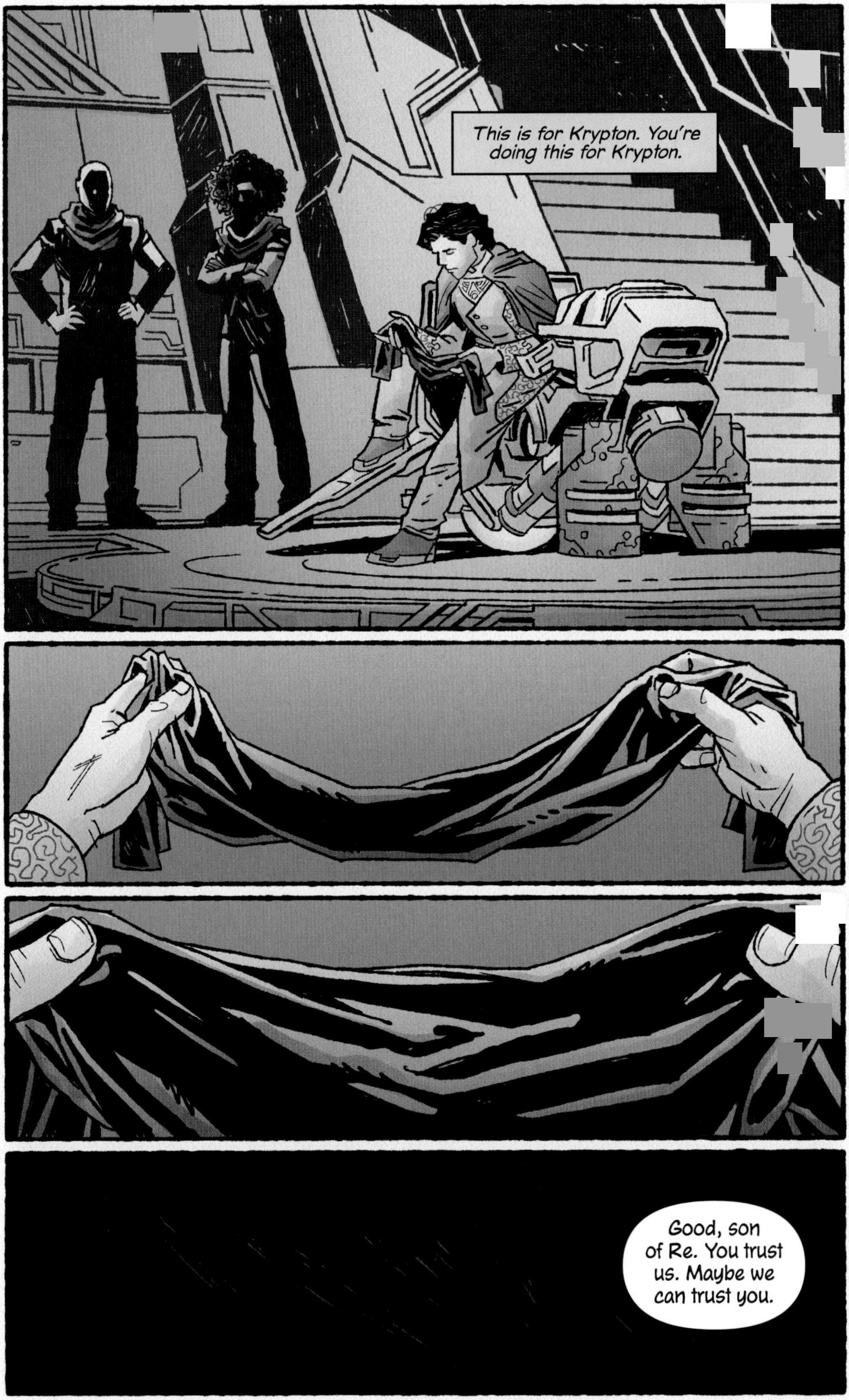
This is for Krypton. You're doing this for Krypton.
Good, son of Re. You trust us. Maybe we can trust you.

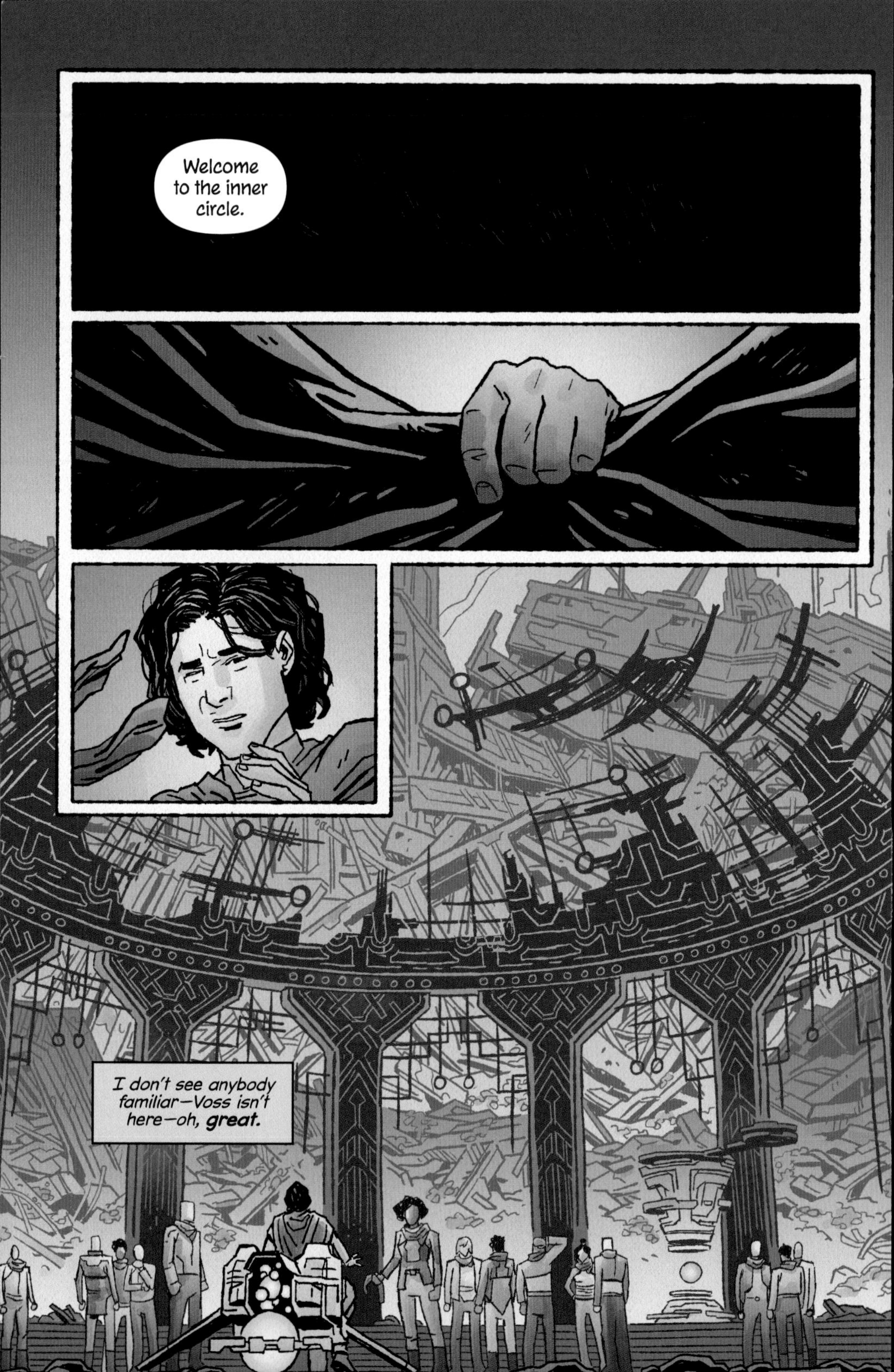
Welcome to the inner circle.
I don't see anybody familiar—Voss isn't here—oh, **great.**

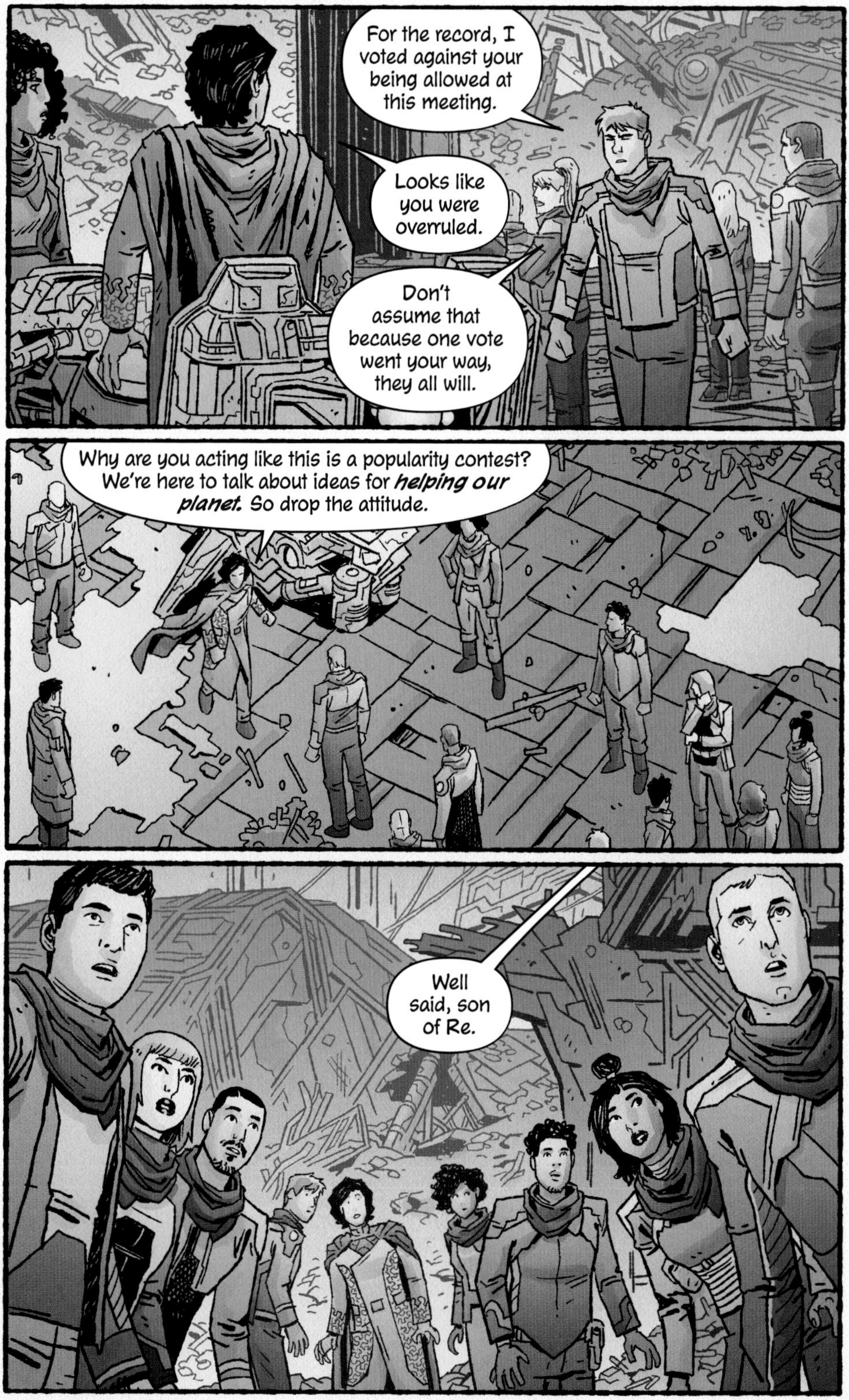
For the record, I voted against your being allowed at this meeting.
Looks like you were overruled.
Don't assume that because one vote went your way, they all will.
Why are you acting like this is a popularity contest? We're here to talk about ideas for *helping our planet.* So drop the attitude.
Well said, son of Re.

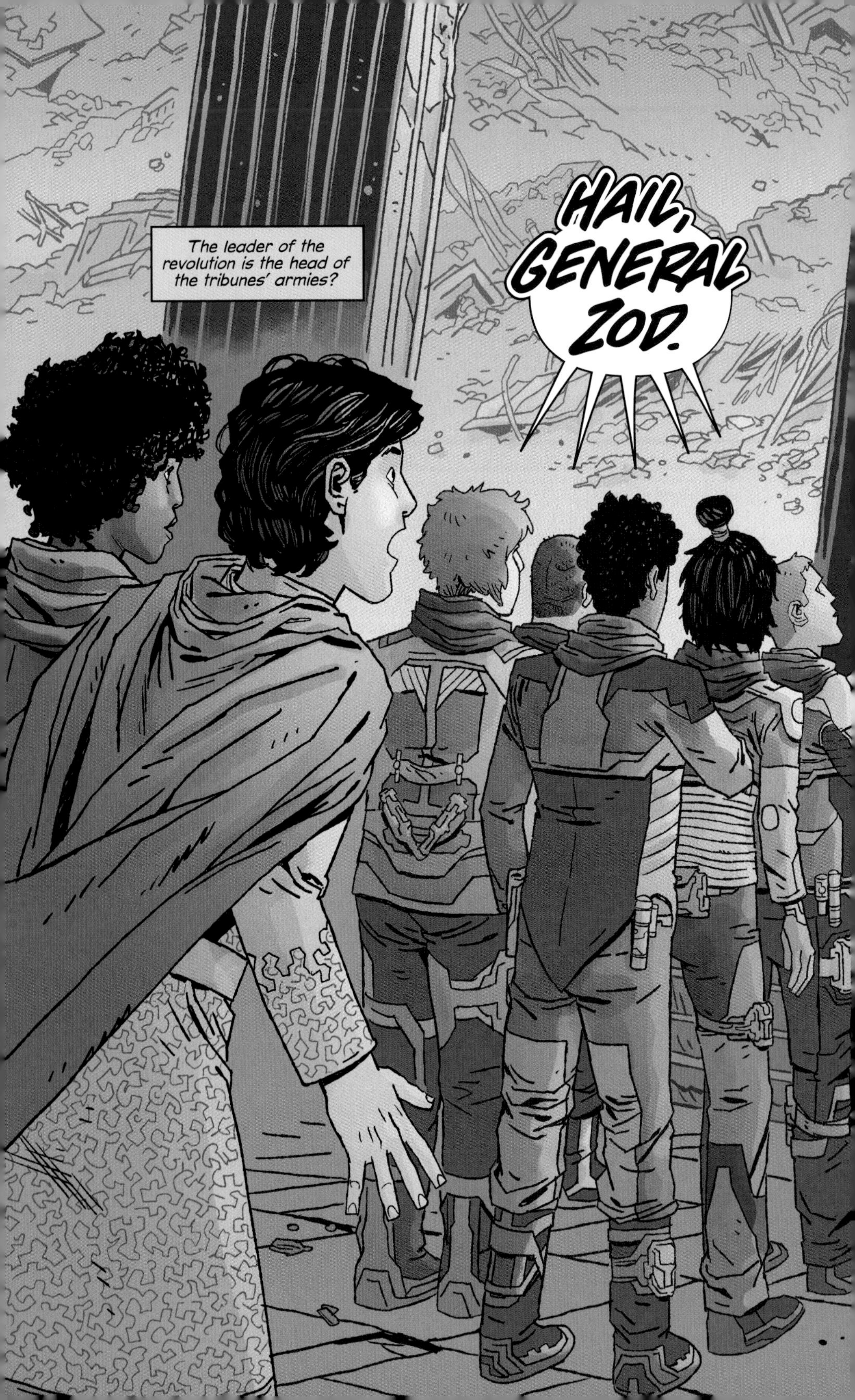
The leader of the revolution is the head of the tribunes' armies?
HAIL, GENERAL ZOD.

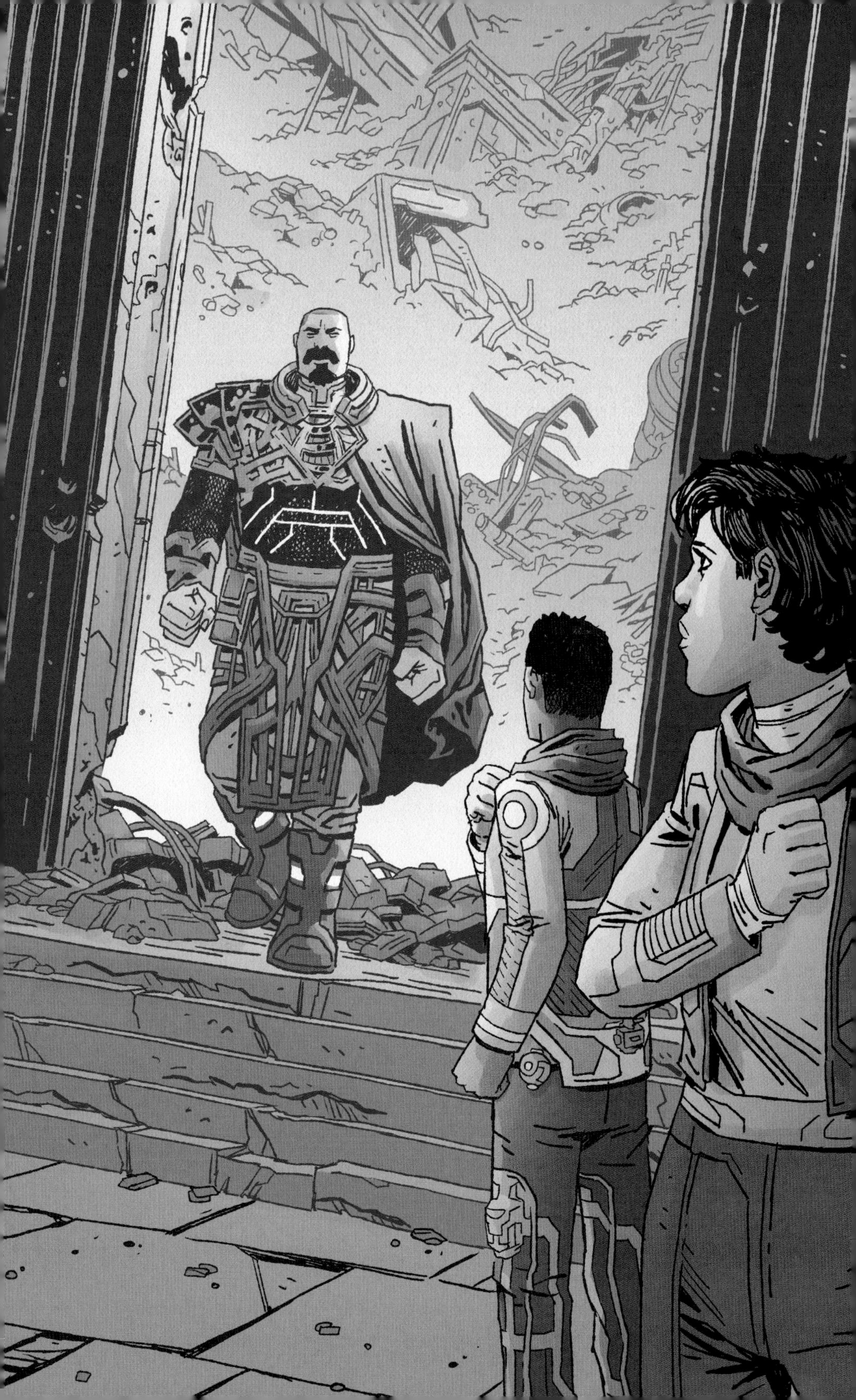

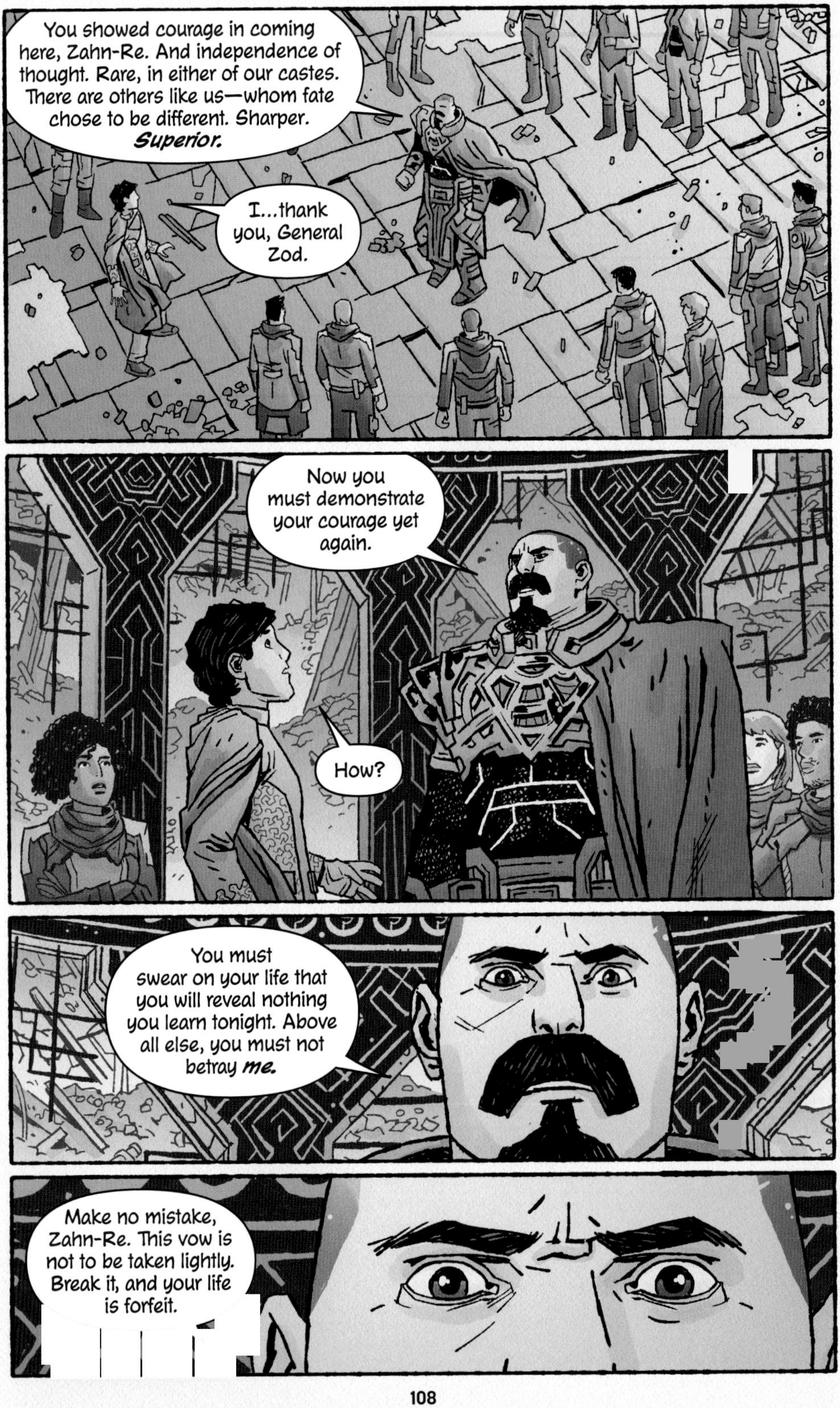
You showed courage in coming here, Zahn-Re. And independence of thought. Rare, in either of our castes. There are others like us—whom fate chose to be different. Sharper. *Superior.*
I...thank you, General Zod.
Now you must demonstrate your courage yet again.
How?
You must swear on your life that you will reveal nothing you learn tonight. Above all else, you must not betray *me.*
Make no mistake, Zahn-Re. This vow is not to be taken lightly. Break it, and your life is forfeit.

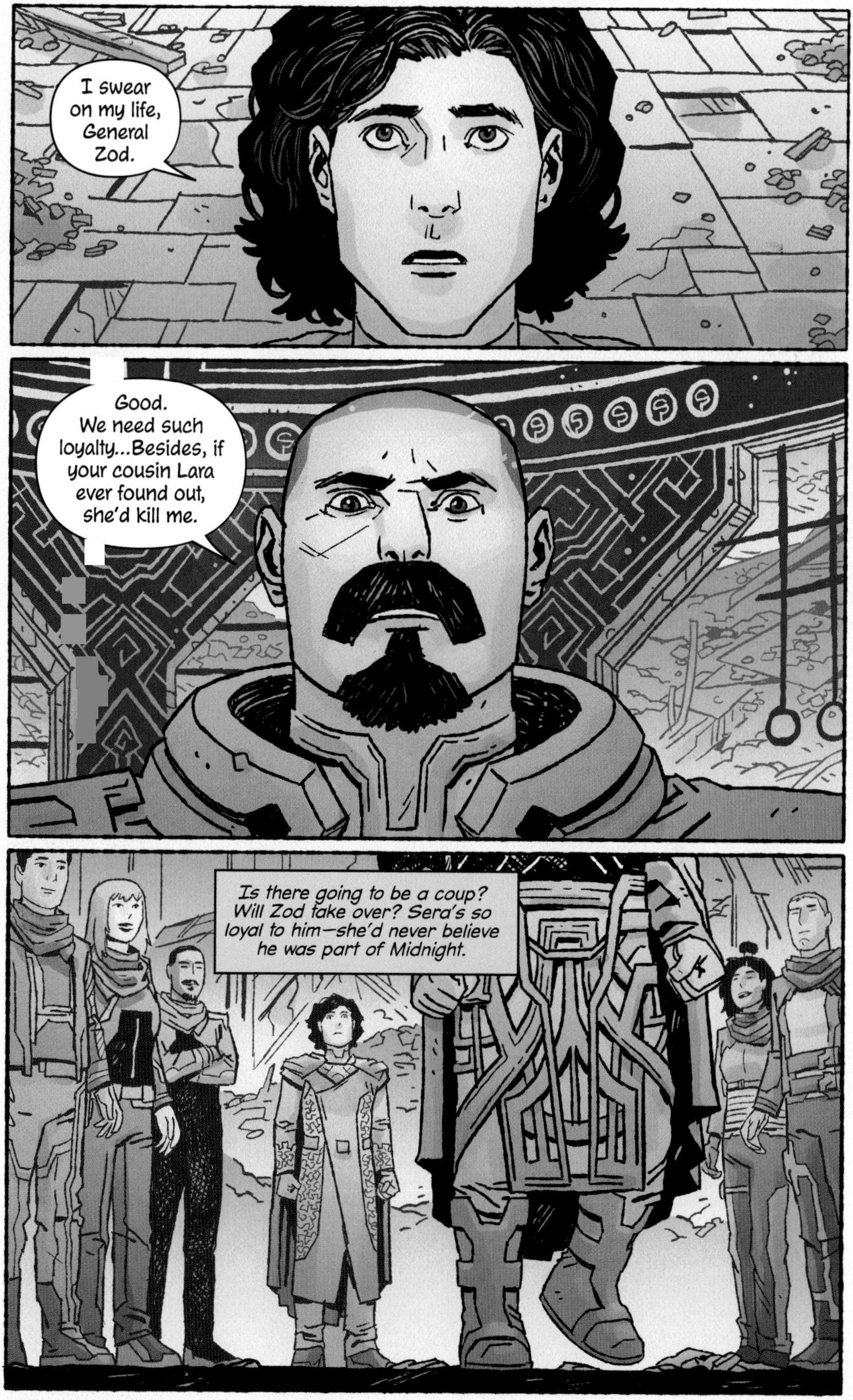
I swear on my life, General Zod.
Good. We need such loyalty...Besides, if your cousin Lara ever found out, she'd kill me.
Is there going to be a coup? Will Zod take over? Sera's so loyal to him—she'd never believe he was part of Midnight.

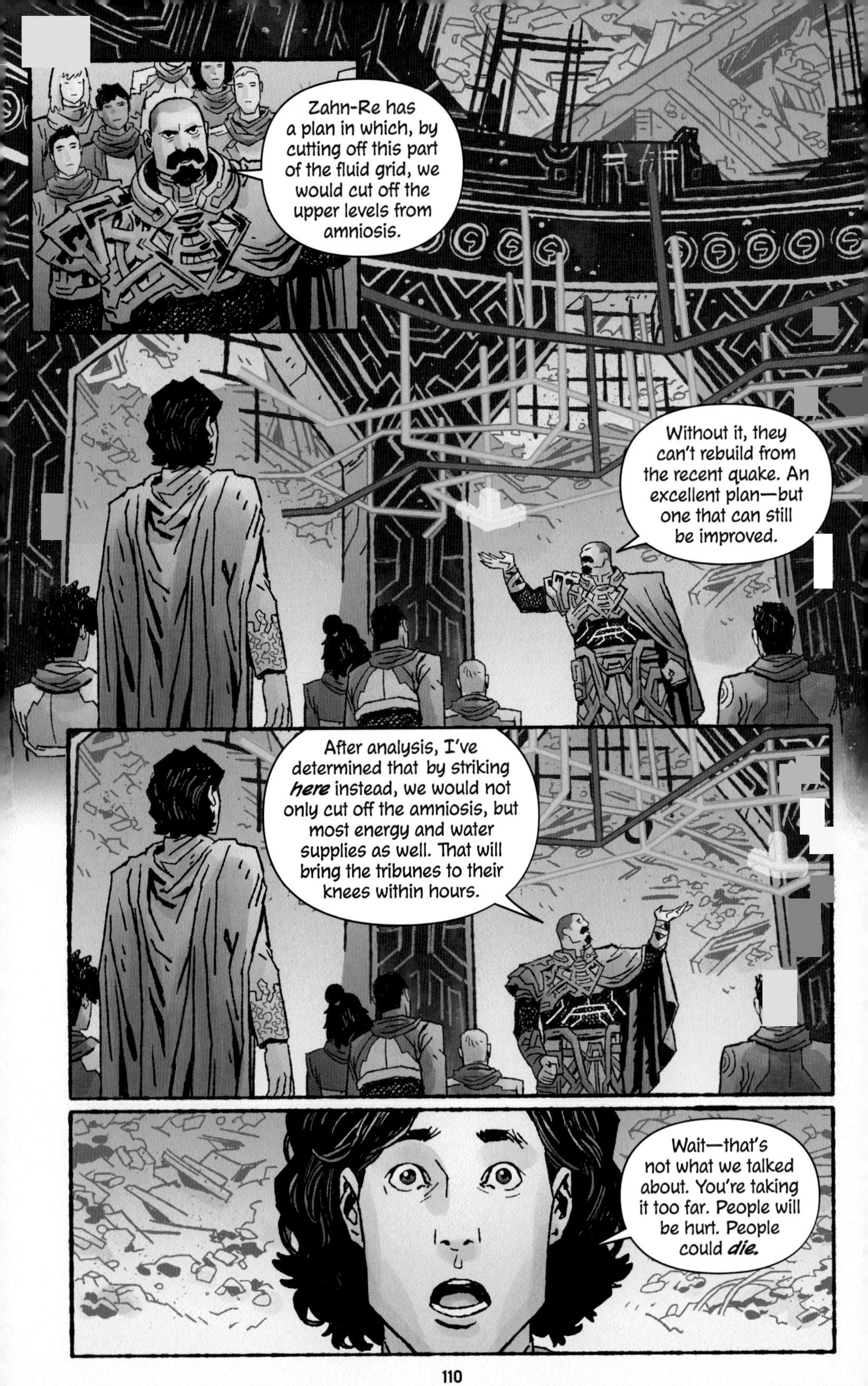
Zahn-Re has a plan in which, by cutting off this part of the fluid grid, we would cut off the upper levels from amniosis.
Without it, they can't rebuild from the recent quake. An excellent plan—but one that can still be improved.
After analysis, I've determined that by striking *here* instead, we would not only cut off the amniosis, but most energy and water supplies as well. That will bring the tribunes to their knees within hours.
Wait—that's not what we talked about. You're taking it too far. People will be hurt. People could *die.*

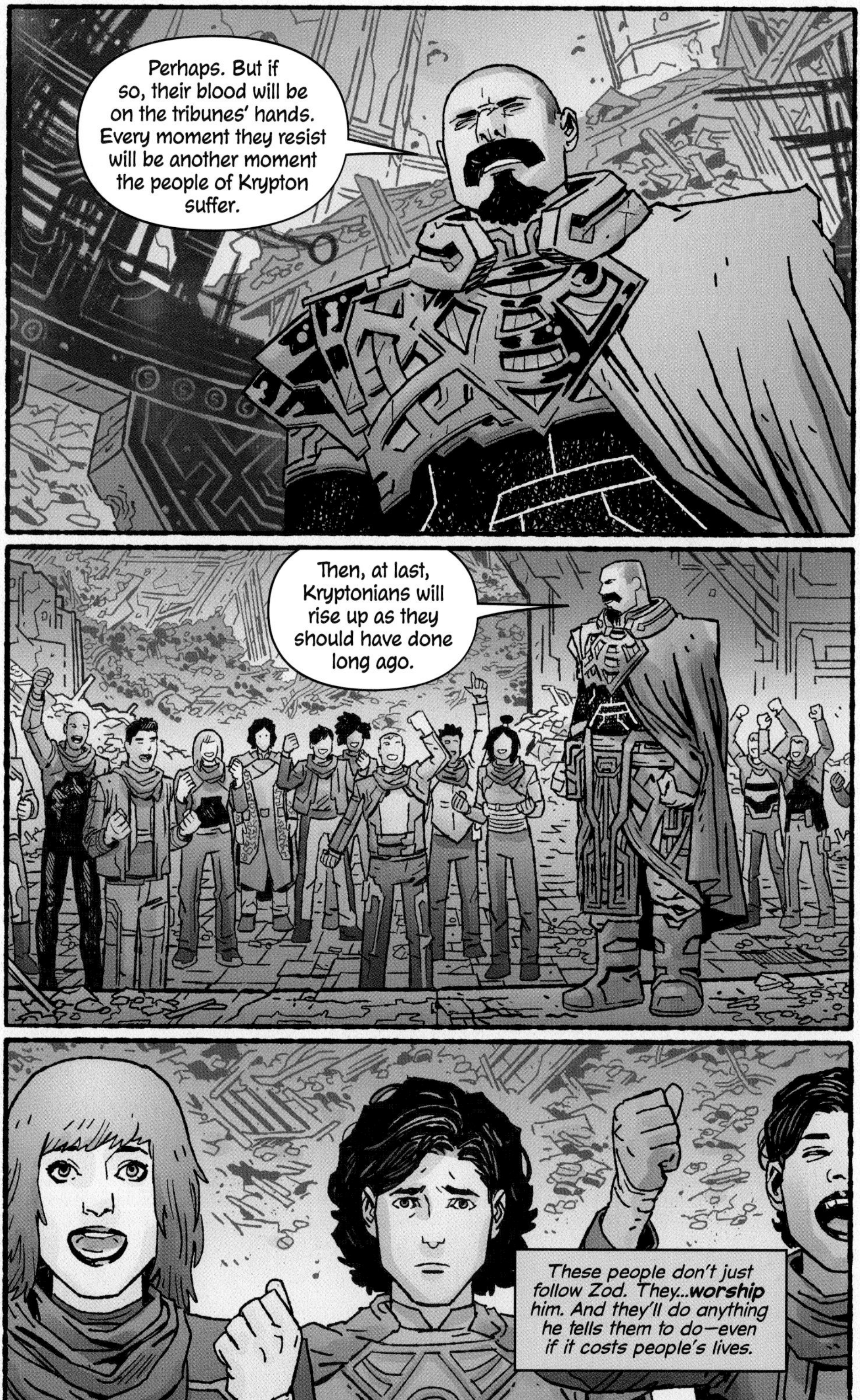
Perhaps. But if so, their blood will be on the tribunes' hands. Every moment they resist will be another moment the people of Krypton suffer.
Then, at last, Kryptonians will rise up as they should have done long ago.
These people don't just follow Zod. They...**worship** him. And they'll do anything he tells them to do—even if it costs people's lives.

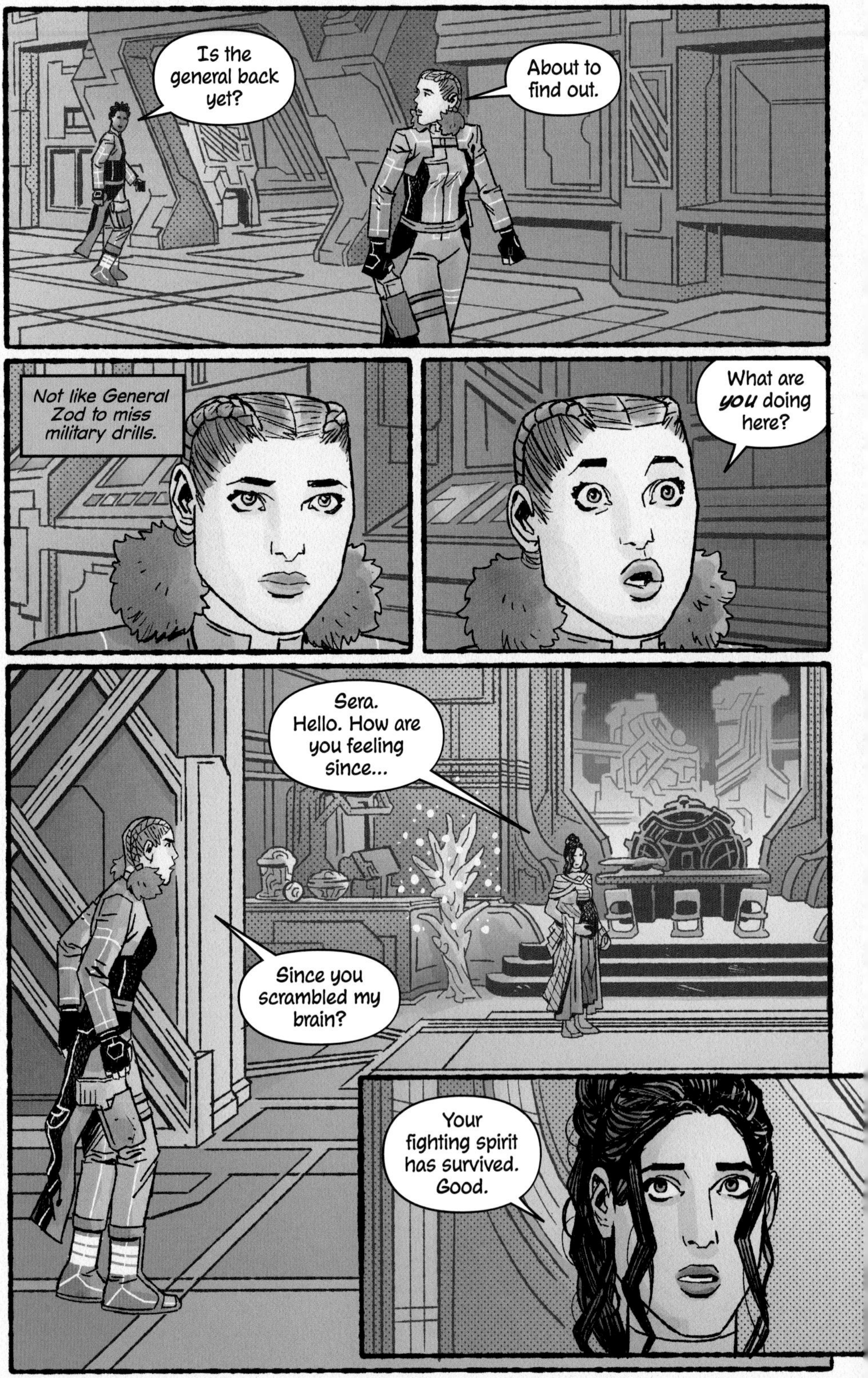
Is the general back yet?
About to find out.
Not like General Zod to miss military drills.
What are *you* doing here?
Sera. Hello. How are you feeling since...
Since you scrambled my brain?
Your fighting spirit has survived. Good.

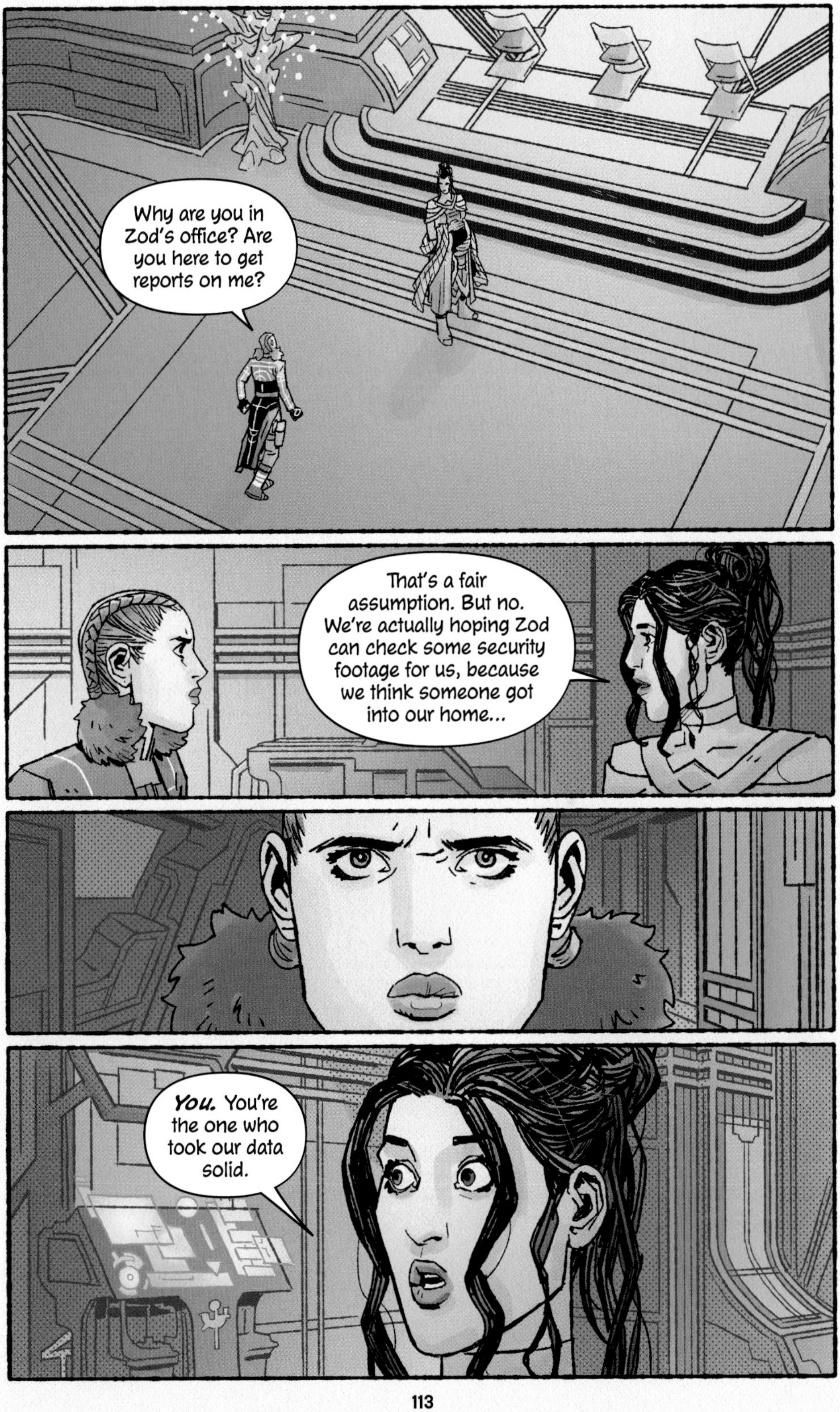
Why are you in Zod's office? Are you here to get reports on me?
That's a fair assumption. But no. We're actually hoping Zod can check some security footage for us, because we think someone got into our home...
You. You're the one who took our data solid.

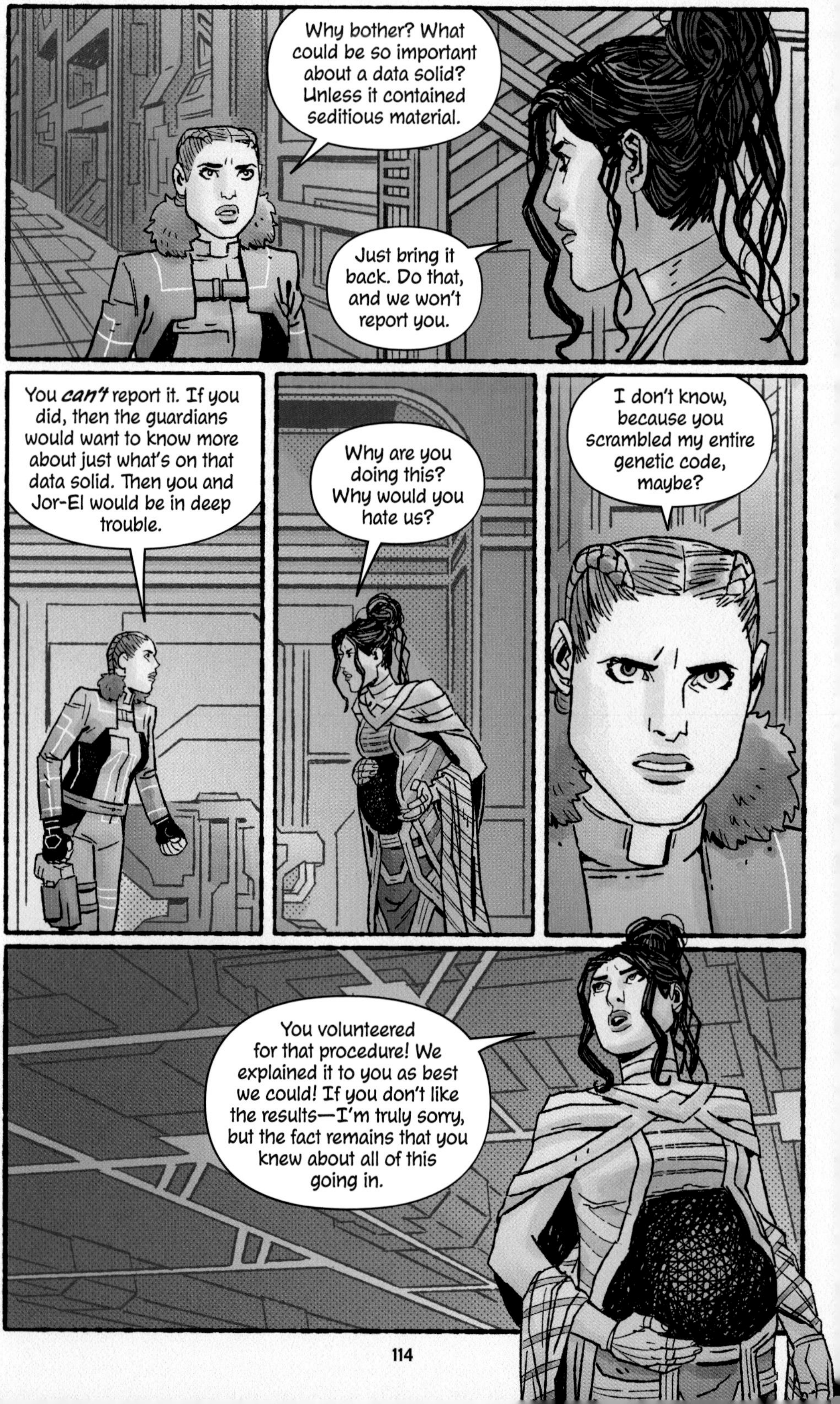
Why bother? What could be so important about a data solid? Unless it contained seditious material.
Just bring it back. Do that, and we won't report you.
You *can't* report it. If you did, then the guardians would want to know more about just what's on that data solid. Then you and Jor-El would be in deep trouble.
Why are you doing this? Why would you hate us?
I don't know, because you scrambled my entire genetic code, maybe?
You volunteered for that procedure! We explained it to you as best we could! If you don't like the results—I'm truly sorry, but the fact remains that you knew about all of this going in.

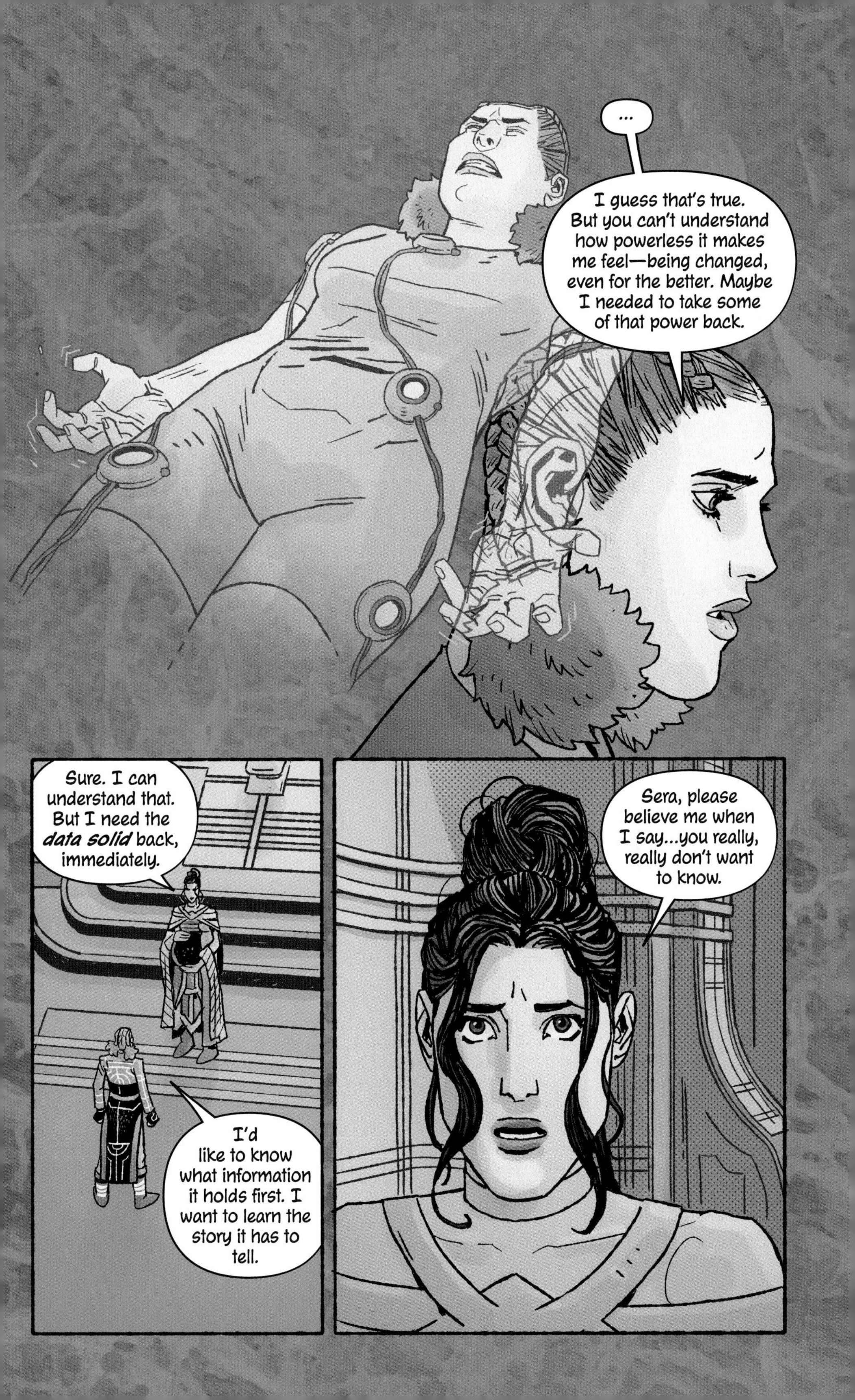
...
I guess that's true. But you can't understand how powerless it makes me feel—being changed, even for the better. Maybe I needed to take some of that power back.
Sure. I can understand that. But I need the *data solid* back, immediately.
I'd like to know what information it holds first. I want to learn the story it has to tell.
Sera, please believe me when I say...you really, really don't want to know.

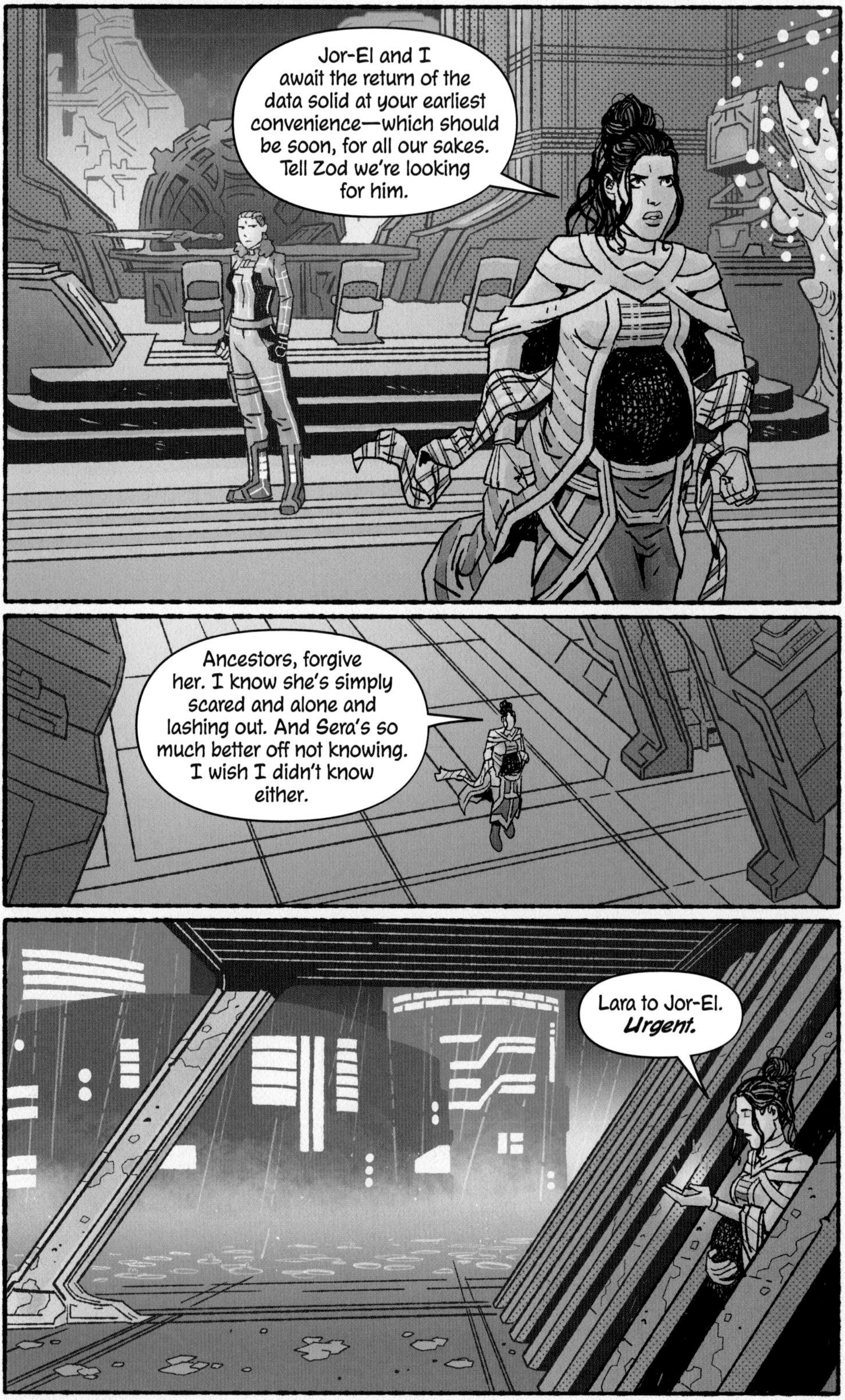
Jor-El and I await the return of the data solid at your earliest convenience—which should be soon, for all our sakes. Tell Zod we're looking for him.
Ancestors, forgive her. I know she's simply scared and alone and lashing out. And Sera's so much better off not knowing. I wish I didn't know either.
Lara to Jor-El. *Urgent.*

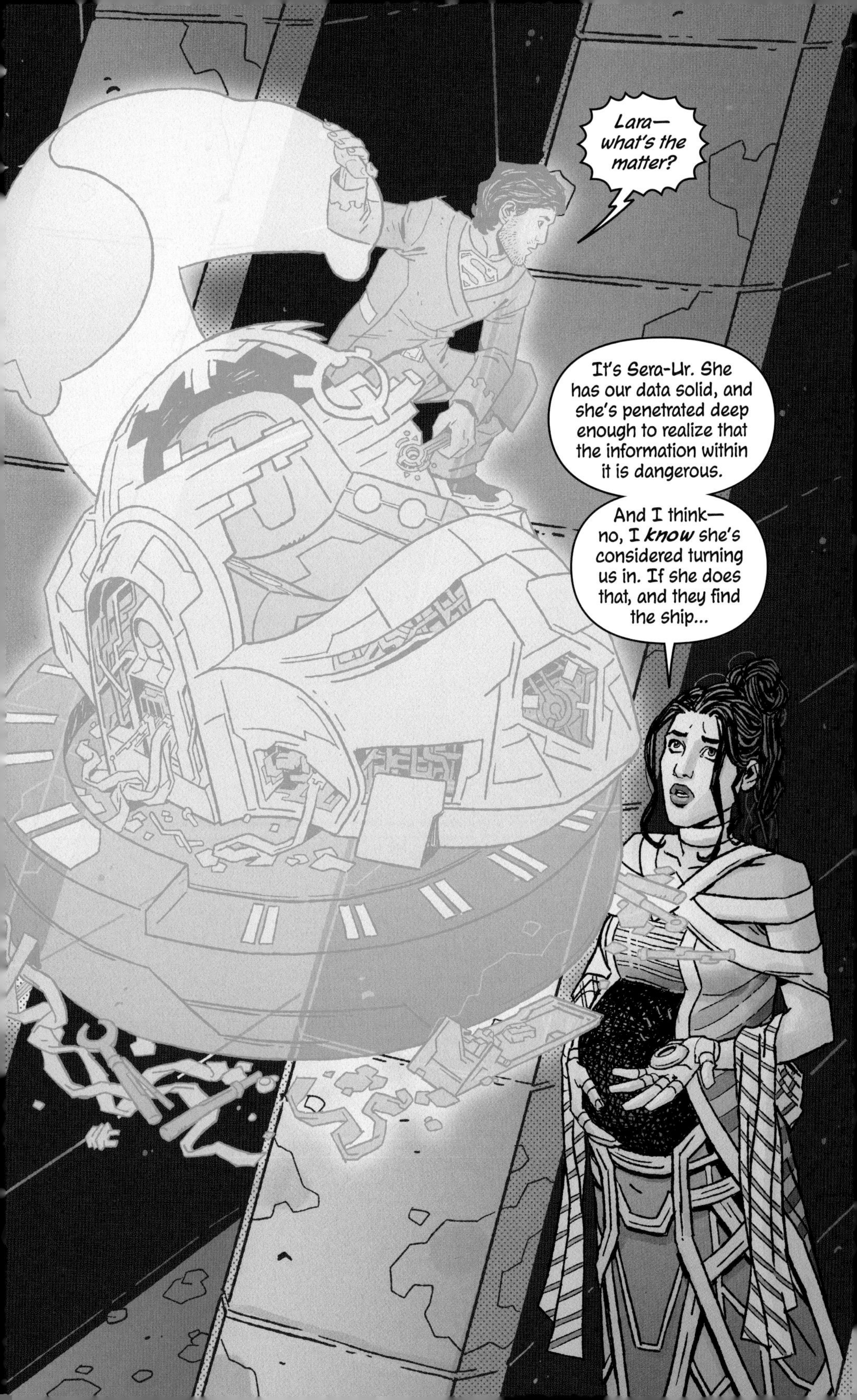
Lara— what's the matter?
It's Sera-Ur. She has our data solid, and she's penetrated deep enough to realize that the information within it is dangerous.
And I think— no, I *know* she's considered turning us in. If she does that, and they find the ship...

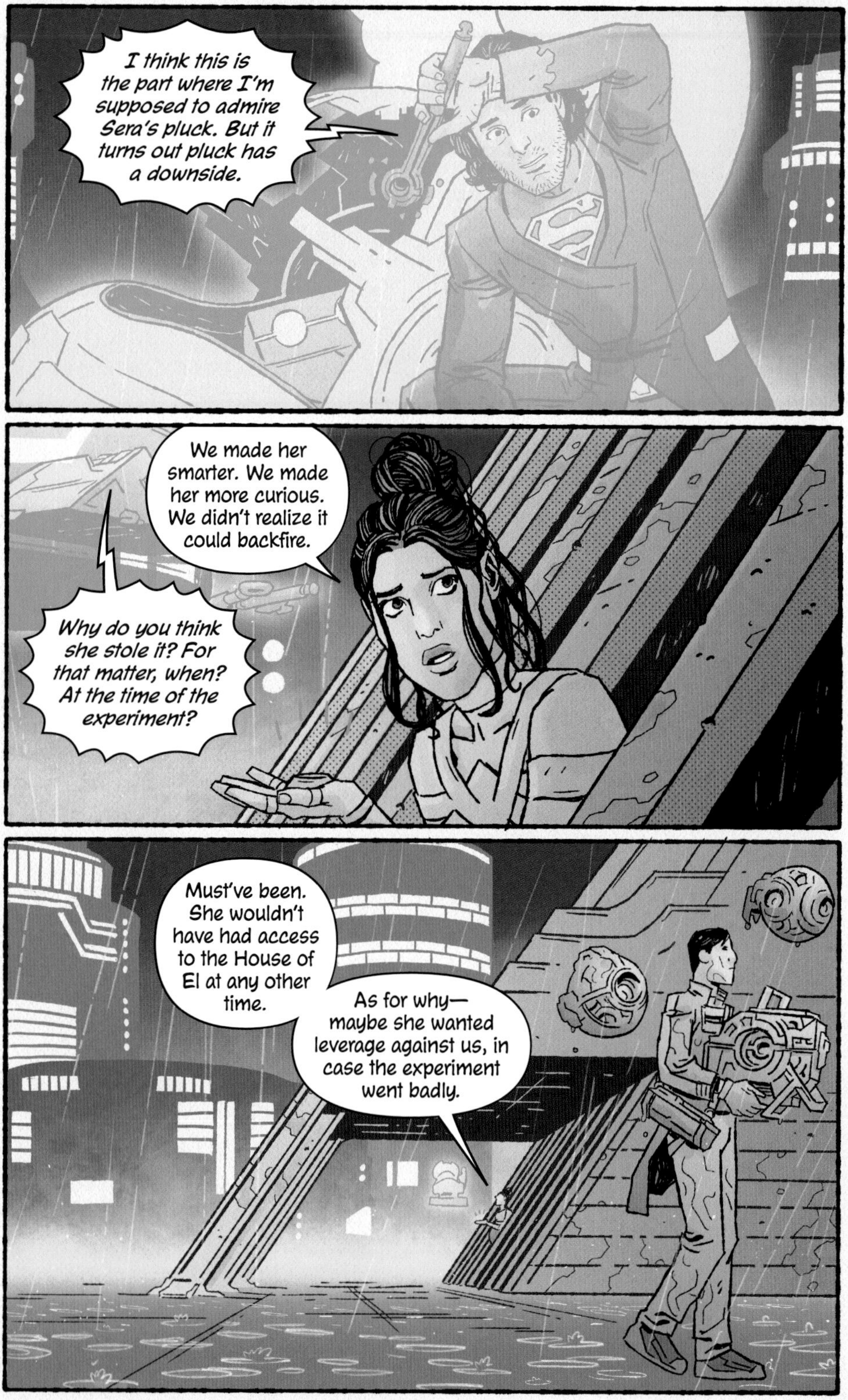
I think this is the part where I'm supposed to admire Sera's pluck. But it turns out pluck has a downside.
We made her smarter. We made her more curious. We didn't realize it could backfire.
Why do you think she stole it? For that matter, when? At the time of the experiment?
Must've been. She wouldn't have had access to the House of El at any other time.
As for why— maybe she wanted leverage against us, in case the experiment went badly.

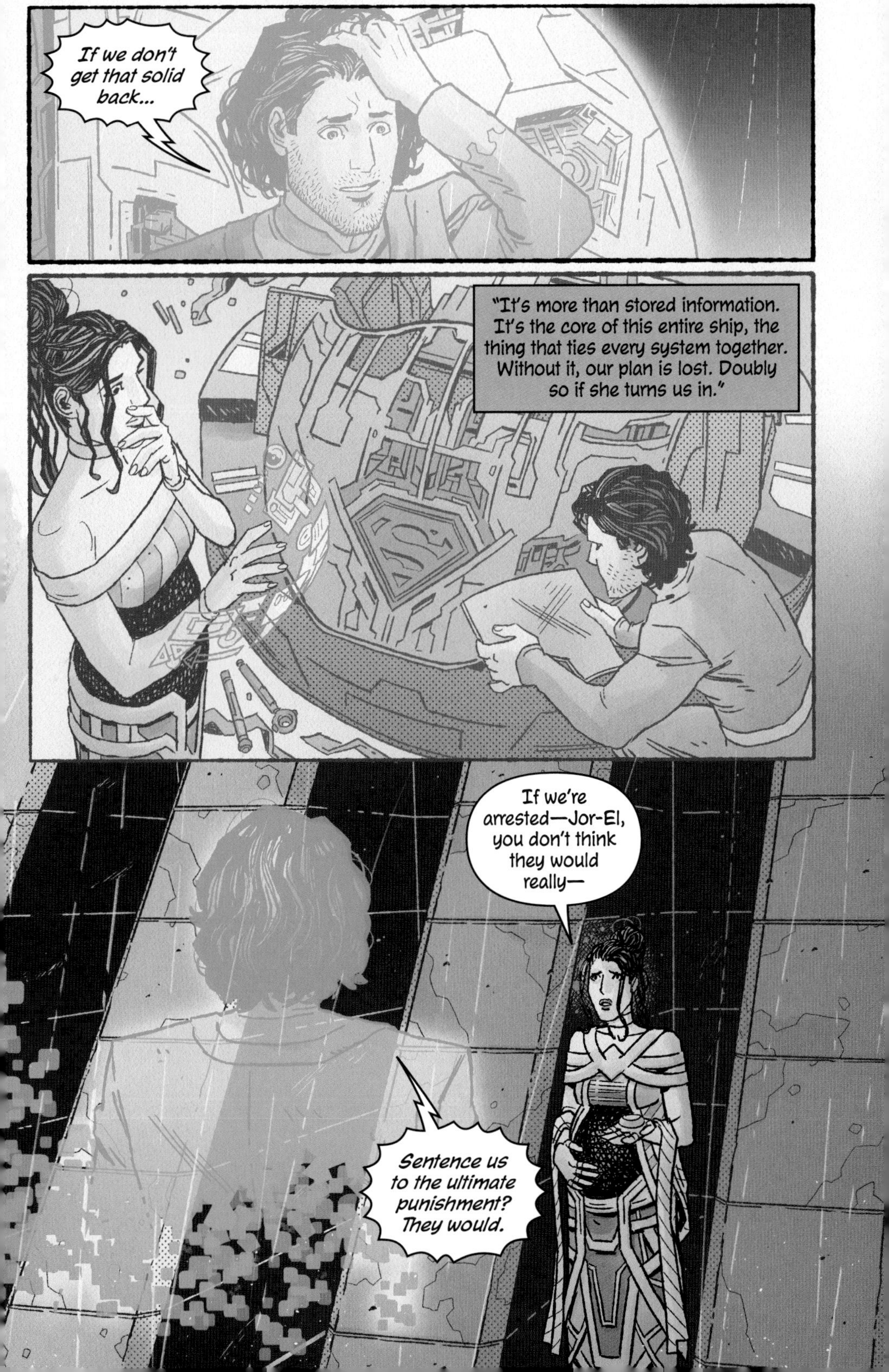

If we don't get that solid back...
"It's more than stored information. It's the core of this entire ship, the thing that ties every system together. Without it, our plan is lost. Doubly so if she turns us in."
If we're arrested—Jor-El, you don't think they would really—
Sentence us to the ultimate punishment? They would.

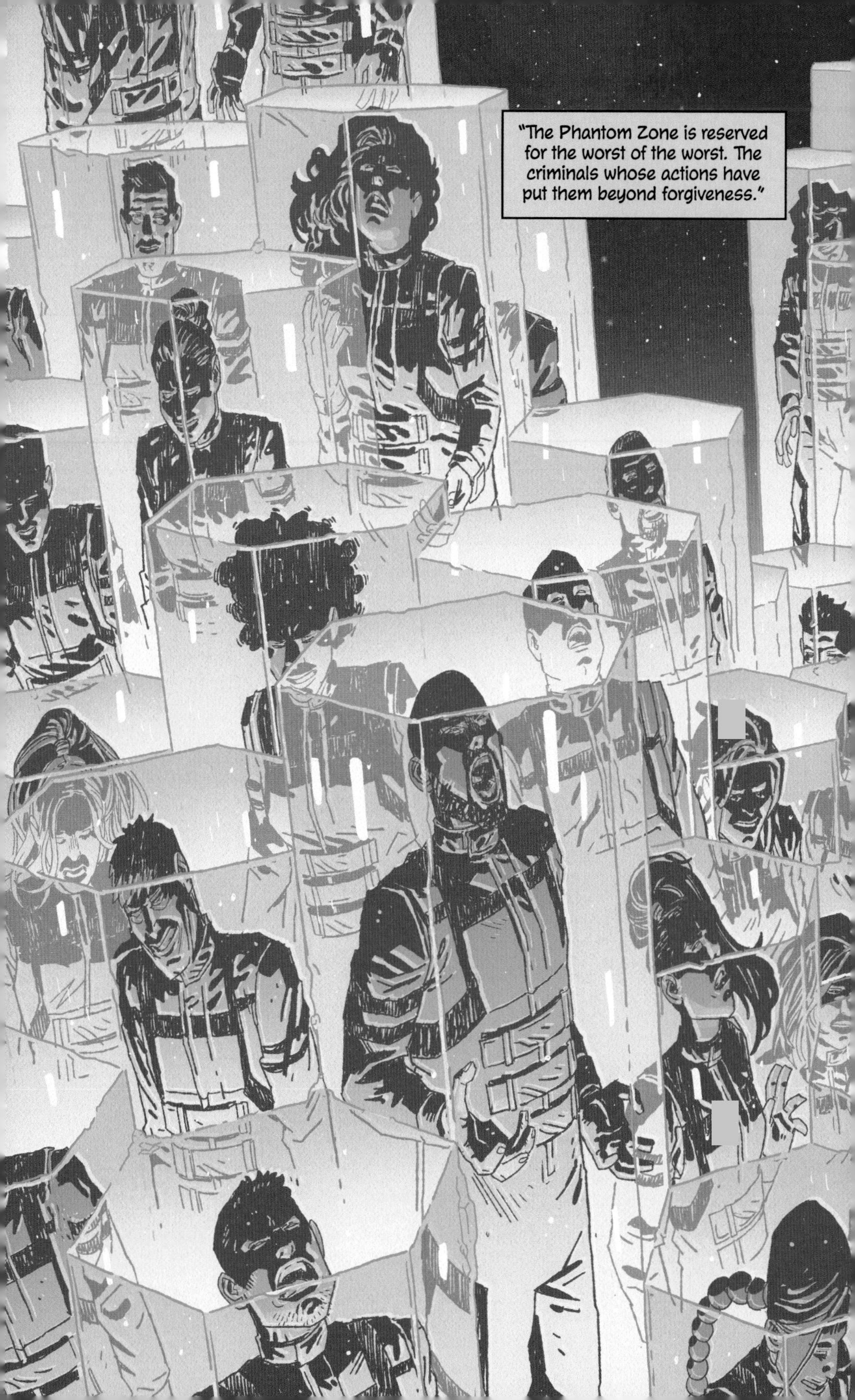
"The Phantom Zone is reserved for the worst of the worst. The criminals whose actions have put them beyond forgiveness."

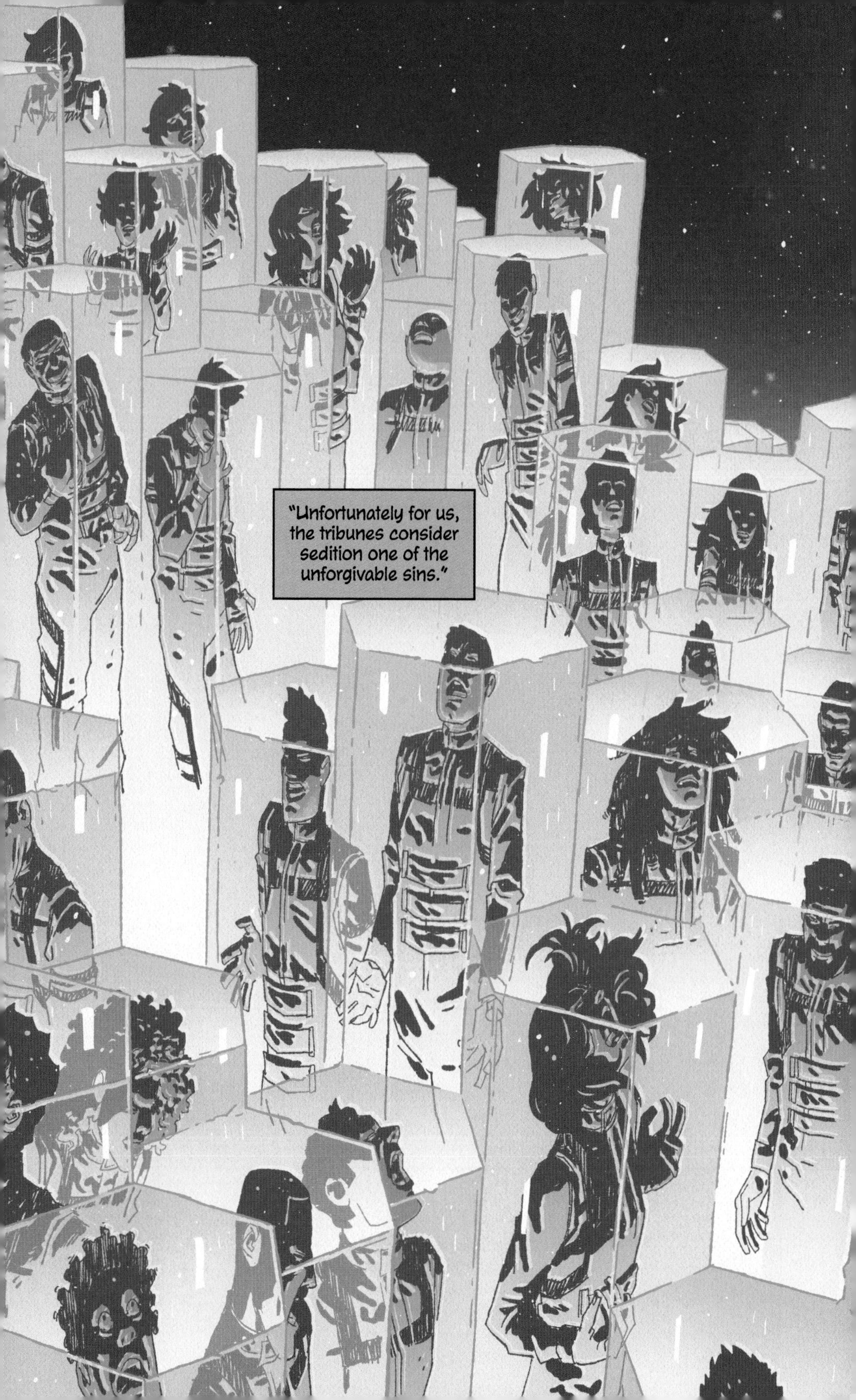
"Unfortunately for us, the tribunes consider sedition one of the unforgivable sins."

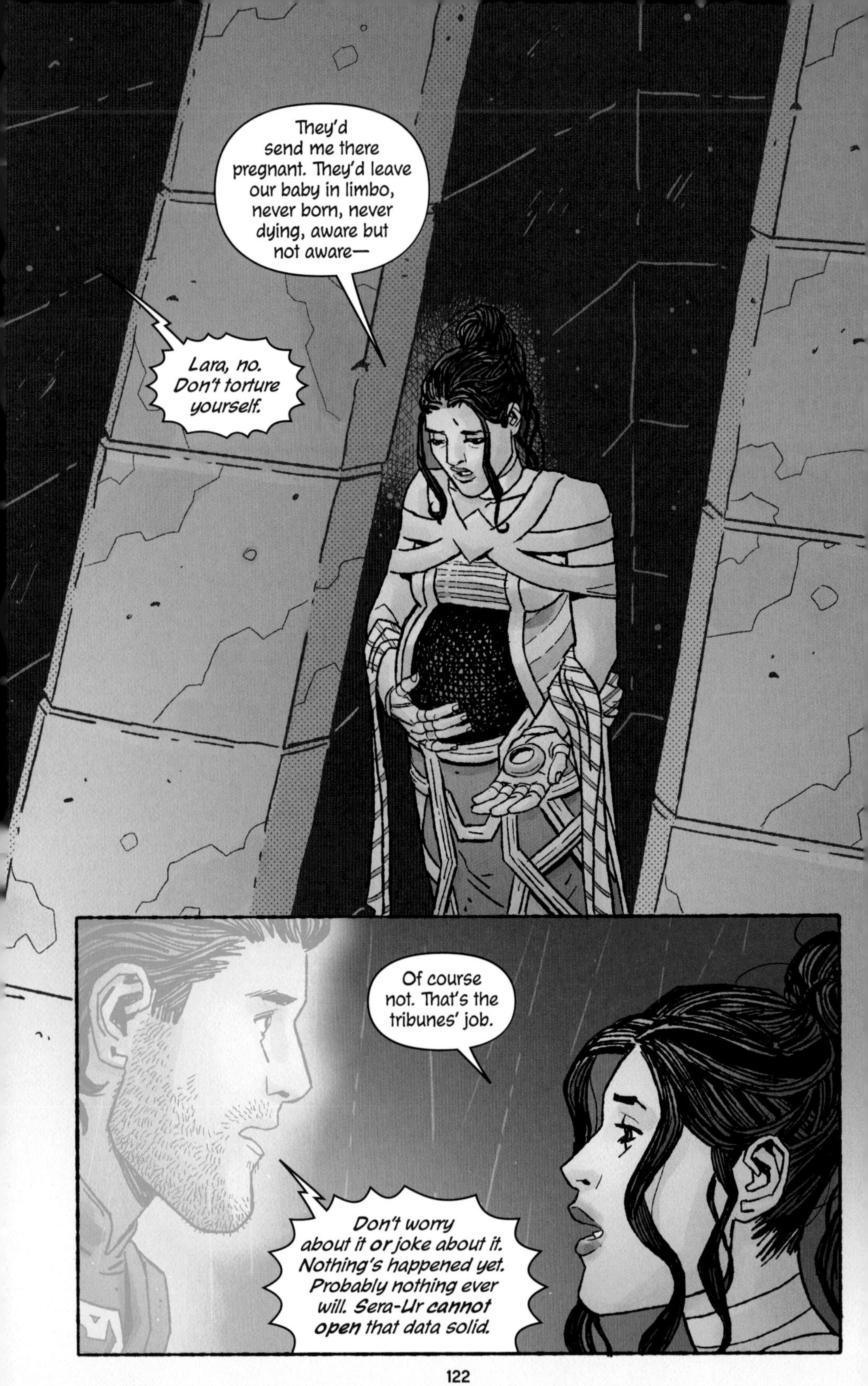
They'd send me there pregnant. They'd leave our baby in limbo, never born, never dying, aware but not aware—
Lara, no. Don't torture yourself.
Of course not. That's the tribunes' job.
Don't worry about it or joke about it. Nothing's happened yet. Probably nothing ever will. Sera-Ur cannot open that data solid.

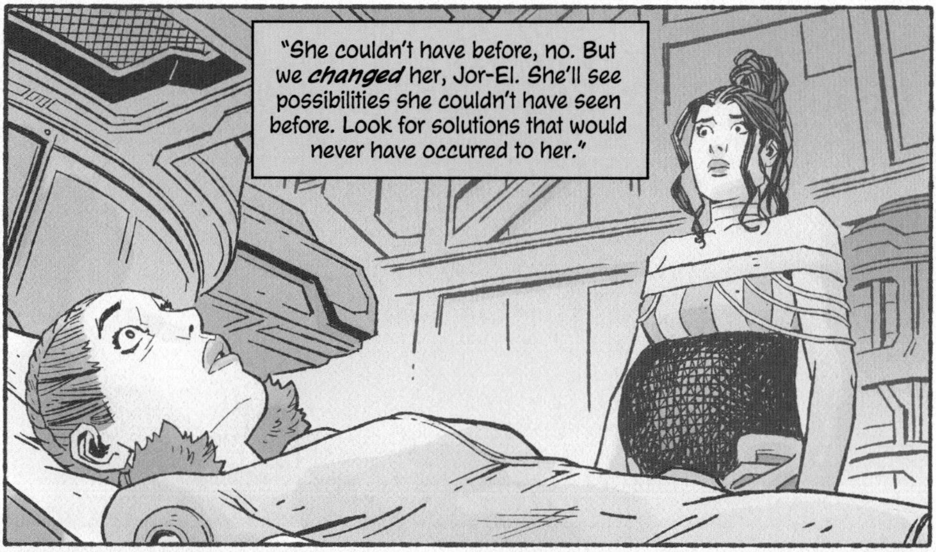
"She couldn't have before, no. But we *changed* her, Jor-El. She'll see possibilities she couldn't have seen before. Look for solutions that would never have occurred to her."

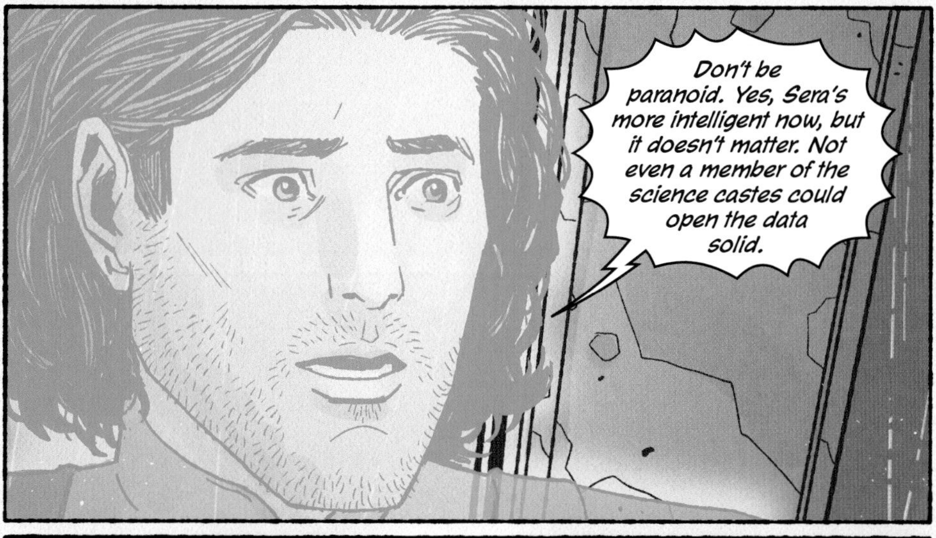
Don't be paranoid. Yes, Sera's more intelligent now, but it doesn't matter. Not even a member of the science castes could open the data solid.

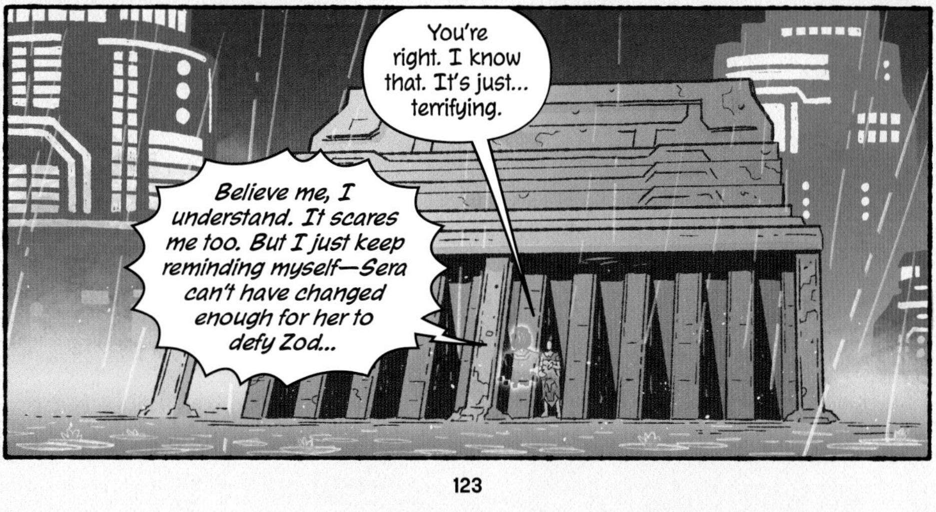
You're right. I know that. It's just... terrifying.
Believe me, I understand. It scares me too. But I just keep reminding myself—Sera can't have changed enough for her to defy Zod...

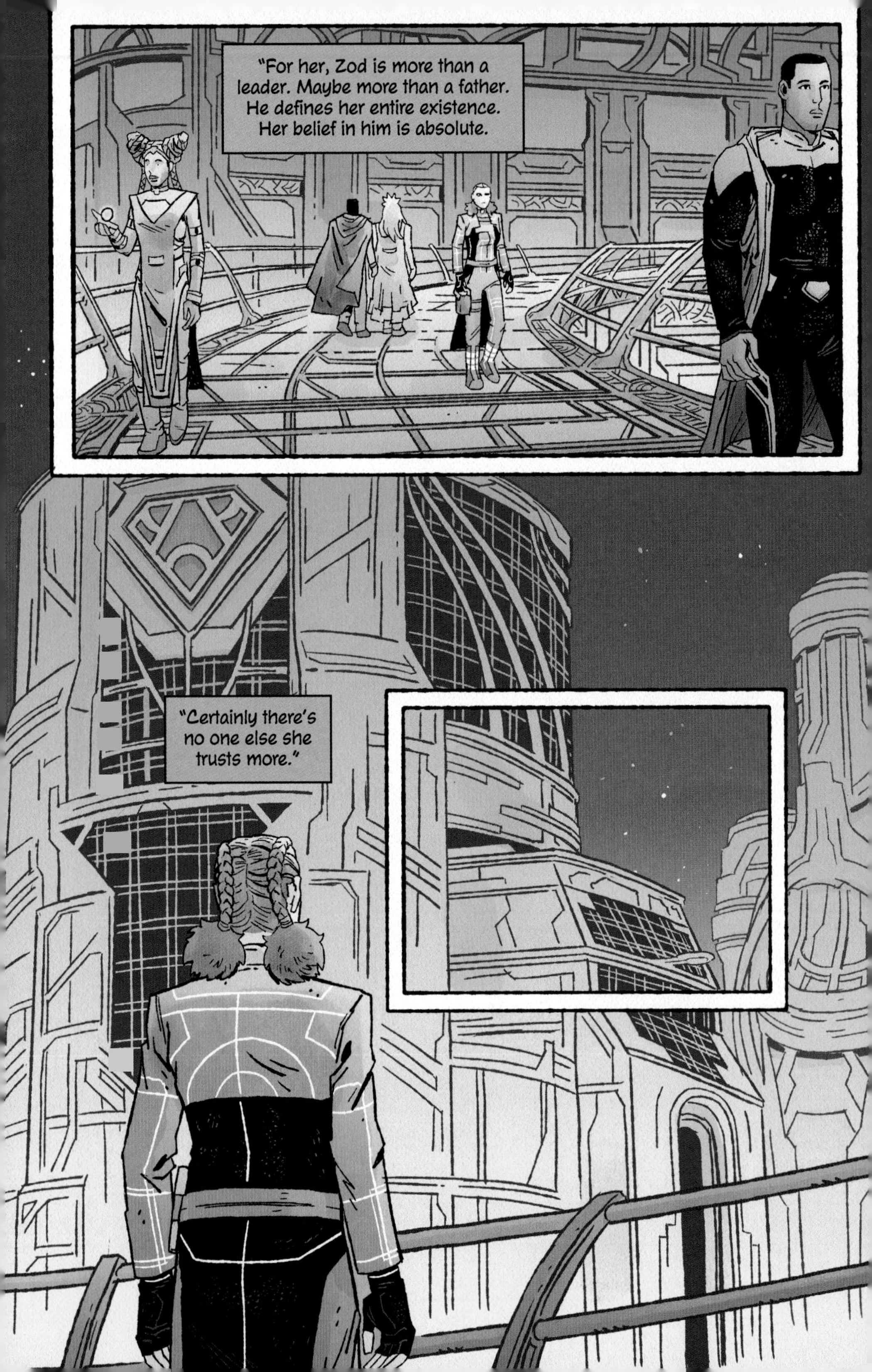
"For her, Zod is more than a leader. Maybe more than a father. He defines her entire existence. Her belief in him is absolute.
"Certainly there's no one else she trusts more."

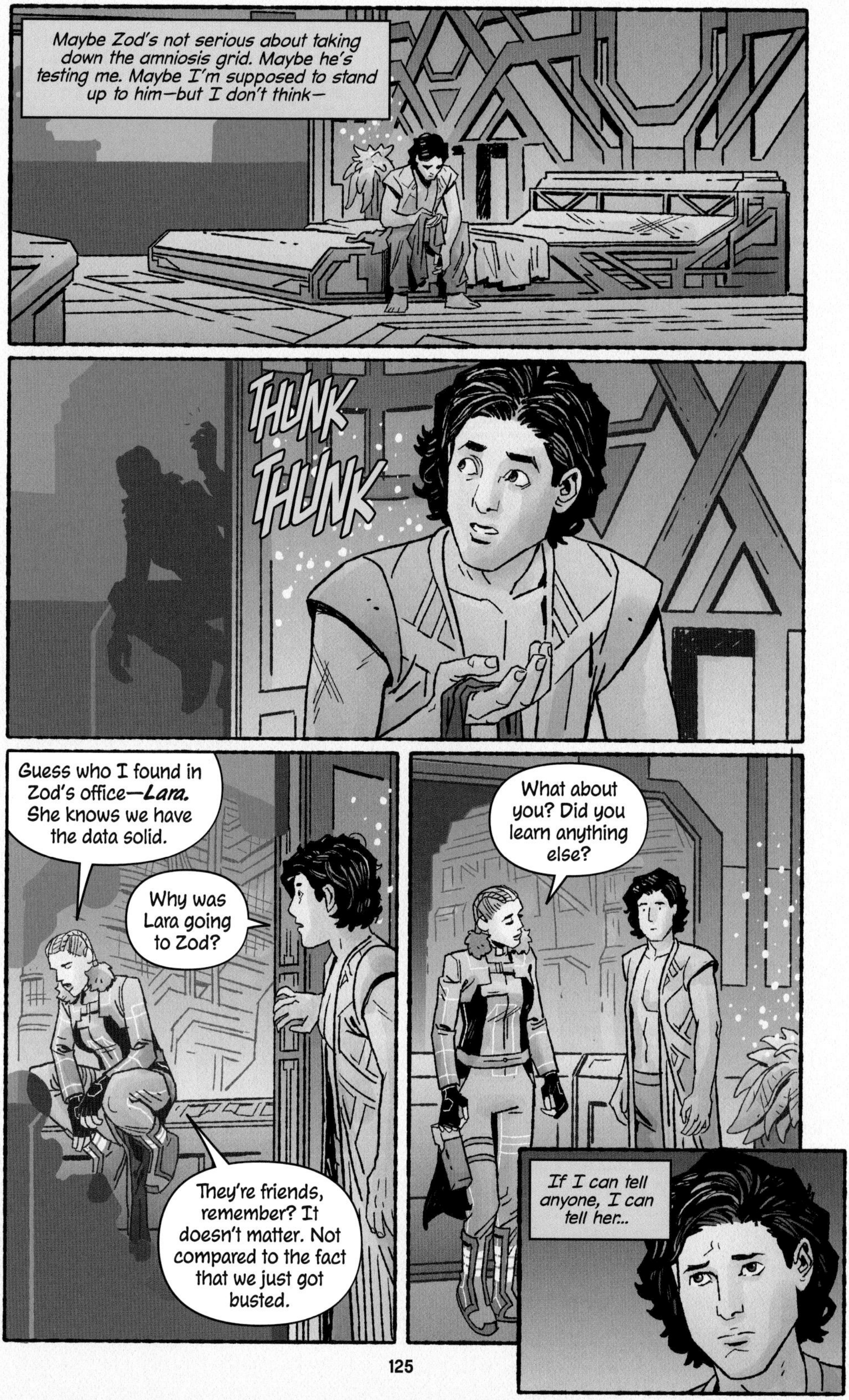
Maybe Zod's not serious about taking down the amniosis grid. Maybe he's testing me. Maybe I'm supposed to stand up to him—but I don't think—
THUNK THUNK
Guess who I found in Zod's office—Lara. She knows we have the data solid.
Why was Lara going to Zod?
They're friends, remember? It doesn't matter. Not compared to the fact that we just got busted.
What about you? Did you learn anything else?
If I can tell anyone, I can tell her...

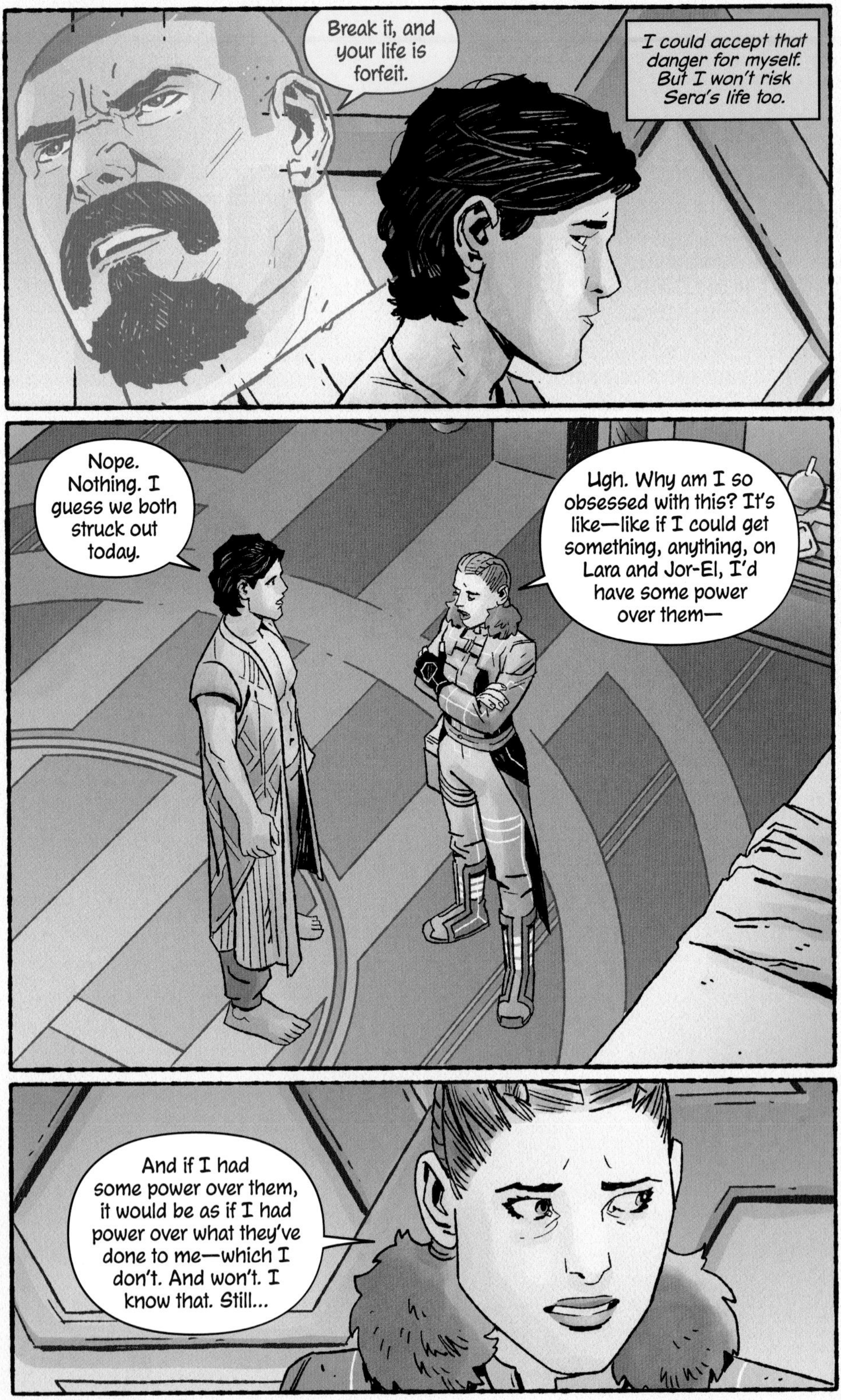
Break it, and your life is forfeit.
I could accept that danger for myself. But I won't risk Sera's life too.
Nope. Nothing. I guess we both struck out today.
Ugh. Why am I so obsessed with this? It's like—like if I could get something, anything, on Lara and Jor-El, I'd have some power over them—
And if I had some power over them, it would be as if I had power over what they've done to me—which I don't. And won't. I know that. Still...

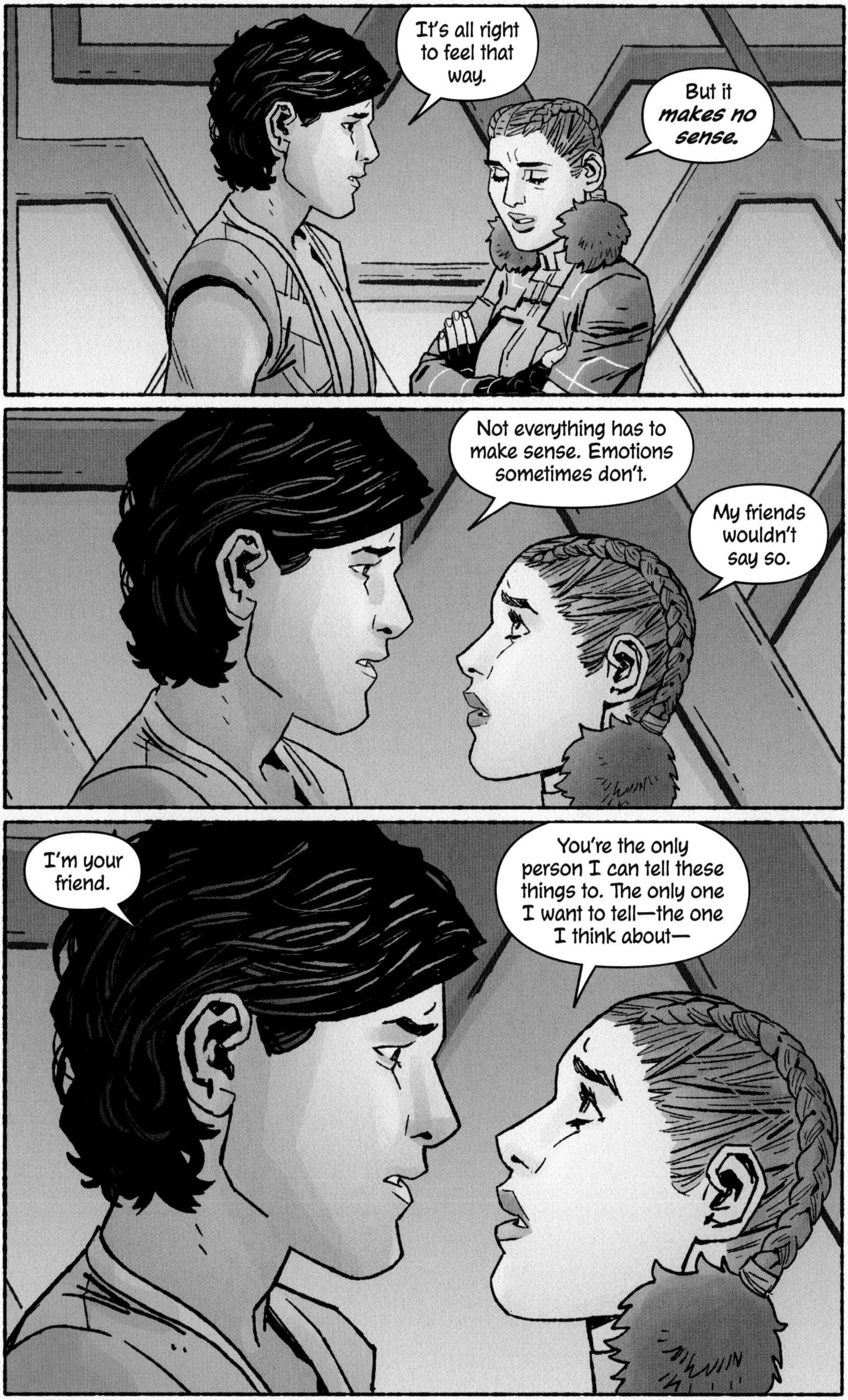
It's all right to feel that way.
But it *makes no sense.*
Not everything has to make sense. Emotions sometimes don't.
My friends wouldn't say so.
I'm your friend.
You're the only person I can tell these things to. The only one I want to tell—the one I think about—

CHAPTER THREE

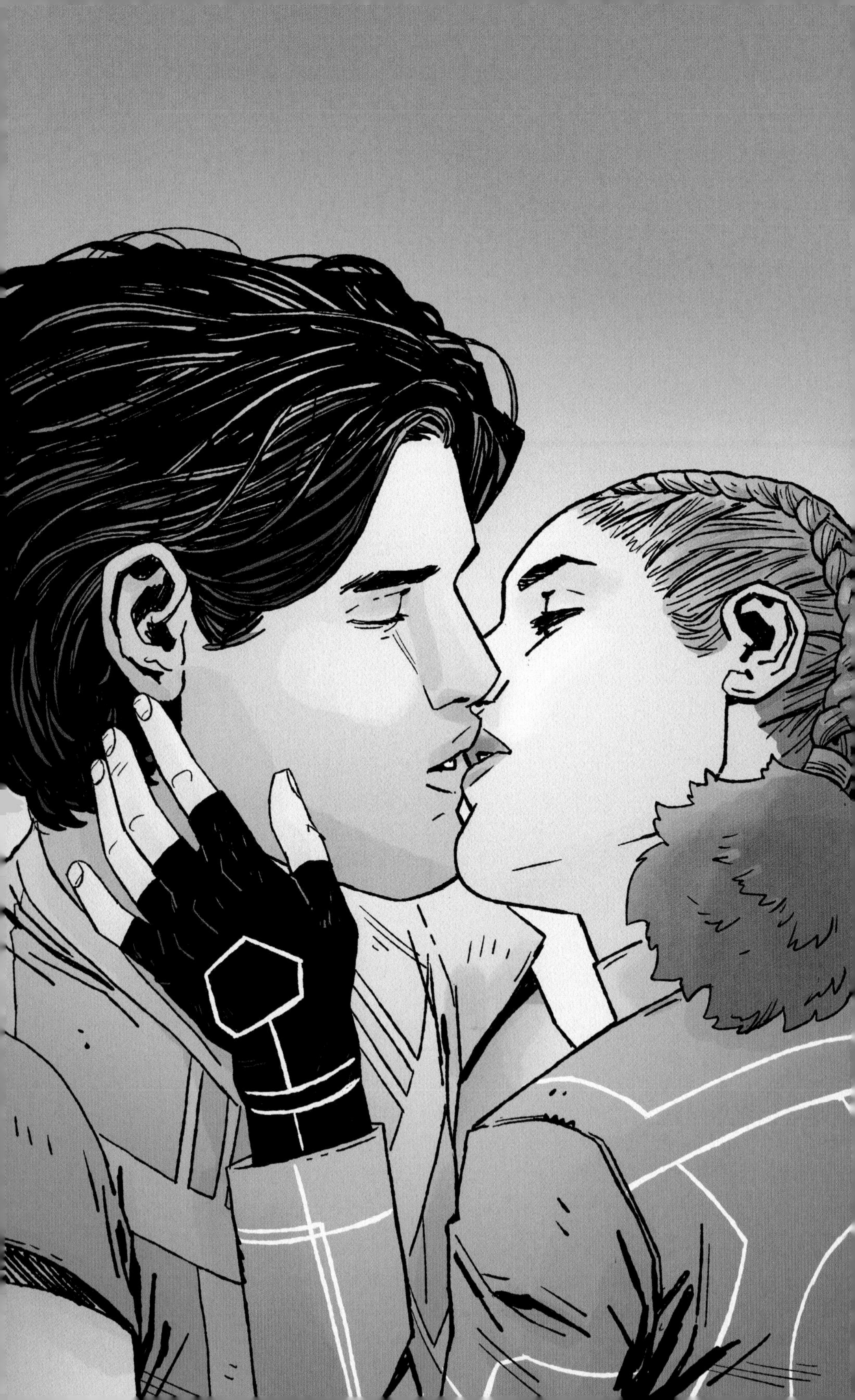

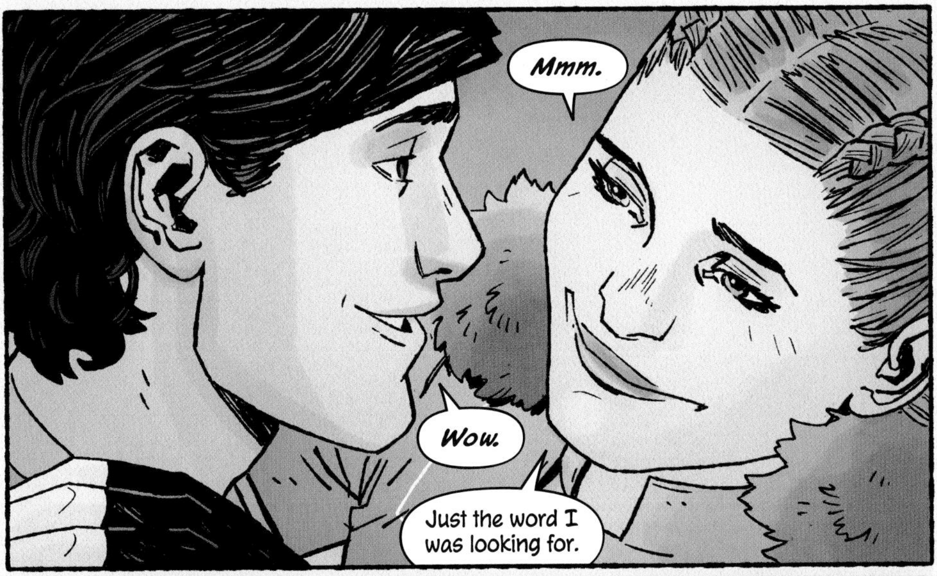
Mmm.
Wow.
Just the word I was looking for.

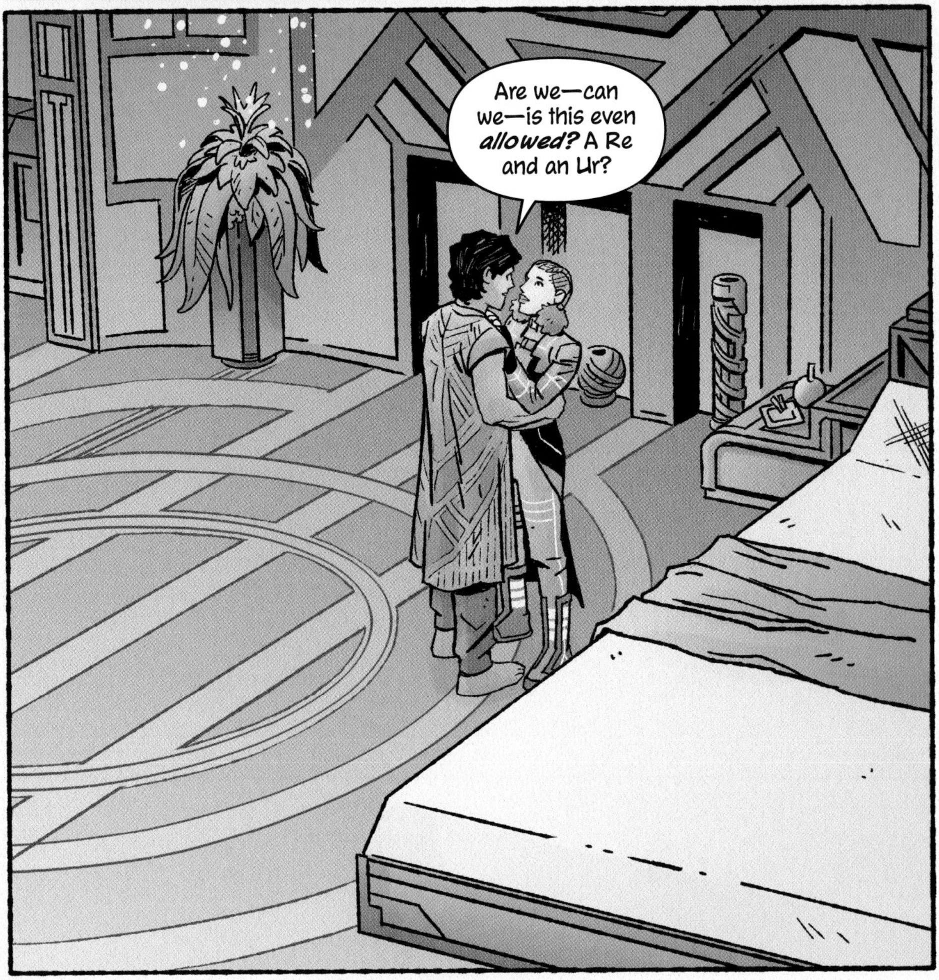
Are we—can we—is this even *allowed?* A Re and an Ur?

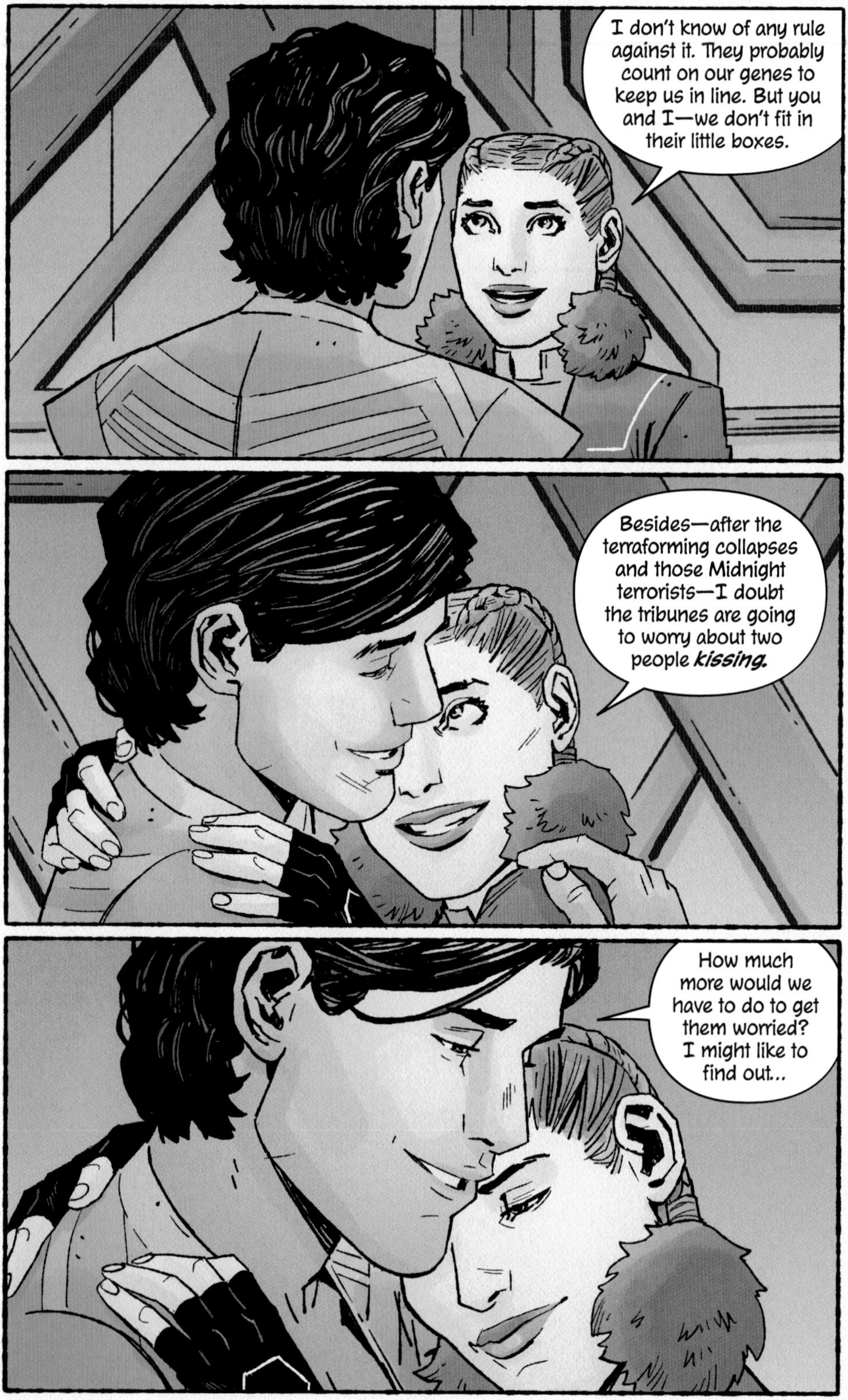
I don't know of any rule against it. They probably count on our genes to keep us in line. But you and I—we don't fit in their little boxes.
Besides—after the terraforming collapses and those Midnight terrorists—I doubt the tribunes are going to worry about two people *kissing.*
How much more would we have to do to get them worried? I might like to find out...

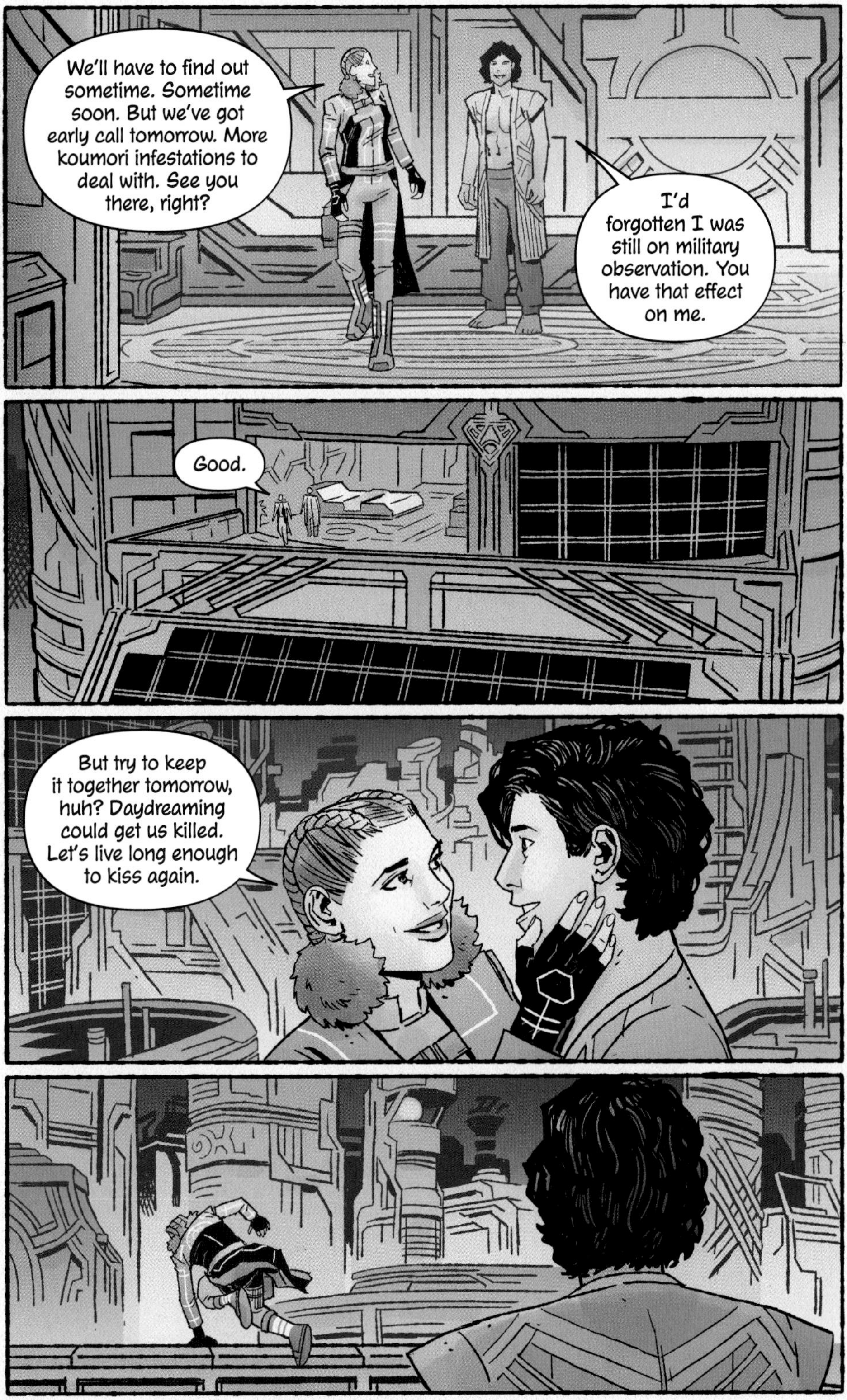

We'll have to find out sometime. Sometime soon. But we've got early call tomorrow. More koumori infestations to deal with. See you there, right?
I'd forgotten I was still on military observation. You have that effect on me.
Good.
But try to keep it together tomorrow, huh? Daydreaming could get us killed. Let's live long enough to kiss again.

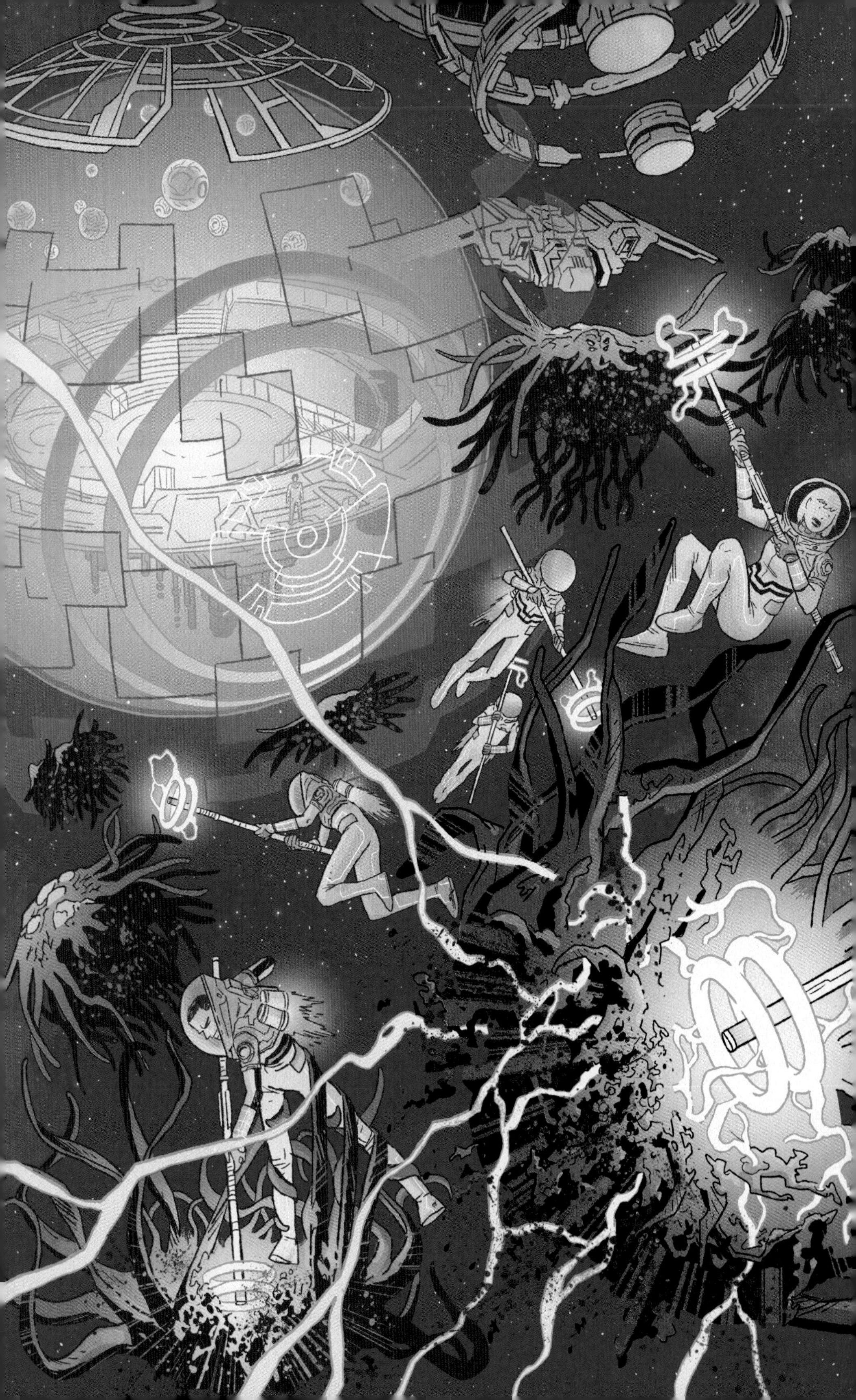

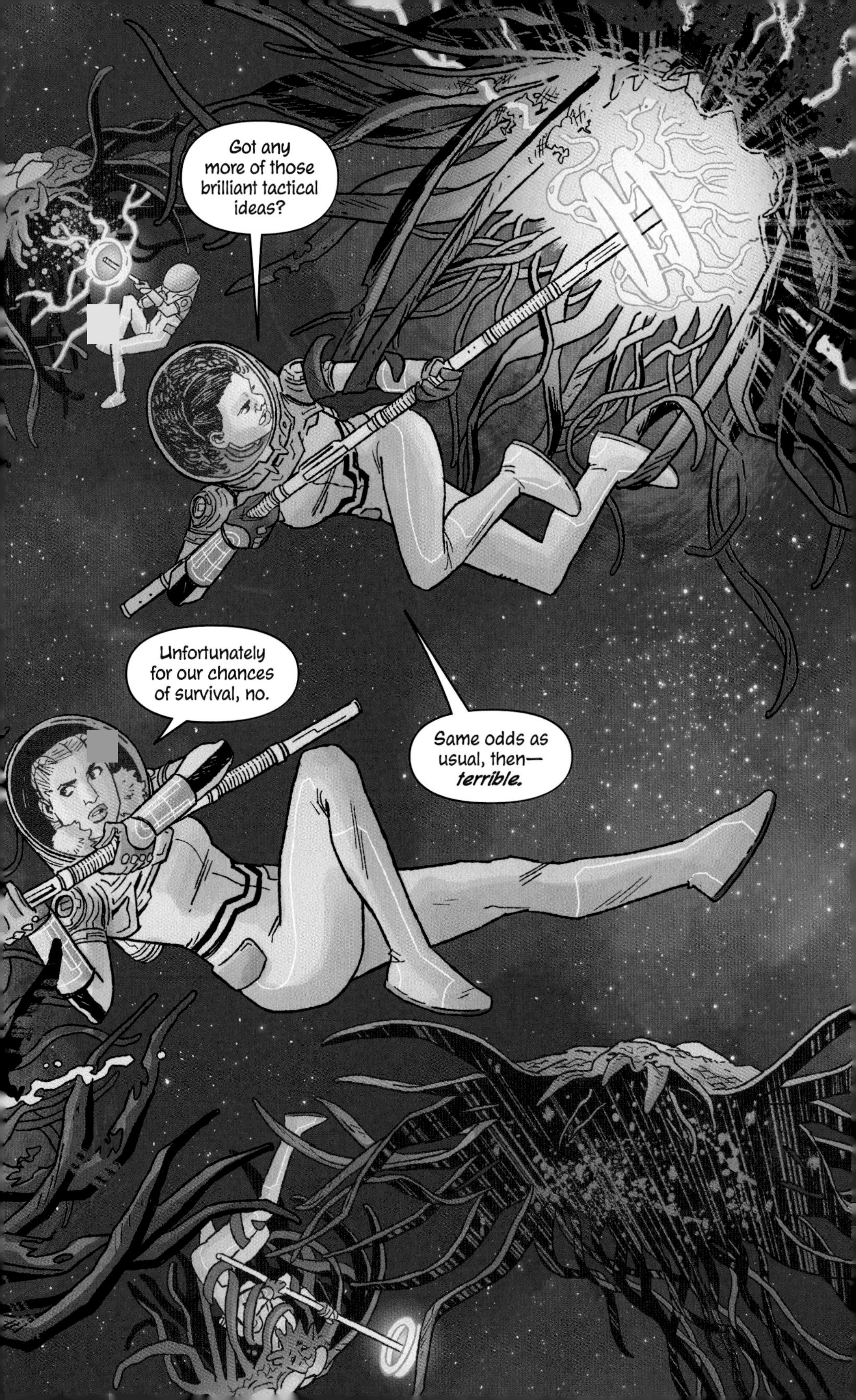
Got any more of those brilliant tactical ideas?
Unfortunately for our chances of survival, no.
Same odds as usual, then—*terrible.*

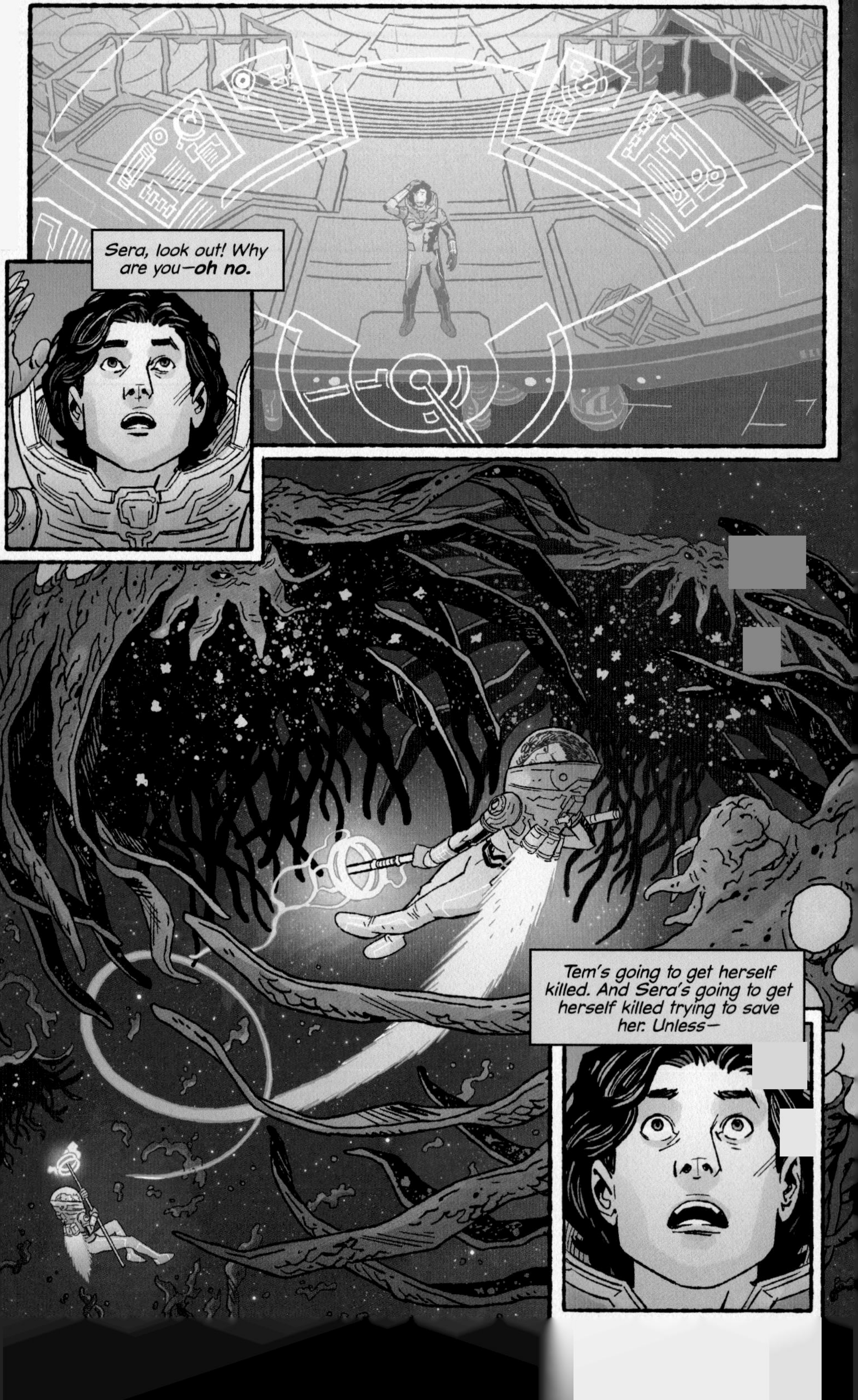
Sera, look out! Why are you—**oh no.**
Tem's going to get herself killed. And Sera's going to get herself killed trying to save her. Unless—

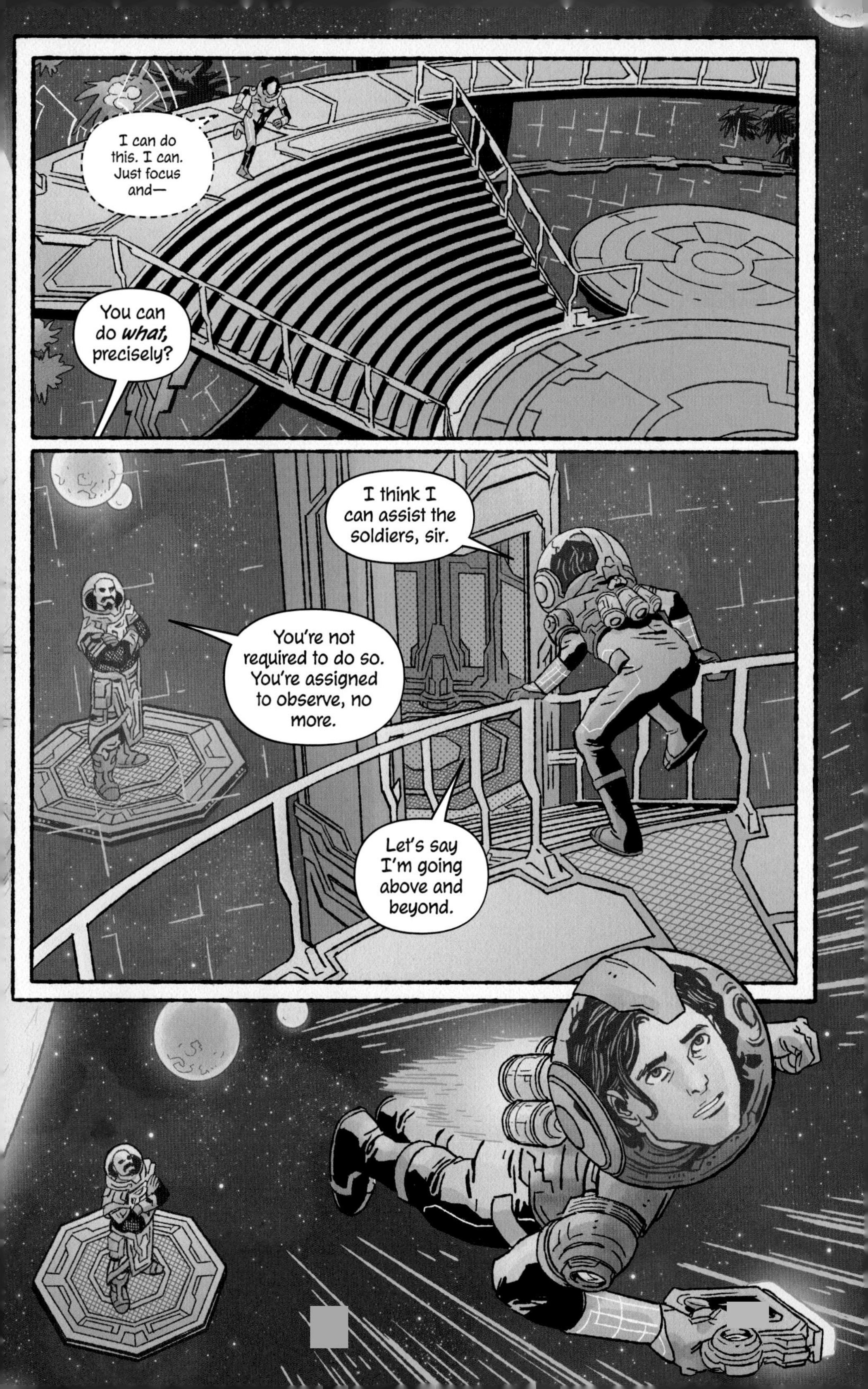
I can do this. I can. Just focus and—
You can do *what,* precisely?
I think I can assist the soldiers, sir.
You're not required to do so. You're assigned to observe, no more.
Let's say I'm going above and beyond.

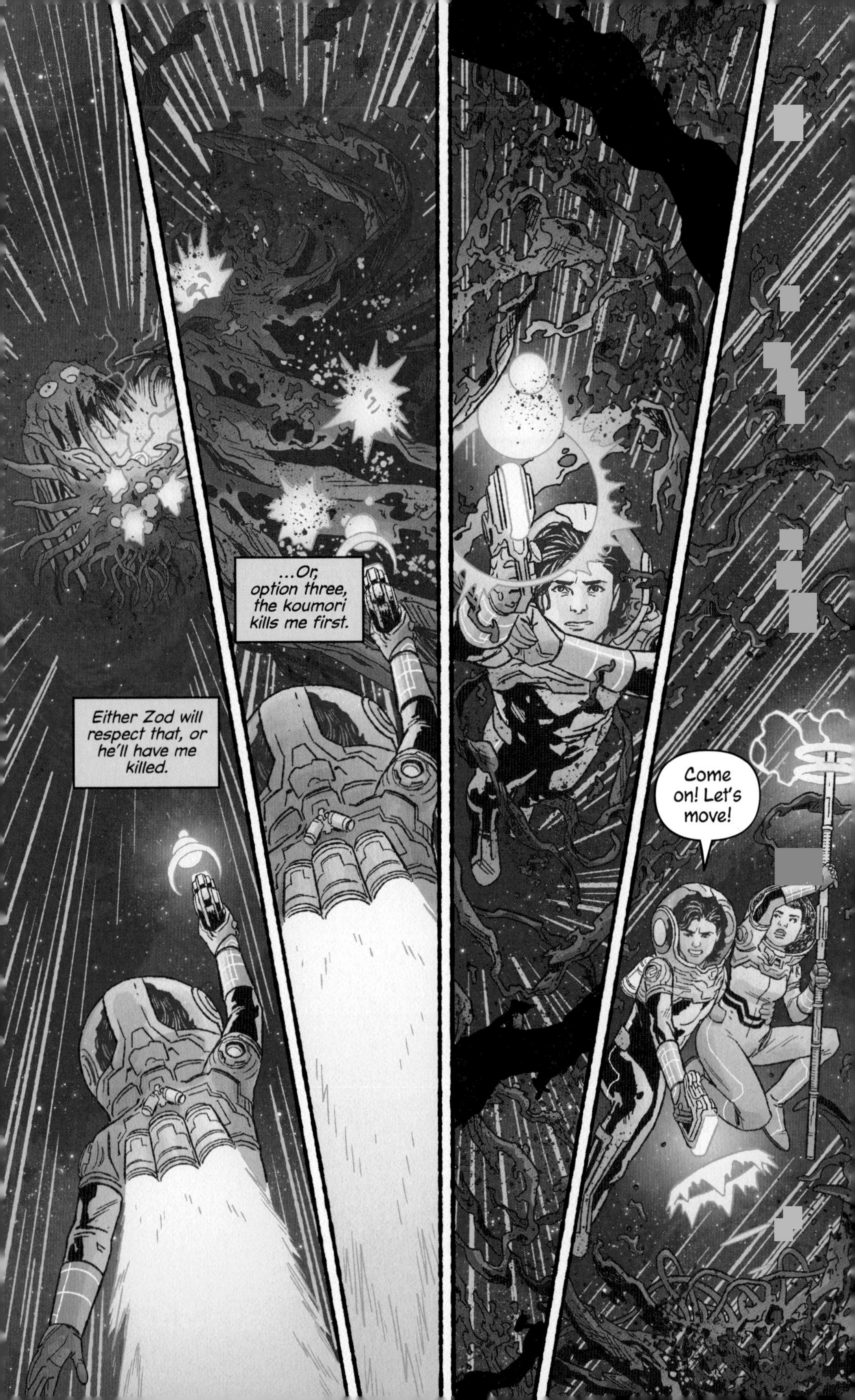
Either Zod will respect that, or he'll have me killed.
...Or, option three, the koumori kills me first.
Come on! Let's move!

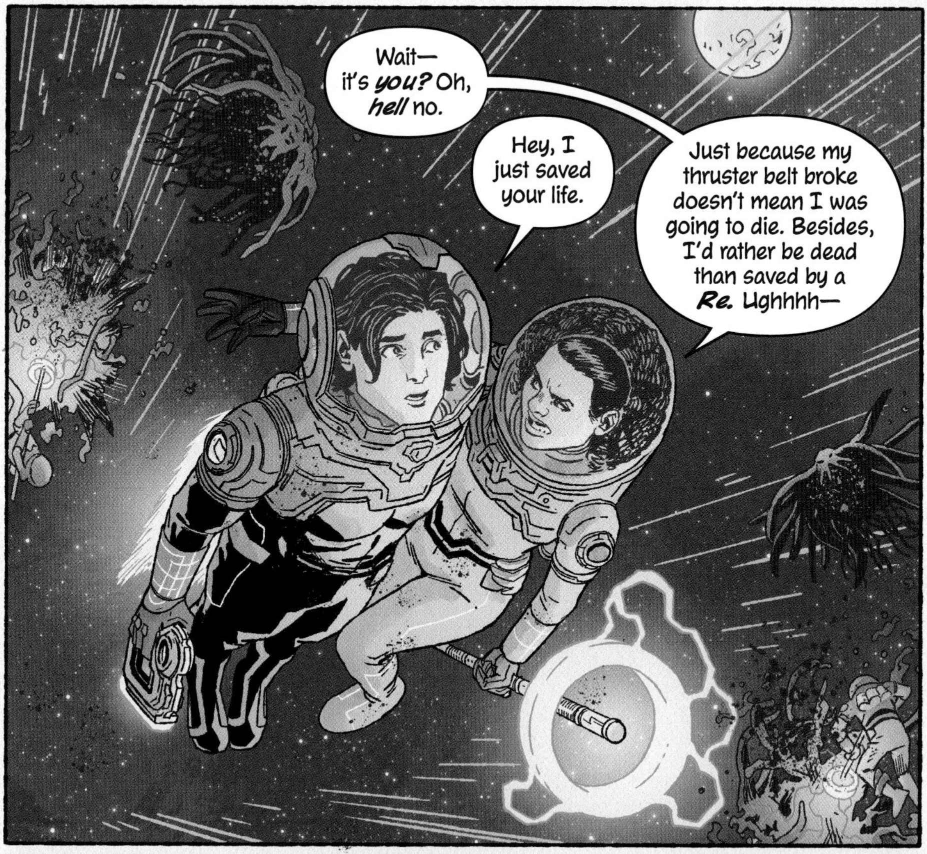
Wait—
it's *you?* Oh, *hell* no.
Hey, I just saved your life.
Just because my thruster belt broke doesn't mean I was going to die. Besides, I'd rather be dead than saved by a *Re.* Ughhhh—

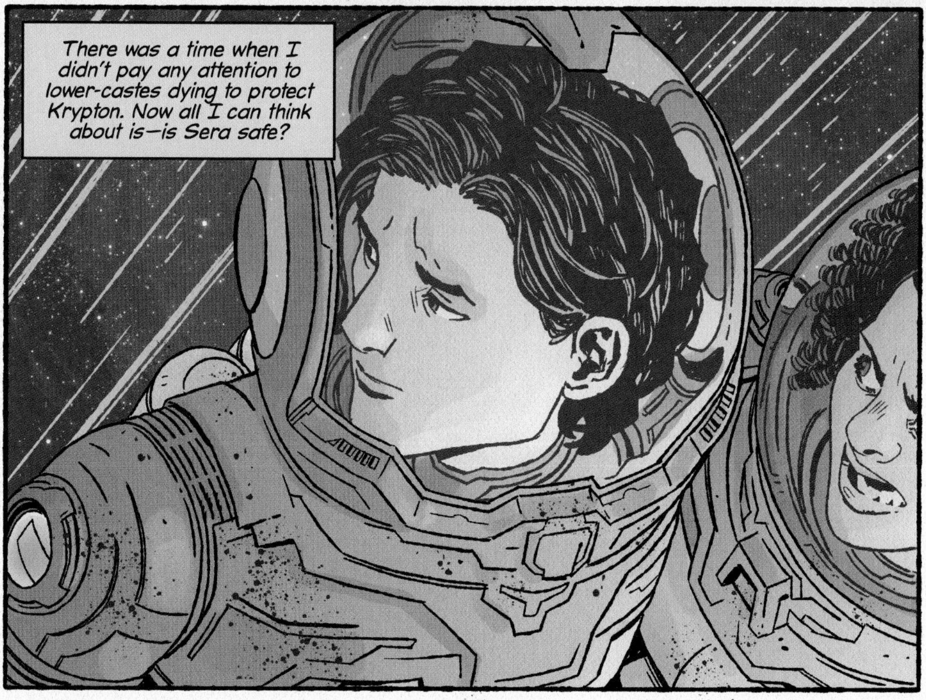
There was a time when I didn't pay any attention to lower-castes dying to protect Krypton. Now all I can think about is—is Sera safe?

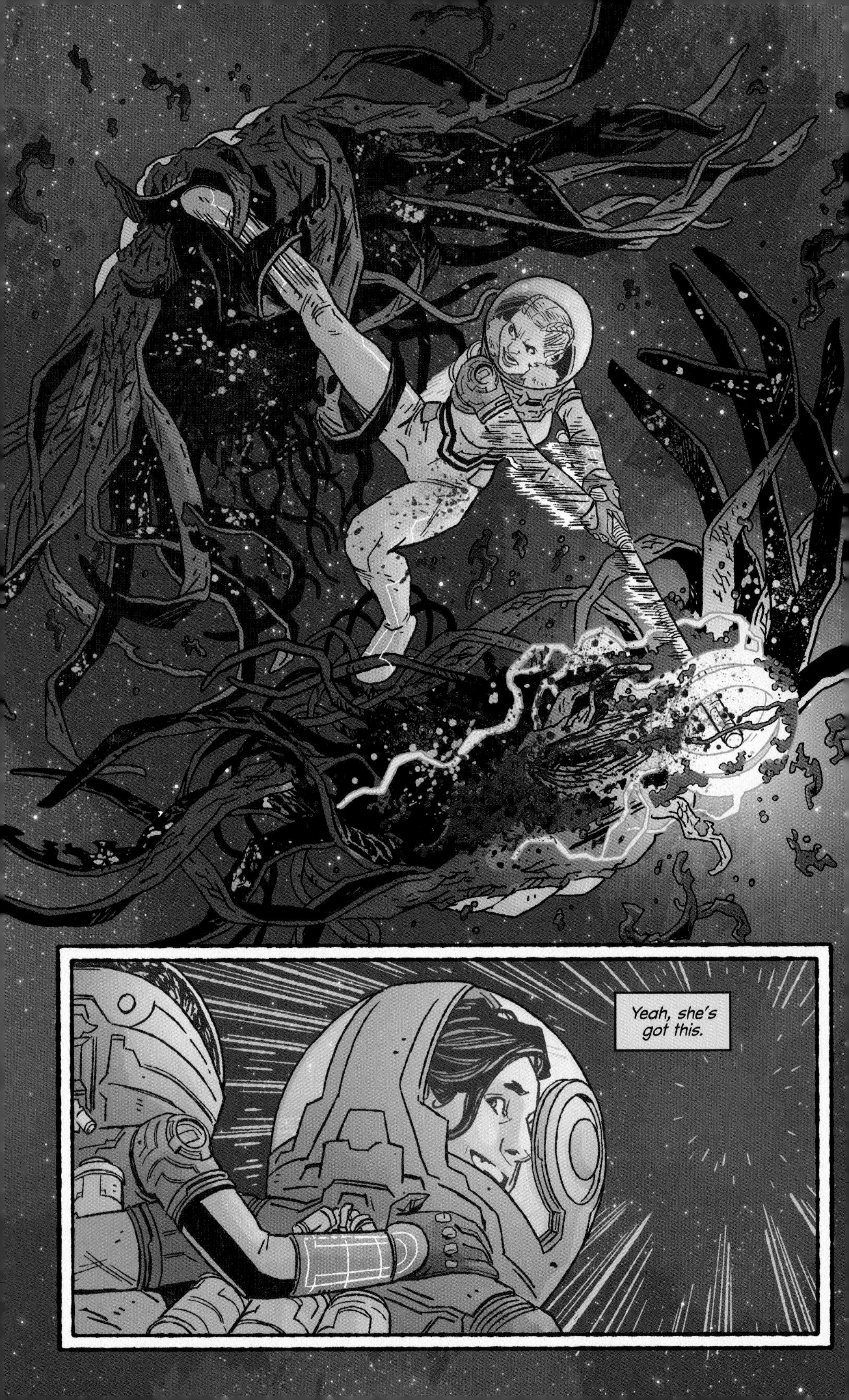
Yeah, she's got this.

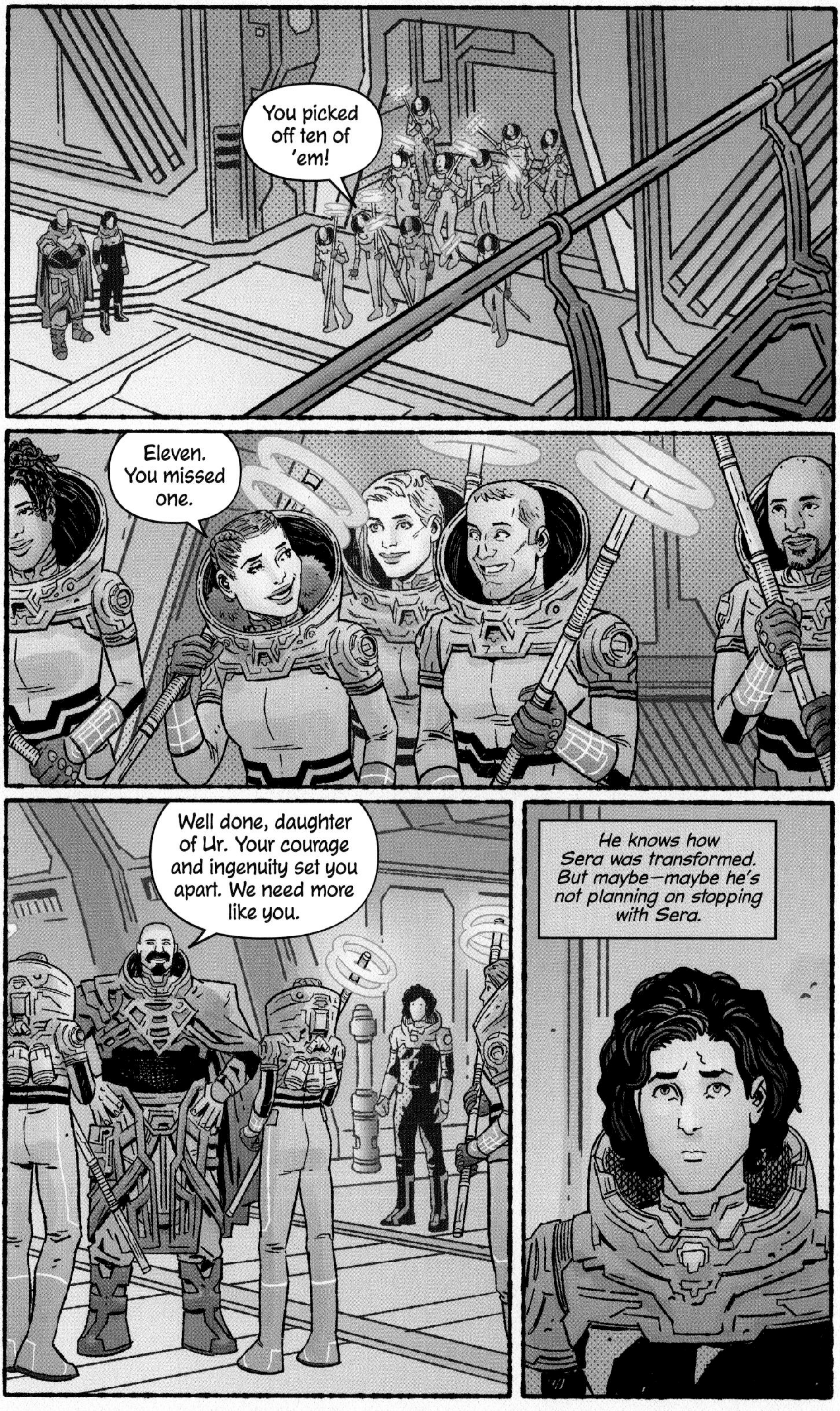
You picked off ten of 'em!
Eleven. You missed one.
Well done, daughter of Ur. Your courage and ingenuity set you apart. We need more like you.
He knows how Sera was transformed. But maybe—maybe he's not planning on stopping with Sera.

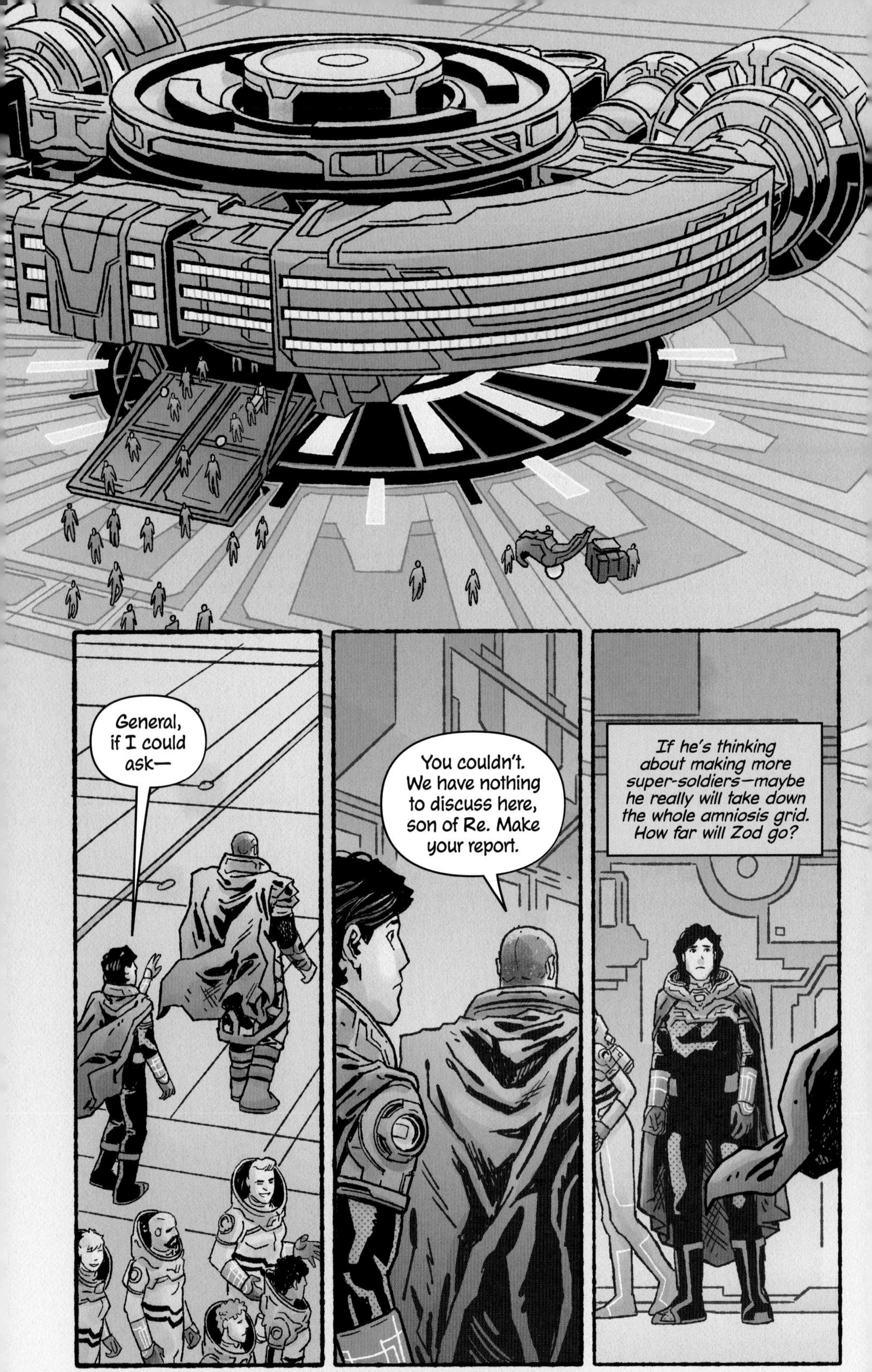

General, if I could ask—
You couldn't. We have nothing to discuss here, son of Re. Make your report.
If he's thinking about making more super-soldiers—maybe he really will take down the whole amniosis grid. How far will Zod go?

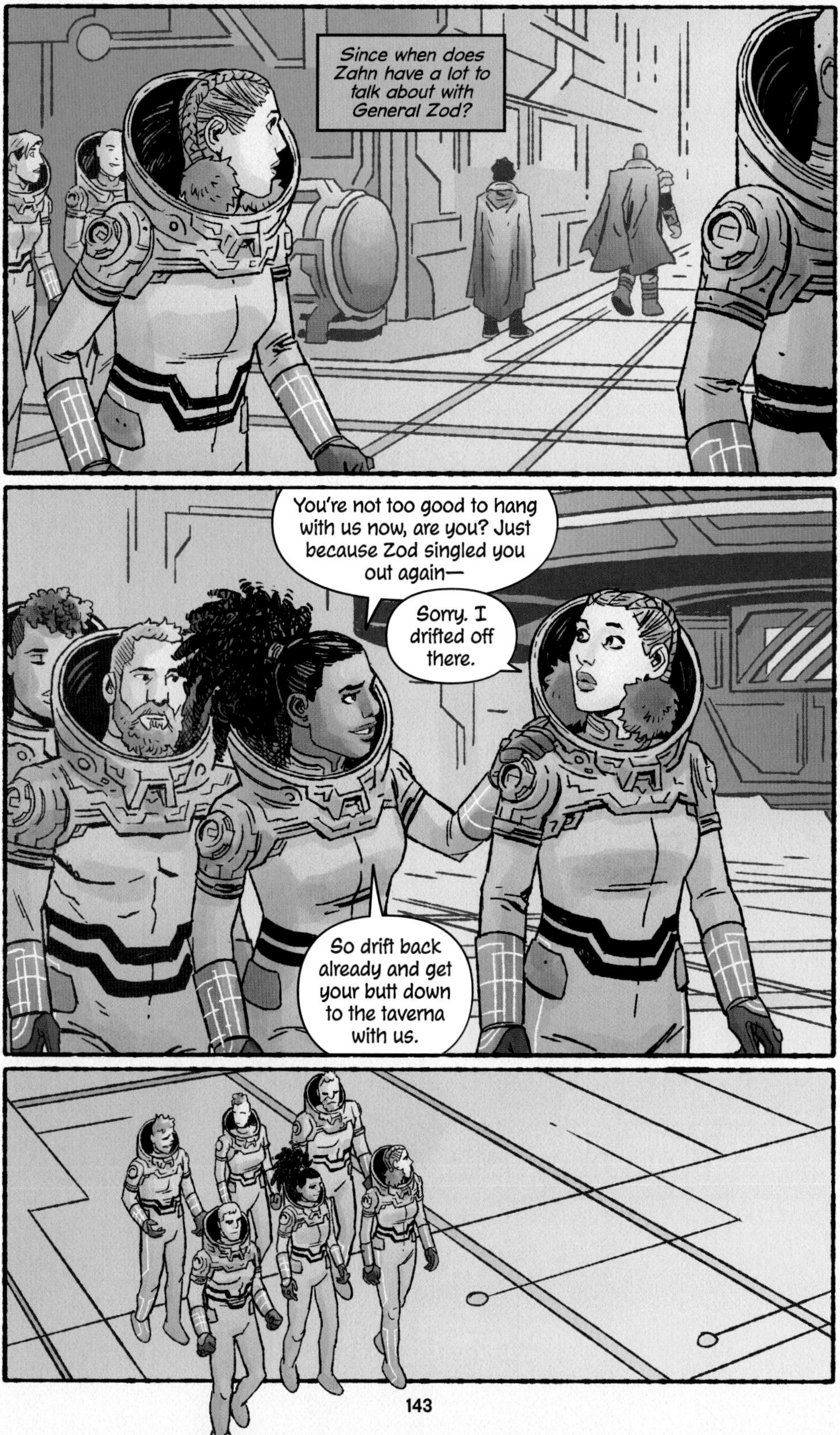
Since when does Zahn have a lot to talk about with General Zod?
You're not too good to hang with us now, are you? Just because Zod singled you out again—
Sorry. I drifted off there.
So drift back already and get your butt down to the taverna with us.

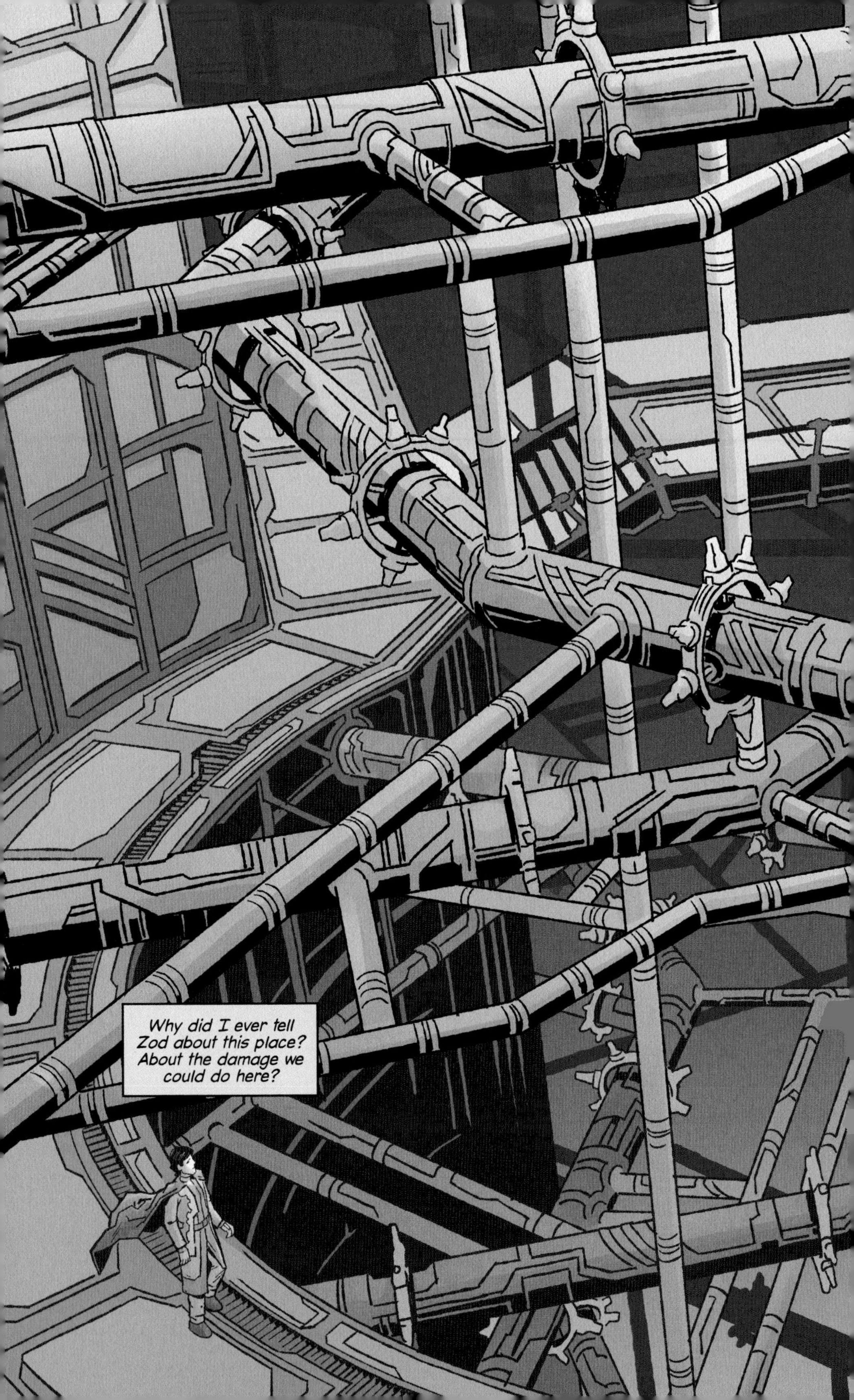
Why did I ever tell Zod about this place? About the damage we could do here?

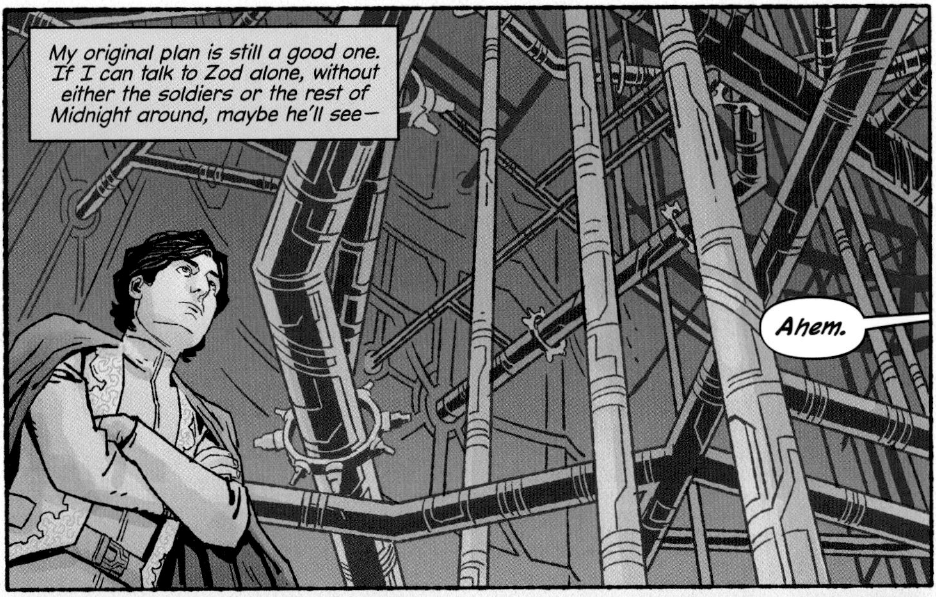
My original plan is still a good one. If I can talk to Zod alone, without either the soldiers or the rest of Midnight around, maybe he'll see—
Ahem.

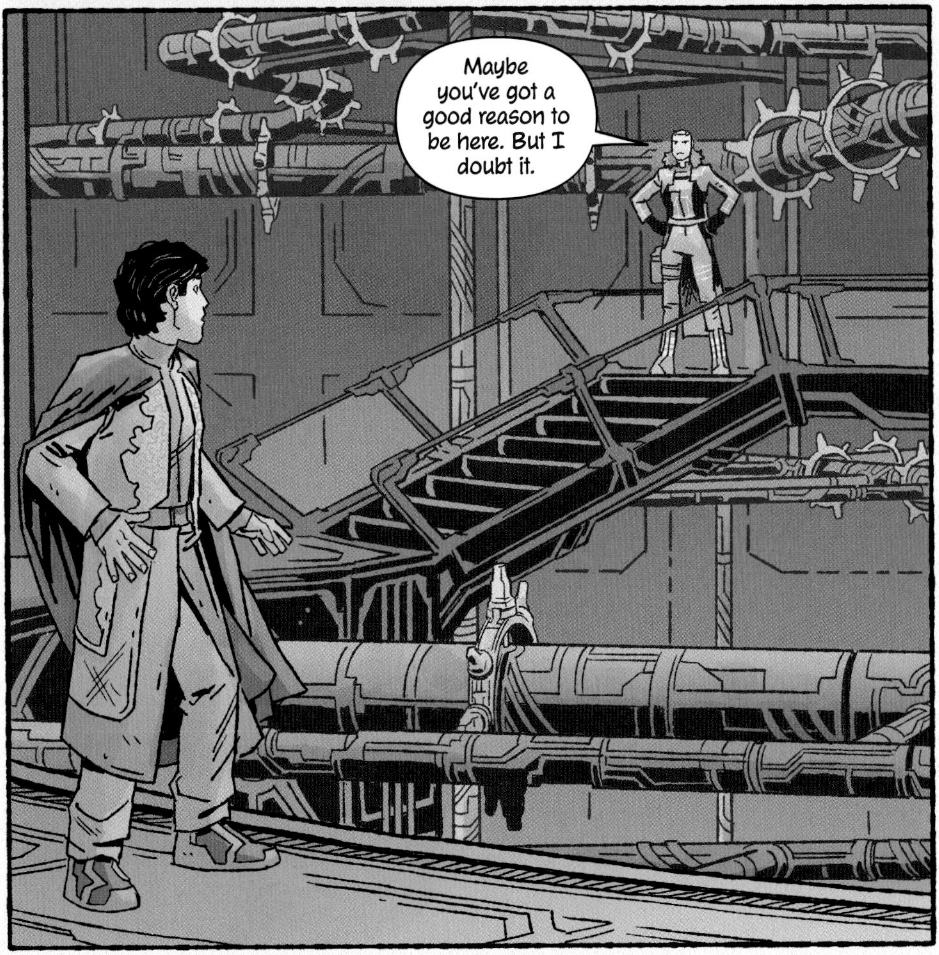
Maybe you've got a good reason to be here. But I doubt it.

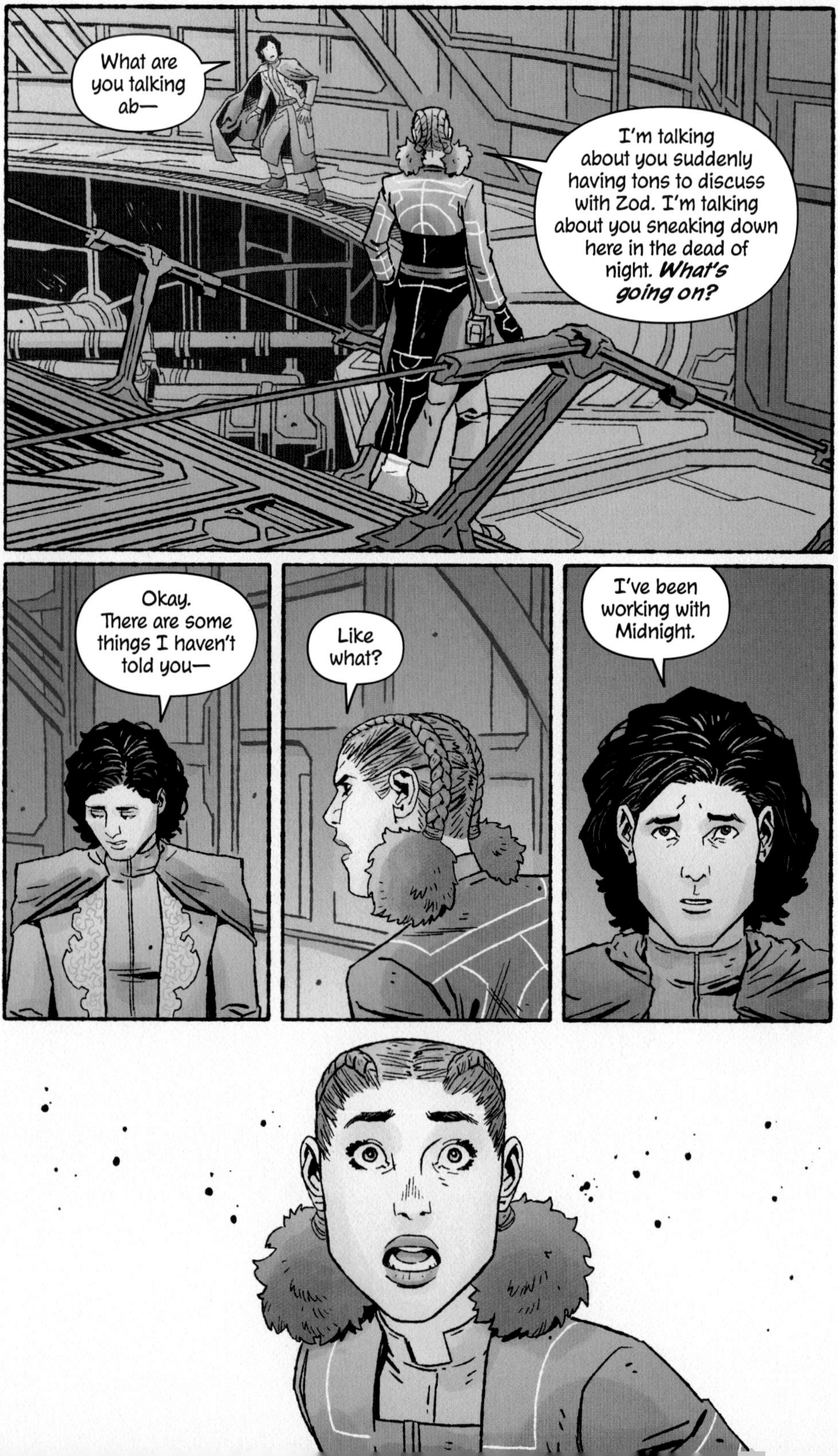
What are you talking ab—
I'm talking about you suddenly having tons to discuss with Zod. I'm talking about you sneaking down here in the dead of night. *What's going on?*
Okay. There are some things I haven't told you—
Like what?
I've been working with Midnight.

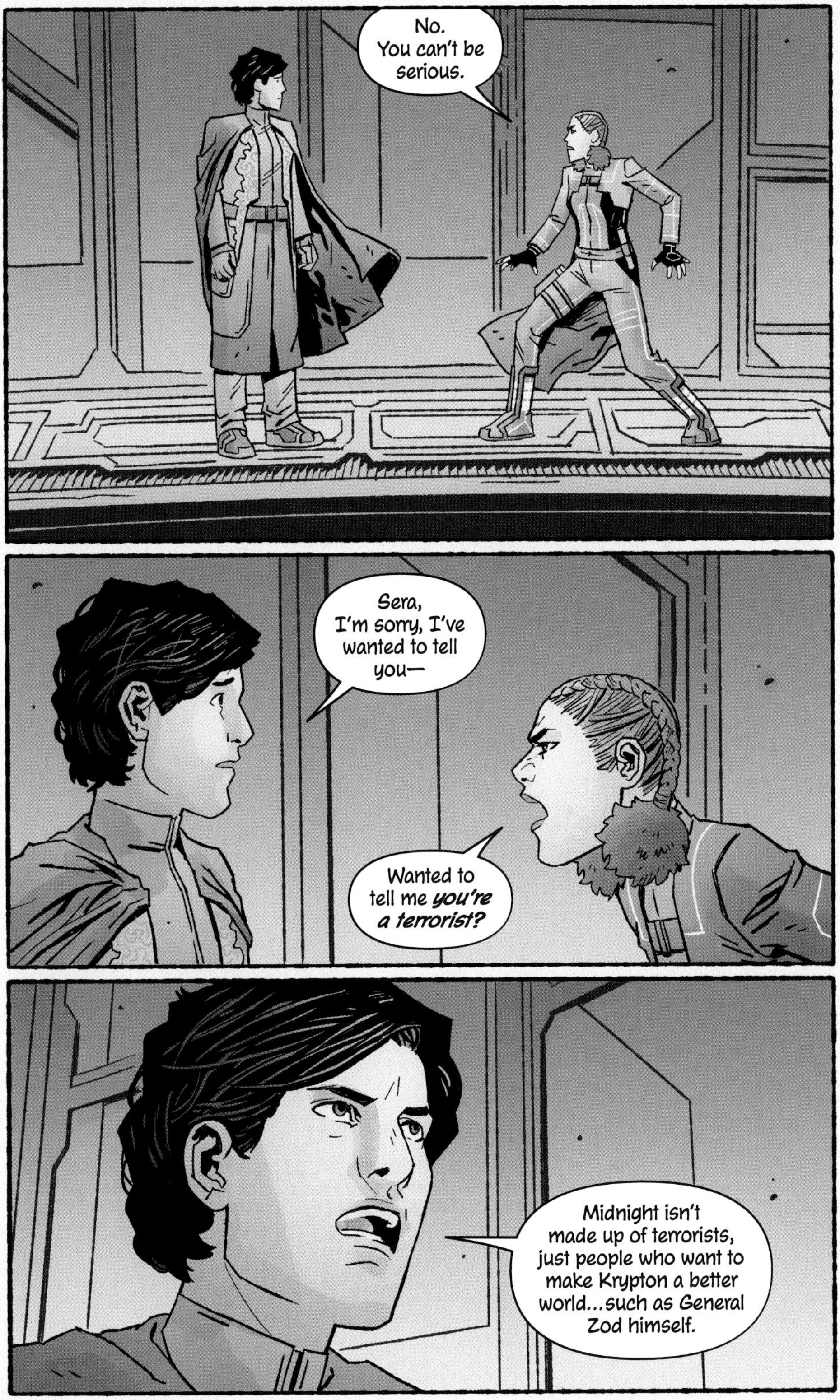
No. You can't be serious.
Sera, I'm sorry, I've wanted to tell you—
Wanted to tell me *you're a terrorist?*
Midnight isn't made up of terrorists, just people who want to make Krypton a better world...such as General Zod himself.

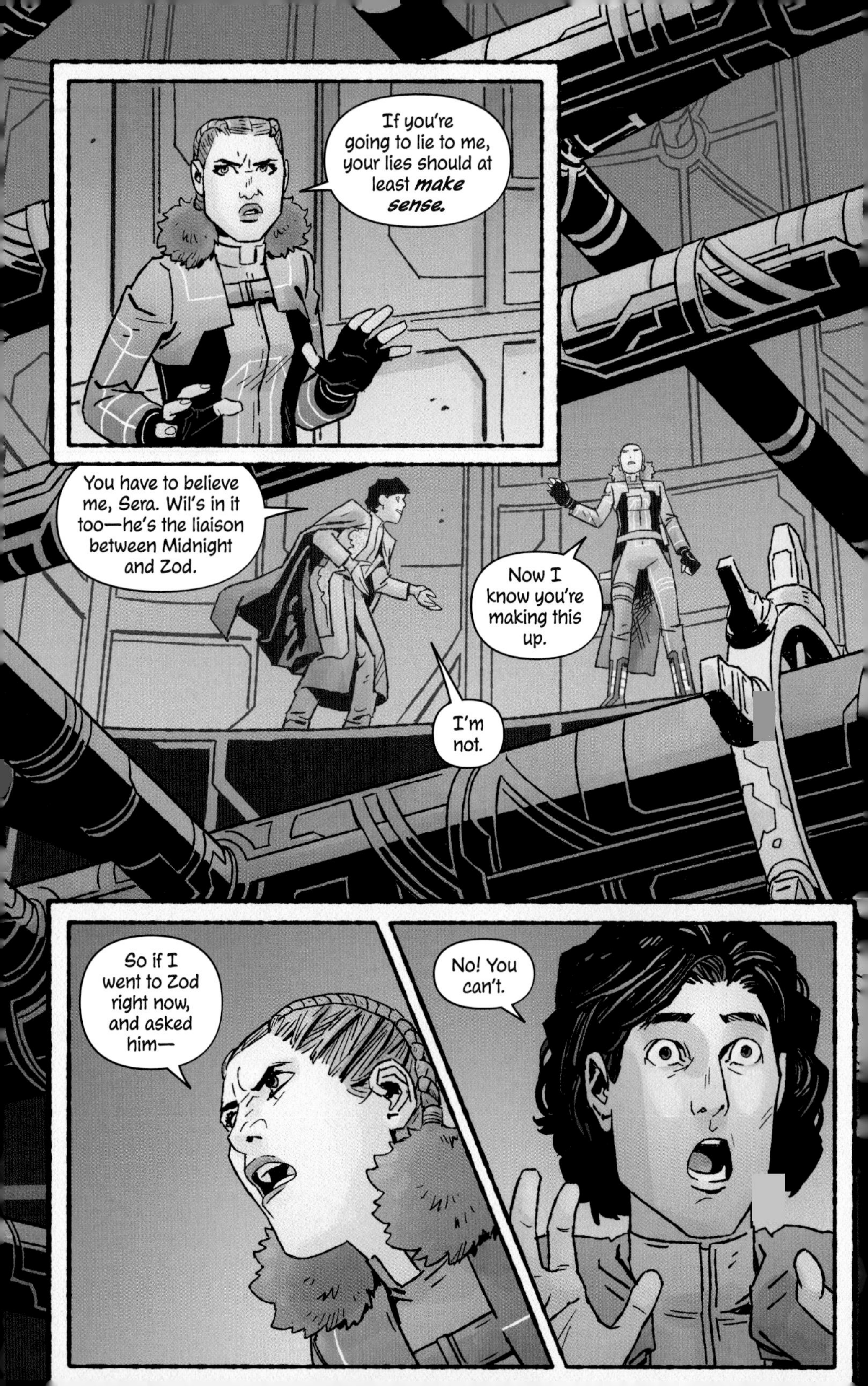
If you're going to lie to me, your lies should at least ***make sense.***
You have to believe me, Sera. Wil's in it too—he's the liaison between Midnight and Zod.
Now I know you're making this up.
I'm not.
So if I went to Zod right now, and asked him—
No! You can't.

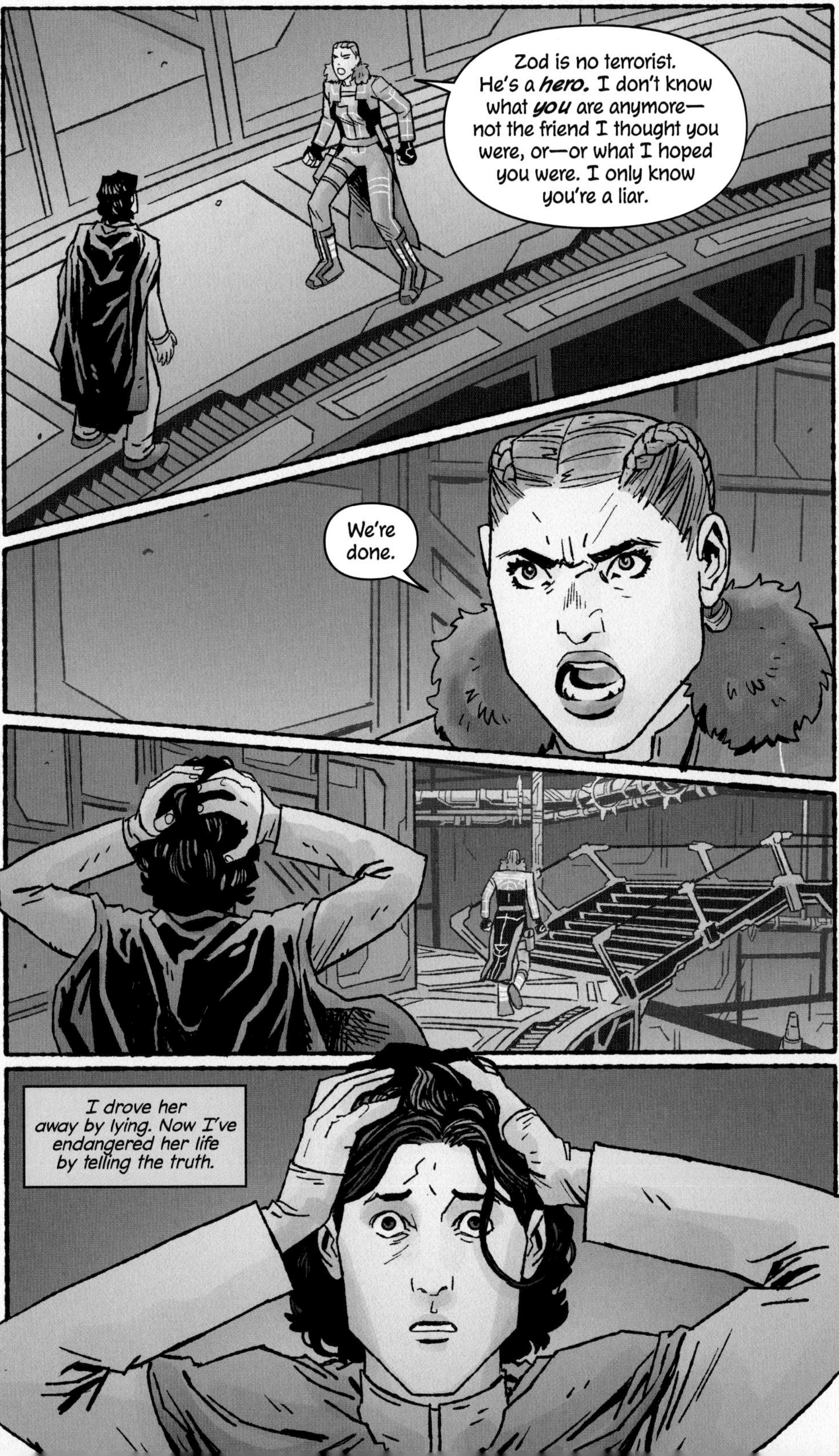
Zod is no terrorist. He's a *hero.* I don't know what *you* are anymore—not the friend I thought you were, or—or what I hoped you were. I only know you're a liar.
We're done.
I drove her away by lying. Now I've endangered her life by telling the truth.

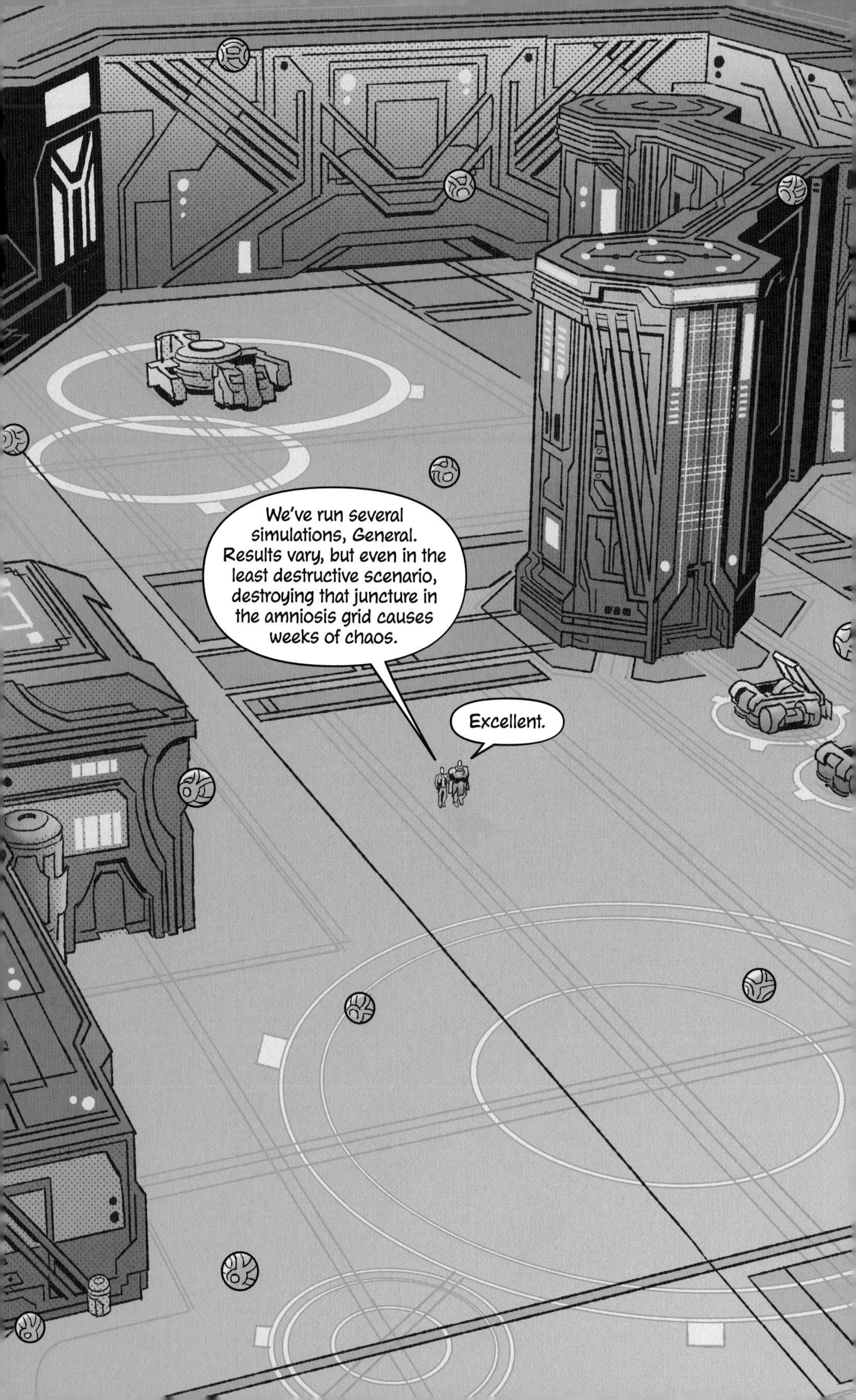
We've run several simulations, General. Results vary, but even in the least destructive scenario, destroying that juncture in the amniosis grid causes weeks of chaos.
Excellent.

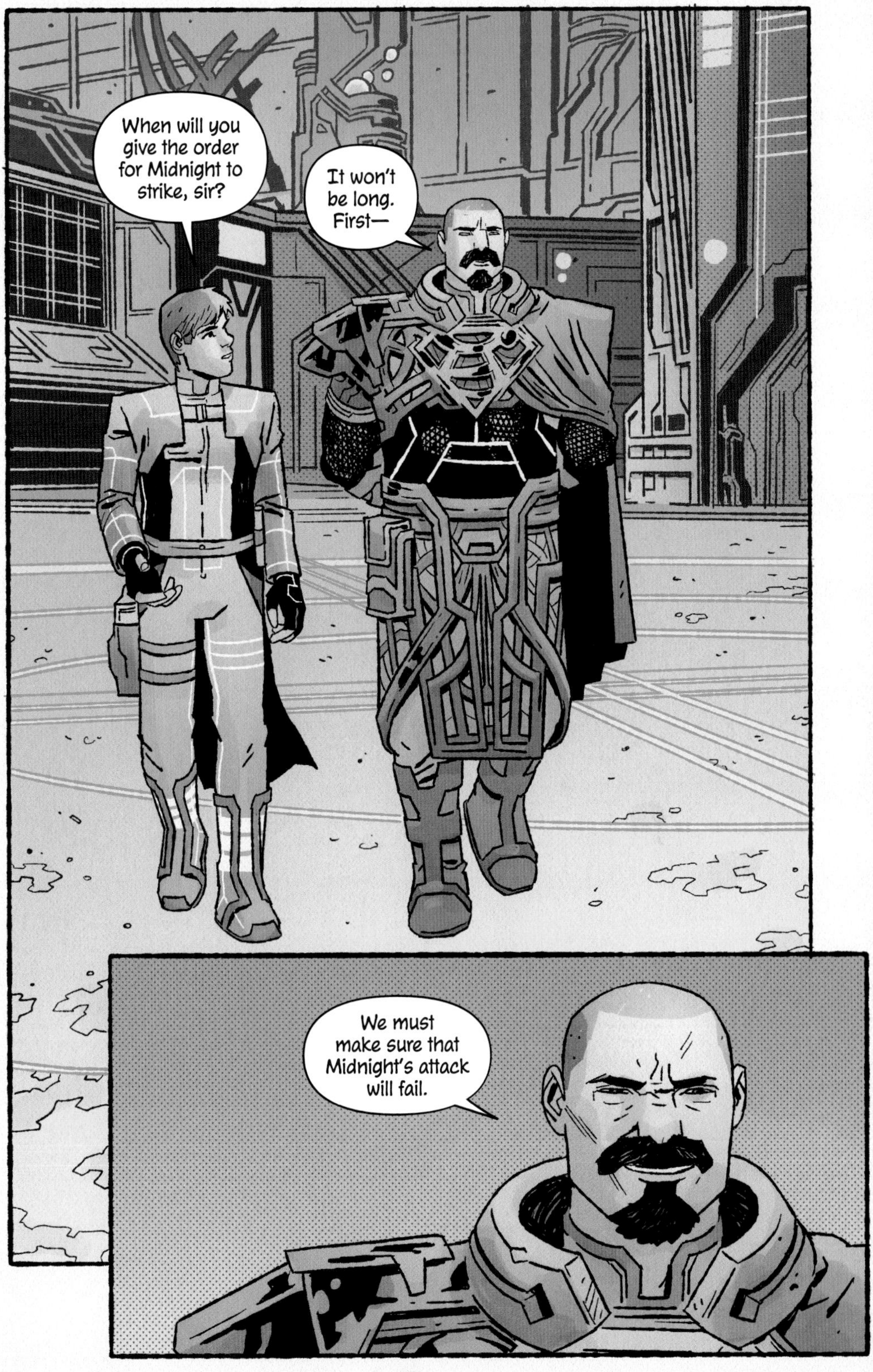
When will you give the order for Midnight to strike, sir?
It won't be long. First—
We must make sure that Midnight's attack will fail.

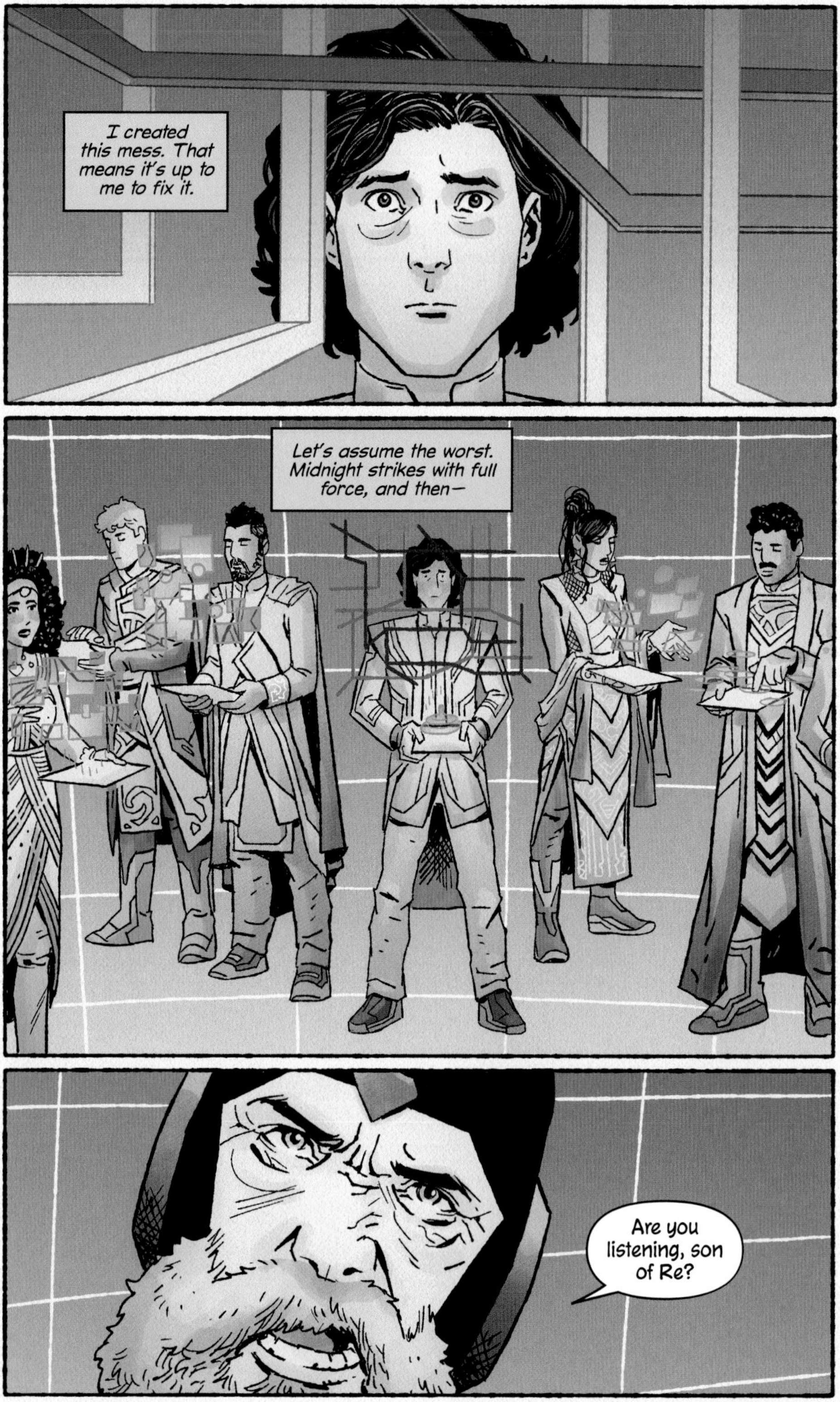
I created this mess. That means it's up to me to fix it.
Let's assume the worst. Midnight strikes with full force, and then—
Are you listening, son of Re?

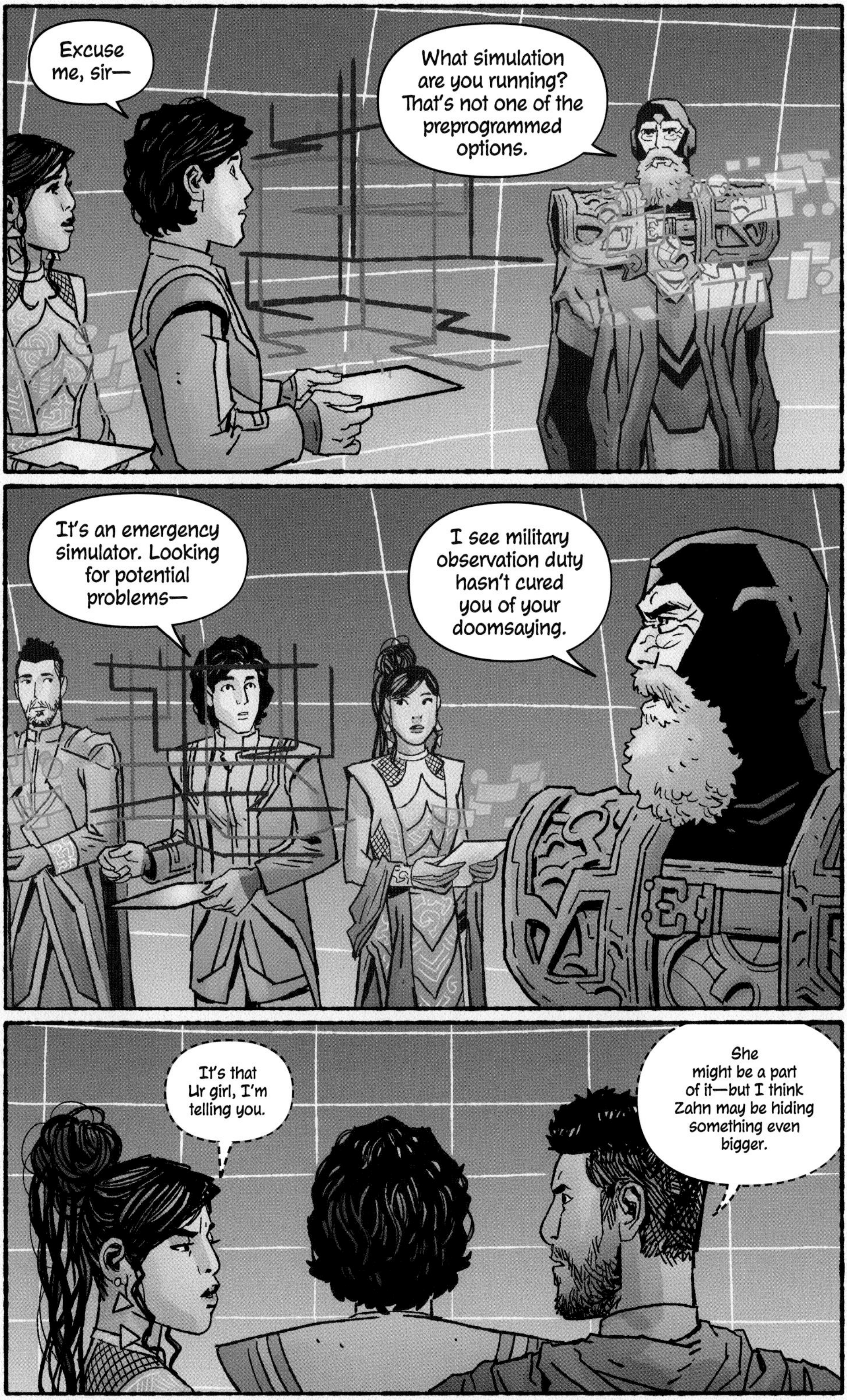
Excuse me, sir—
What simulation are you running? That's not one of the preprogrammed options.
It's an emergency simulator. Looking for potential problems—
I see military observation duty hasn't cured you of your doomsaying.
It's that Ur girl, I'm telling you.
She might be a part of it—but I think Zahn may be hiding something even bigger.

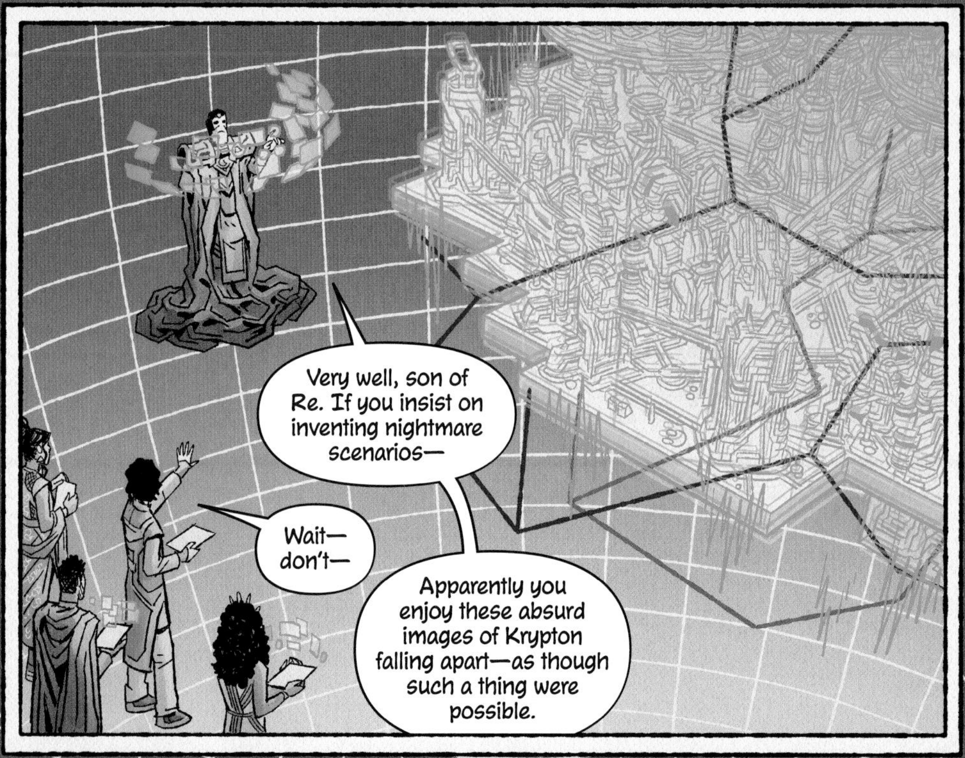
Very well, son of Re. If you insist on inventing nightmare scenarios—
Wait—don't—
Apparently you enjoy these absurd images of Krypton falling apart—as though such a thing were possible.

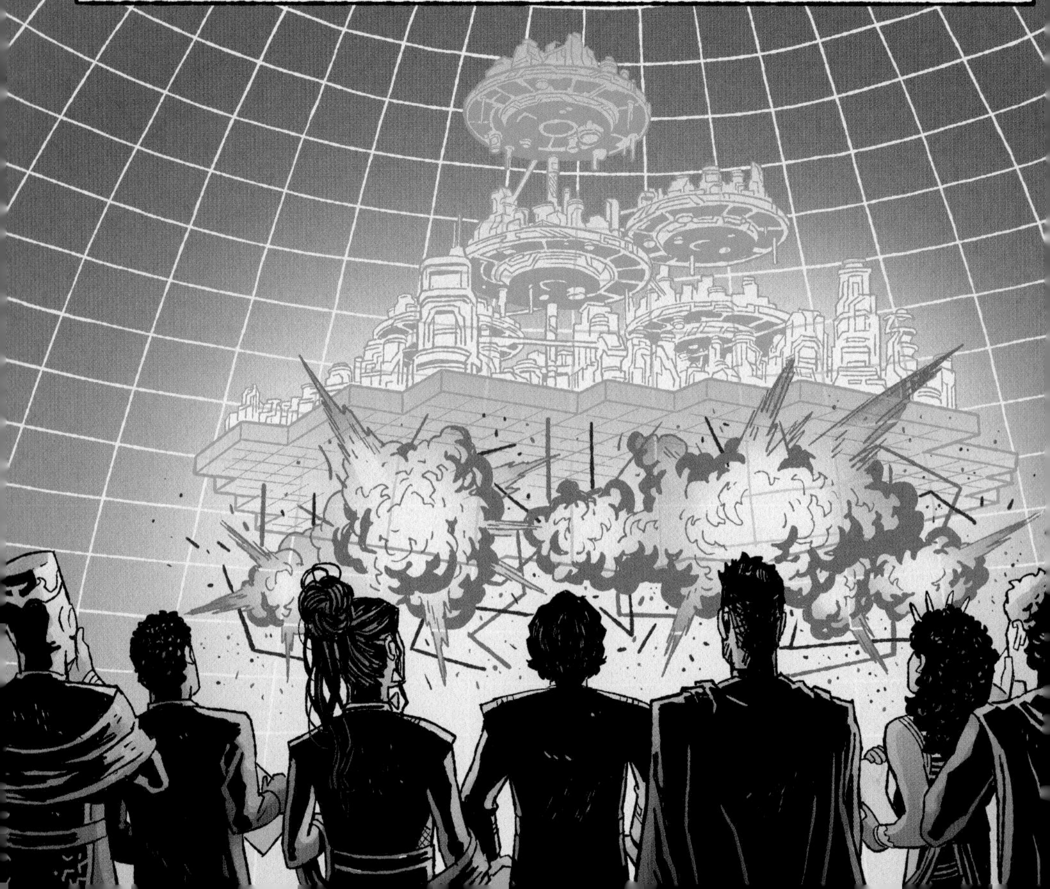

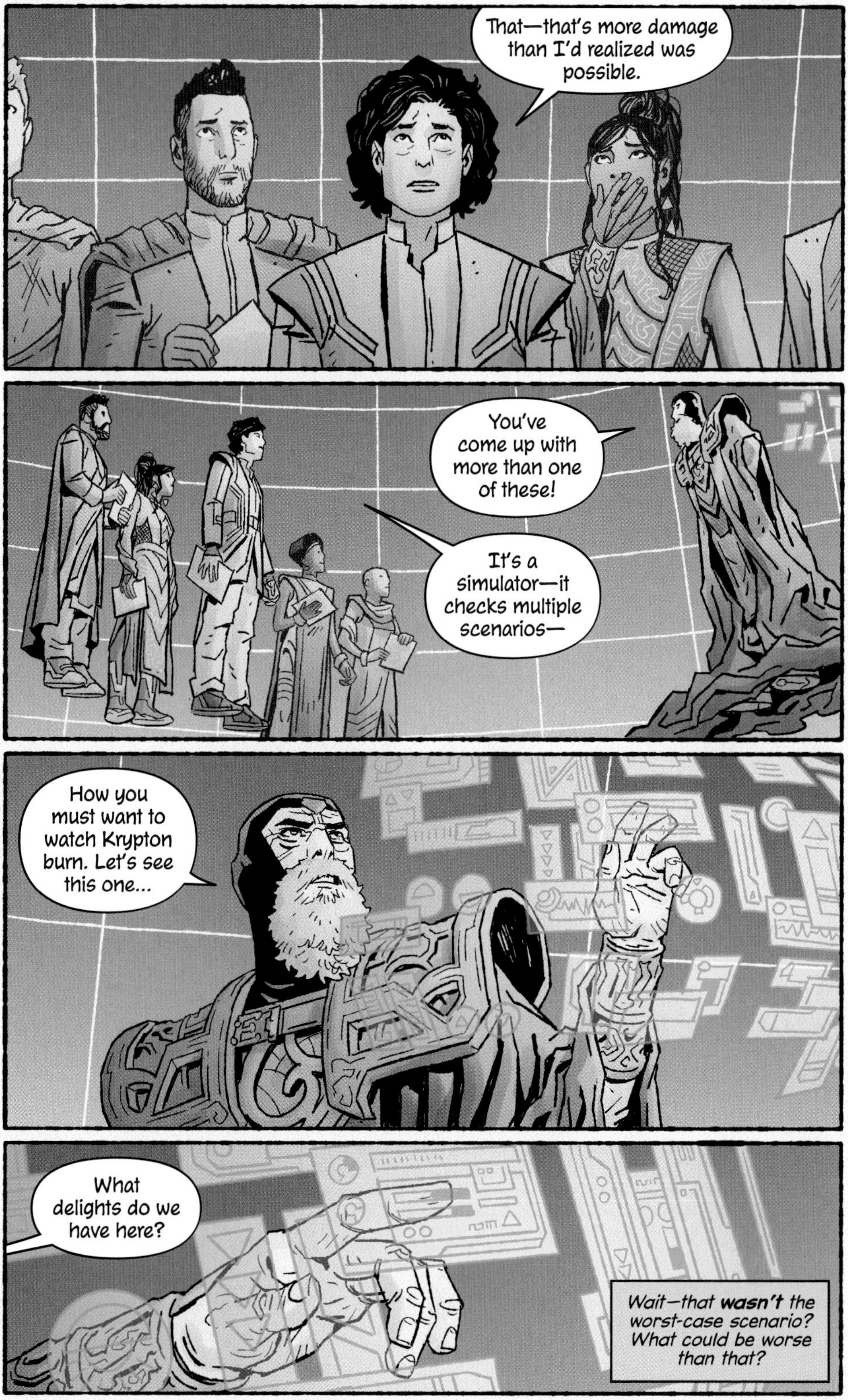
That—that's more damage than I'd realized was possible.
You've come up with more than one of these!
It's a simulator—it checks multiple scenarios—
How you must want to watch Krypton burn. Let's see this one...
What delights do we have here?
*Wait—that **wasn't** the worst-case scenario? What could be worse than that?*

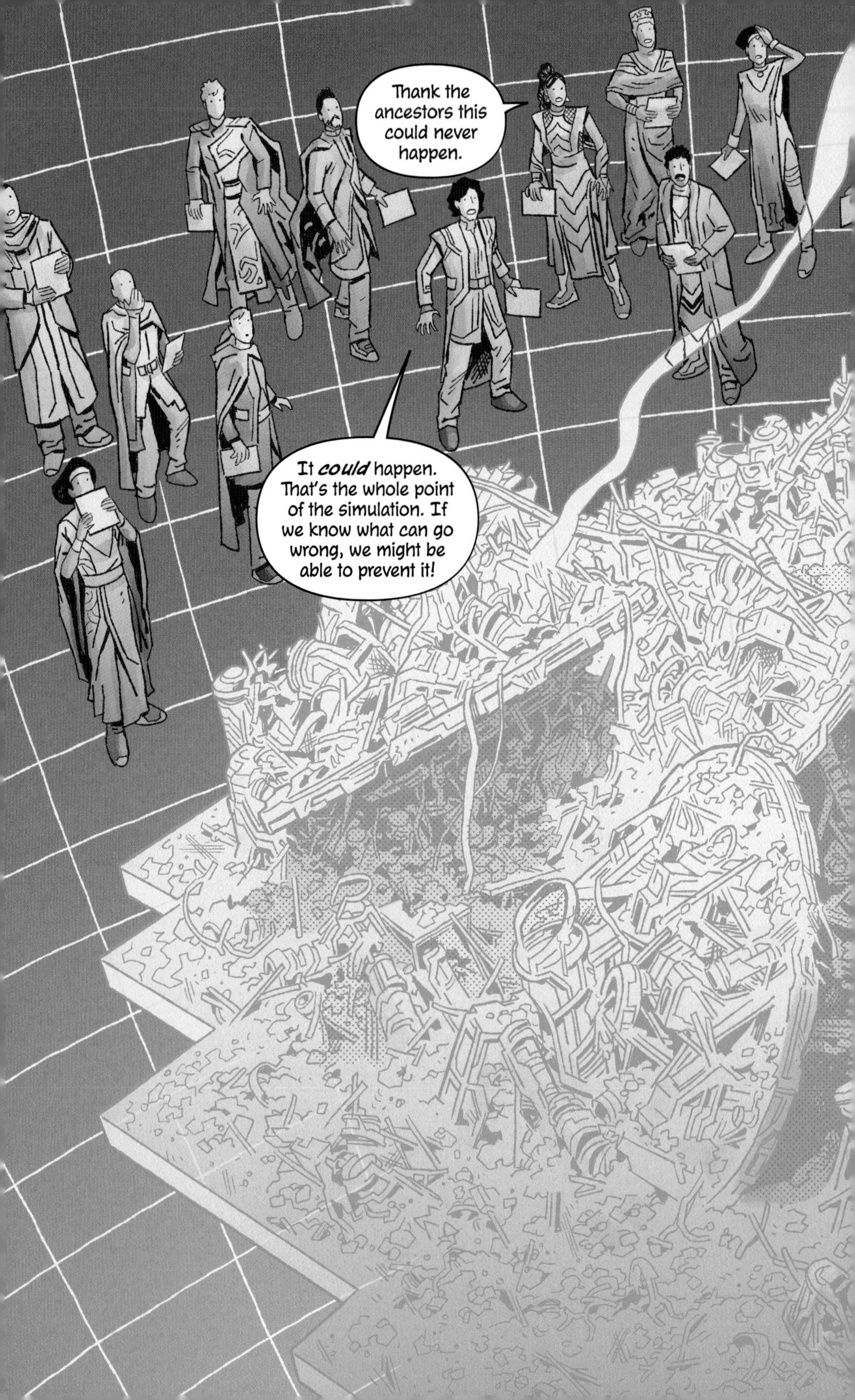
Thank the ancestors this could never happen.
It *could* happen. That's the whole point of the simulation. If we know what can go wrong, we might be able to prevent it!

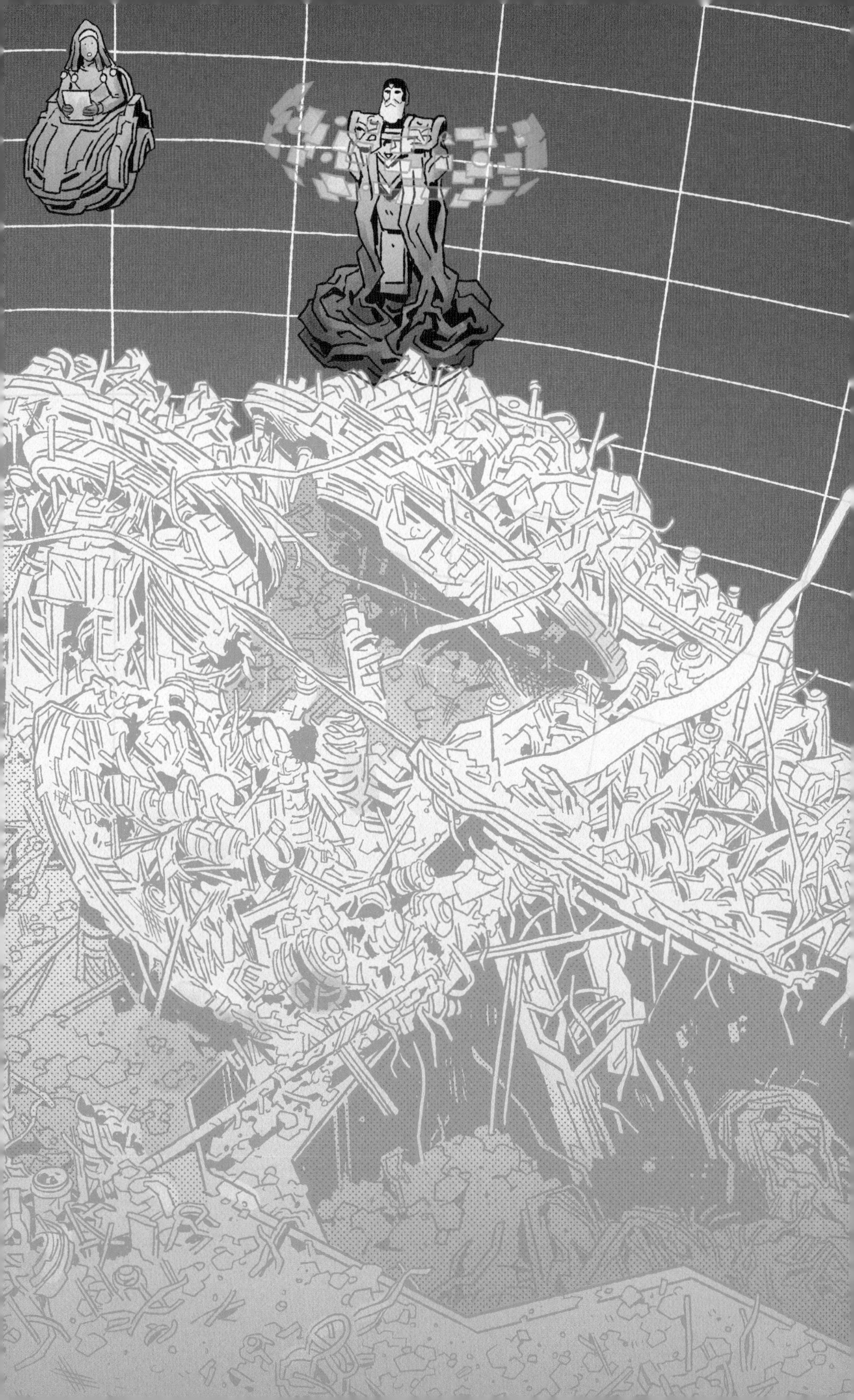

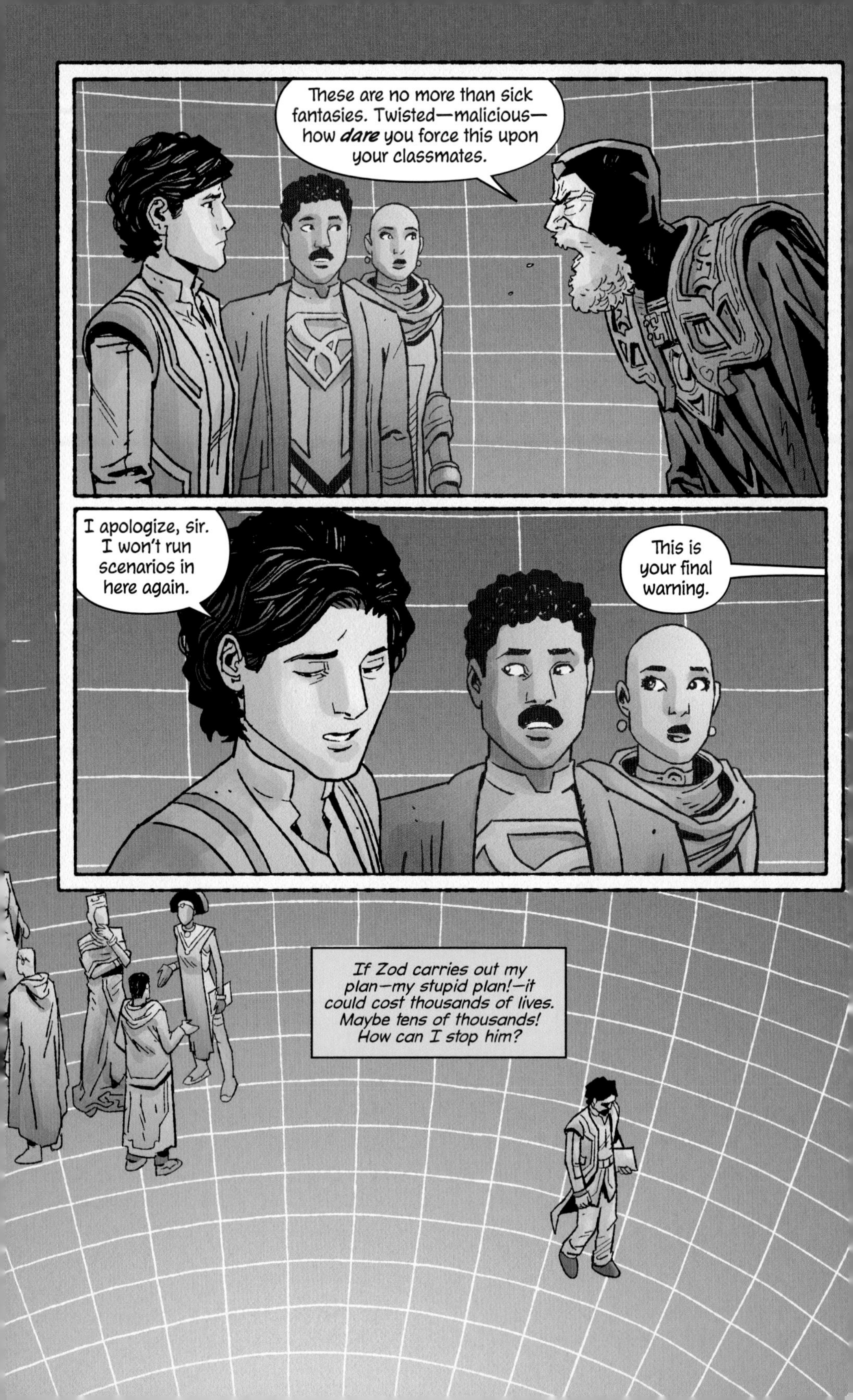
These are no more than sick fantasies. Twisted—malicious—how *dare* you force this upon your classmates.
I apologize, sir. I won't run scenarios in here again.
This is your final warning.
If Zod carries out my plan—my stupid plan!—it could cost thousands of lives. Maybe tens of thousands! How can I stop him?

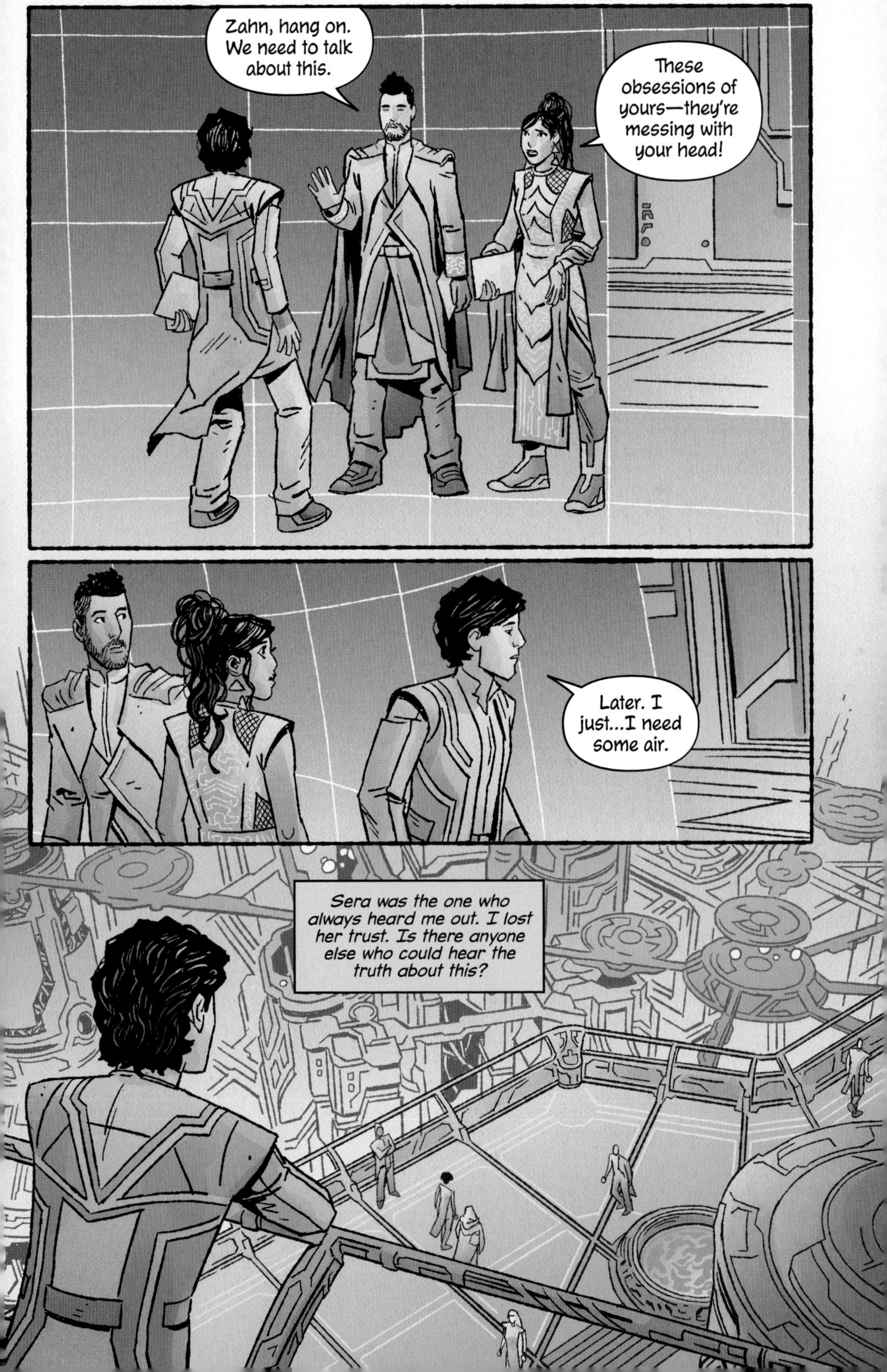
Zahn, hang on. We need to talk about this.
These obsessions of yours—they're messing with your head!
Later. I just...I need some air.
Sera was the one who always heard me out. I lost her trust. Is there anyone else who could hear the truth about this?

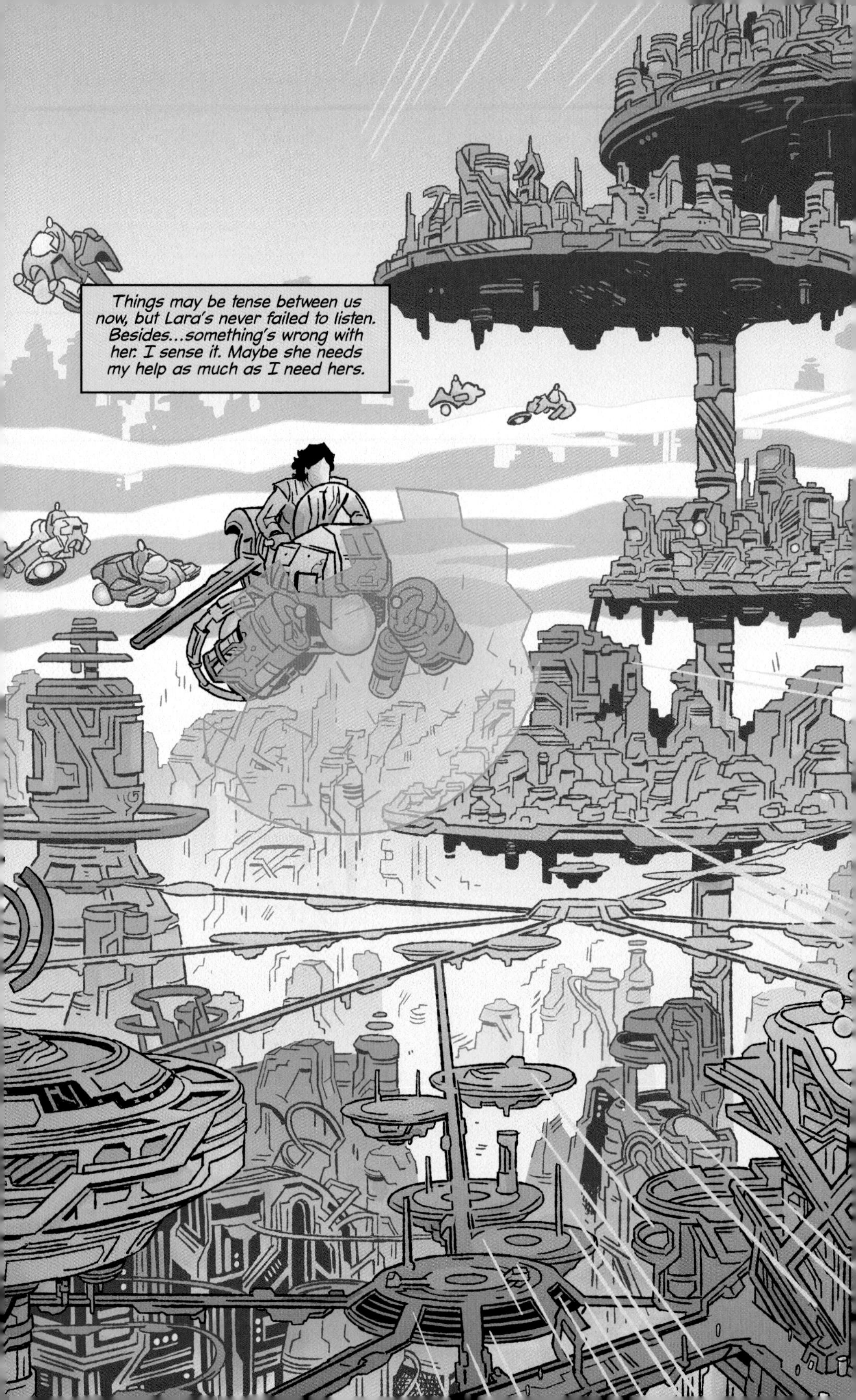
Things may be tense between us now, but Lara's never failed to listen. Besides...something's wrong with her. I sense it. Maybe she needs my help as much as I need hers.

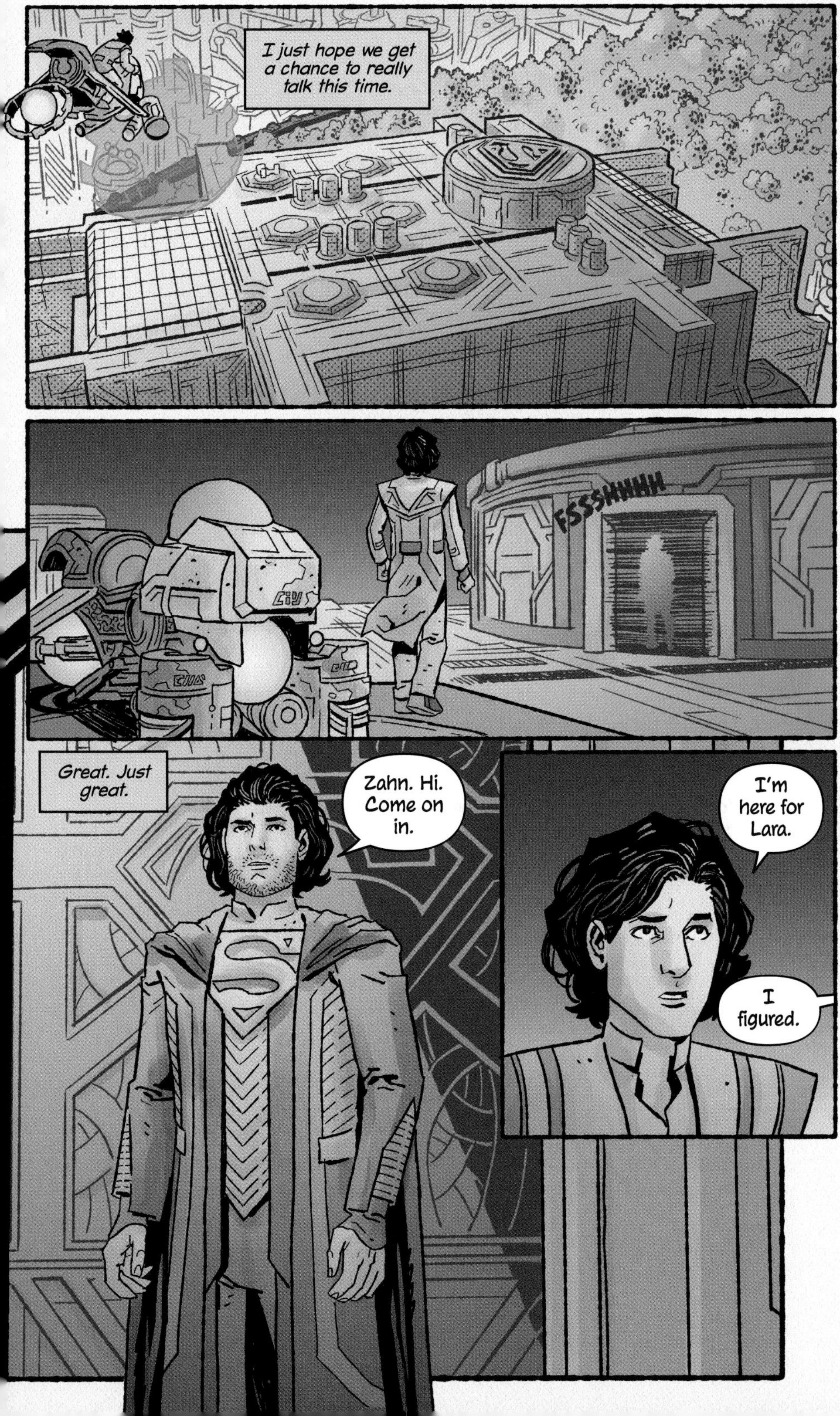
I just hope we get a chance to really talk this time.
FSSSHHHH
Great. Just great.
Zahn. Hi. Come on in.
I'm here for Lara.
I figured.

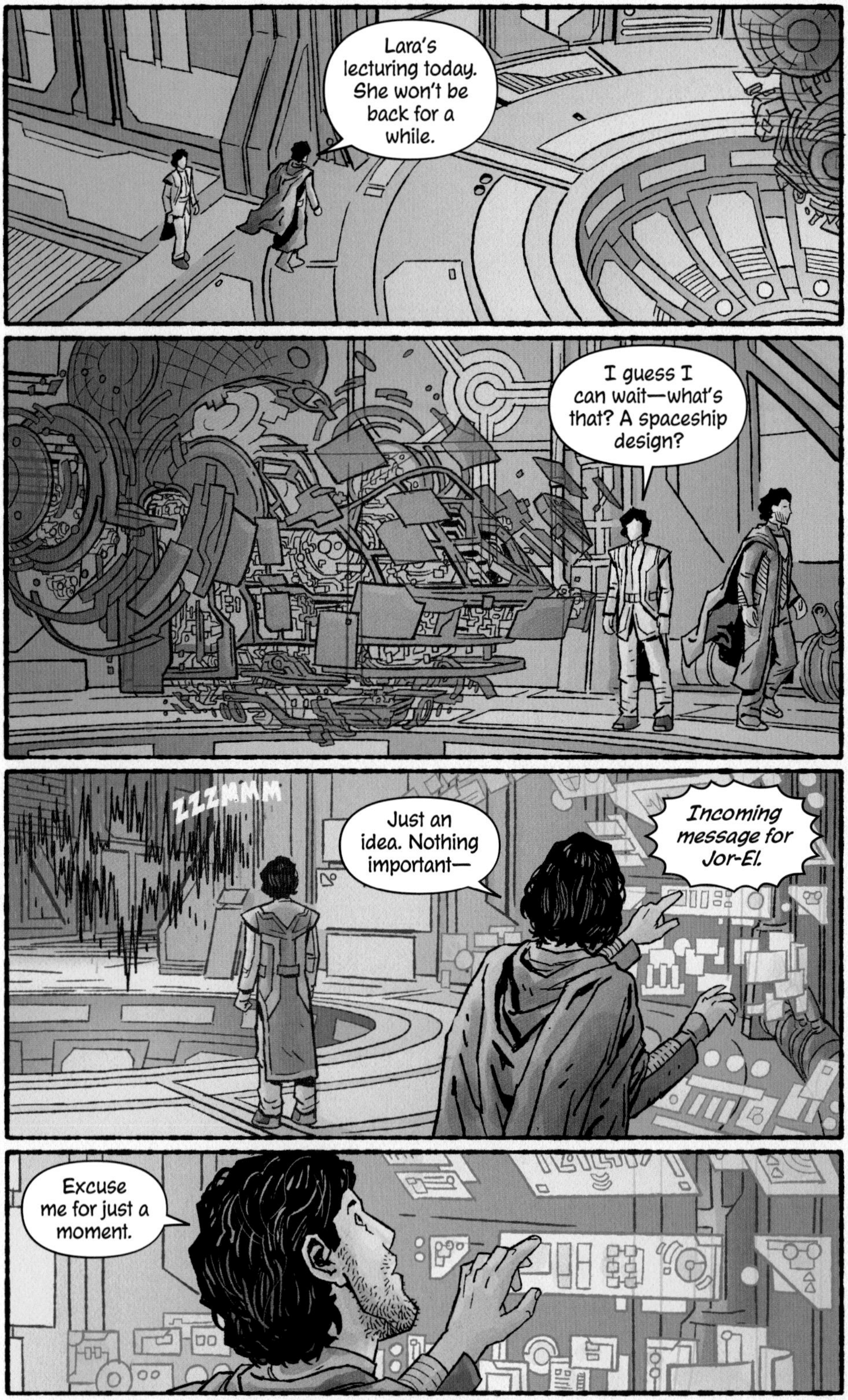
Lara's lecturing today. She won't be back for a while.
I guess I can wait—what's that? A spaceship design?
ZZZMMM
Just an idea. Nothing important—
Incoming message for Jor-El.
Excuse me for just a moment.

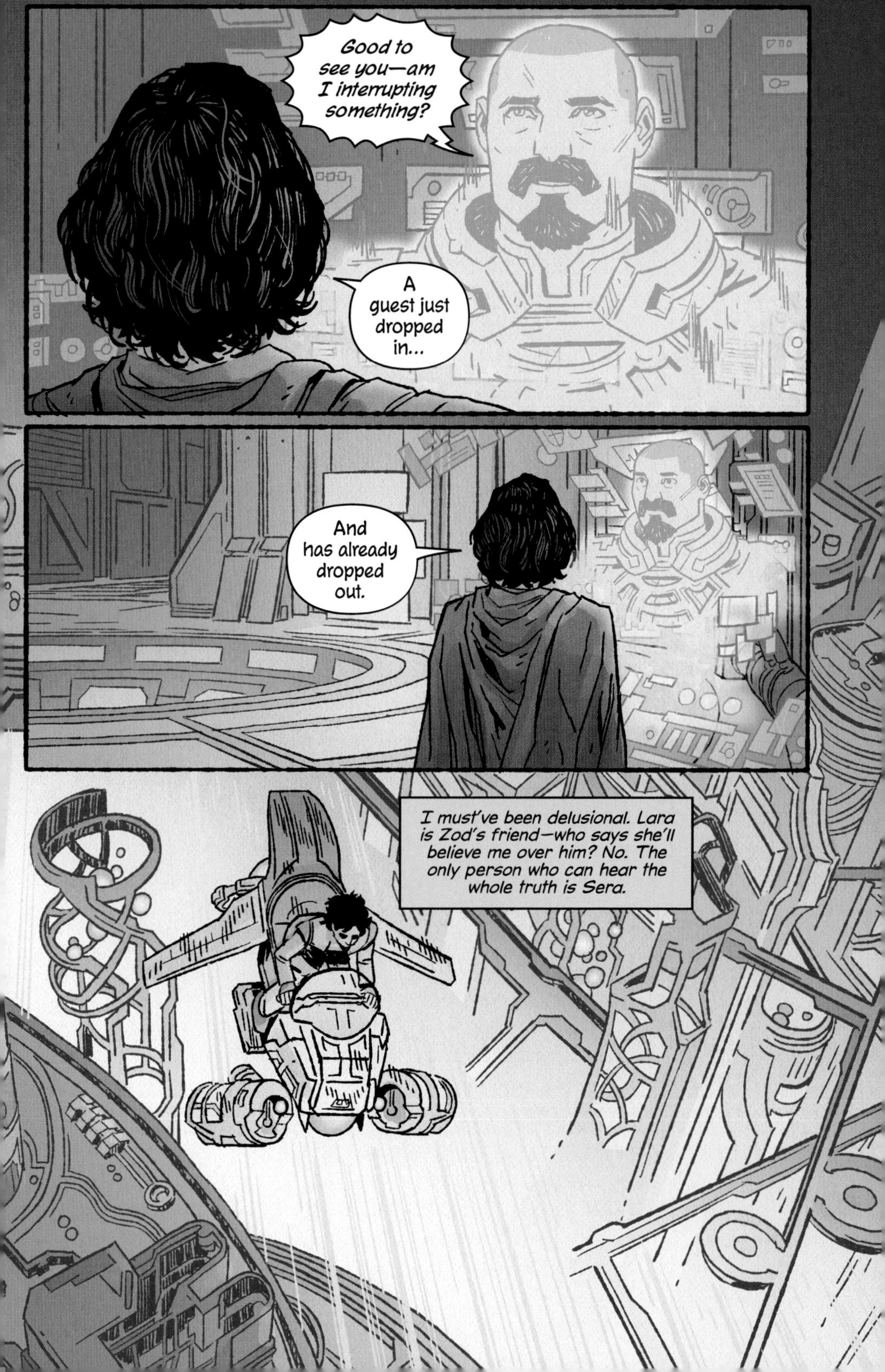
Good to see you—am I interrupting something?
A guest just dropped in...
And has already dropped out.
I must've been delusional. Lara is Zod's friend—who says she'll believe me over him? No. The only person who can hear the whole truth is Sera.

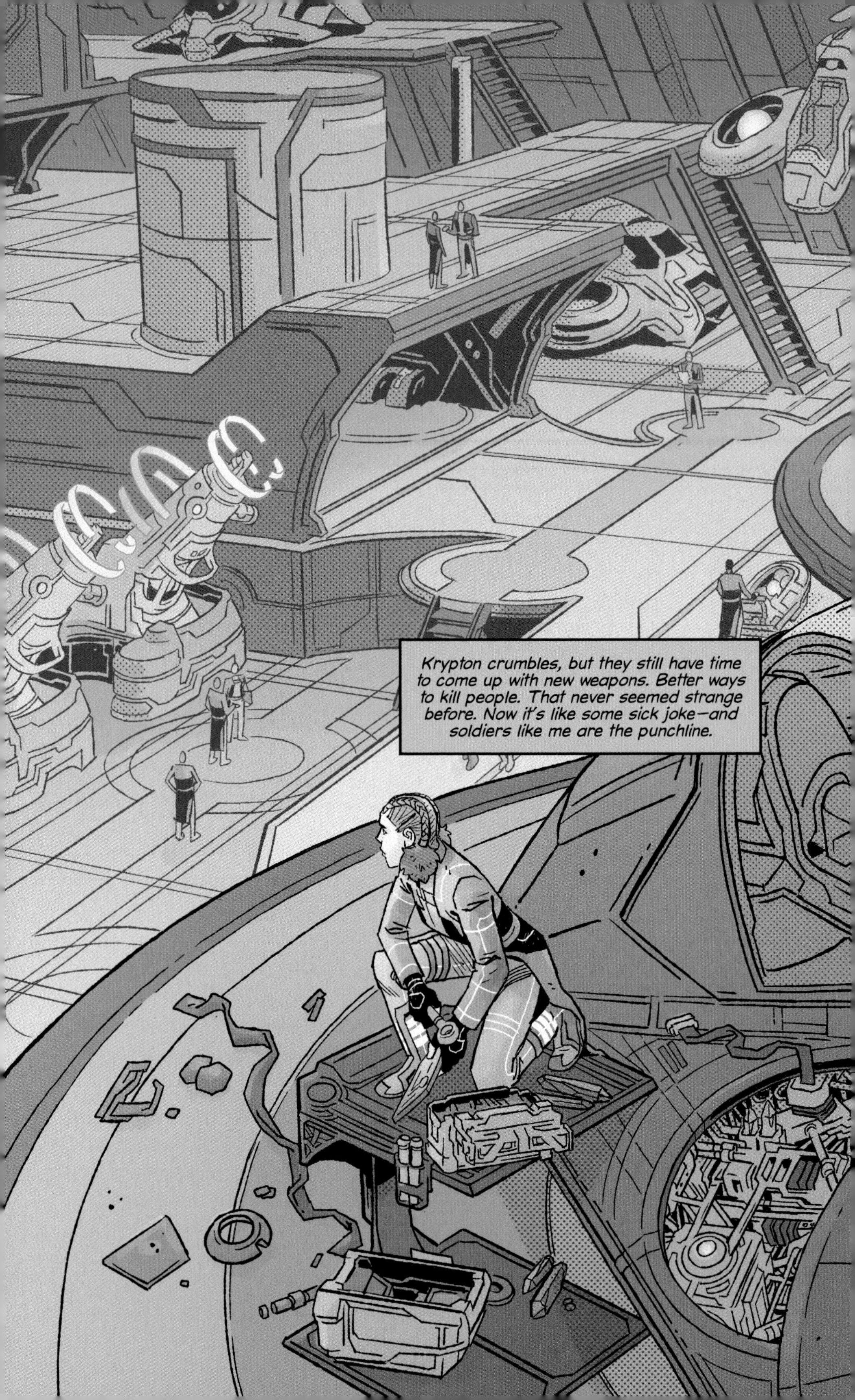
Krypton crumbles, but they still have time to come up with new weapons. Better ways to kill people. That never seemed strange before. Now it's like some sick joke—and soldiers like me are the punchline.

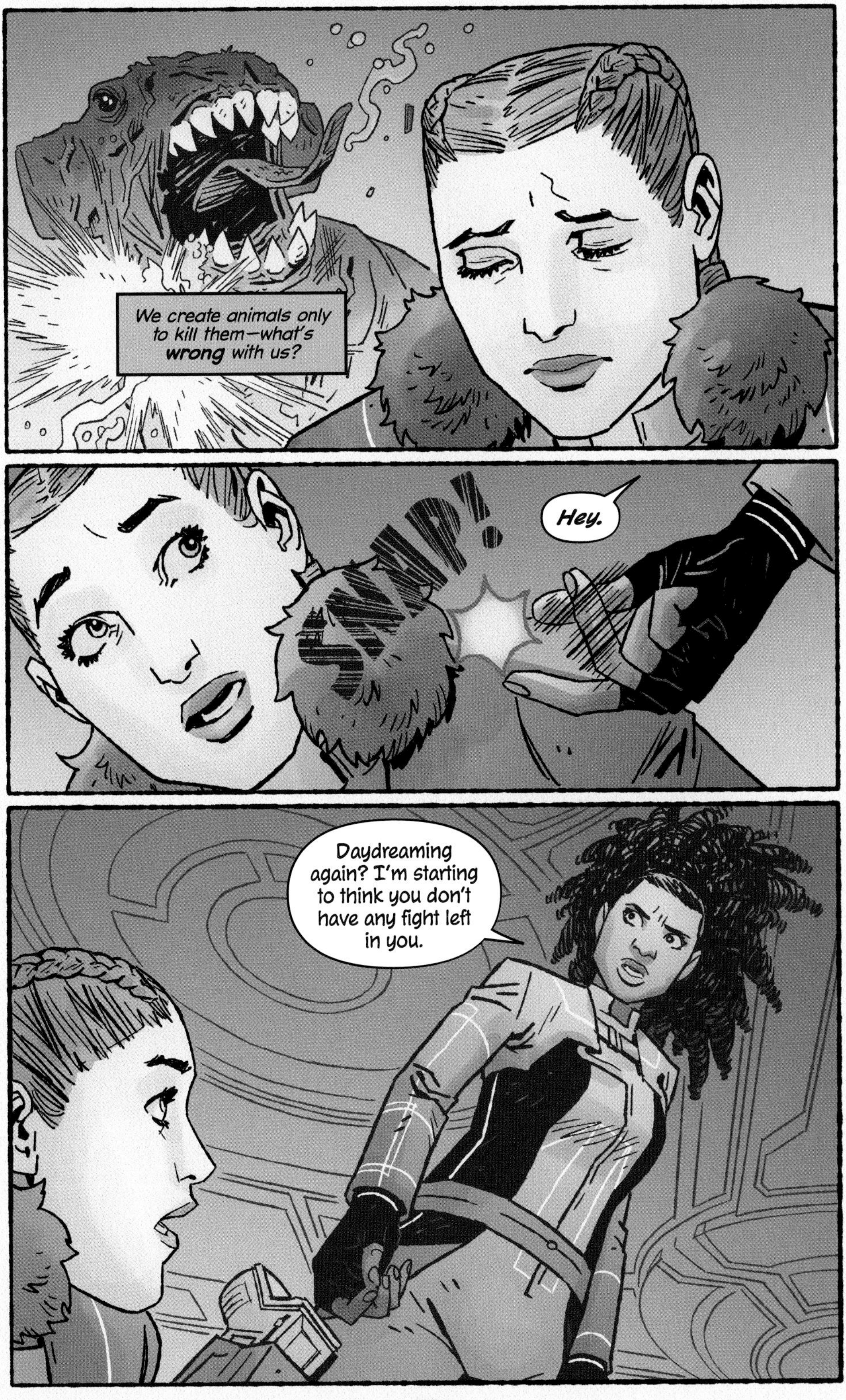
We create animals only to kill them—what's **wrong** with us?
SNAP!
Hey.
Daydreaming again? I'm starting to think you don't have any fight left in you.

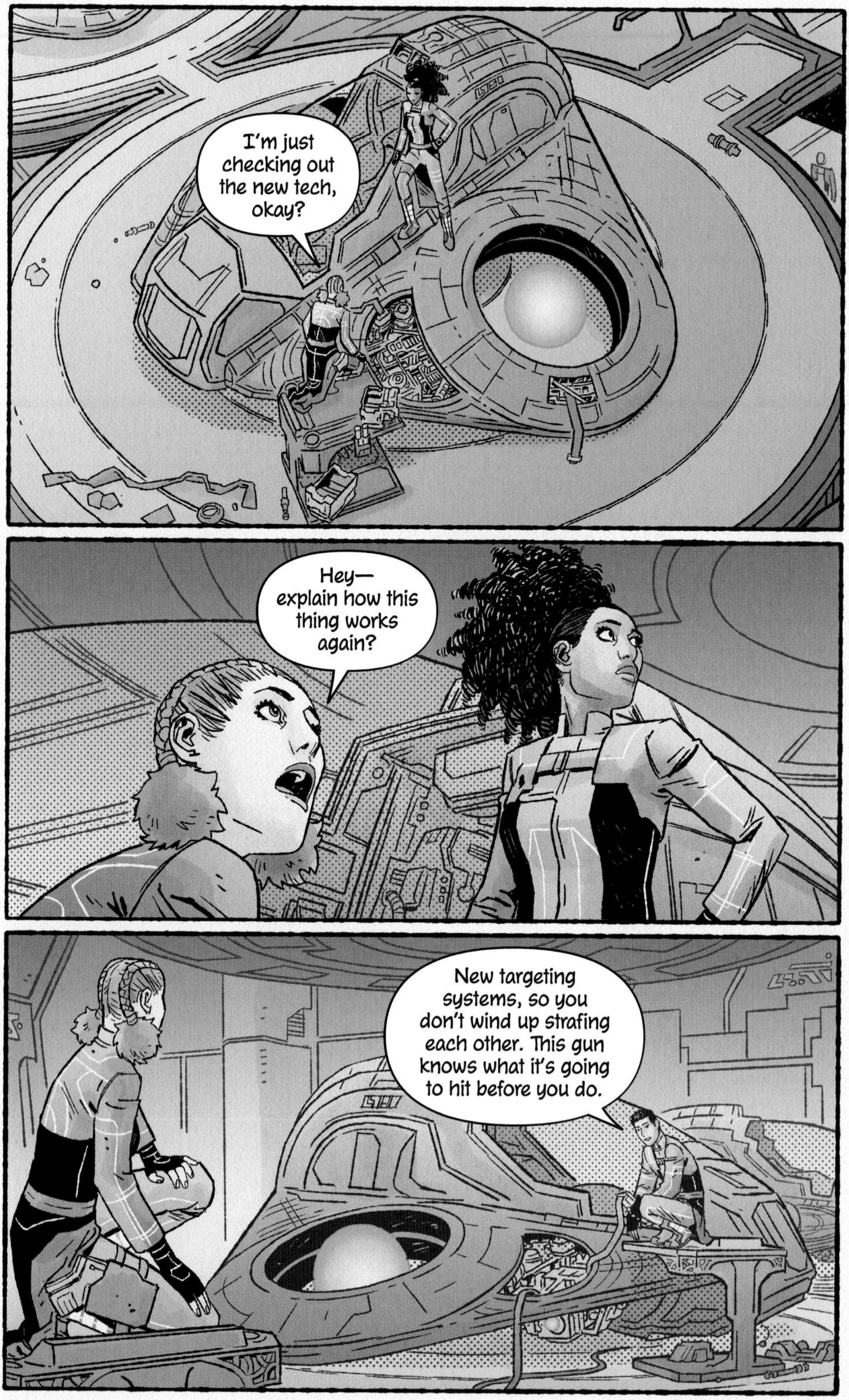
I'm just checking out the new tech, okay?
Hey— explain how this thing works again?
New targeting systems, so you don't wind up strafing each other. This gun knows what it's going to hit before you do.

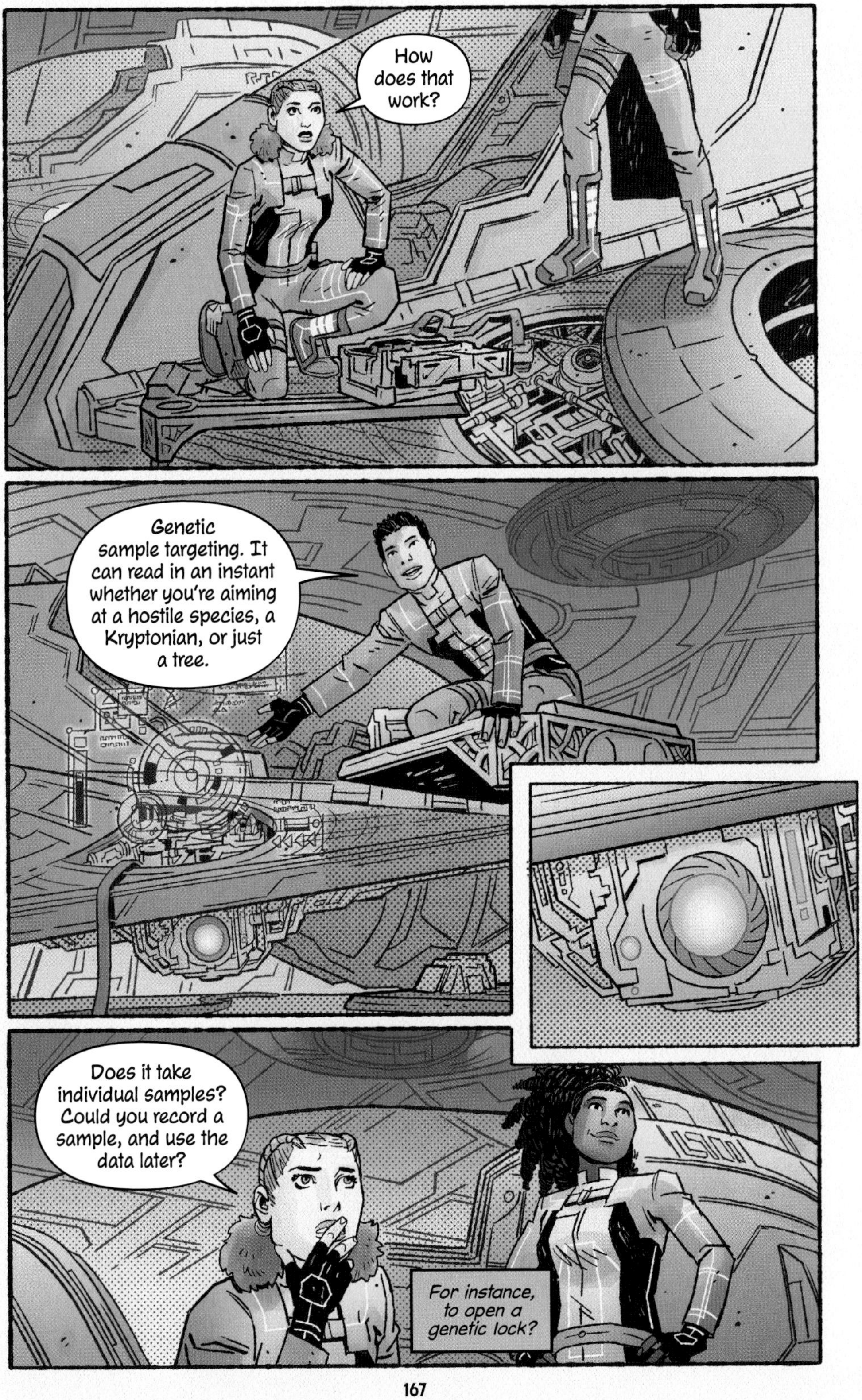
How does that work?
Genetic sample targeting. It can read in an instant whether you're aiming at a hostile species, a Kryptonian, or just a tree.
Does it take individual samples? Could you record a sample, and use the data later?
For instance, to open a genetic lock?

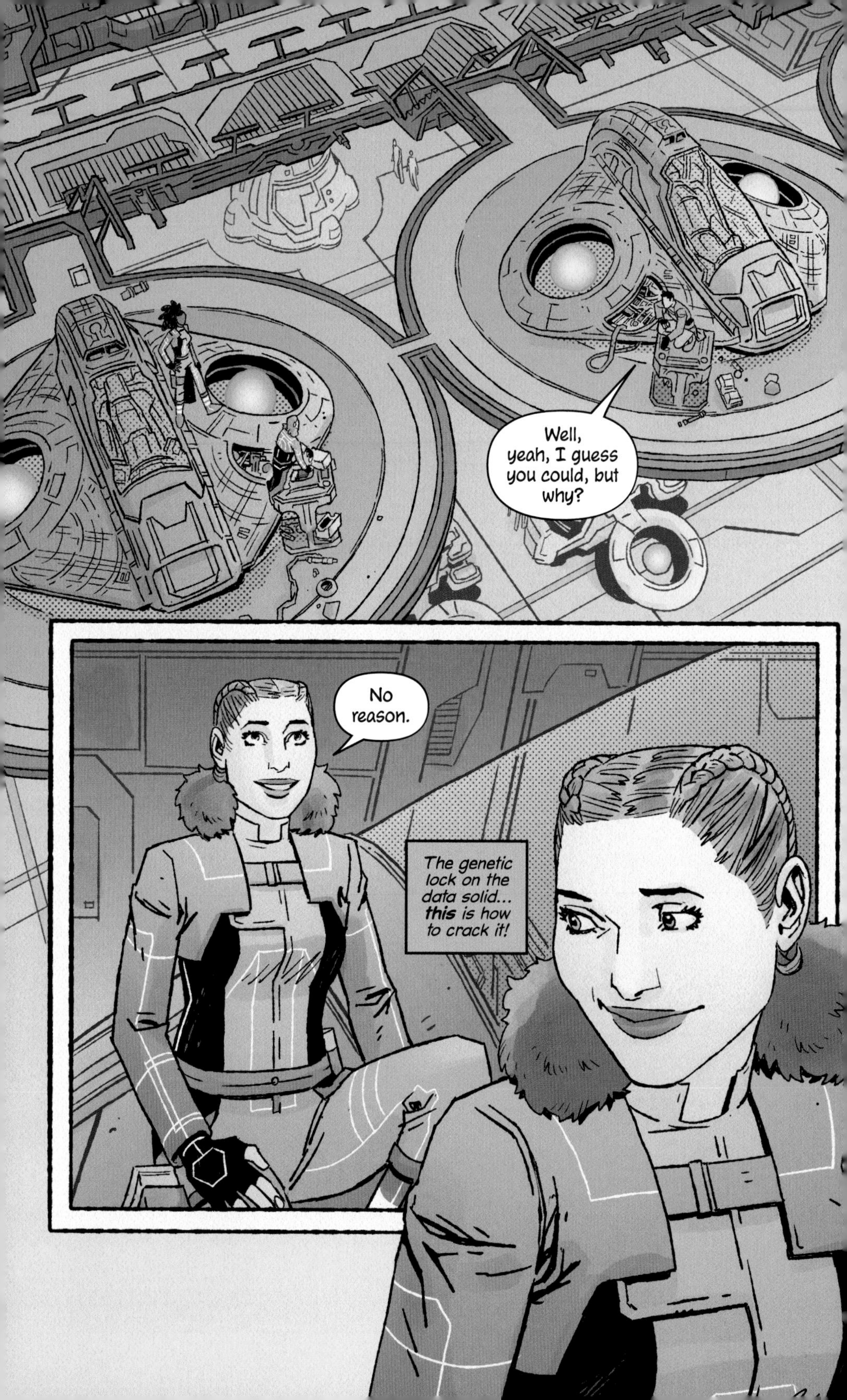
Well, yeah, I guess you could, but why?
No reason.
The genetic lock on the data solid... **this** is how to crack it!

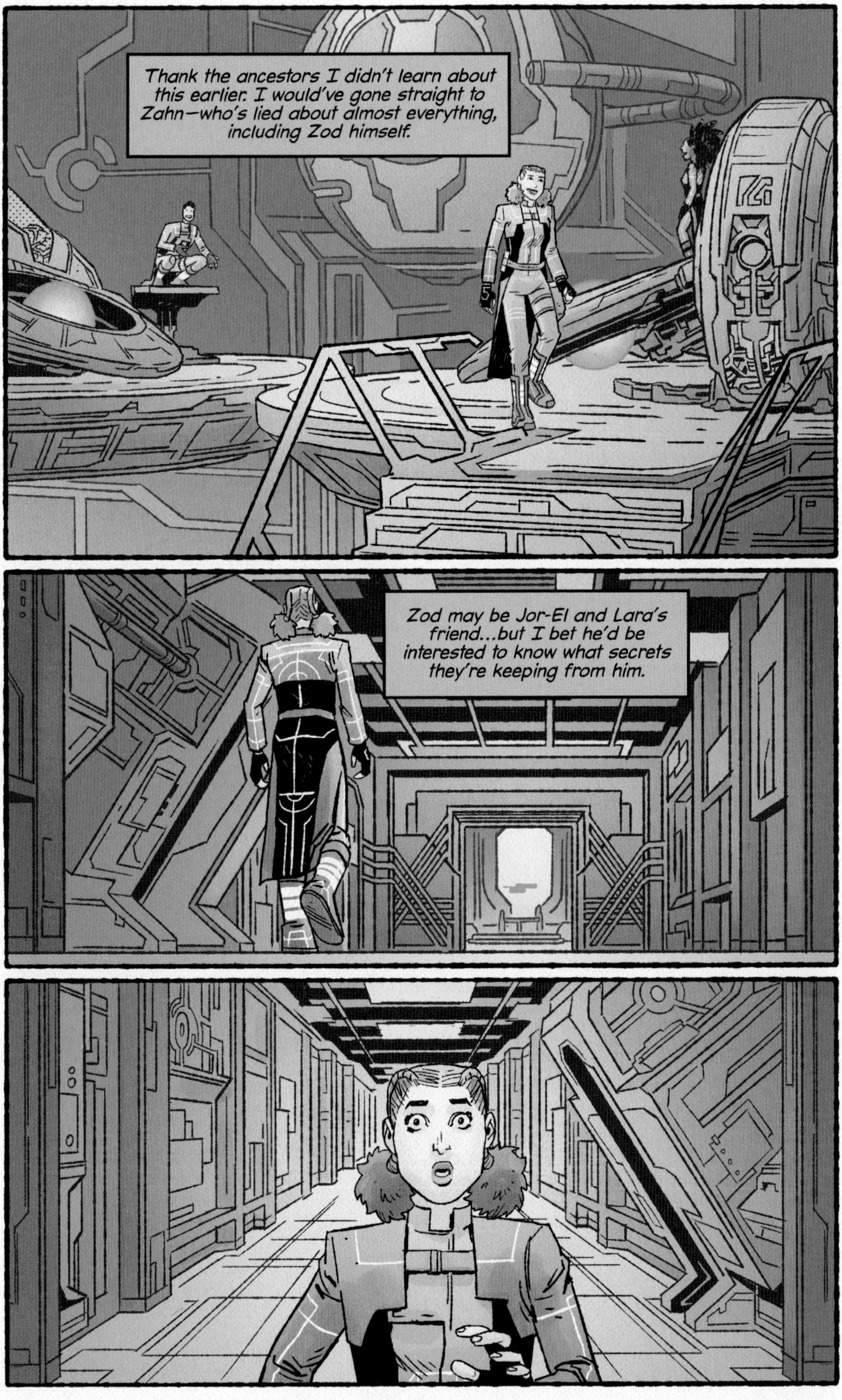

Thank the ancestors I didn't learn about this earlier. I would've gone straight to Zahn—who's lied about almost everything, including Zod himself.
Zod may be Jor-El and Lara's friend...but I bet he'd be interested to know what secrets they're keeping from him.

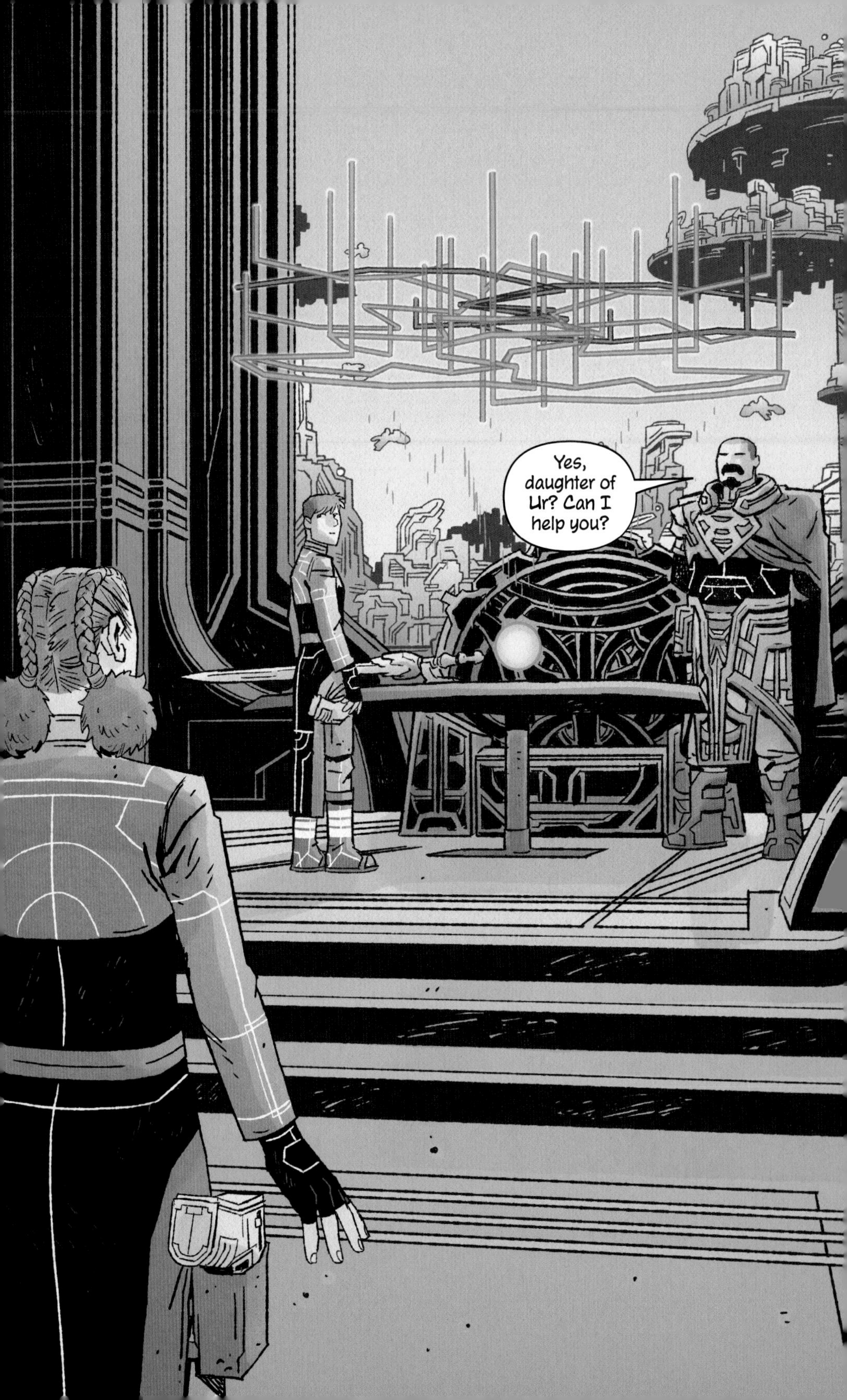
Yes, daughter of Ur? Can I help you?

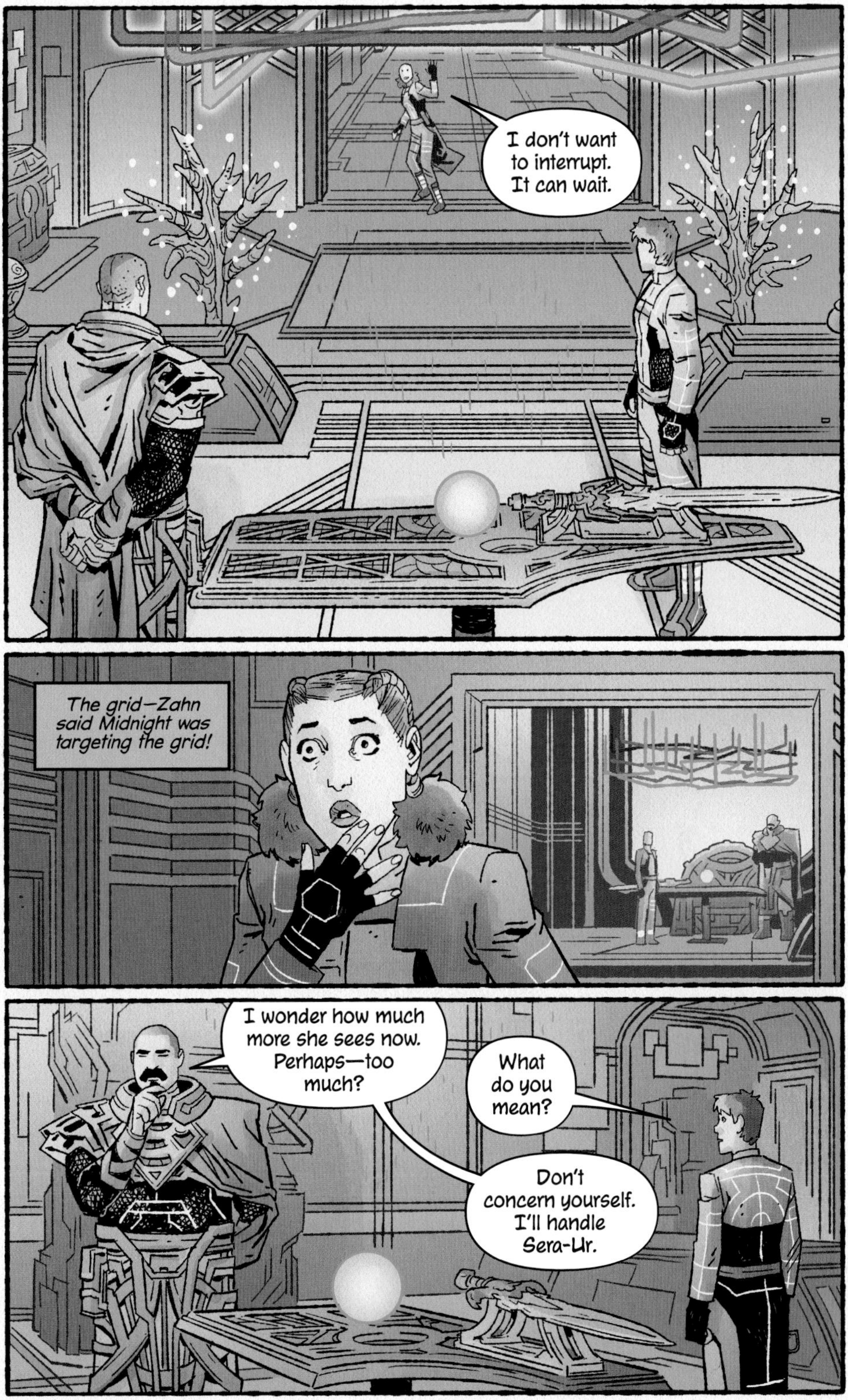
I don't want to interrupt. It can wait.
The grid—Zahn said Midnight was targeting the grid!
I wonder how much more she sees now. Perhaps—too much?
What do you mean?
Don't concern yourself. I'll handle Sera-Ur.

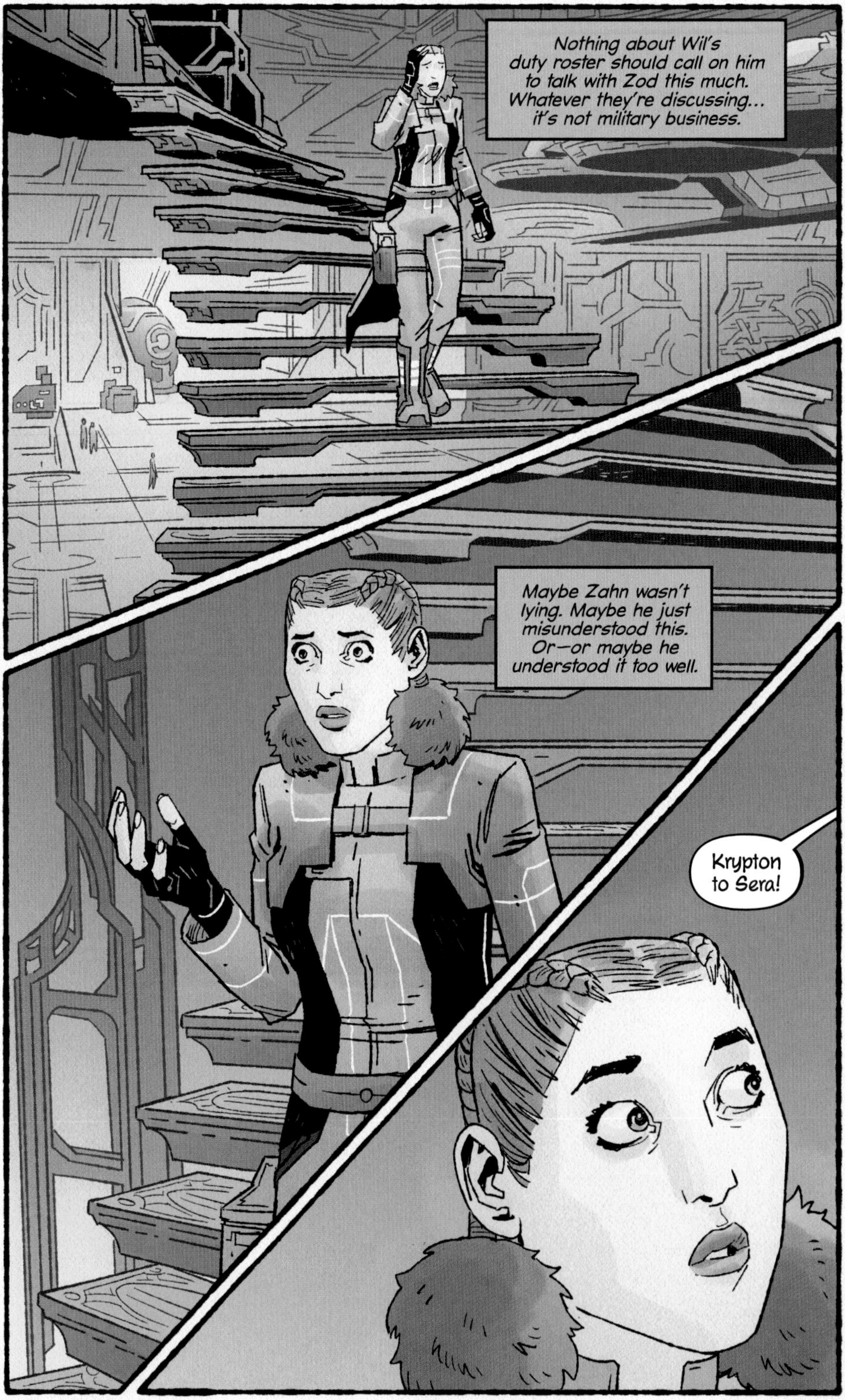
Nothing about Wil's duty roster should call on him to talk with Zod this much. Whatever they're discussing... it's not military business.
Maybe Zahn wasn't lying. Maybe he just misunderstood this. Or—or maybe he understood it too well.
Krypton to Sera!

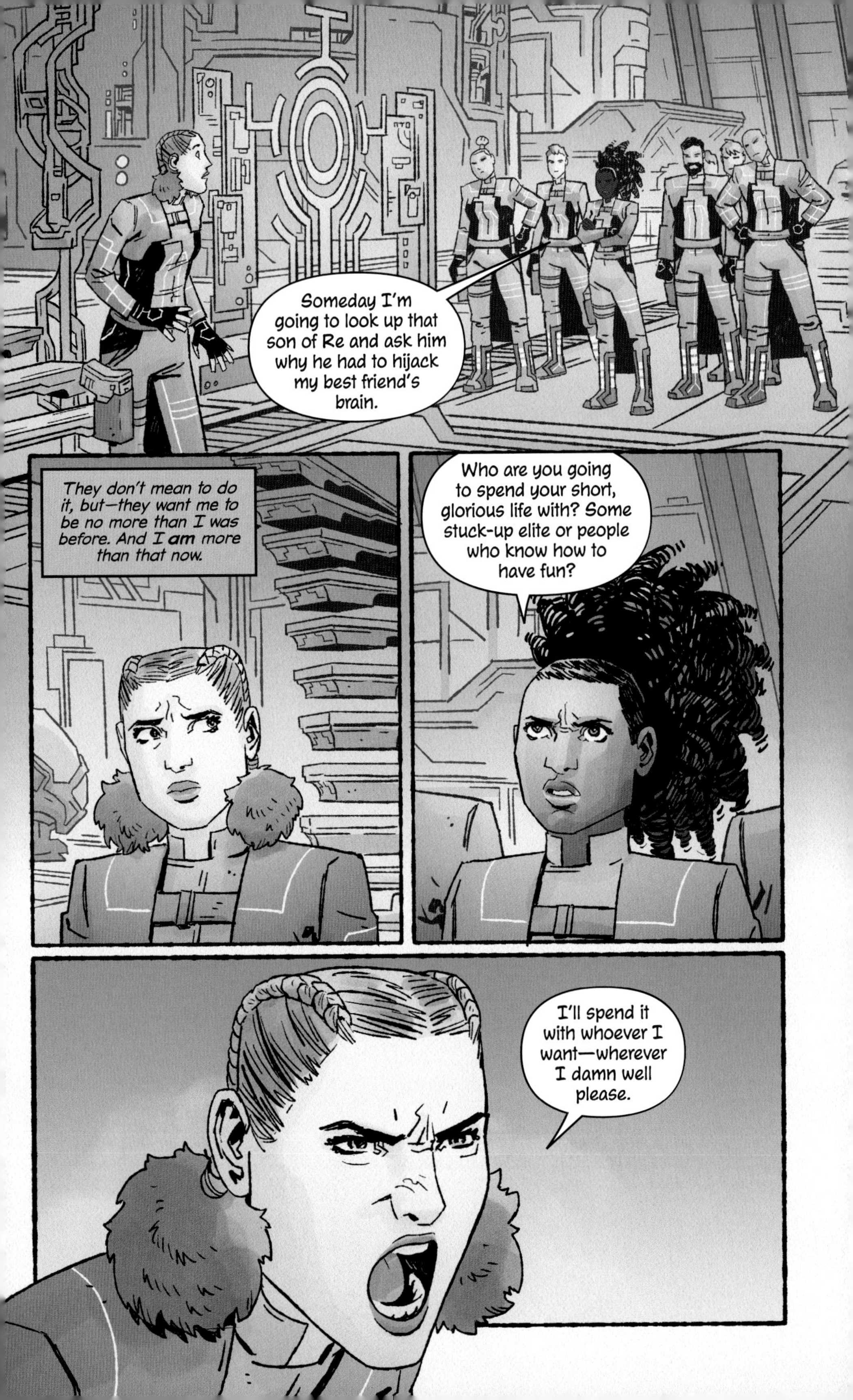
Someday I'm going to look up that son of Re and ask him why he had to hijack my best friend's brain.
They don't mean to do it, but—they want me to be no more than I was before. And I **am** more than that now.
Who are you going to spend your short, glorious life with? Some stuck-up elite or people who know how to have fun?
I'll spend it with whoever I want—wherever I damn well please.

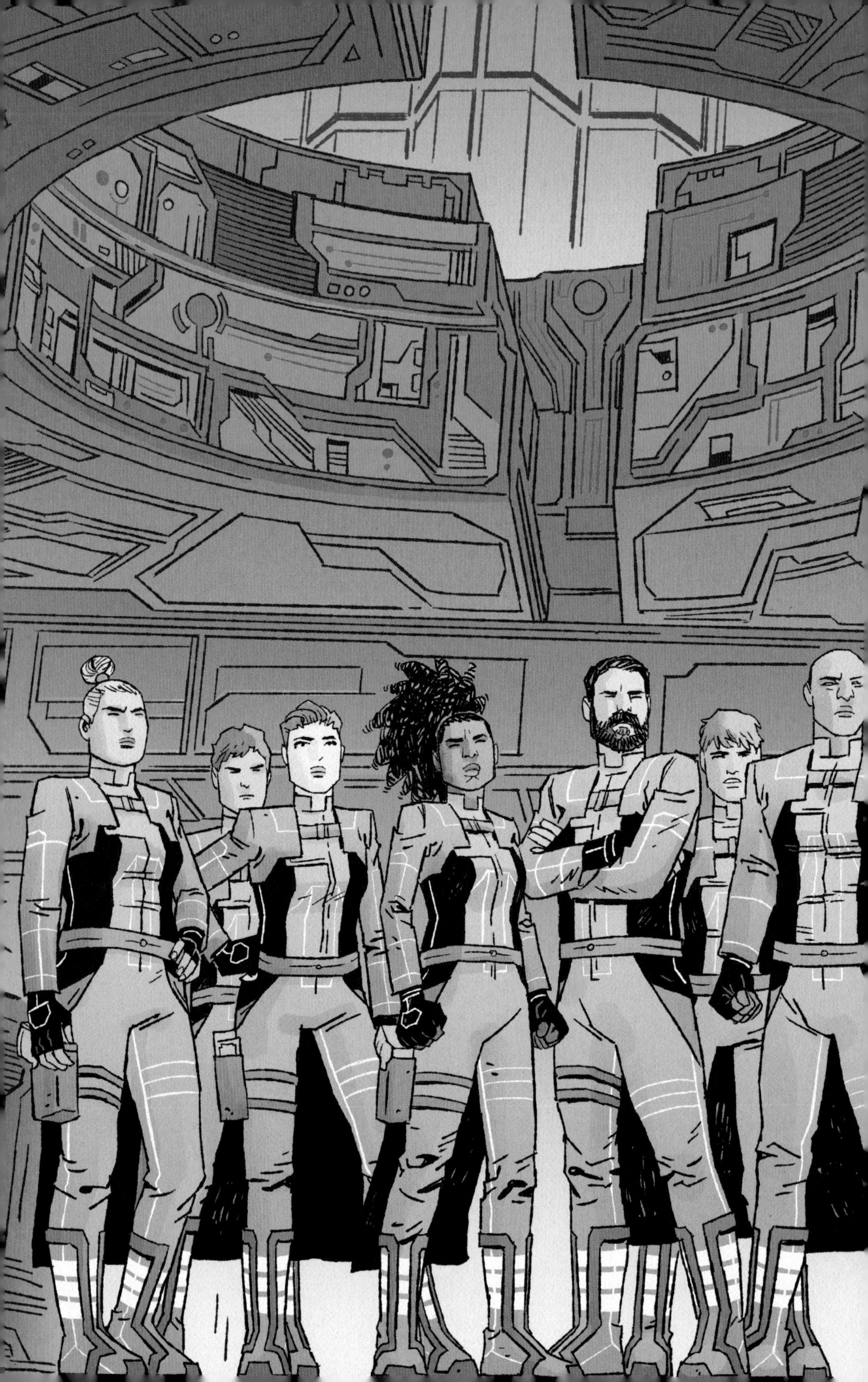

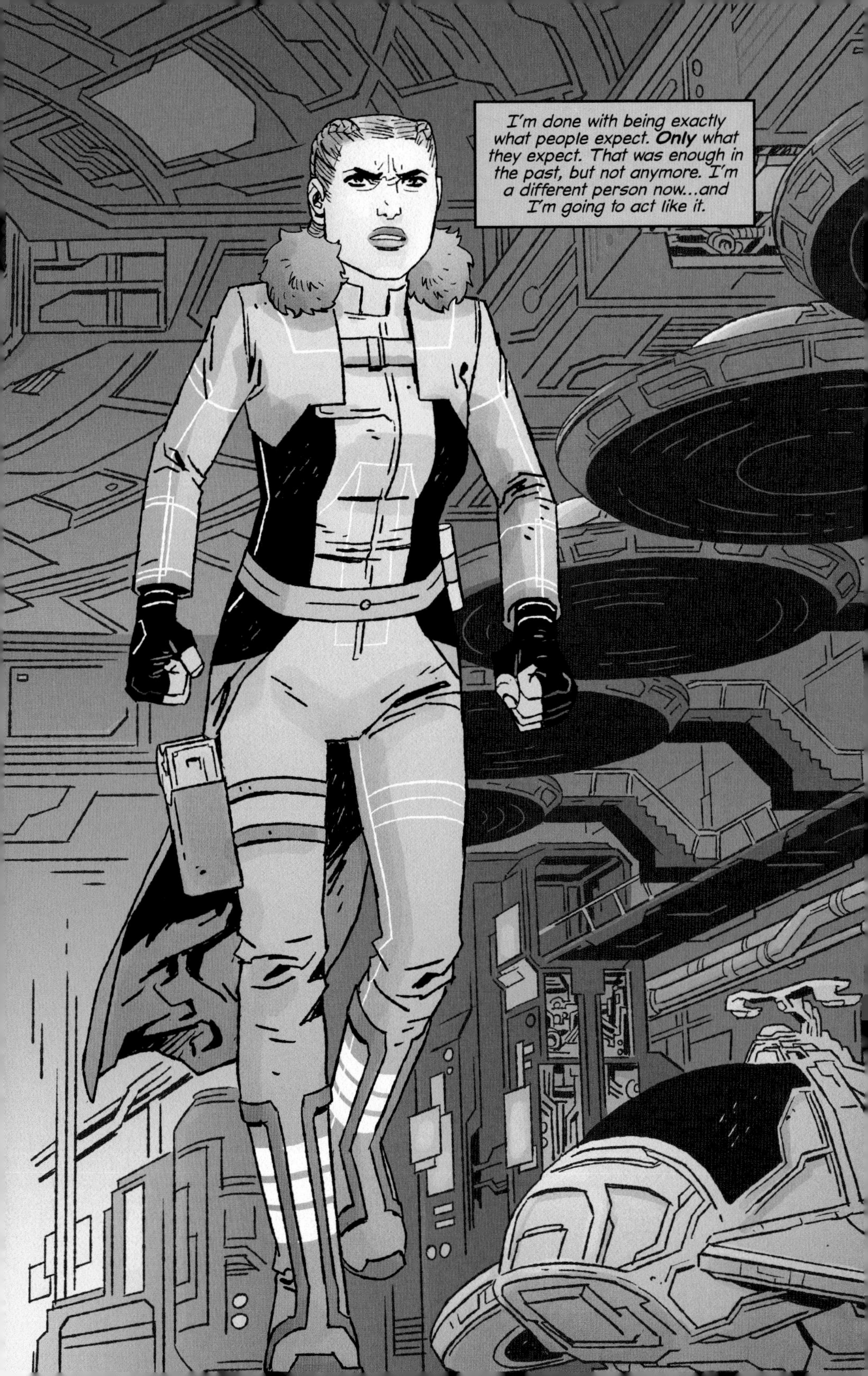
I'm done with being exactly what people expect. **Only** what they expect. That was enough in the past, but not anymore. I'm a different person now...and I'm going to act like it.

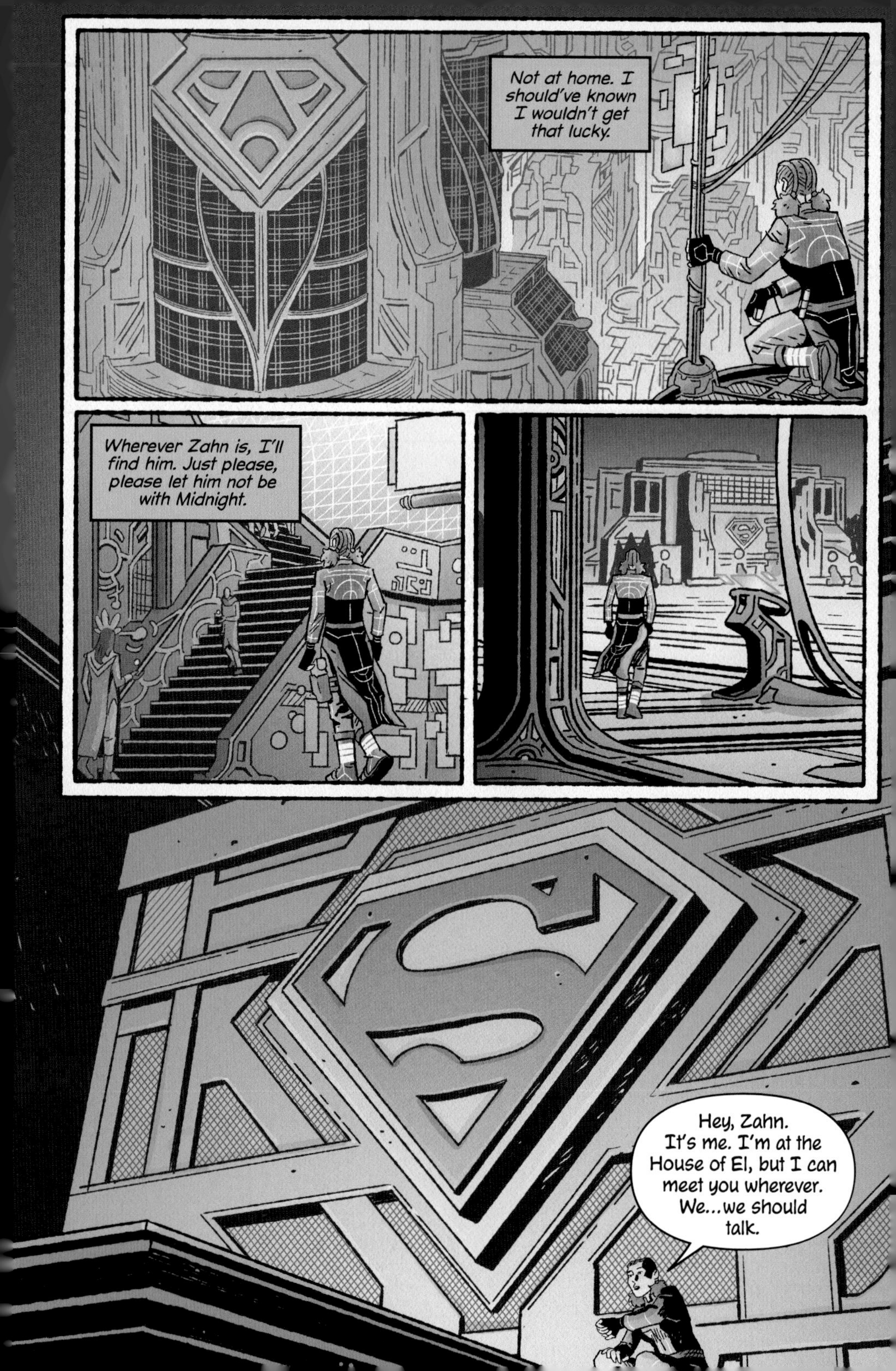
Not at home. I should've known I wouldn't get that lucky.
Wherever Zahn is, I'll find him. Just please, please let him not be with Midnight.
Hey, Zahn. It's me. I'm at the House of El, but I can meet you wherever. We...we should talk.

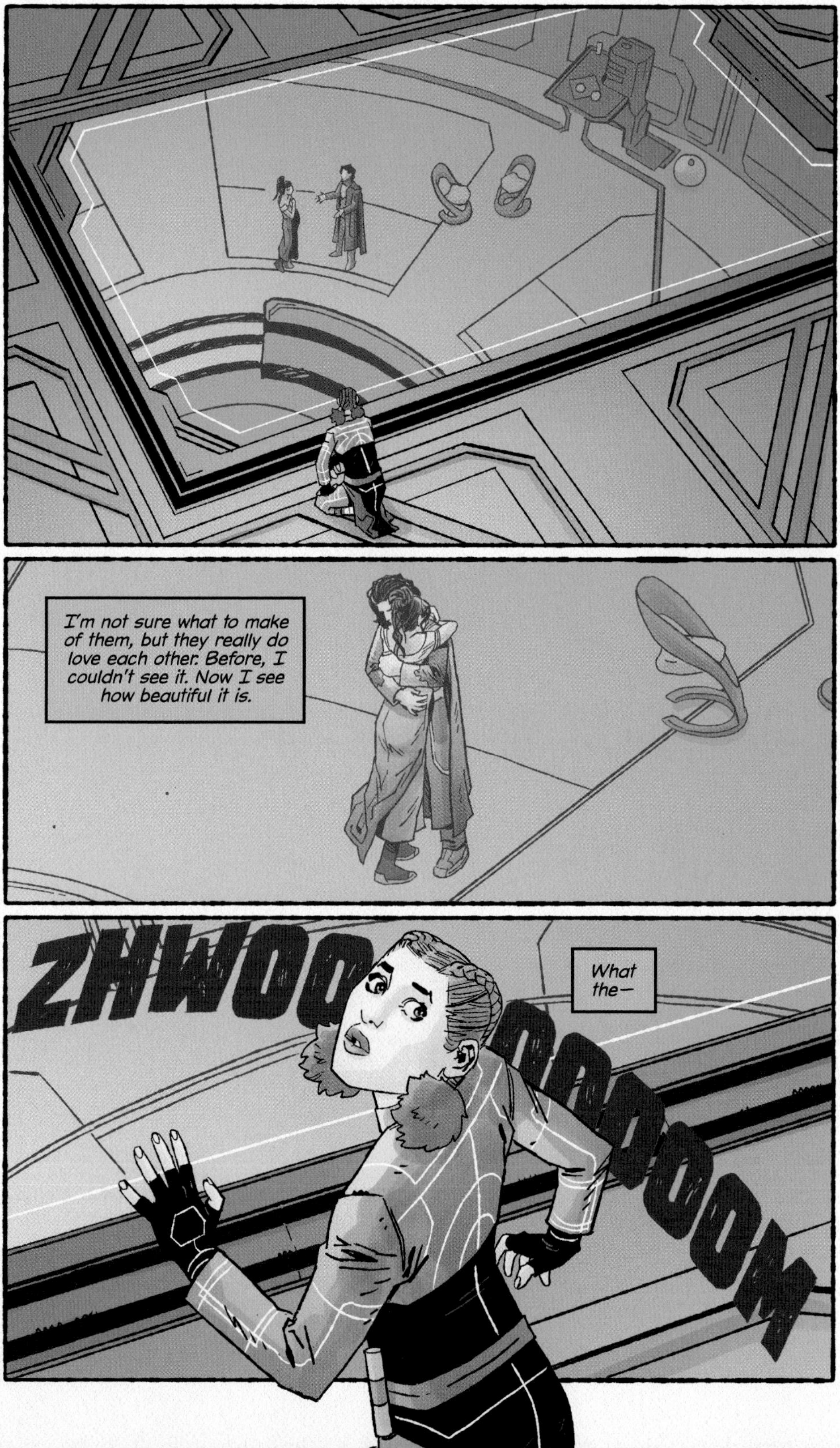
I'm not sure what to make of them, but they really do love each other. Before, I couldn't see it. Now I see how beautiful it is.
ZHWOOOOOOOOOOOM
What the—

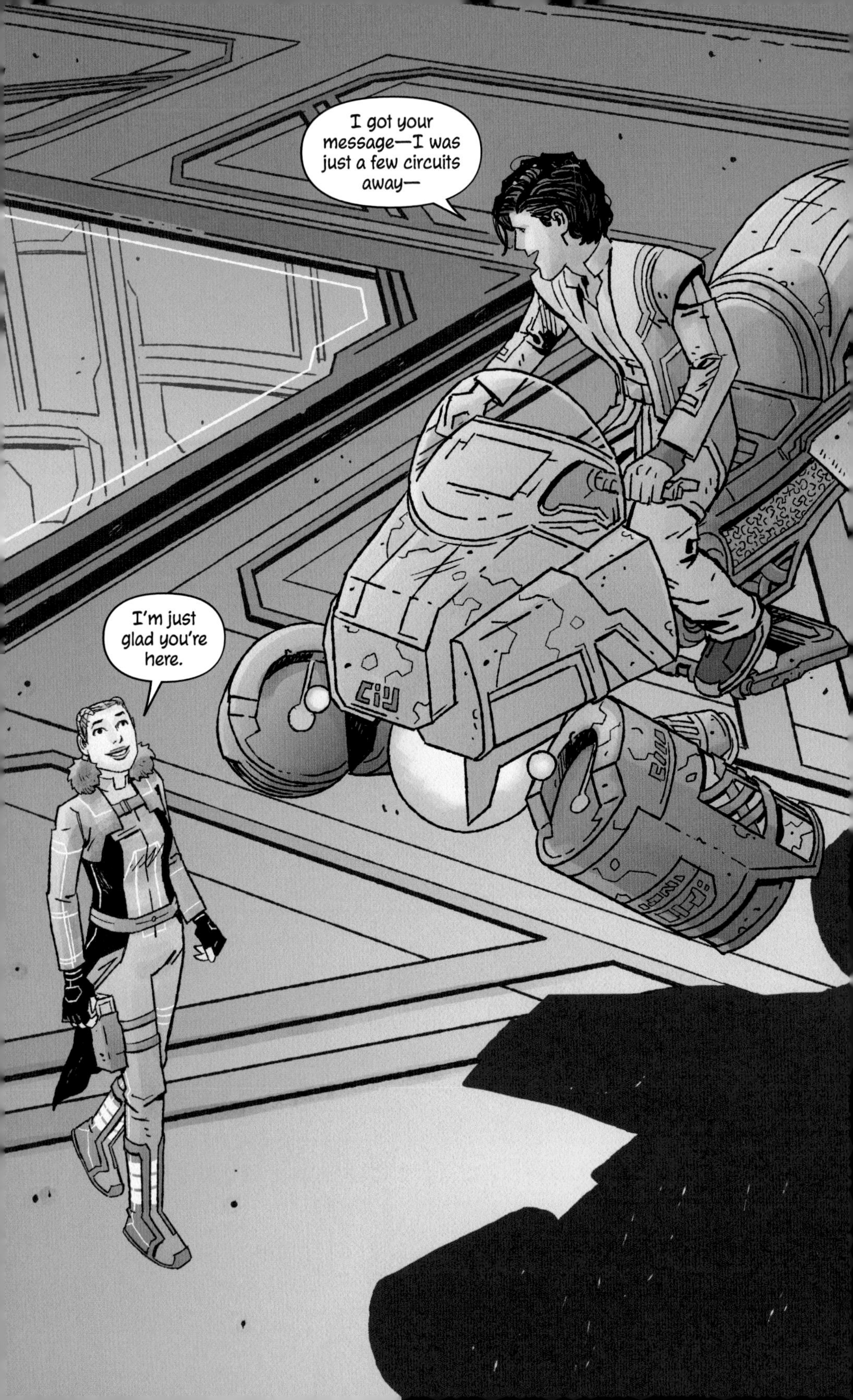
I got your message—I was just a few circuits away—
I'm just glad you're here.

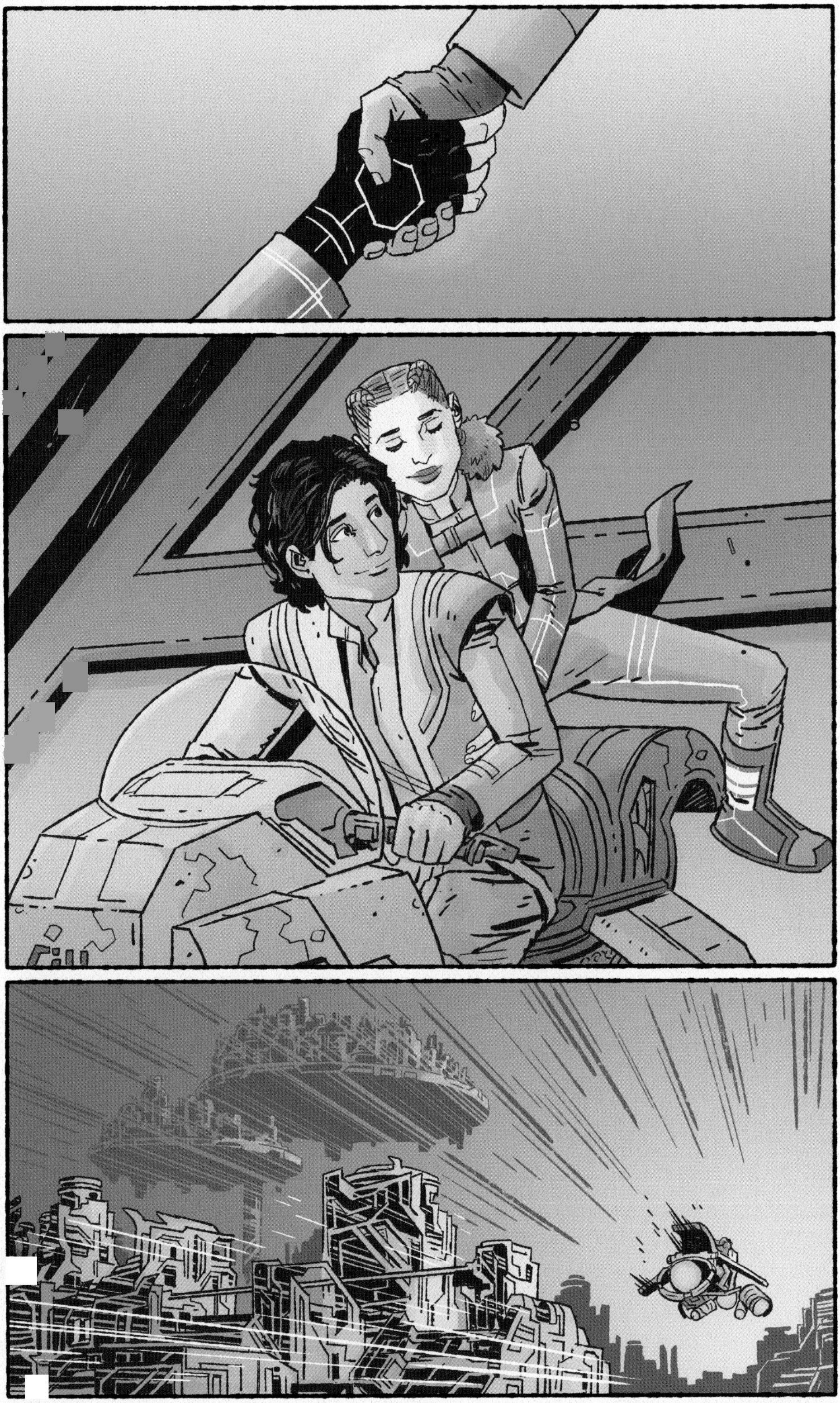

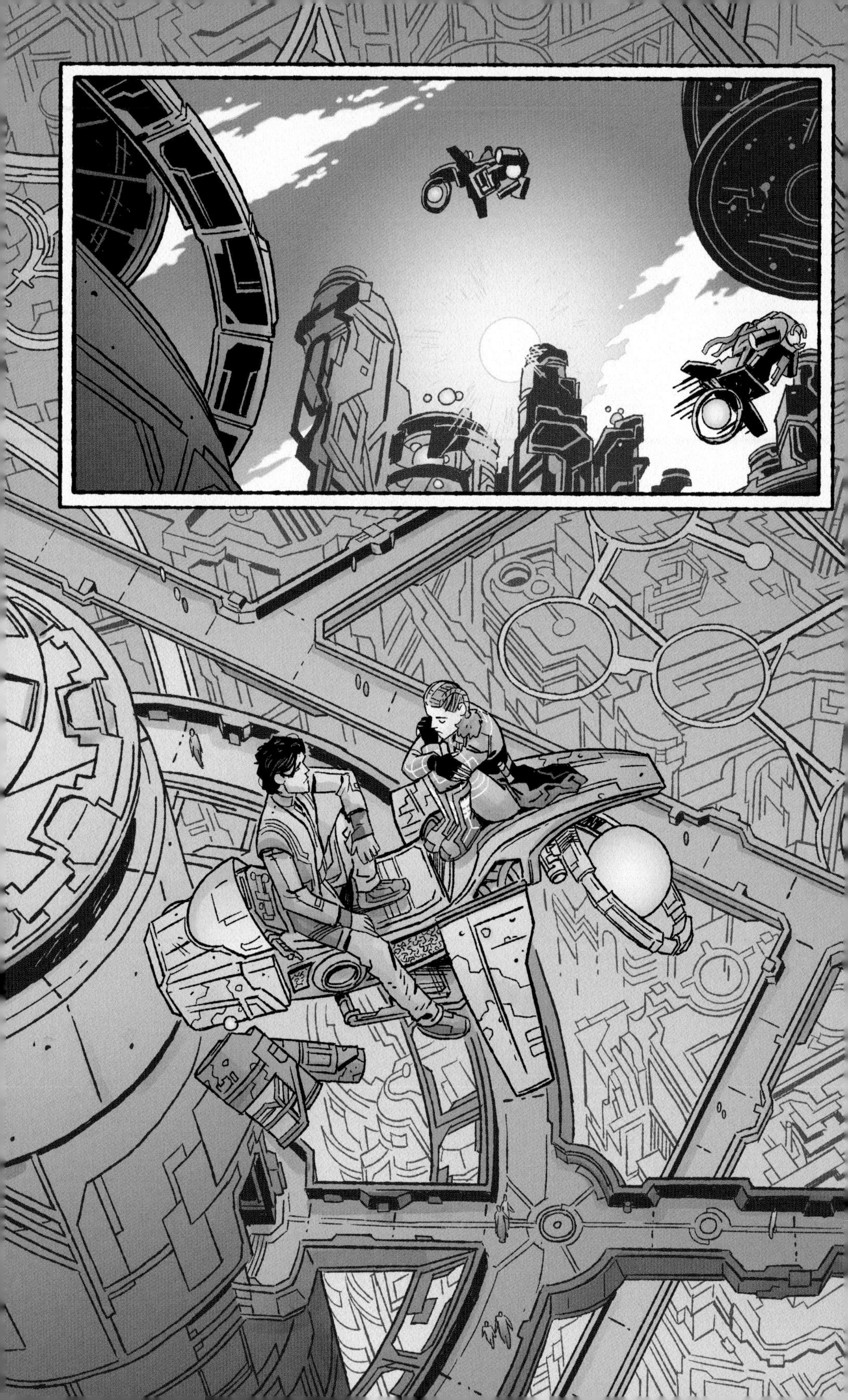

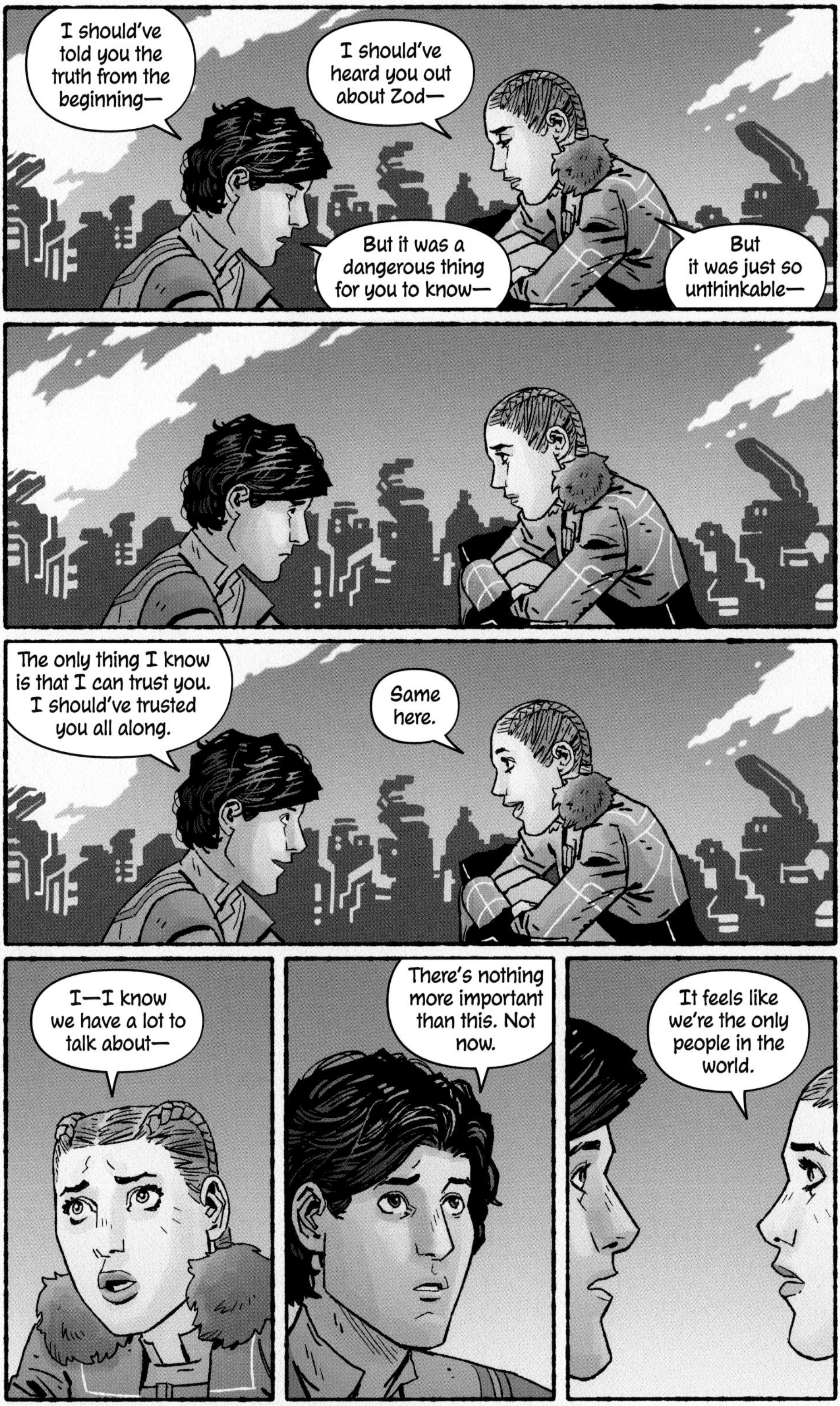
I should've told you the truth from the beginning—
I should've heard you out about Zod—
But it was a dangerous thing for you to know—
But it was just so unthinkable—
The only thing I know is that I can trust you. I should've trusted you all along.
Same here.
I—I know we have a lot to talk about—
There's nothing more important than this. Not now.
It feels like we're the only people in the world.

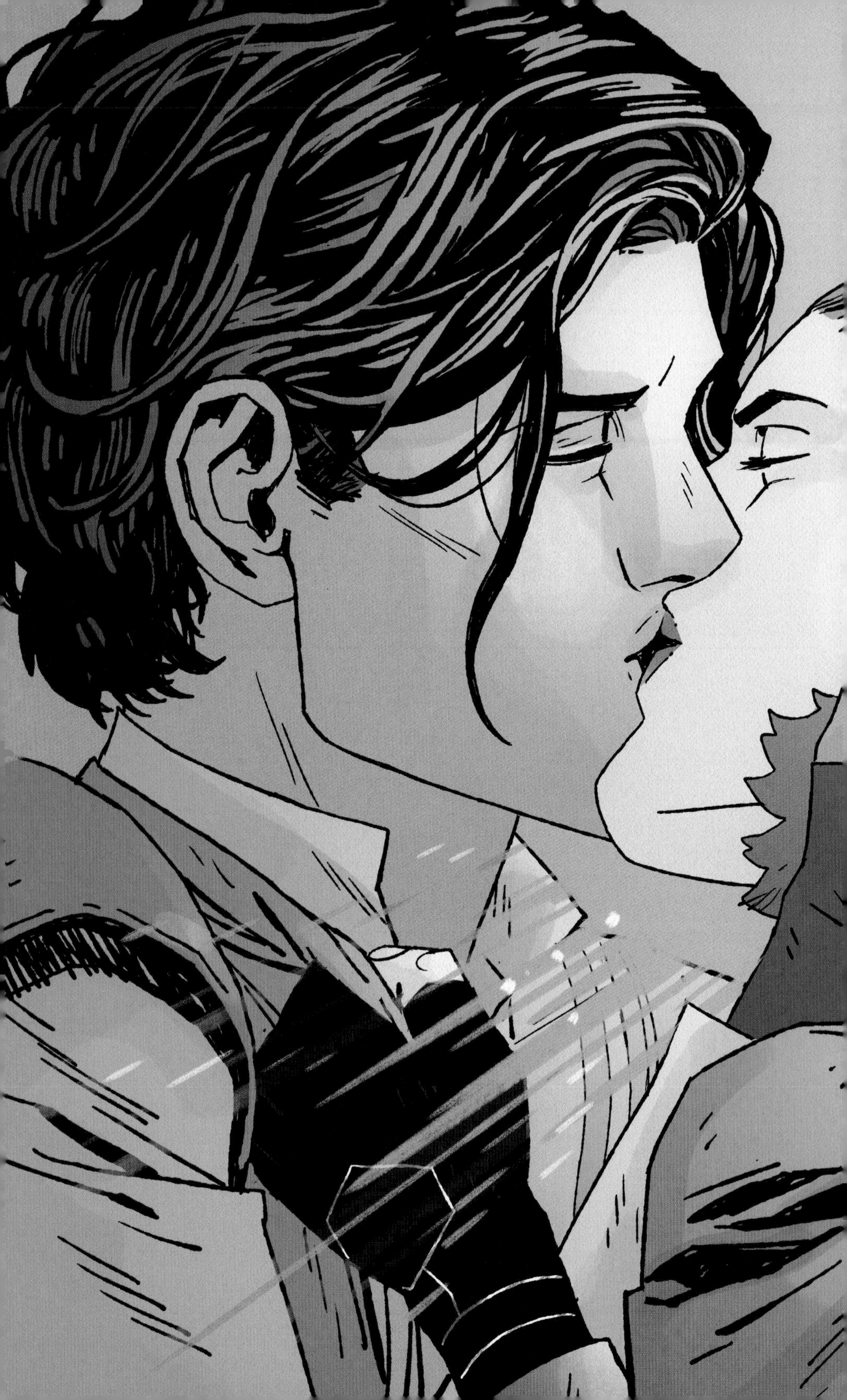

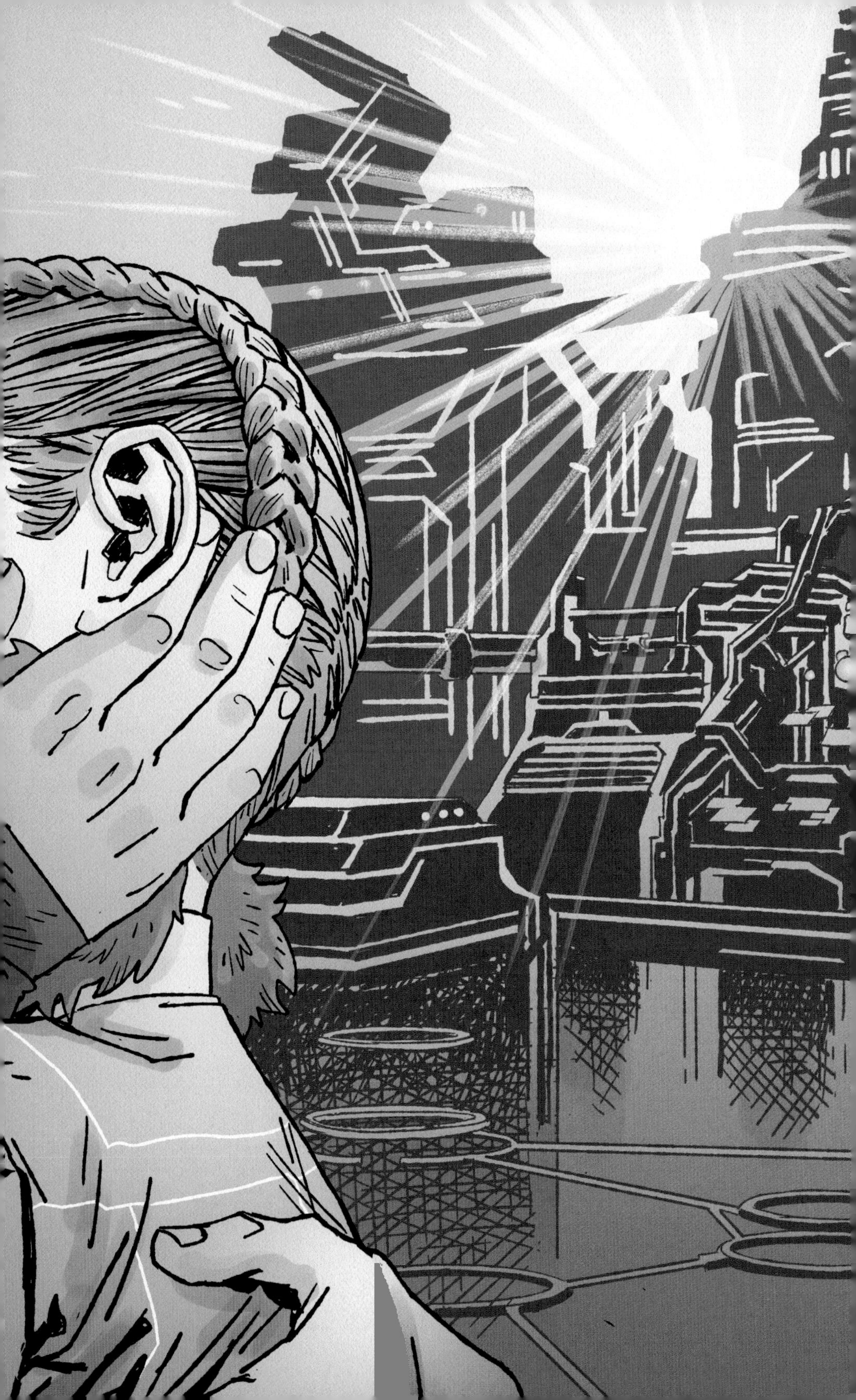

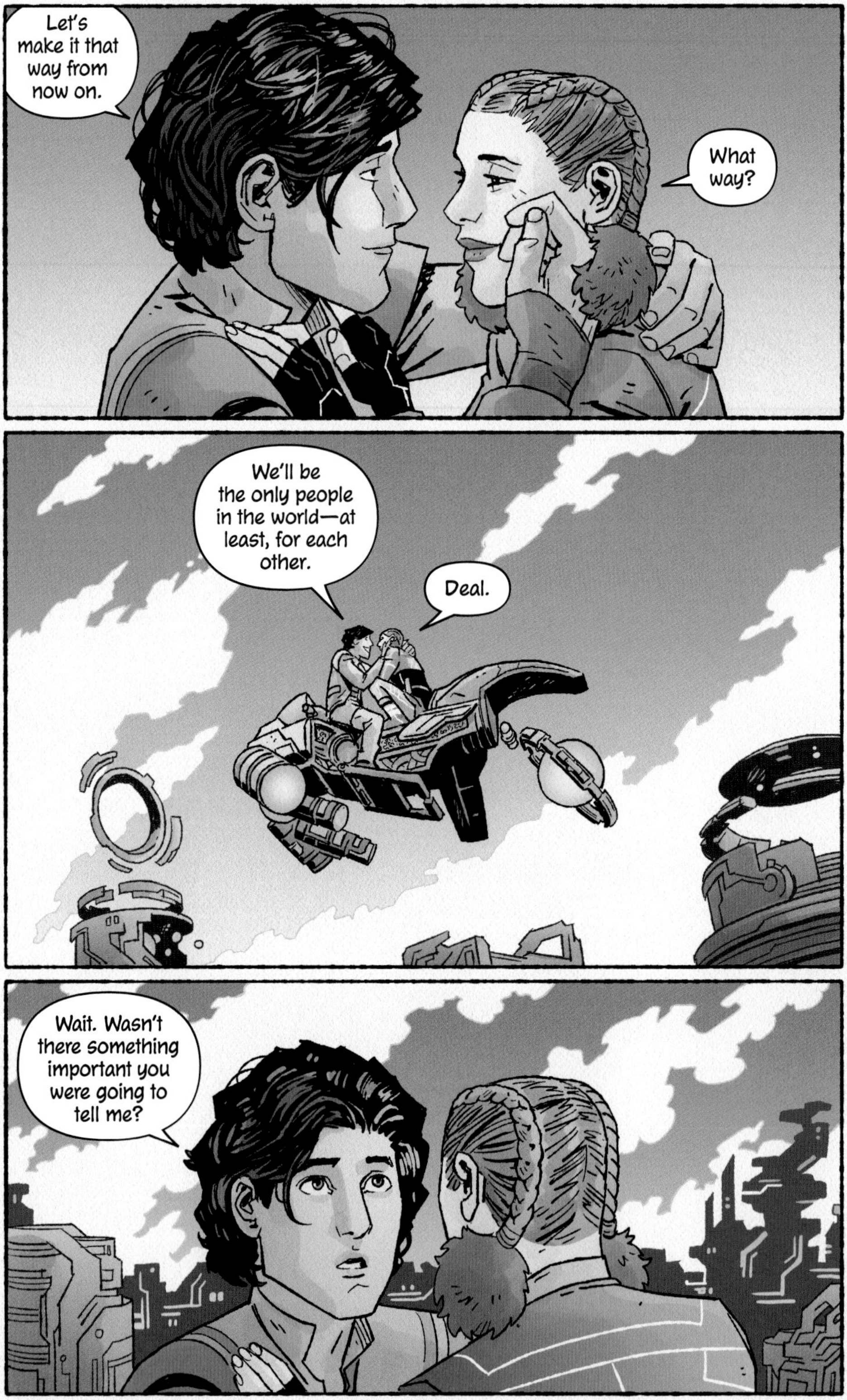
Let's make it that way from now on.
What way?
We'll be the only people in the world—at least, for each other.
Deal.
Wait. Wasn't there something important you were going to tell me?

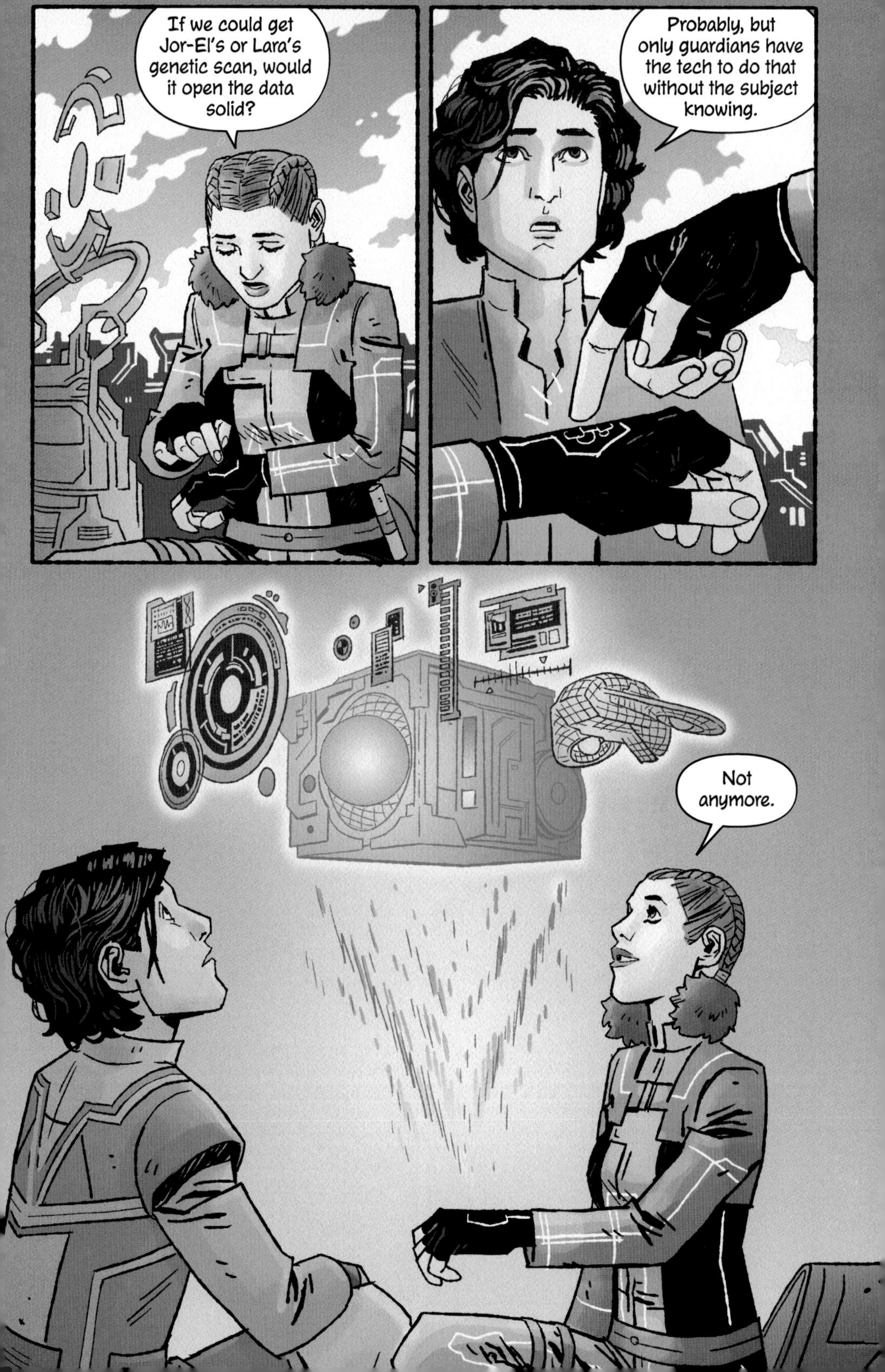
If we could get Jor-El's or Lara's genetic scan, would it open the data solid?
Probably, but only guardians have the tech to do that without the subject knowing.
Not anymore.

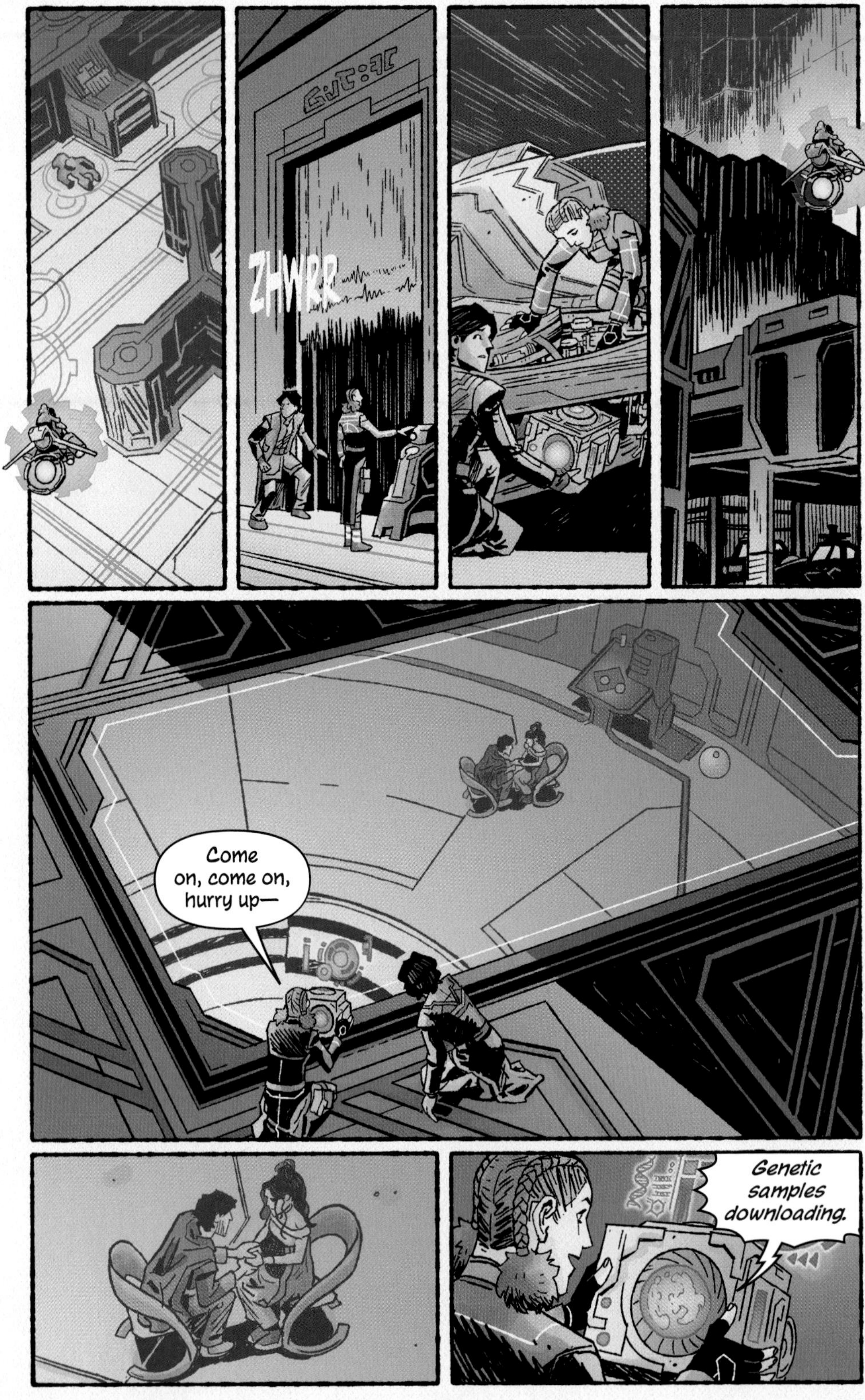
ZHWRR
Come on, come on, hurry up—
Genetic samples downloading.

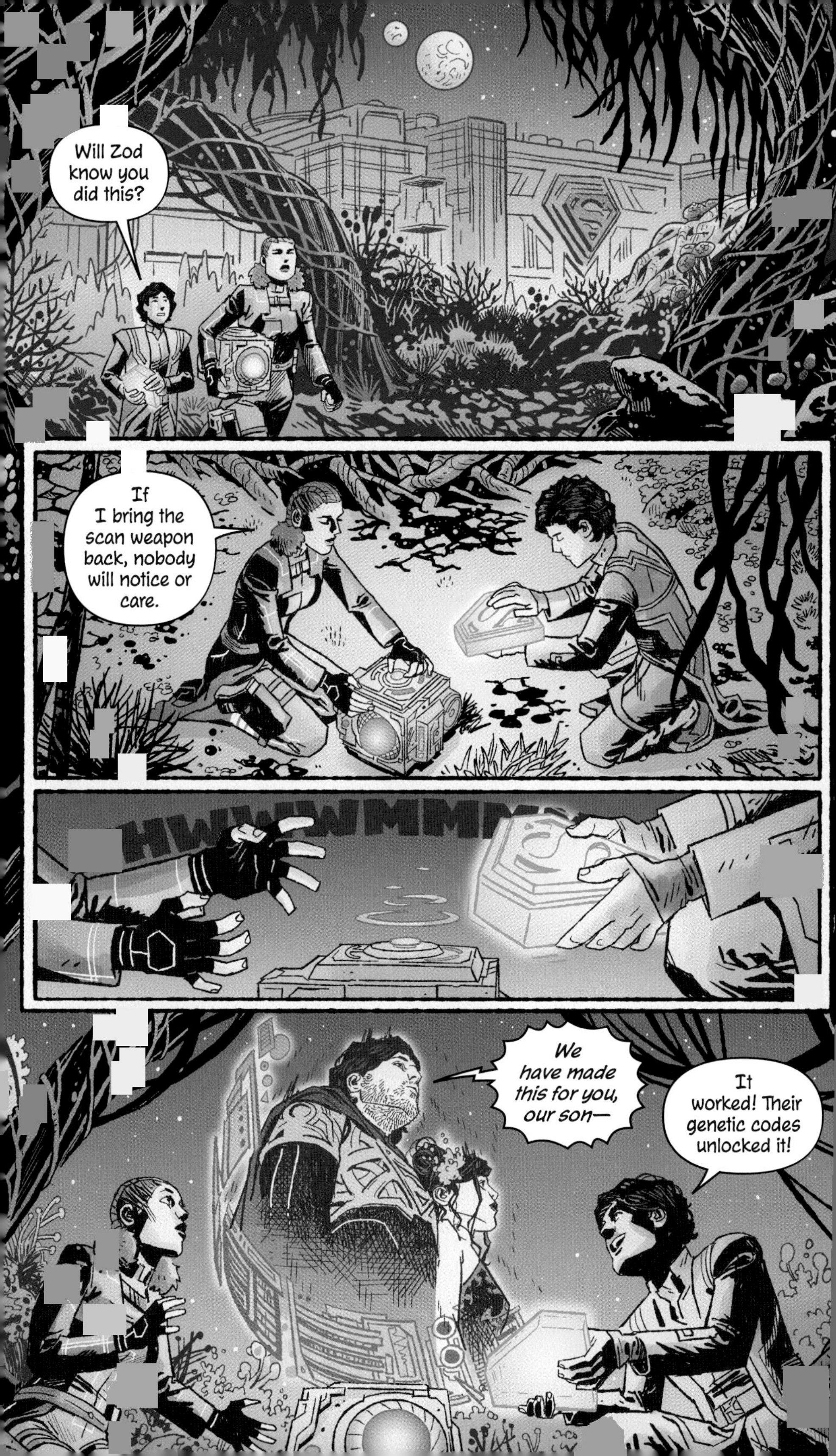
Will Zod know you did this?
If I bring the scan weapon back, nobody will notice or care.
HWWWWMMM
We have made this for you, our son—
It worked! Their genetic codes unlocked it!

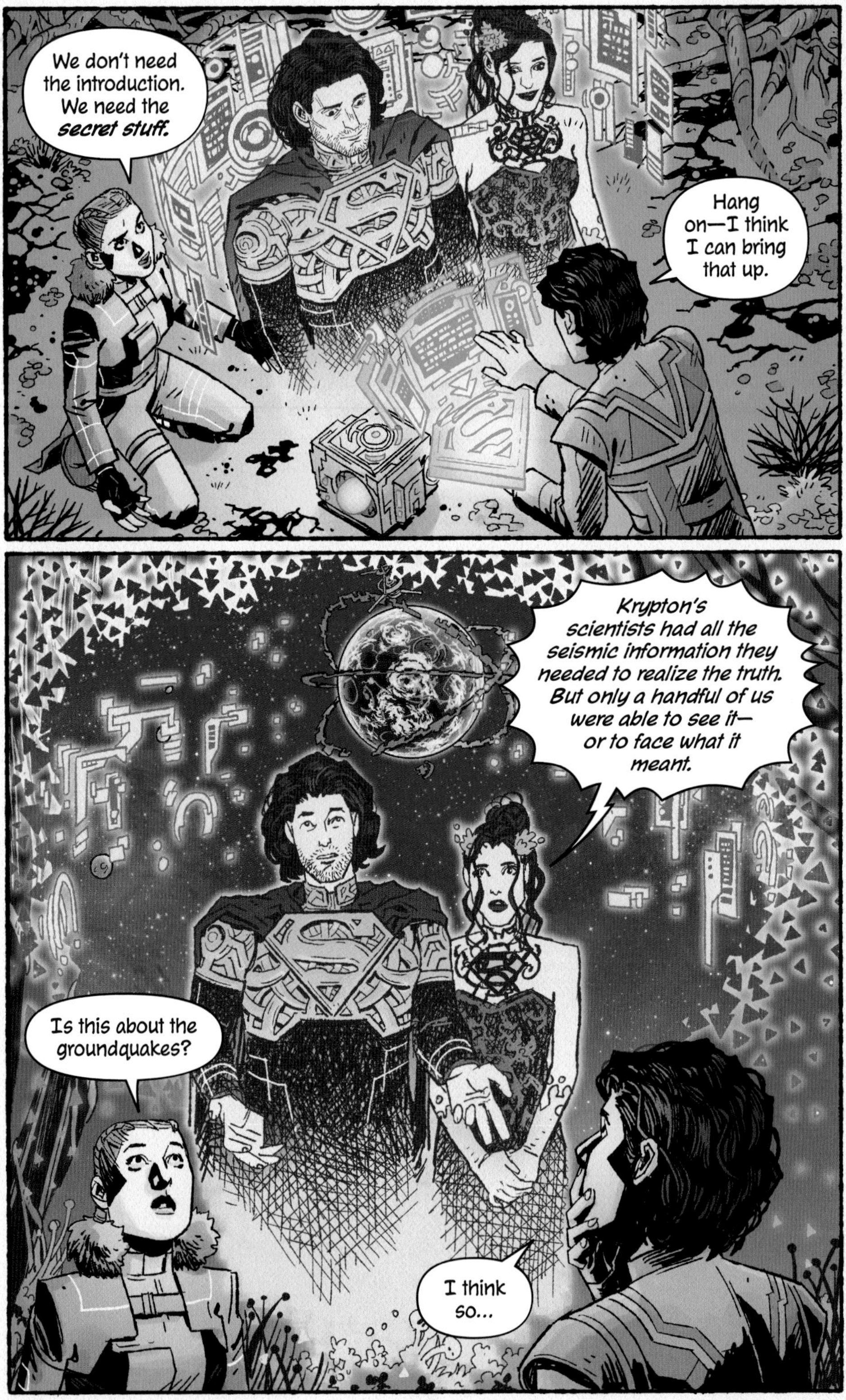
We don't need the introduction. We need the *secret stuff.*
Hang on—I think I can bring that up.
Krypton's scientists had all the seismic information they needed to realize the truth. But only a handful of us were able to see it— or to face what it meant.
Is this about the groundquakes?
I think so...

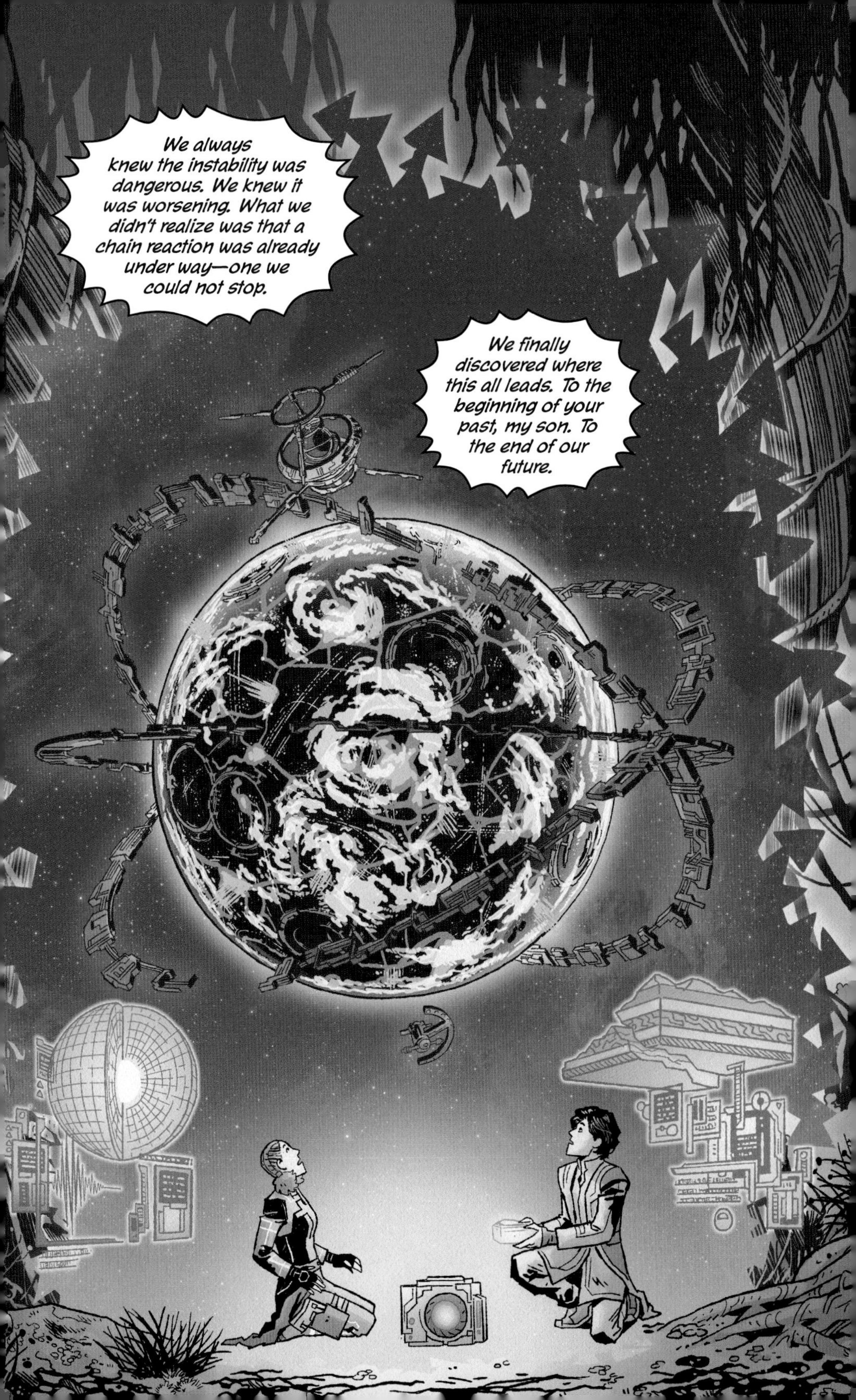
We always knew the instability was dangerous. We knew it was worsening. What we didn't realize was that a chain reaction was already under way—one we could not stop.
We finally discovered where this all leads. To the beginning of your past, my son. To the end of our future.

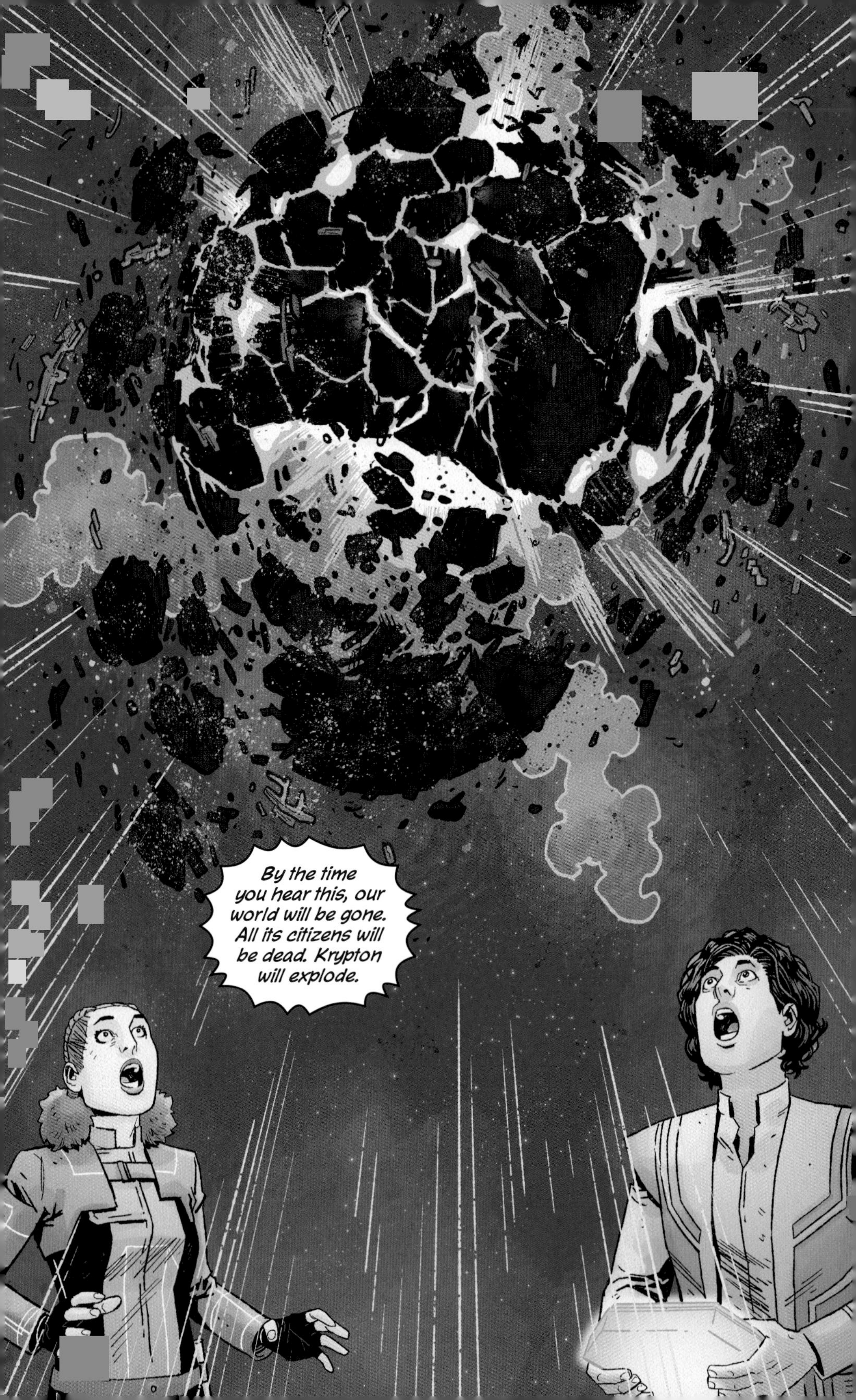
By the time you hear this, our world will be gone. All its citizens will be dead. Krypton will explode.

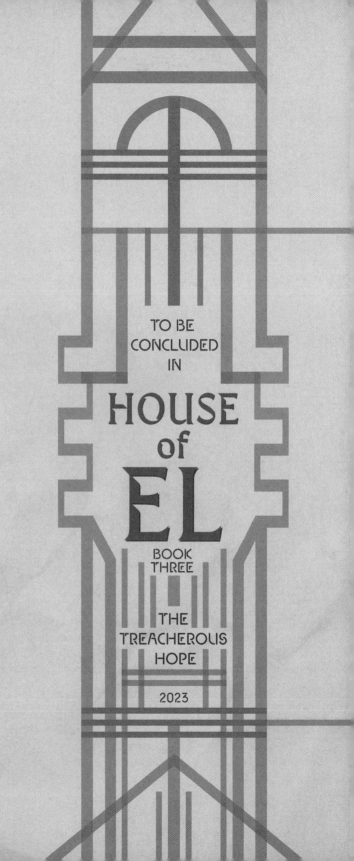

TO BE
CONCLUDED
IN

HOUSE of EL

BOOK
THREE

THE
TREACHEROUS
HOPE

2023

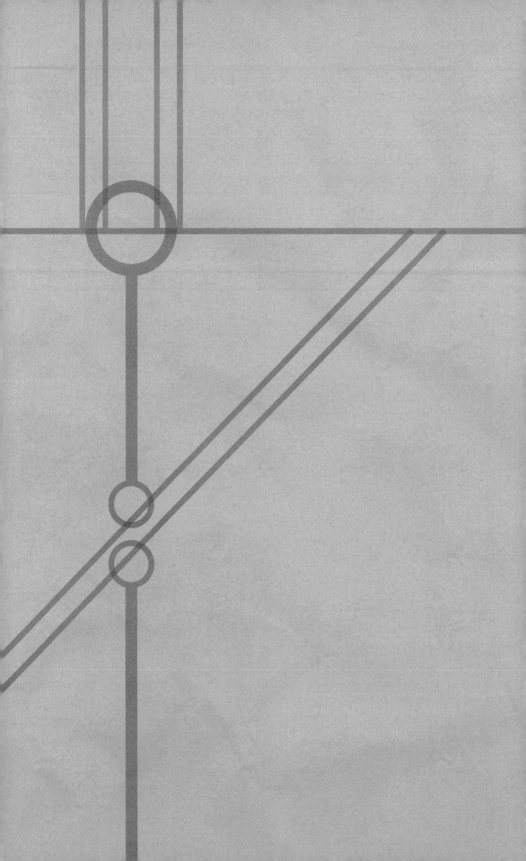

CLAUDIA GRAY

is the *New York Times* bestselling author of many science fiction and paranormal fantasy books for young adults, including the Constellation series, the Firebird series, the Evernight series, the Spellcaster series, and *Fateful*. She's also had a chance to work in a galaxy far, far away as the author of the Star Wars novels *Lost Stars*, *Bloodline*, *Master & Apprentice*, and *Leia, Princess of Alderaan*. Born a fangirl, she loves obsessing over geeky movies and TV shows, as well as watching any series with British people solving murders in picturesque settings. She will take your Jane Austen trivia challenge any day, anytime. Currently she lives in New Orleans.

ERIC ZAWADZKI

is a Canadian comic book artist who is most well known for his work on *The Dregs* and *Eternal*. He most recently co-created *Heart Attack* for Skybound/Image Comics. Zawadzki lives in Calgary with his wife and two hairless cats.

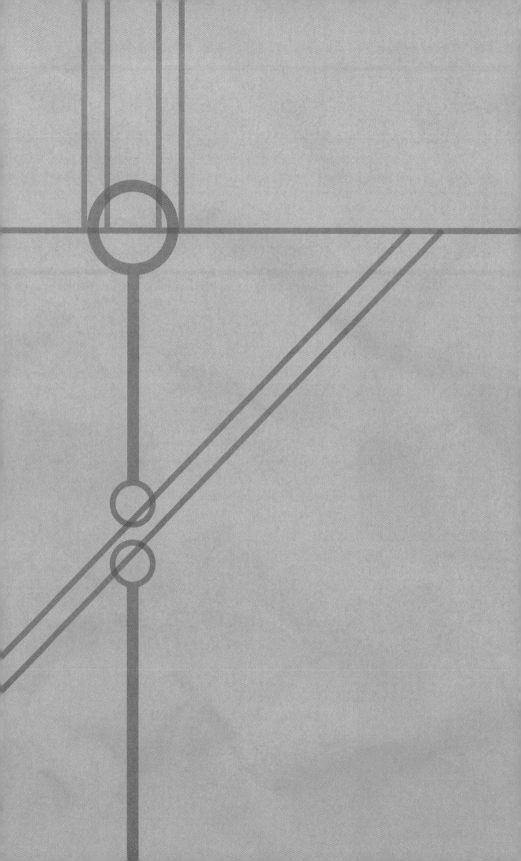

HOUSE OF EL returns in 2023 for the final chapter in the trilogy. Time is running out for Sera, Zahn, and the entire planet of Krypton as it moves towards its inevitable fate. What desperate measures will Zod take to head off disaster? Could Sera and Zahn have come to acknowledge their feelings for each other just as their lives are about to end? Will baby Kal-el truly be the only survivor of this doomed world? Be here for HOUSE OF EL BOOK THREE: THE TREACHEROUS HOPE.

new york times bestselling author
CLAUDIA GRAY
illustrated by ERIC ZAWADZKI
HOUSE of EL
book three:
THE TREACHEROUS HOPE

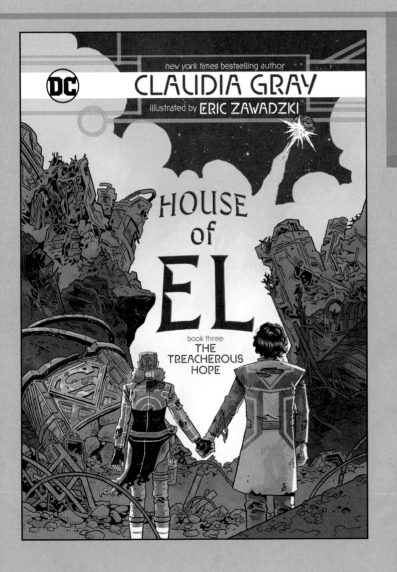

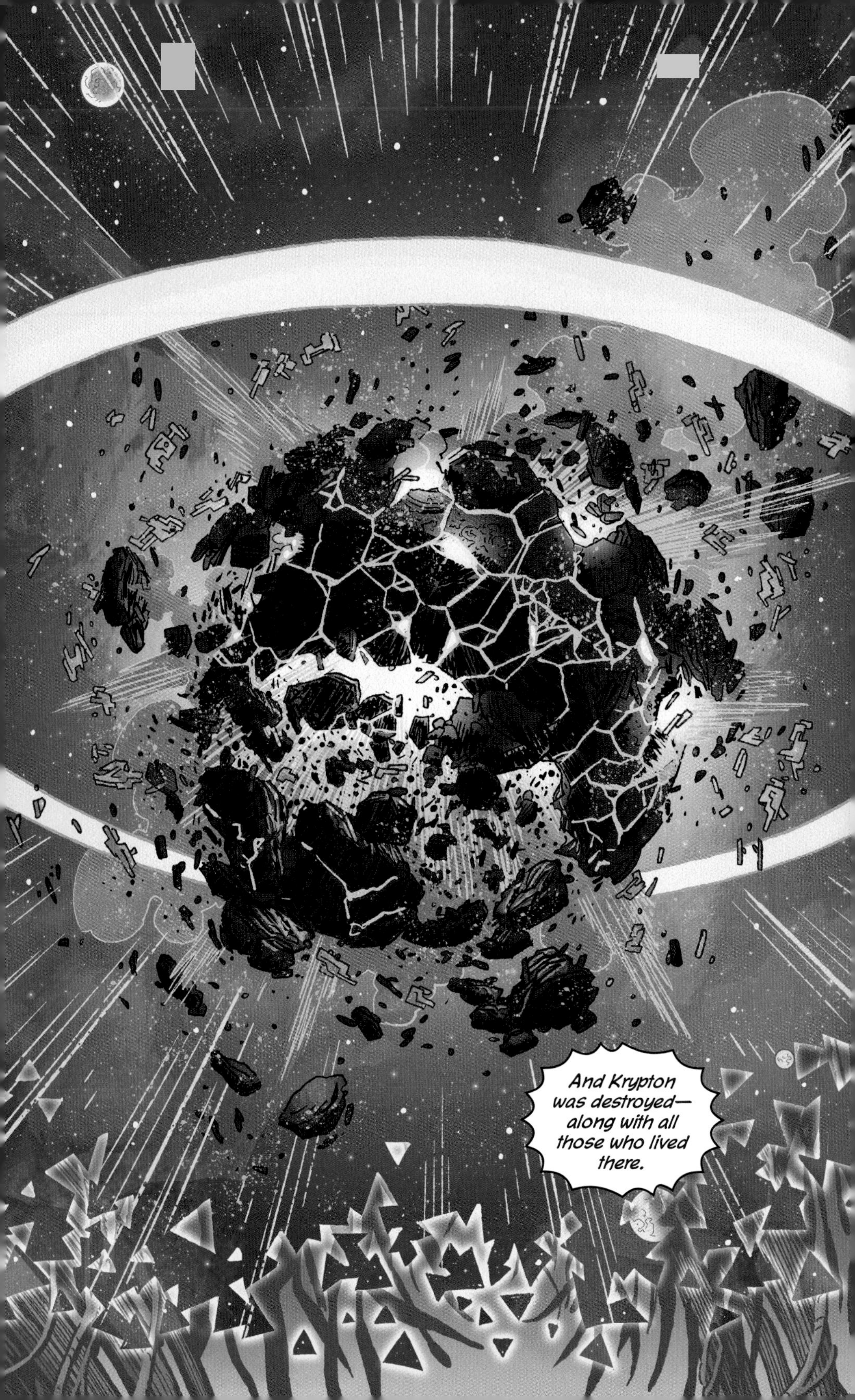
And Krypton was destroyed— along with all those who lived there.

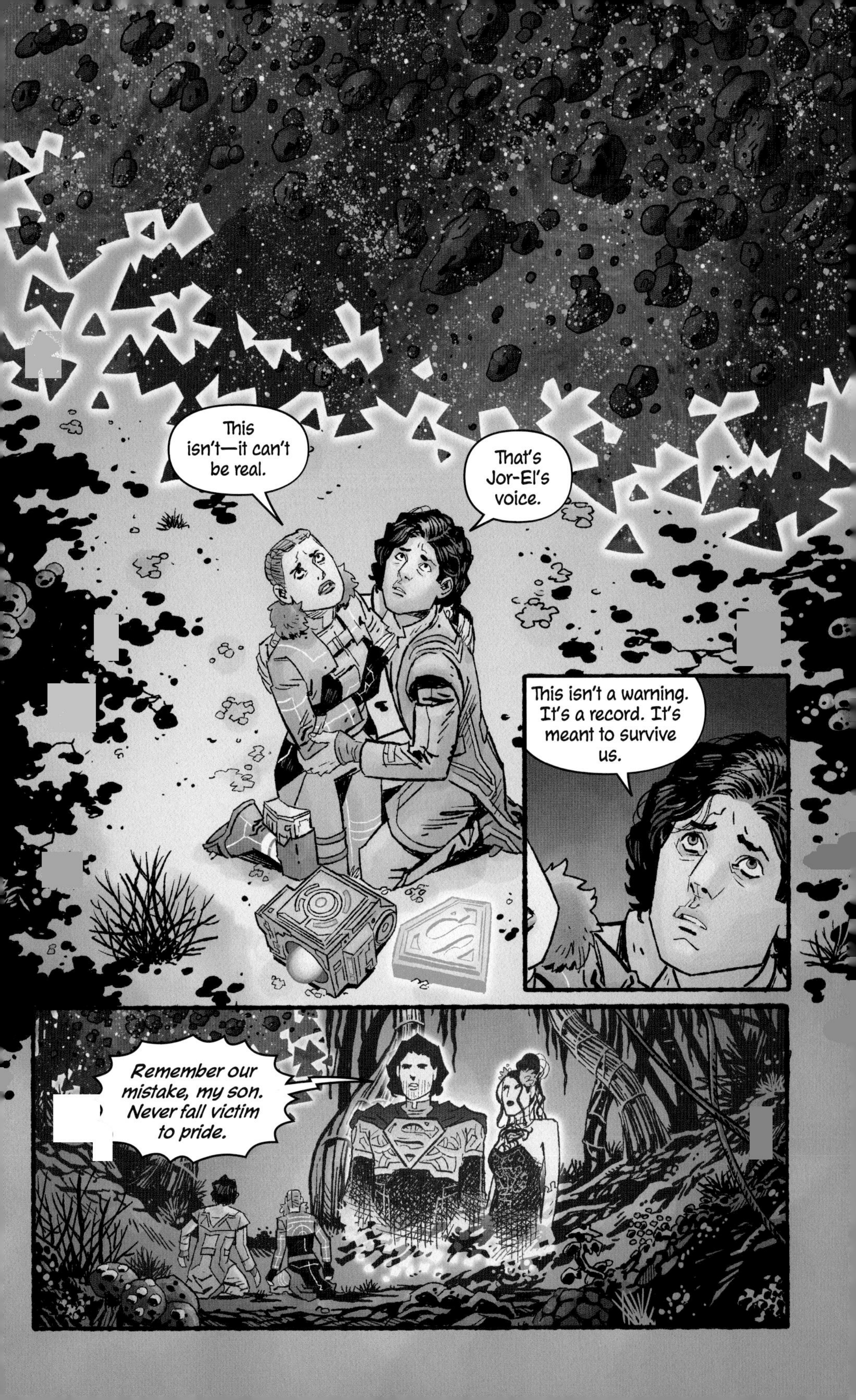
This isn't—it can't be real.
That's Jor-El's voice.
This isn't a warning. It's a record. It's meant to survive us.
Remember our mistake, my son. Never fall victim to pride.

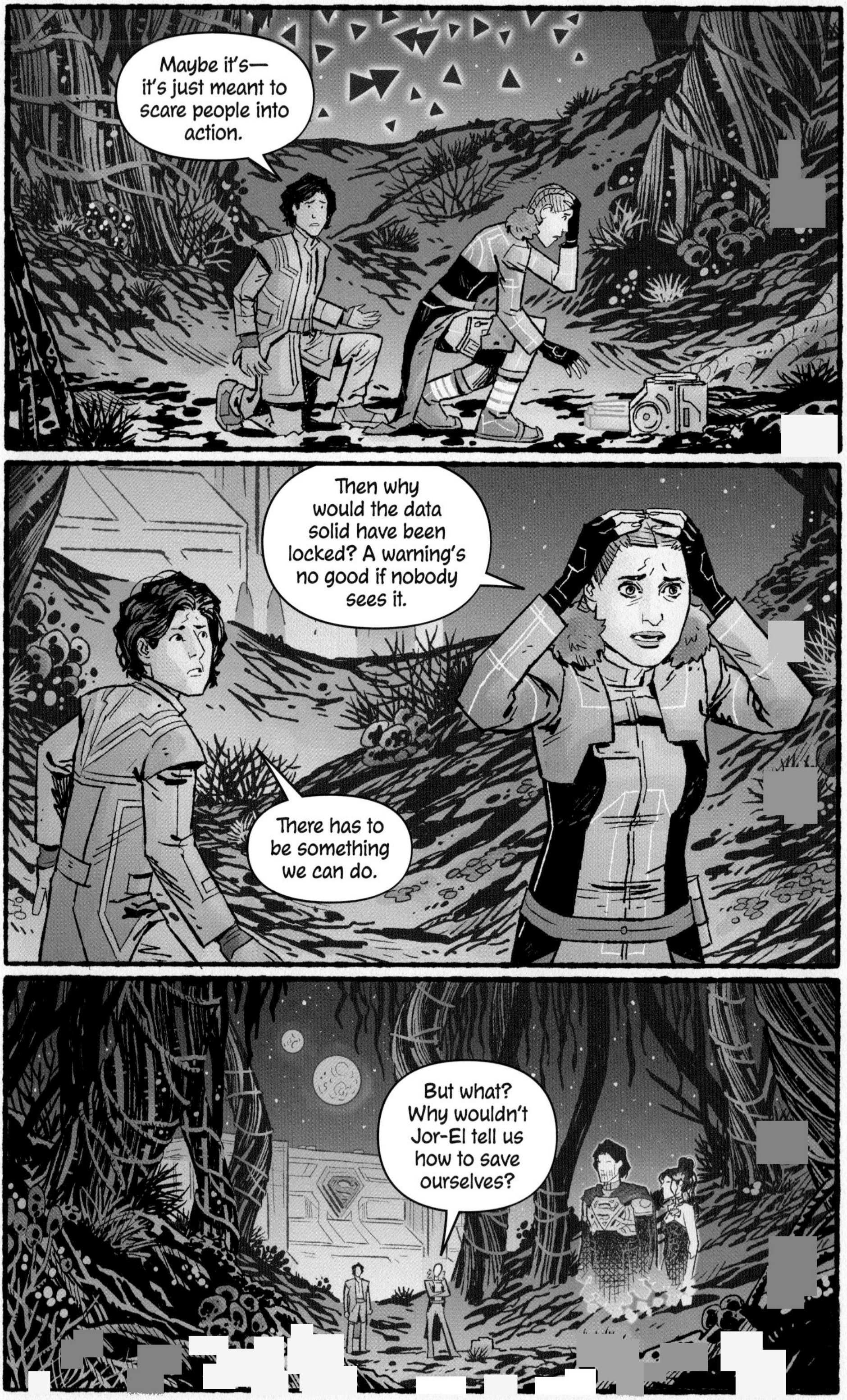
Maybe it's— it's just meant to scare people into action.
Then why would the data solid have been locked? A warning's no good if nobody sees it.
There has to be something we can do.
But what? Why wouldn't Jor-El tell us how to save ourselves?

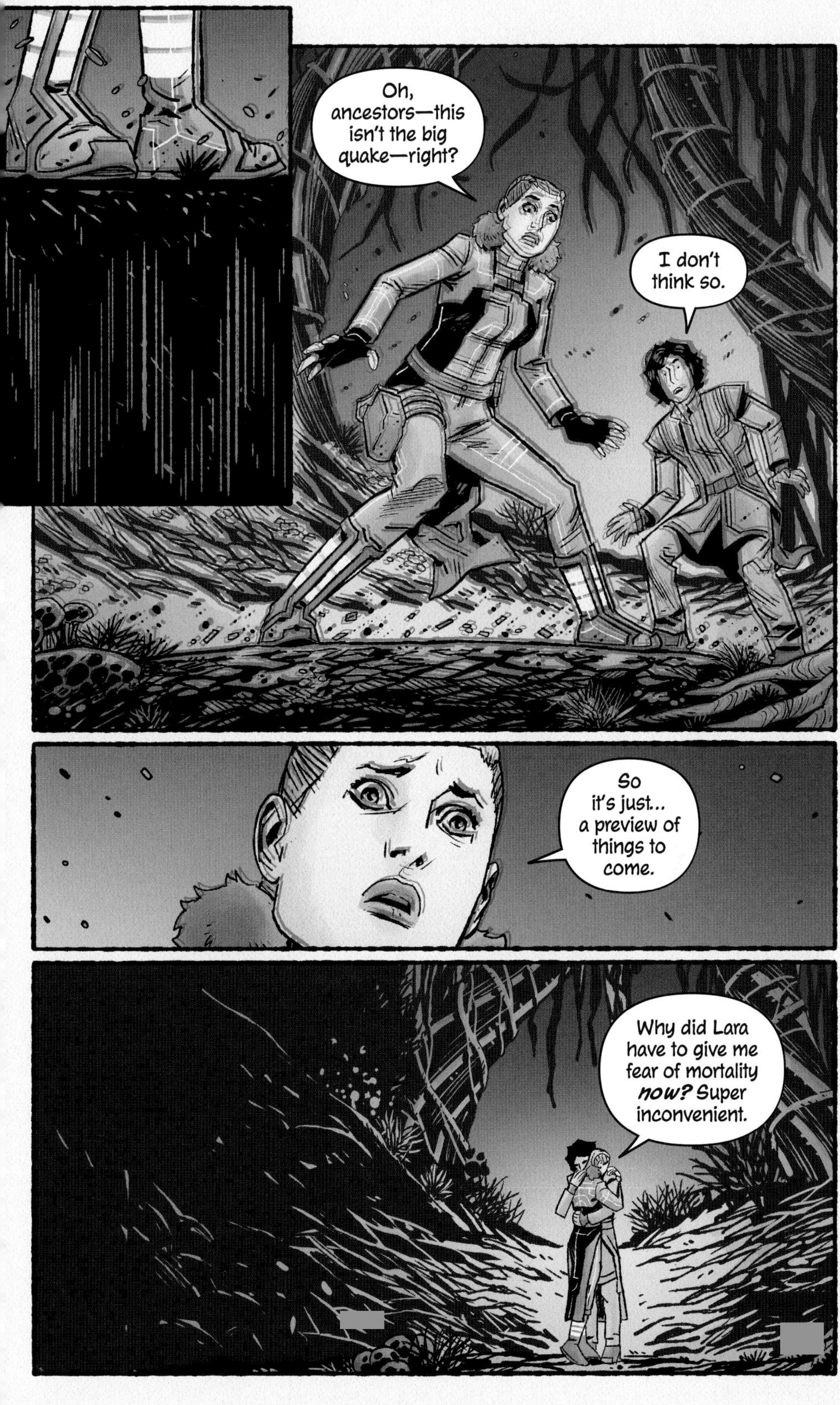
Oh, ancestors—this isn't the big quake—right?
I don't think so.
So it's just... a preview of things to come.
Why did Lara have to give me fear of mortality *now?* Super inconvenient.

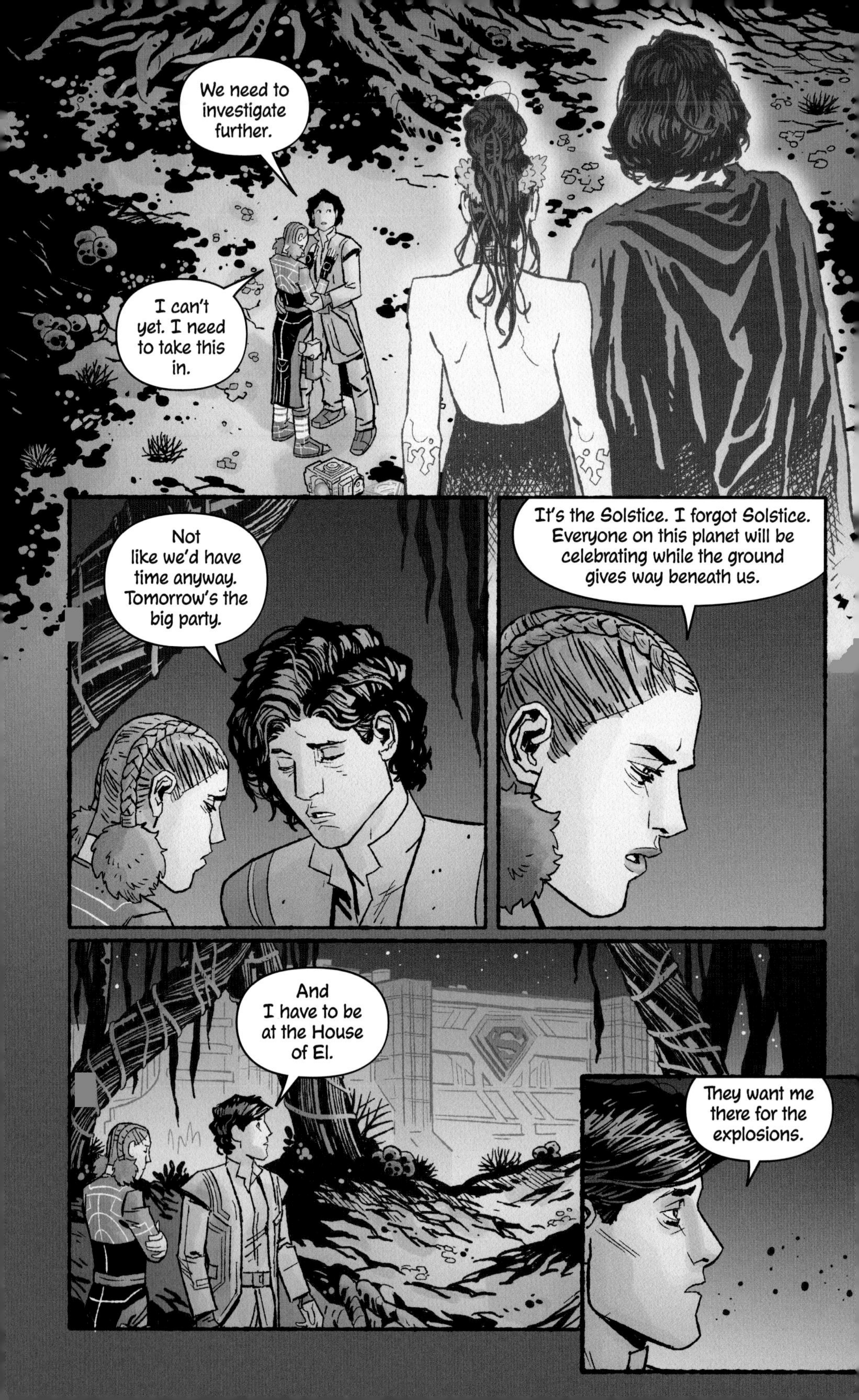
We need to investigate further.
I can't yet. I need to take this in.
Not like we'd have time anyway. Tomorrow's the big party.
It's the Solstice. I forgot Solstice. Everyone on this planet will be celebrating while the ground gives way beneath us.
And I have to be at the House of El.
They want me there for the explosions.

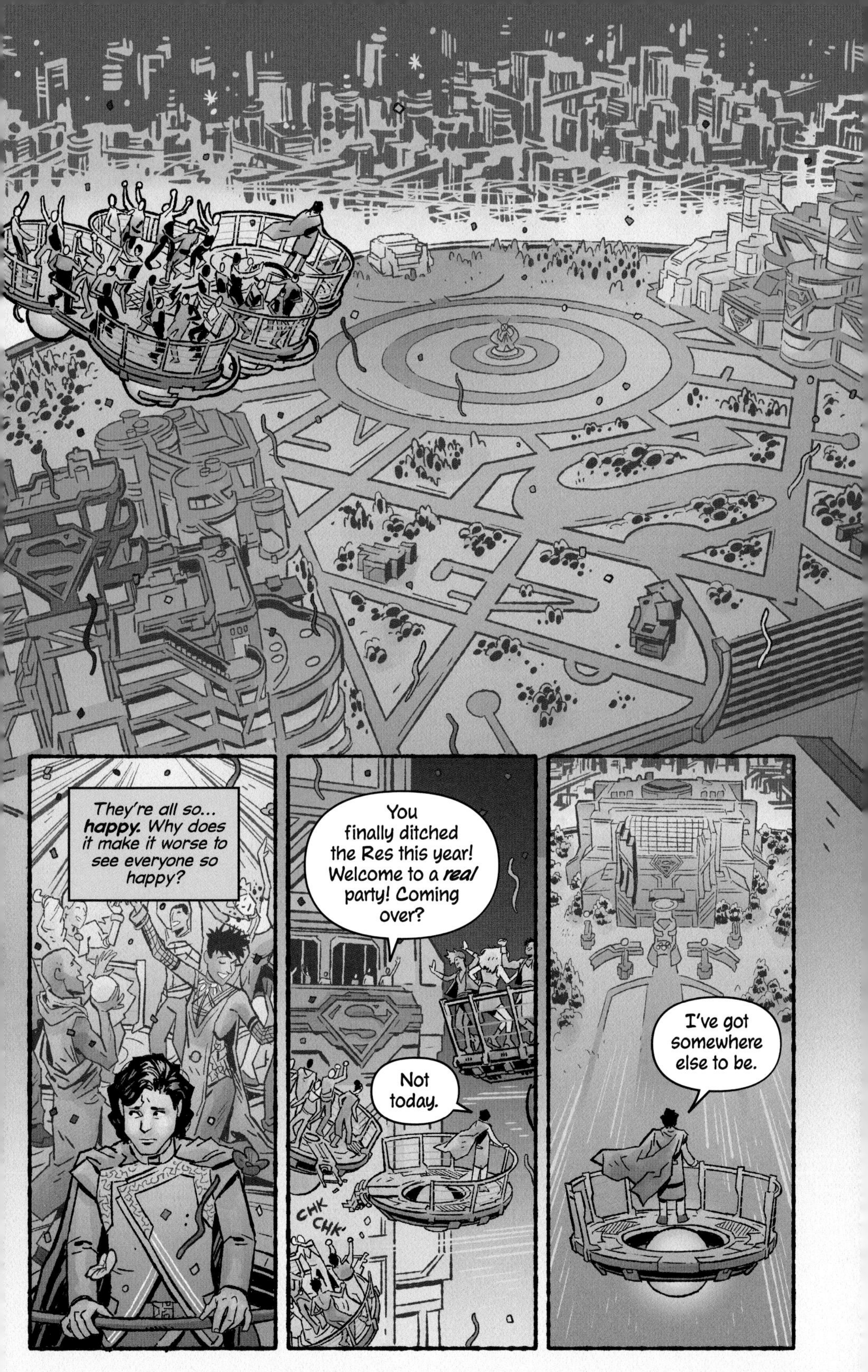
They're all so... **happy.** Why does it make it worse to see everyone so happy?
You finally ditched the Res this year! Welcome to a ***real*** party! Coming over?
Not today.
CHK CHK'
I've got somewhere else to be.

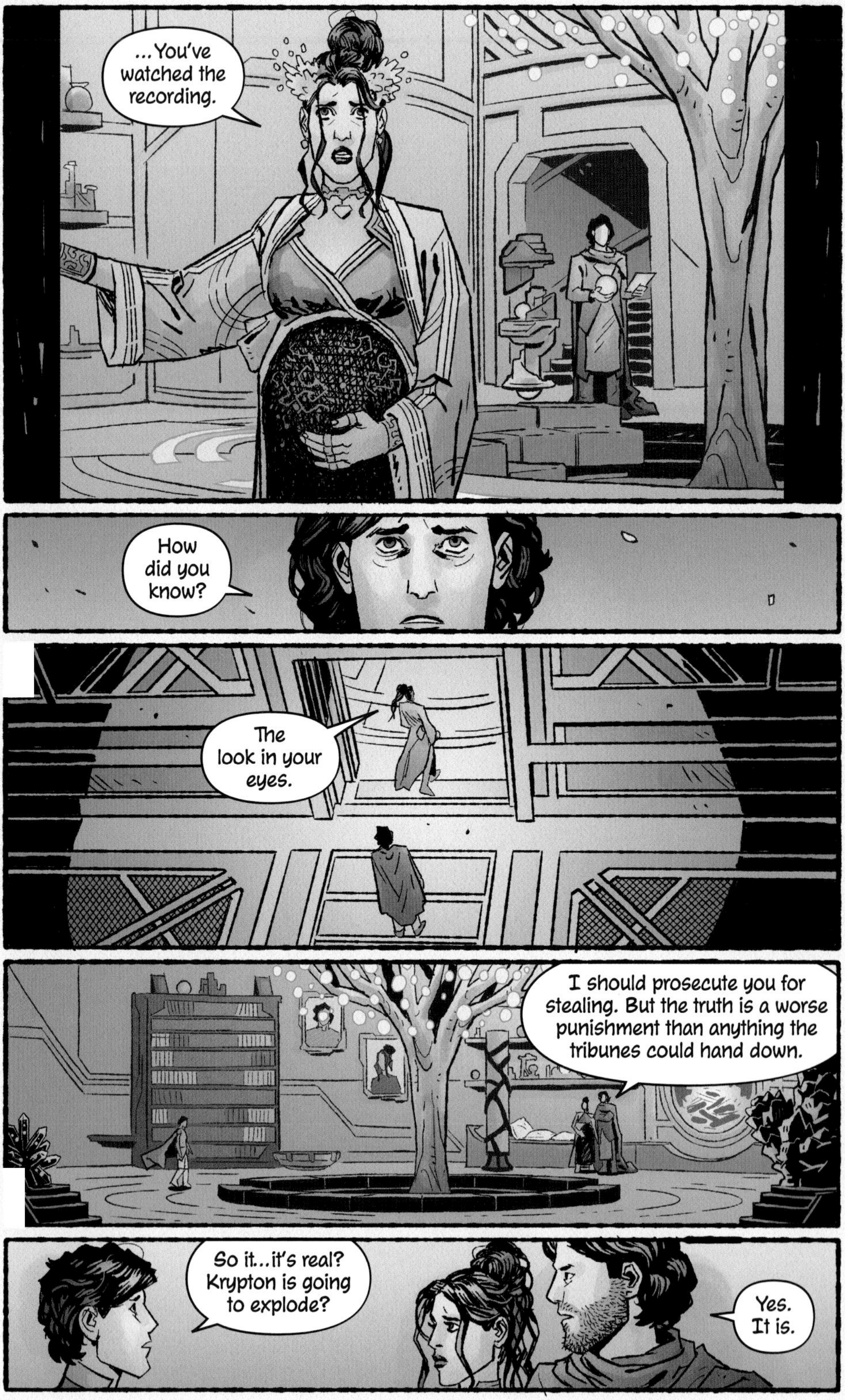
...You've watched the recording.
How did you know?
The look in your eyes.
I should prosecute you for stealing. But the truth is a worse punishment than anything the tribunes could hand down.
So it...it's real? Krypton is going to explode?
Yes. It is.

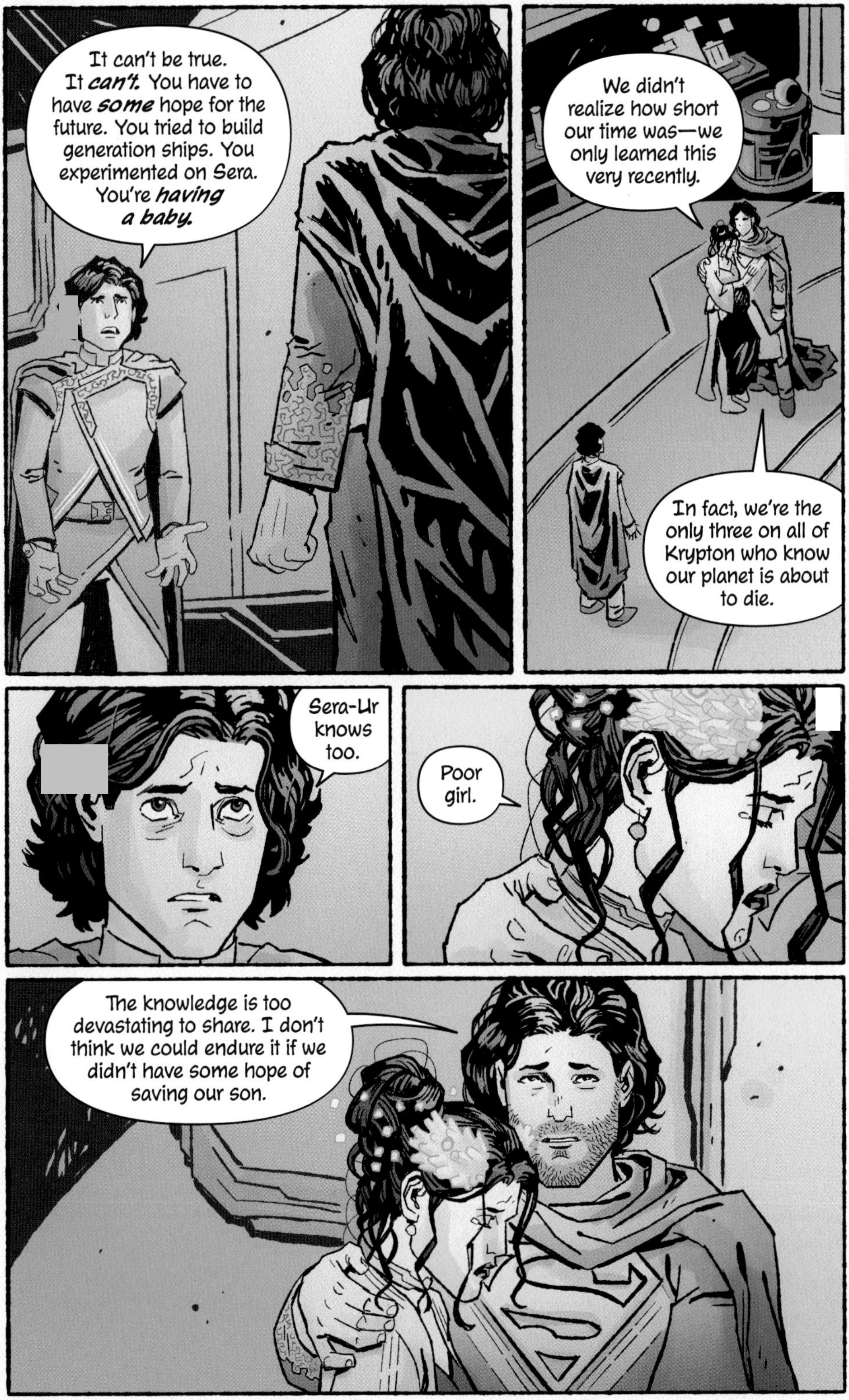
It can't be true. It *can't.* You have to have *some* hope for the future. You tried to build generation ships. You experimented on Sera. You're *having a baby.*
We didn't realize how short our time was—we only learned this very recently.
In fact, we're the only three on all of Krypton who know our planet is about to die.
Sera-Ur knows too.
Poor girl.
The knowledge is too devastating to share. I don't think we could endure it if we didn't have some hope of saving our son.

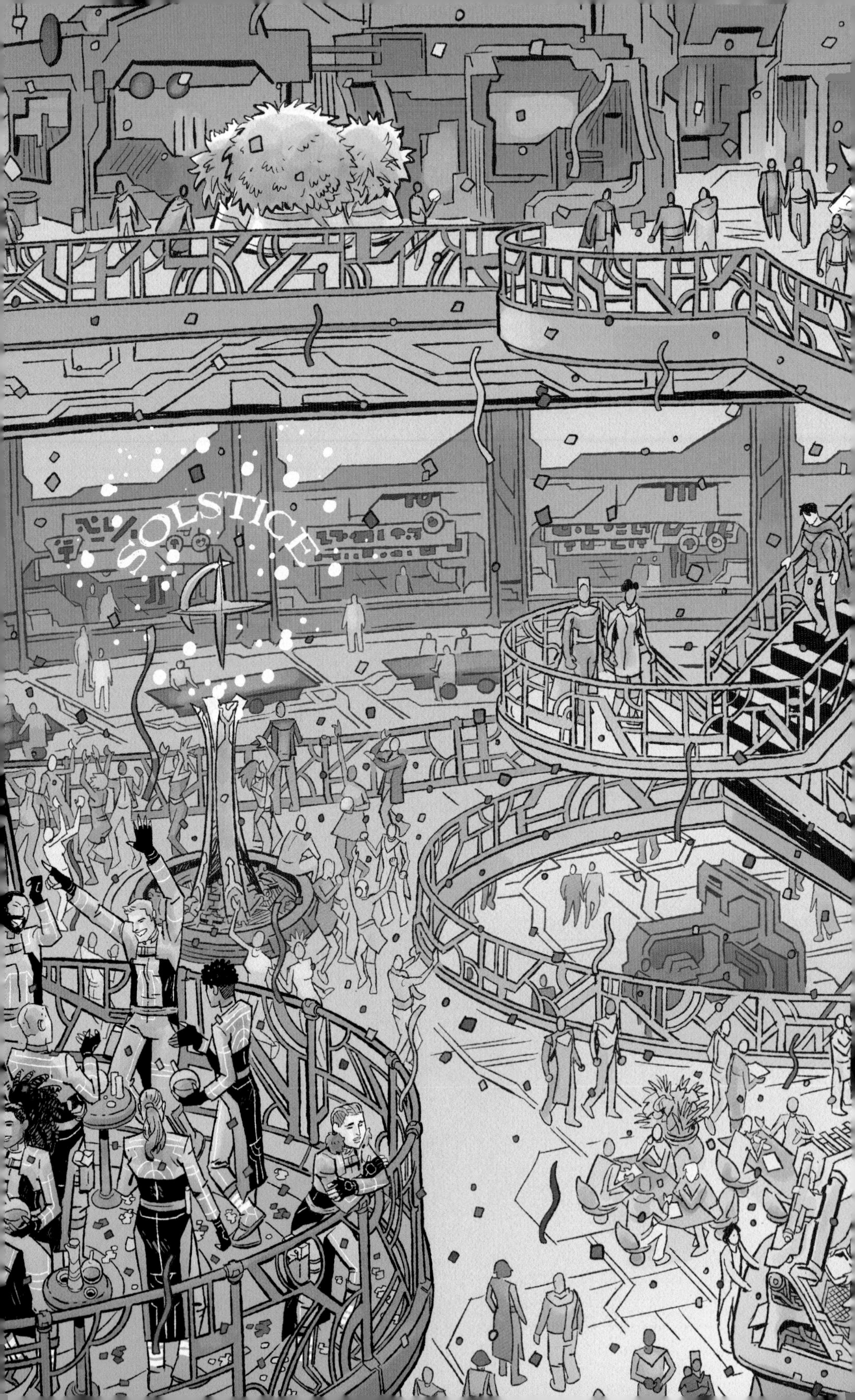
SOLSTICE

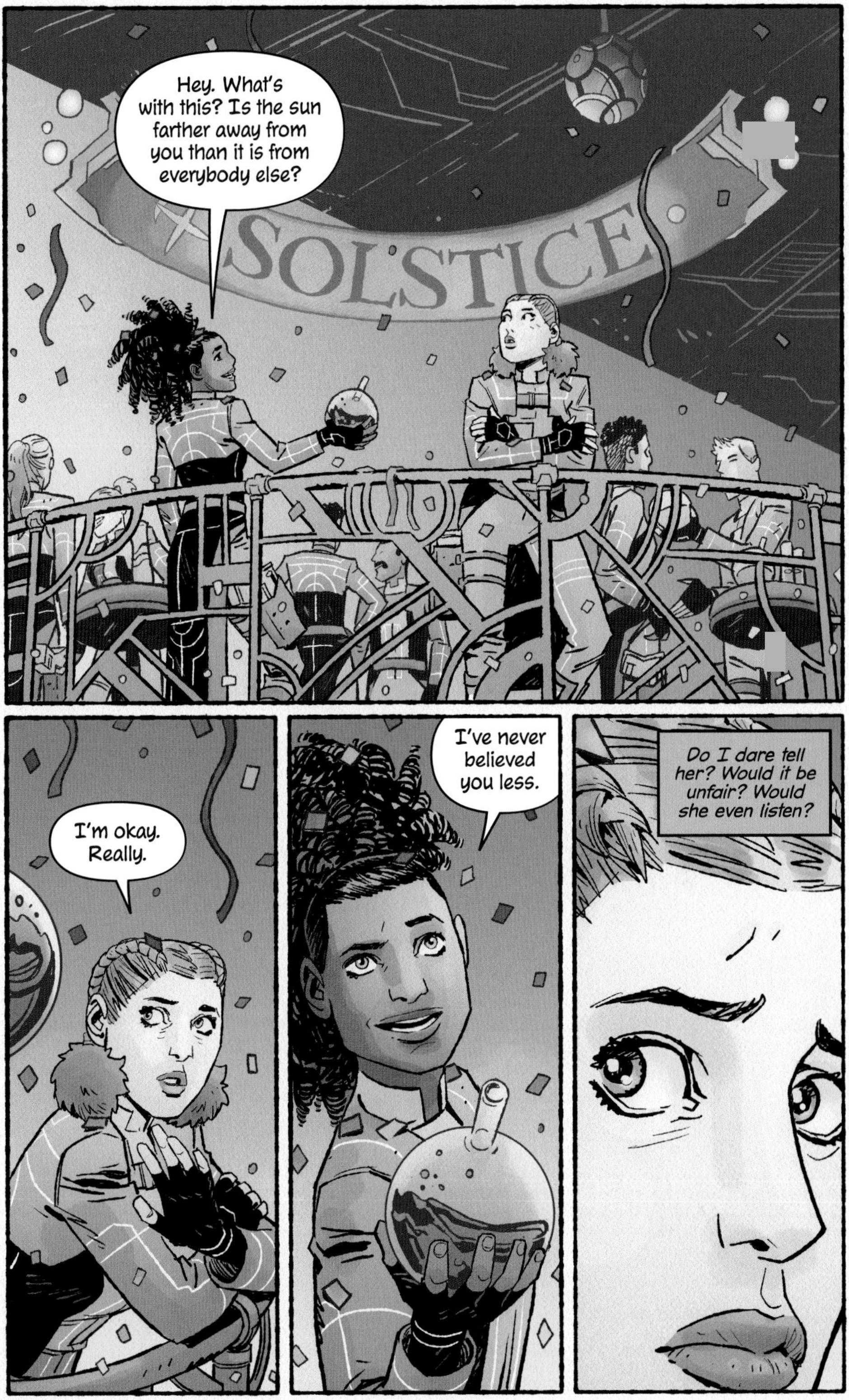
SOLSTICE
Hey. What's with this? Is the sun farther away from you than it is from everybody else?
I'm okay. Really.
I've never believed you less.
Do I dare tell her? Would it be unfair? Would she even listen?

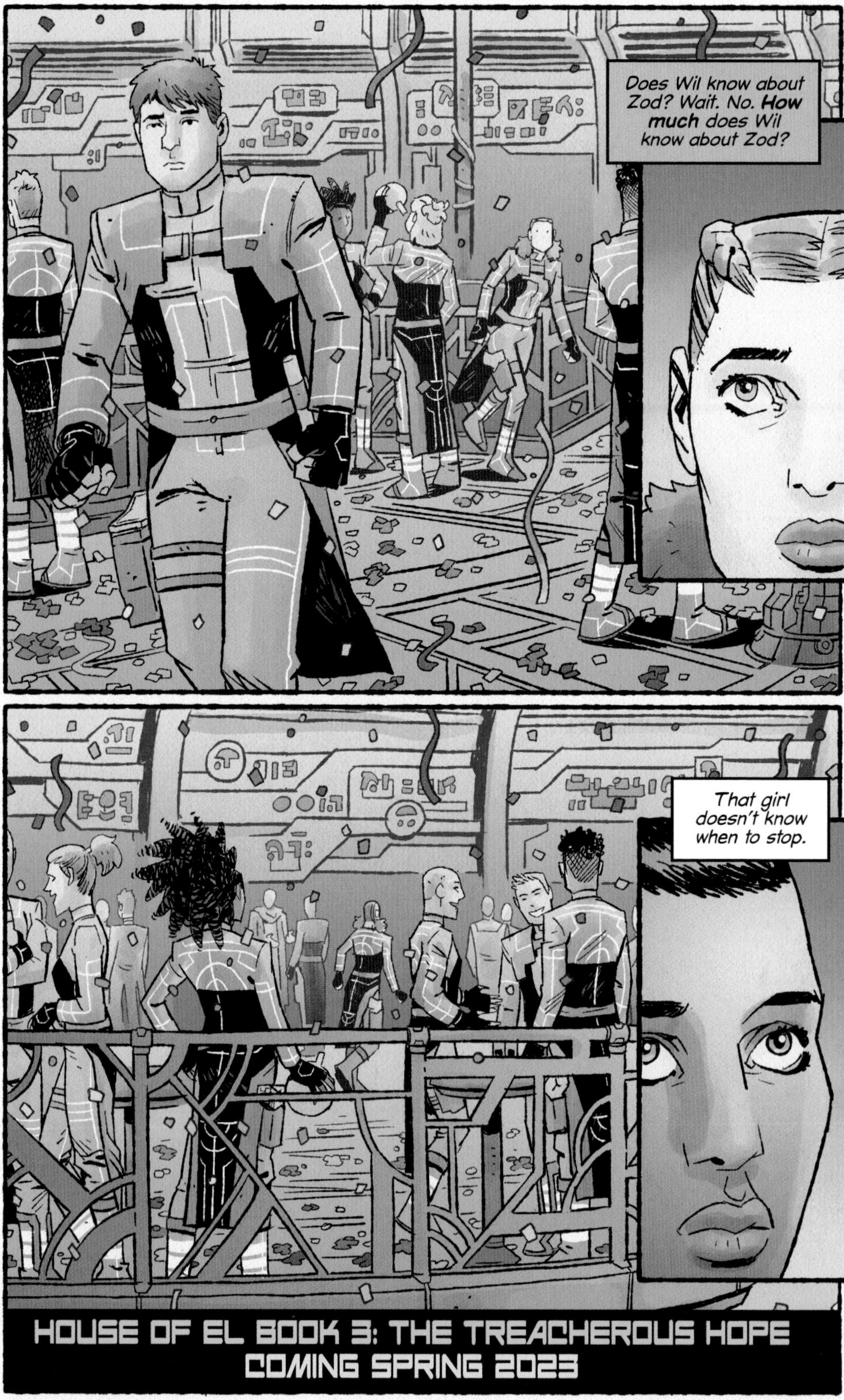
Does Wil know about Zod? Wait. No. **How much** does Wil know about Zod?
That girl doesn't know when to stop.
HOUSE OF EL BOOK 3: THE TREACHEROUS HOPE
COMING SPRING 2023

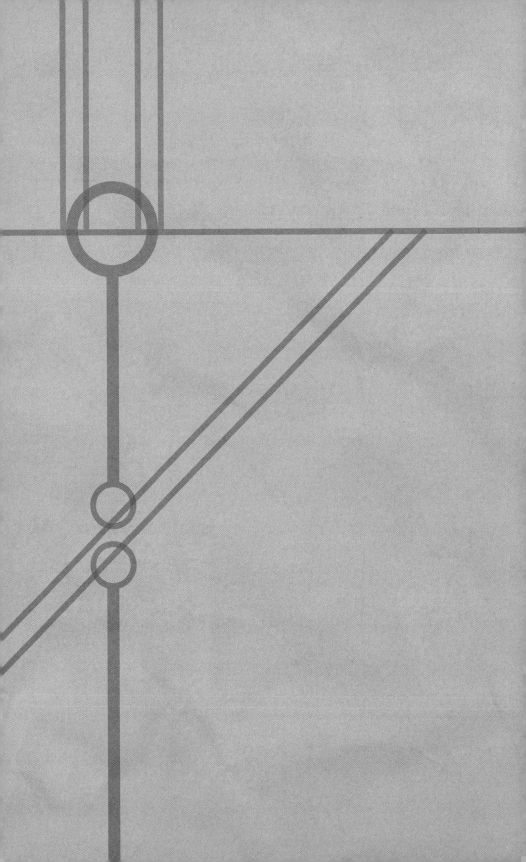

LOOKING FOR FANTASTIC FICTION FROM OUR WRITERS AND ARTISTS?
CHECK OUT THESE TITLES!

"A riveting new portrayal of the ocean's fiercest princess."
—Marissa Meyer, #1 New York Times bestselling author of The Lunar Chronicles
NEW YORK TIMES BESTSELLING AUTHOR
danielle paige
MERA
tidebreaker
A GRAPHIC NOVEL
ILLUSTRATED BY
stephen byrne

MERA: TIDEBREAKER

Danielle Paige,
Stephen Byrne

A powerful story that explores duty, love, heroism, and freedom... told through the eyes of an independent undersea princess.

ISBN: 978-1-4012-8339-1

Based on the New York Times Bestselling Novel by
SARAH J. MAAS
DC
CATWOMAN
SOULSTEALER
Adapted by
LOUISE SIMONSON
Illustrated by
SAMANTHA DODGE

CATWOMAN: SOULSTEALER

Sarah J. Maas
Louise Simonson
Samantha Dodge

When the Bat's away, the Cat returns to Gotham City, where she must fight Batwing and the League of Assassins!

ISBN: 978-1-4012-9641-4

/* #1 New York Times Bestselling Author of This Is Where It Ends */
Marieke Nijkamp
The Oracle Code_
//A Graphic Novel
//Illustrated by
Manuel Preitano

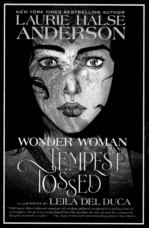

THE ORACLE CODE

Marieke Nijkamp,
Manuel Preitano

A haunting mystery in a rehabilitation center where Barbara Gordon must battle the phantoms of her past before they consume her future.

ISBN: 978-1-4012-9066-5

"The superhero book I've always wanted and needed—heartwarming, vibrantly alive, a loving portrayal of Cassandra Cain that will leave readers hungry for more."
—Marjorie Liu, New York Times bestselling author of Monstress
Shadow OF THE Batgirl
SARAH KUHN
NICOLE GOUX

SHADOW OF THE BATGIRL

Sarah Kuhn,
Nicole Goux

The harrowing story of a girl who overcomes the odds to find her unique identity.

ISBN: 978-1-4012-8978-2

NEW YORK TIMES BESTSELLING AUTHOR
LAURIE HALSE ANDERSON
WONDER WOMAN
TEMPEST TOSSED
ILLUSTRATED BY LEILA DEL DUCA

WONDER WOMAN: TEMPEST TOSSED

Laurie Halse Anderson,
Leila Del Duca

Cut off from her island home and fellow Amazons, Princess Diana of Themyscira finds herself a refugee in an unfamiliar land.

ISBN: 978-1-4012-8645-3

TEEN TITANS: RAVEN

ISBN: 978-1-4012-8623-1

TEEN TITANS: BEAST BOY

ISBN: 978-1-4012-8719-1

TEEN TITANS: BEAST BOY LOVES RAVEN

ISBN: 978-1-4012-8719-1

Kami Garcia, Gabriel Picolo

The *New York Times* bestselling series about first loves, faithful friendships, family secrets, and finding your true self.

THE NEW YORK TIMES BESTSELLING SERIES
KAMI GARCIA
"Friendships, family secrets, and a teenage boy who can turn into animals. What's not to love?"
—Gene Luen Yang, New York Times bestselling author of American Born Chinese
THE NEW YORK TIMES BESTSELLING SERIES
KAMI GARCIA
DC
KAMI GARCIA
GABRIEL PICOLO
THE NEW YORK TIMES BESTSELLING SERIES
TEEN TITANS
BEAST BOY loves RAVEN